THE YOUNG MADONNA

Lynn Wood

Fall Into a Story Books

Copyright © 2016 Lynn Wood

ISBN: 979-8-9903029-3-8

Cover Design: BookCoverZone
Library of Congress Control Number: 2018675309
Printed in the United States of America

This book was published and briefly available in 2015/2016 under its original title:
Mary Elle...The Chosen One and Updated in 2024

CONTENTS

TITLES BY LYNN WOOD

Fiction:

The Young Madonna

The Catalyst

Coming Soon:

Introducing Maxwell Cole and The Honor & Protect Series:

Secrets, Lies & Betrayals

Norman Brides Series:

Keeper of the Stone

Finders Keepers

The Promise Keeper

The Complete Keeper Trilogy

Non-Fiction:

Lessons In Illumination

...A Beginner's Guide to the Eternal Way

Yoga Behind the Veil

...A Journey of Self-Discovery

PROLOGUE

The little girl waited in line for her turn with Father Byrnes. His line was the longest. Father John's line was empty. Did it make him sad no one wanted to go to him? She felt a little guilty at the thought, but the prospect of the priest's discomfort was not enough to encourage her to switch lines.

She exchanged a nervous, silent glance with her friend, Mary Jean, and noted her friend's hands, like her own, were trembling. It was Mary Jean's turn. The red light changed to white above the door and the classmate who was in line in front of them shuffled out of the confessional with a decidedly relieved, if pious, expression on her face as she made her way to the altar to offer her penance.

Mary Elle sent Mary Jean an encouraging nod to ease her friend's anxiety as she prepared to enter the confessional. She watched nervously as Mary Jean approached the half-open door and then pulled it open wide enough for her to slip through. When the door closed behind her it was with a finality Mary Elle found troubling.

She knew what it looked like inside. Sister Liadore showed them. It was just a little room with a kneeler placed in front of the screen separating the two rooms where the priest sat listening to the penitent confess their sins. Some of the other kids chose face to face confession, but Mary Elle liked the idea of the secret little room. If she was going to lie to a priest, she thought it would be easier if she didn't have to look him in the eye.

It seemed like she waited forever for the red light over the door to change to white. Mary Jean emerged a few moments later with her hands clasped in prayer position. Their glances met and Mary Jean rolled her eyes heavenward in a gesture Mary Elle interpreted as, 'well, at least that's over,' and then her friend passed by her on her way to the altar.

Mary Elle drew a deep, shuddering breath, wiped her suddenly sweaty palms on her plaid jumper and then stepped through the partially open door. She turned to shut the door firmly behind her and knew the time had come to face her fears. She took a single step, and then knelt in front of the screen. A moment later she heard the screen slide open. When her voice emerged it was in a soft, shaky whisper. She wondered if the priest could tell how nervous she was.

"Bless me, Father, for I have sinned. This is my first confession…."

CHAPTER ONE

The stranger crept closer towards the sleeping woman curled on her side in a fetal position. He presumed her defensive position was an attempt to ward off the cold hovering over the room. As if she somehow sensed his silent approach, the young woman sighed in her sleep and rolled onto her back, revealing to his curious gaze young, exquisitely formed features.

In sleep the woman exuded a childlike purity. He knew from the purpose of his assignment he should not be surprised by the girl's innocence, and yet he acknowledged he was. He would not have believed it possible for such purity to still exist in a world dominated by blood and faithlessness. How had this ordinary woman escaped the violence of a world that derived singular delight in spilling the blood of the innocent, as if those responsible could somehow expiate their own sins by dragging their victims to hell with them?

Her rhythmic breaths were a visible whisper between them, giving testament to the cold. He watched her burrow deeper beneath the layer of quilts she used to combat the chill and for a moment he paused in the completion of his duty. An unfamiliar sense of indecision and fleeting regret pressed against his usually implacable will. With an impatient gesture he tossed aside their silent challenge to his purpose and bent close to the sleeping woman, whispering her name.

"Mary Elle."

The girl instinctively raised a hand to sweep aside his uninvited entry into her quiet slumber. His objective complete, the intruder left his victim to her dreams, knowing the innocence that fostered them, and the purity he'd been surprised to discover in so unlikely a steward, had been shattered forever.

CHAPTER TWO

"Mary Elle, Mary Elle." This time it was a child's voice hailing her, floating wispily through the veil separating wakefulness from sleep, rousing Mary Elle enough to disturb her yet not enough to bring her fully awake. Pleased at the sleeping woman's irritated muttering and taking it as evidence of having captured her attention, the little girl revealed the reason for her visit.

Mary Elle's brows drew together in a puzzled frown. Even in sleep her subconscious rejected the direction of her dreams. In them a little girl nervously clutched a much larger hand and peered trustingly up into the eyes smiling gently down at her. Despite her companion's attempts at reassurance, Mary Elle could sense the young girl's fear. It was a fear bordering on terror. The tiny hand clutching the large masculine one was shaking uncontrollably, presenting a sharp contrast to the brave front she was desperately trying to project. It was obvious she didn't want to be there... wherever there was.

As if the visitor to her dreams was anxious for Mary Elle to understand the source of her dread, the little girl closed the remaining gap between them and merged their thoughts. Immediately Mary Elle felt the steady rhythm of her slumberous breaths ramp up in communion with the girl's barely restrained panic. She braced herself against the onslaught of foreign worries chasing themselves around her head. Her mother assured her a great honor was being bestowed upon her, but the little girl would have preferred the distinction be given to another. She blinked away her tears, determined not to shame her parents by weeping.

In sleep, Mary Elle reached up to swipe impatiently at her damp eyes. Then schooling her features she glanced back over her shoulder to assure herself her mother was still there. Relieved, she attempted to persuade her faltering will it wasn't too late for her to change her mind. Her mother wouldn't force her.

Even as she took heart from her mother's reassuring smile, encouraging her on her way, Mary acknowledged it was too late for her to flee back to the safety of her mother's loving arms. It had begun. She bent her head to hide the tears she was unable to hold back any longer. Sensing her misgiving, her companion gave her hand a gentle squeeze.

"I'm afraid," she confided in a shame-filled whisper.

CHAPTER THREE

In the way of dreamers, Mary Elle understood she was caught up in a fantasy but no matter how desperately she struggled against its tangled, spidery web she was unable to free herself. The little girl kept calling her name until finally Mary Elle conceded defeat and gave up trying to convince herself she was imagining things. With more exasperation than either fear or welcome, she sat up in bed and exclaimed out loud into the dark silence surrounding her, "What? What do you want?"

As if content with the evidence of having secured her attention, the young girl fell silent. For a moment Mary Elle caught a vision of her smiling face before she faded back under the cover of darkness.

"Thanks a lot," Mary Elle muttered, as irritated with herself as her imaginary visitor, and wondered briefly if the spicy pizza she indulged in for dinner was responsible for her hallucinations. After peering around her dark room, just to assure herself she was indeed alone, she lay back down, drawing the heavy quilts up to her chin before rolling over, hoping to escape back into sleep for a few precious hours before she had to get up for work. The shrill sound of her alarm announcing morning's unwelcome arrival jolted her back to reality before she even closed her eyes.

"Great, just great," she sighed aloud, unconcerned by her solitary conversation. She lived alone. Sometimes she spoke her thoughts out loud just to relieve the silence.

With a disciplined resolve cultivated mostly from financial necessity, Mary Elle squashed the temptation to burrow deeper beneath the quilts and turned to silence the buzzing alarm. Bracing herself, she climbed out of bed and hurried across the room to the adjoining bathroom, reminding herself to pick up a portable heater at the hardware store on her way home from work.

It didn't seem to matter where she set the thermostat for the central heating and cooling system. Without supplementary measures, the temperature in the house never climbed above a brisk sixty five, except during the summer months when only an act of nature brought the reading below eighty.

Her friend, Crystal, was appalled by her refusal to notify the landlord of her problems with the heating and air conditioning system, but Mary Elle shrugged off her concerns. She was willing to tolerate the inconvenience because she feared the consequences of lodging a complaint. Her rent was so ridiculously cheap she was afraid the cost of the repairs would amount to more than her annual rent payments. In which case, she reasoned, her landlord might conclude continuing to lease the house to her was more trouble than it was worth. Since she couldn't afford another place remotely as nice as the old converted chapel she called home, she was willing to sleep in layers and beneath a mountain of quilts in the winter, shed both in the summer, and keep her grievances to herself.

Besides, her secluded abode came with mitigating charms offsetting her inability to regulate the temperature and the uncertainty of hot water. She offered up a little prayer today would not prove to be one of those days she would have to make do without the latter and turned on the shower as far to the hot side of the dial as it would go. She stripped out of the old sweats she slept in and released a gratified sigh at the sight of the steam rising behind the glass shower door.

Whispering her heartfelt appreciation in the direction of heaven, she stepped into the casket-sized cubicle and decided she would skip the chore of washing and drying her waist length hair.   A simple braid proved both expedient and professional when the need arose.   Monday mornings were challenging enough without complicating the beginning of the work week with hair care.   At least this one promised to be quieter than usual. The last day of final exams before the long holiday break tended to pass in a seldom heard but welcome hush echoing off the vaulted ceilings and marble hallways of St. Mary's where she taught.

CHAPTER FOUR

She was back. Mary Elle groaned and covered her ears, even going so far as to pull the pillow over her head to drown out the sound of her own name echoing around and around inside her head. Of course her small act of defiance proved predictably useless. Imaginary voices couldn't be silenced so easily. Mary Elle was beginning to doubt they could be silenced by any means. Night after night the little girl returned to disturb her dreams. Mary Elle sensed her young visitor's anxiety but she didn't have the slightest idea what she was supposed to do to alleviate it. Equally frustrating, the childish voice never shared the reason for her late night visits.

Finally, in what had become a nightly signal of her surrender Mary Elle threw the covers aside and sat up in bed. "What? What do you want? How can I help you if you won't tell me what's wrong?"

When the girl's response finally came, Mary Elle heard her unseen visitor's simple request as clearly as if she was sitting across from her in bed. "I want you to paint me a picture."

Except to Mary Elle the girl's appeal was anything but simple. The words stabbed at her heart with a pain leaving her breathless, cleaving open a wound she only just managed to half convince herself was beginning to heal. Her young companion forgotten, Mary Elle swiped at the bitter tears stinging her eyes and accepted sleep would continue to elude her for the remainder of the night.

For the length of her entire life Mary Elle clung to a single ambition, despite the mounting evidence it would continue to evade her reach. She yearned for the talent to paint the way other women craved great beauty. Over the years she convinced herself if she just studied hard enough, practiced long enough and simply refused to let go of her hope of becoming an artist, her dream would come true.

But it was not to be. After years of pitiful self-denial, she was finally forced to accept the bitter truth. She was not destined to paint. Some dreams, no matter how desperately pursued, remained forever out of reach. Whatever the secret, whatever indefinable quality separated the merely proficient from the genius of the true artist, she lacked it.

Apparently the little girl who was disturbing her dreams lately didn't get the memo. Mary Elle wasn't sure why it fell on her to break the disappointing news, but she did so, with stilted words and stiff lips, "I can't paint. I wish I could. You're wasting your time. You'll have to find someone else."

Mary Elle closed her eyes against the wrenching grief the confession tore through her. In the span of a single breath the past three years were stripped away and she was transported back to her college apartment in Boston. In her mind's eye she saw herself with desolate tears streaming down her face, tossing her art supplies into large, plastic garbage bags before hauling them out to the dumpster behind her apartment building. If she couldn't paint, she refused to be confronted daily with the tools of her failure. Maybe she should have sold her supplies as her friends urged, but to Mary Elle that would have been worse. The thought of someone else using her brushes, canvases and easels to craft what she was unable to would have stripped her of whatever will she retained to begin building a new life for herself from the ashes of her previous one.

The girl's response, when it finally came, effectively broke through the wall of Mary Elle's shattered memories, "No. You are the chosen one. If you won't help me, there is no one else."

Mary Elle shook her head in denial, dropping its heavy weight into her hands, trying desperately to convince herself their entire absurd conversation was a product of her imagination run amok. 'The chosen one'. What in the world did that mean?'

By the time she recovered enough to ask her unseen companion for clarification, it was too late. She was alone in the room and in her head.

Sighing in frustration, she thrust a trembling hand through her long hair. 'The chosen one.' That was laughable. She was never chosen for anything in her life. There was nothing unique or special about her. It hardly seemed fair she was being forced to confront her painful limitations all over again. Weren't dreams where you fled to escape your inadequacies?

In a huff, Mary Elle settled back down in bed and drew the heavy quilts up to her chin, silently acknowledging falling back to sleep would prove impossible with her thoughts so restless. For long silent moments she lay staring up at the ceiling where the light of the moon and the heavy wind whistling outside her windows combined to cast the lively shadows dancing across her line of vision and playing out on the stark white canvas above her head. It occurred to her for one frightful moment she might be losing her grip on reality, but she quickly dismissed the notion.

The girl she imagined she heard calling her name and telling her she was the chosen one was just a dream... a really odd dream maybe, but that's the way some dreams were. Odd. Bordering on the bizarre, sucking you into the quagmire separating fantasy from reality until the dreamer couldn't tell one from the other. Everyone had them. There were entire branches of science and pseudo-science devoted to the study and interpretation of odd dreams. Psychiatrists, shamans, spiritualists, fortune tellers. Some people built their entire careers around the practice. There was nothing for her to worry about.

Besides, it didn't take an expert to interpret hers. Obviously she was still harboring some unresolved issues over her decision to abandon her art. Maybe she could have been a little gentler in the way she handled things, but sometimes the pain of walking away was so great, compassion was not an option. It was as if she was involved in an unhealthy relationship she held onto for too long. When faced with such a circumstance, yes, certainly it would be nice if the two sides could part as friends, but the critical element was escaping the unhealthy situation intact. If the only way to accomplish that goal was to cut one's losses and run like hell, than that's what one did in order to survive.

And that's what she did when she moved to Pittsburgh in search of a new life. She packed up her paints and brushes, her charcoals and books. She took down her easels and carefully, painstakingly dismantled the fresh canvases waiting for her to fill them with her vision. There was nothing resembling gentleness about the process. After she separated the canvases from the frames, she took them apart in a fit of violent, resentful destruction she never imagined herself capable of.

When the time came to leave Boston, she discovered she could stow the entirety of her personal belongings in her little compact car. Her painting supplies, before she destroyed them, were pretty much the extent of them. The furniture in her apartment belonged to the landlord. Her clothes and laptop fit in the backseat of her car. When she left school, heading south and west towards Pittsburgh, she left most of her life, along with the myriad pieces of her shattered heart, behind in the old dumpster.

She supposed the devastation she buried so mercilessly beneath her resolve to grow up and get over herself; not everyone got to play the part of Cinderella in the drama of life, was likely responsible for her bizarre dreams of late. Maybe it was a good sign. Maybe it meant she was ready to face her demons and deal with them like the responsible adult she promised herself she would become when she graduated from college. For now, though, she was simply too tired to do battle with her lingering issues tonight.

Maybe she should attempt to rationalize herself back to

sleep. The girl wasn't real. None of it was real. Mary Elle circled the questionably comforting mantra around and around through her thoughts until she finally surrendered to her exhaustion. The moment she did, the little girl was there, staring at her with sad, apprehensive eyes. As if she was afraid Mary Elle would leave her there alone in the dark.

Groaning in protest, Mary Elle sat up in bed and abandoned all pretense of sleep. She couldn't stand it. Even if the little girl existed only in her imagination, she couldn't simply leave her there alone in the no man's land separating dreams from wakefulness. A bit disgusted by her easy capitulation to her young visitor's emotional blackmail, Mary Elle mentally tacked on an additional weakness to her list of limitations. She was a pushover. A tearful plea, an innocent girl, and she was lost.

Chiding herself for being an idiot, Mary Elle crawled out of bed and headed in the direction of the narrow, winding stairs leading to the bell tower where the big iron bell still hung on its thick, braided rope from back in the day when her small home served as a private family chapel for a wealthy industrialist. There was no heat at all in the cramped space. Her breath escaped her lips in visible puffs.

The light from the moon reflected through the stained glass windows circling the cupola capping the bell tower. Since the tiny tower room lacked electricity as well as heat Mary Elle kept an oil lantern hanging near the entrance at the top of the stairs. She lit it now, not for the first time concluding the original owner carried his bid for historical authenticity a bit too far. Still, she conceded the light from the glass lantern was enough for her to see her way across the narrow space to where her guilty indulgence in the form of her tiny stash of art supplies rested, long neglected against the far wall.

The glow from the moonlight appeared to frame them momentarily, providing unwelcome emphasis for the enormity of the step she was about to take. She was forced to swallow back the knot of barely suppressed panic rising in her chest and threatening to become lodged in her throat. Was she ready for this? Maybe she should reconsider subjecting herself to the painful memories that would be resurrected the instant her fingers closed around a paint brush.

Shaking off her hesitation and telling herself not to add any more drama to the bizarre situation she stumbled into, she crossed the room and knelt on the stone floor to sort through her supplies. They were pitiful to her eyes. A single virgin sketchpad sat propped against the stone wall. A box of unopened charcoals lay next to her favorite brush; the one she was unable to bring herself to part with when she left Boston. In the corner, her closed easel leaned against the wall along with a single rolled up blank canvas.

Mary Elle settled into a cross-legged position and rested her head and back against the cold, stone wall. As soon as she closed her eyes, the memories seeped through her defenses she so carefully erected to keep them at bay. The smells assaulted her first. The pungent odor of turpentine and oil paint made her dizzy with longing. Her hands slid from long-remembered habit along the sweats she slept in, trying to rid her fingers of their memories of wet paint.

The instinctive movement was accompanied instantly by the sound of her mother's frustrated voice calling up the stairs, nagging her to change before she picked up a paint brush, tacking on the oft-repeated reminder clothes were expensive and so were shoes. They couldn't afford to replace them every other week as a result of Mary Elle's carelessness.

Her eyes drifted to the unused sketch pad by her side. It looked lonely there, as if it too was waiting for her to rescue it from its solitary, purposeless existence. Reluctantly, with nerves tingling along her reach, she stretched out her hand to retrieve the blank paper. It was cold to the touch. She placed the tablet on her lap before cautiously turning to the first page, almost surprised to confront its vacant surface. What was she supposed to do with so much emptiness?

Her professors were right. She lacked creativity. What

in the world was she doing? She slammed the pad closed and leaned her head back against the wall. Instantly, the little girl's anxious features swam before her vision.

If only she possessed the talent to capture the expression in her eyes... both anxious and excited at once...or the way her long, dark hair fell down her back in a sleek mantle, how her innocent, very young face was uplifted to the other face beyond Mary Elle's line of sight. There was awe there too. An awe combining bemused wonder with near reverence at the identity of her mysterious companion.

Almost in a daze, Mary Elle reached for the box of unopened charcoals and slid one out. Her fingers closed familiarly around it. Instantly, her long neglected soul leapt to life. How could she be so dismally inept at a practice she found such joy in? Pushing aside her doubts, she gripped the pencil with more confidence, and recalling the girl's eyes, set out to capture them. It was a modest goal and one she promised herself she would be content with. Surely all her years of study and training would enable her to re-create a young girl's expressive eyes on paper.

Long silent moments later, her eyes stared down at those of her now silent companion she could almost feel watching her efforts from just beyond her shoulder. At the evidence of her small accomplishment, Mary Elle set another modest ambition for herself: to give those eyes context in an oval face, with an olive complexion and a tail of long ebony hair braided for modesty's sake.

Mary Elle lost track of the time and the cold seeping into her limbs from the stone floor despite the layers of clothes she wore to ward it off. For the first time in years she allowed herself the debatably foolish indulgence of unleashing her dreams from their imprisonment she insisted upon when she accepted the harsh reality of adulthood. While her vision flew unfettered, she felt the subject of her efforts abandon her watchful stance at her side and wander around the room, her attention focused on the scenes depicted in the stained glass above her.

At one point Mary Elle became aware of her now silent companion pausing for what seemed an inordinate amount of time beneath one of the scenes. Curious, she glanced up to see which one captured her young visitor's attention. The Crucifixion. Mary Elle felt an icy shiver slide up her spine that had nothing to do with the chill in the room. Part of her wanted to jump up from where she sat and race over to shield the child's eyes. Surely, even in glass, the scene was too violent for one so young.

As if compelled to follow the girl's line of sight, Mary Elle's vision drifted upward to focus on the bloody scene. Her perusal didn't last long. She found the images disturbing in a way she long suspected others did not. Certainly the young girl she was laboring to capture on paper didn't turn her gaze away. She seemed fascinated by the events lit by moonlight and shimmering softly in glass. Mary Elle sat staring at her, wondering who she was and what in the world she was doing in Pittsburgh, of all places.

The small puzzle was enough of a distraction to bring her focus to the lateness of the hour. Releasing a tired sigh, she reluctantly acknowledged she could no longer ignore the cramp in her hand and the stiffness of her protesting limbs from sitting cross-legged on the cold stone for so long. She released the charcoal she still gripped in her right hand and let it bounce unheeded across the hard floor while she stretched out her legs, shaking out the cramps.

To avoid confronting what she feared would provide indisputable evidence of the mediocrity of her talent, she busied herself with small movements, stretching out her fingers, clenching and unclenching the muscles in her legs to return feeling to her toes, all the while deliberately keeping her gaze averted from the open page in her lap.

All she knew for certain was it was no longer empty. What else it contained, she wasn't yet prepared to confront. She didn't think she could face again the evidence of her own failure, understanding the cost of having the burgeoning happiness bubbling up inside her ruthlessly crushed beneath the weight of even her own suspect objectivity.

'What did it matter what anyone else thought?' she countered silently. She enjoyed her art so much. Couldn't she just be happy with the joy it gave her without evaluating it to death? Maybe that was the purpose of the little girl's visit to her dreams, to encourage her to pick up her own again.

But of course she would look. She needed to know. Bracing herself, Mary Elle stole a hesitant peek at the open page on her lap. 'No, that couldn't be right,' she rebuked herself. She wasn't seeing clearly. It was obvious her objectivity was more suspect than she realized.

She must be evaluating her efforts through the eyes of her dream-self, not her true mind's eye. Maybe she was still asleep. Surely that was the only reasonable explanation because never in her wildest fantasies did she believe she could be capable of producing the images staring back at her.

She might not be an expert, but nor was she a complete neophyte. Absent her ability to create it, Mary Elle indulged her love of art through the study of it. Maybe the little girl from her dream was some famous, long-dead artist who was channeling her talent through Mary Elle's hand.

As crazy as it sounded, it made more sense than the idea the skill to produce the sketches in front of her were just dropped upon her unsuspecting head by a benevolent God. She lifted her head, seeking answers from her unusual visitor only to discover, just like a dream, she vanished in the light of day.

Shaking her head to clear her thoughts, Mary Elle glanced back down at the page in her lap. This couldn't be right. She couldn't be seeing what she thought she was seeing. She decided what the situation demanded was some honest objectivity. Fortunately she knew just where to find it.

Closing the cover gently so as not to smudge the images, she laid the pad aside and jumped to her feet, cringing in pain when her stiff limbs protested her sudden movement. She shook out her legs, then paused to scoop up her phone before heading towards the stairs, her eyes widening in amazement when she saw the time. It was ten forty.

How long was up there? All she remembered was it was dark when she climbed the tower stairs. Maybe she was trapped in some kind of fugue state for the past several hours. Shaking her head in wonder she let her eyes sweep back towards the stained glass window depicting the Crucifixion. There was still no sign of her young visitor. Mary Elle wasn't certain if she should be relieved or disappointed by her absence. Was her imagination responsible for supplying the innocent features to go along with the anxious voice disturbing her dreams?

She couldn't help but wonder at what point harmless dreams and fantasies descended into the darker domain of hallucinations and psychosis. Shrugging the question away with a lightheartedness belying the seriousness of her query, Mary Elle grinned. If a little insanity was the price of the gift she was given, she would pay it gladly. They could lock her away in a padded cell with her paints and canvases and she would only wave benignly in her keepers' direction as she shooed them out the door.

Half an hour later, showered, dressed and ready to set off in pursuit of objectivity, Mary Elle retrieved the sketchpad from where it rested on her unmade bed. She stole a quick peek inside just to assure herself her earlier impression remained unchanged and her creation wasn't transformed while she was distracted with more mundane demands of daily life into something resembling her usual, pedestrian offerings.

Relieved, she grinned back at the image of the little girl staring up at her from the page. For a moment she thought she detected an answering twinkle in her dark eyes. Mary Elle was tempted to bend down and kiss her sweet face, but refrained from doing so because she didn't want to risk smudging the charcoal. Instead she carefully closed the pad, tucked it under her arm, and tripped happily down the stairs and out her front door.

CHAPTER FIVE

Even though winter's official arrival was just days away, bright sunlight chased aside the icy cold of the past few weeks and brought a grateful smile to Mary Elle's lips. Holiday shopping was in full swing on Walnut Street in the affluent neighborhood of Shadyside where her best friend presided over her whimsical shop of whatnots and such. Caught up in the excitement and holiday spirit of her fellow shoppers, Mary Elle didn't even mind when she was forced to park three blocks away and climb the steep street to her friend's shop.

The barely suppressed desperation on the faces of those she passed reminded her of her own unfinished holiday shopping. Shrugging off the unwelcome reminder, she fairly bounced up the crowded walk with a secret grin flirting along her lips until she arrived at the entrance to her friend's store, *Witchy, Wantya.*

Her smile widened at the fanciful script scrawled in freehand across the large window and its accompanying display. All manner of whimsy was cunningly presented for the buyer's consideration. Twinkling white Christmas lights framed the window and beckoned both the curious and frazzled alike to step inside to share in the magic, and perhaps purchase some for themselves. Witches, fairies and magicians all arrayed in their holiday finery sat conversing on stools and stones around a pot of witch's brew and singing Christmas carols. Santa stood nearby, smiling indulgently on the gathering, while elves played a game of hide and seek in the woods where shy sprites hid between the tangled branches.

No one would accuse her best friend of lacking creativity,

Mary Elle concluded with a wry smile. A frustrated art student like herself, Crystal found a more satisfying outlet for her love of art than teaching Romance languages to barely interested high school students. Clutching her sketchpad under her arm, Mary Elle passed through the entrance, smiling at the tinkling of wind chimes proclaiming her arrival.

Crystal glanced up with a ready smile from where she manned the humming register and chatted with a customer while she wrapped the other's purchases in the shop's distinctive silver wrap. Her friend nodded with the satisfied gleam of a successful proprietor in the direction of the waiting line of customers, most of whom were cradling multiple selections in their arms. Her gesture indicated she was going to be more than a few minutes before she could respond to the reason prompting Mary Elle's unannounced visit. At Mary Elle's answering nod, Crystal returned her focus to her customers and to arranging a large, deep violet bow around the festive silver box she was wrapping.

Sighing away her frustration at the delay, Mary Elle strode purposefully across the shop, stepped next to her friend behind the counter, and flashed a friendly smile in the direction of the next customer in line.

"May I help you?" She offered.

It wasn't the first time she manned her friend's shop. It was how the two initially met. It was Crystal who handed her a life-line in the form of a part-time job when Mary Elle arrived in the valley. Their shared love of art provided the seed from which their burgeoning friendship took root.

With holiday shopping in full swing, it was almost closing time before they found an opportunity to catch their collective breaths. Crystal turned in Mary Elle's direction as the last customer, her arms weighed down by shopping bags filled with shiny silver packages, left the shop. As the door closed behind her, Crystal broke out in a spontaneous little jig.

"We killed it today. I don't know how to thank you enough for helping me out. My temporary holiday help called out right before opening and I gave Jessica the day off for her future daughter-in-law's bridal shower. How did you know I needed you? We must be connected on some telepathic level. I'm going to put the closed sign on the door and take you to dinner. I'm also going to pay you for the hours you put in today." When Mary Elle would have protested, Crystal interrupted her, "Don't bother arguing. We both know you need the money, and there's no way I would have been able to handle the rush today without you. So I'm paying you time and a half and that's that."

Mary Elle laughed, throwing up her hands in surrender. "Maybe I'll spend my bounty here in the shop. I wrapped so many cute things today. I coveted them all. You have such a gift, Crystal."

It was fun to watch her tattooed and pierced best friend blush with pleasure at her compliment, then sputter awkwardly trying to deflect it. To give her time to recover her composure, Mary Elle slid out from behind the counter and strode towards the door. With her hand on the closed sign she sent an inquiring look in Crystal's direction. At her affirming nod, Mary Elle switched the sign from open to closed with a flourish, then let her glance sweep through the space separating them. The small shop looked like a hurricane just passed through. "We should probably restore order before we leave."

Ignoring her suggestion, Crystal grabbed both of their purses from the drawer beneath the register and joined her at the door. "That's the elves' job. I pay them in cookies from the bakery down the street. Let's go. I need a drink."

Grinning, Mary Elle pulled her arm free from her friend's determined grasp, held up one finger in a gesture to wait, and hurried to collect her sketchpad.

Eyeing it curiously as Mary Elle re-joined her at the door, Crystal asked, "What's that?"

"The reason for my impromptu visit today. I'll explain when we get to the restaurant. Where should we go?"

"It was a big day. Let's splurge."

It wasn't until they were seated in the booth of the upscale family-run Italian restaurant a few blocks from the shop and were waiting for their drinks to arrive, Crystal gestured to the sketchpad Mary Elle tucked away next to her on the bench in the booth.

Struggling with a sudden bout of nervousness, Mary Elle reluctantly reached for it. "I wanted to show you something... to get your opinion...your honest opinion."

"All right," Crystal replied, her expression revealing her curiosity.

When Mary Elle made no move to pass the pad across the table, Crystal prompted, "Can I see whatever it is you want my opinion on?"

"I suppose so." Mary Elle set the sketchbook on the table. Then with the tips of her fingers, pushed it slowly across the booth and into Crystal's waiting grip. With a quick, curious glance at Mary Elle's anxious expression, Crystal lifted the pad from the table and set it in her lap. Propping it up against the table top, she flipped back the cover. Mary Elle couldn't discern anything from her friend's initial reaction. Finally unable to bear the suspense any longer, she prompted anxiously, "Well, what do you think?"

"Did you do this?"

Mary Elle felt the telling color rise in her cheeks. "I don't want that to influence your opinion."

One brow arched over her friend's piercing green gaze as their glances met. "I thought you said you couldn't draw."

"I didn't say I couldn't draw, only that I wasn't very good at it."

Crystal let her gaze drop back down to the page in front of her, then raised it again to meet Mary Elle's worried glance. "If this is your idea of not being very good at it, remind me not to share any of my work with you."

"It's not awful, is it?" Mary Elle asked in a hushed voice, finally beginning to believe the evidence of her own eyes.

Crystal laughed. "Honey, I don't know who your art professors were but they must have been blind. This is not only not awful; it's fantastic, amazing, incredible...you have a real gift. Why in the world are you wasting your time teaching Latin?"

Mary Elle blinked away the tears filling her eyes and blurring her vision. "I've never done anything like it. To be honest, I'm not even sure I really did it."

"What do you mean?" Crystal demanded in obvious confusion, with laughter dancing in her expressive eyes.

Mary Elle released a heart-felt sigh and reluctantly went on to explain about her strange dreams and the little girl's request of her.

Eyeing her incredulously, Crystal challenged, "So what, you think the girl in the picture is somehow responsible for the improvement in your artistic ability?"

"I know it sounds crazy, but we're not talking about a slight enhancement here. More like a quantum leap. Maybe both of us are seeing her through rose-colored glasses. You're my friend. You don't want to hurt my feelings. And I don't want to be forced to accept, again, I lack any real artistic ability."

After a final incredulous glance at the page, Crystal closed the cover and passed the pad back across the booth top. "Let me be blunt. You're wrong and so was every art professor who claimed you lacked talent. Are you going to paint her?"

Mary Elle's head shot up at the question. "What?"

"Are you going to paint her? Pastels won't do her justice. She deserves to be done in oil."

"This is so crazy," Mary Elle whispered more to herself than in response to her friend's smiling observation. At the same time the waiter arrived with their drinks.

Crystal reached for their glasses and after passing one to Mary Elle, raised her own for a somewhat mocking but admiring tribute. "And so a master is born..."

Unsatisfied, she quickly shook her head, and tried again,

"No, given the circumstances, maybe born is a poor choice. How about chosen?" She paused again, still unsatisfied, then found the appropriate salute. "No....I think, a master... *Awakens.*"

CHAPTER SIX

"If you could be a little less...well, a little less of everything, we could finally finish this and give us both a much-needed break from each other. She's just a little girl. Can't you tone it down a bit?" Mary Elle mumbled beneath her breath at the source of her irritation. She was determined this weekend would bring about the conclusion of her latest experiment with art. Over the long winter months, she took Crystal's advice and attempted to re-create the girl from her dreams in oil. She was actually quite pleased with the way her initial subject turned out. It was her silent companion she was inexplicably having so much trouble with. Part of her difficulty she knew arose from the fact she had no idea who he was. From the size of his hand, she guessed him to be a grown man. The girl's father, maybe?

But no matter her numerous, discarded attempts, she was unable to capture the right dimensions. She rejected dozens of failed efforts. She couldn't understand why she was having so much trouble. All she needed to do was portray a man's hand clasping a smaller child's one, and an adult male arm concealed by his cloak. It should be the easiest part of the painting. She should be able to reproduce the image from her mind's eye without any unnatural expansion of her previous talent.

In contrast, the girl's face flew off the edge of her brush and virtually re-created itself on canvas. Mary Elle had yet to give her subjects context. She needed to finish the stupid hand and arm first. Who was he anyway? And why was he giving her such a hard time?

She put down the stubby charcoal and stretched out her

hand, using the fingers of her other hand to bend back the ones working the pencil. Leaning back on her elbows she stared up at the light passing through the stained glass, casting colorful shadows on the stone floor around her. She kept going until she was settled flat on her back and she lay staring up at one of the glass scenes above her. It was a familiar setting, not unlike the one she was trying to create.

"Of course," she whispered into the silence, turning her focus back to the canvas. She compared the half-finished painting with the scene in the window, wondering if that's where her inspiration came from.

The girls shared general characteristics. They were both very young, perhaps three or four years old, with long dark hair, but that was where the similarities ended. The young Madonna in the window was not holding any one's hand. Instead she was looking back over her shoulder, as if saying goodbye to the life and family she knew to date.

Mary Elle turned back to her painting. Then looked back at her sketches of the hand clasping the girl's and the arm it was attached to. "So that's who you are. You're not supposed to be in the picture yet...no pun intended."

With renewed purpose Mary Elle sat up and reached for the pad and a fresh charcoal. She understood now why all her efforts to date were so unsatisfactory. She was drawing a man's hand and a man's arm, but the little girl's champion was not a man. No, God would not rely on a man to protect the child destined to become his son's mother on earth.

He would call out the big guns. Who bigger than an angel, an archangel at that? Which explained why the little girl's expression mirrored such faith and awe as she stared up at her unseen companion.

For a moment, Mary Elle's hand hung suspended over the page while she debated how to capture an archangel's grasp. She tried to envision what he looked like in the eyes of the young virgin. She immediately dismissed the rather insipid characterizations of angels so often depicted in art. The ones resembling young boys graced with soft feminine features and wings, floating around on clouds and whiling away their time in heaven playing harps. Somehow she didn't think God's most magnificent creations would be content with such an insipid existence.

"Maybe you could give me a hint here. How am I supposed to know what an archangel looks like?" A deliberate silence was the only response to her rather desperate plea. "Fine, but don't blame me if you don't like the way you turn out."

The last rejoinder was tacked on in a frustrated, whispered muttering barely audible in the silence of her cramped cell. She felt an odd wariness hovering in the air and recognized it was coming from her. She was suddenly conscious of a new caution guiding her thoughts and it was with an almost respectful purpose she put pencil to paper and tried again.

Closing her eyes, she tried to bring into focus the memories from her dream. Even though the young virgin was the clear center of the scene replaying itself in her thoughts, he was there, close-by, an awe-inspiring, even terrifying presence.

She concentrated on where the girl's hand rested in his. Though it resembled a man's, it was not flesh and blood. The cloak covering his arm resembled spun gold and shone softly in the bright light of early afternoon. "All right, all right, I'll try," she whispered and could almost feel his impatience at her inadequacies. "I know. You don't like her being alone. She's vulnerable here. I'm doing my best."

Gaining confidence as she felt her silent companion's grudging approval of her halting efforts, Mary Elle moved swiftly from charcoal to oil. The tension hovering in the air relaxed noticeably as she painted the virgin's protector into the picture. When she was finished, she put down the brush and leaned back on her heels, pleased with the result. The rest of the scene could wait...the background, the crowds, and finally the facade of the ancient temple. The subject of her painting was safe now. It was all right for her to take a break.

Exhausted, Mary Elle lay on the hard floor and closed her eyes. She was sound asleep moments later, her head pillowed on her bent arm. Unbeknownst to her, the colored light from the stained glass above danced around her, enclosing her in a protective circle where she lay sleeping.

Contrary to Mary Elle's assumption she would finish the painting the same weekend, it ended up taking her several more weeks to satisfy herself with the end result. Since her dreams' focus was on the subjects of her painting, Mary Elle was obliged to spend a considerable amount of time researching the appropriate background for the young virgin and her angelic protector. She searched online sources for depictions of the architecture of the times, looking for ideas of a typical street scene, the details of the priestly vestments and the clothing of the onlookers in the crowd. Would animals make up a part of the scene? Should the road be depicted in dirt or stone? What about trees and other plant life? Would the area surrounding the temple appear prosperous and well-kept under Roman rule or would it be in a state of disrepair? Did a slight breeze provide relief from the blistering heat of a blazing sun, or was the air heavy and still?

Mary Elle carefully assembled each pertinent detail, letting them sift through her thoughts, moving the pieces around until she could see how the scene appeared the fateful morning, hear it, smell and even taste it on the tip of her tongue. When she was ready, she set out to transfer the images in her head to the waiting canvas where a little girl, holding the hand of an archangel waited patiently for Mary Elle to complete the request she put to her in a dream.

Mary Elle wasn't aware of a distinct moment when she thought to herself, 'Oh good, it's finally finished.' One breath she was holding the brush in her hand, the next she was laying it down on the stained rag beneath the easel where the canvas rested.

Wide-eyed, her astonished, fixed gaze examined the completed painting. Taking in the results of her efforts, Mary Elle was more uncertain than ever she was the one responsible for its genius, despite the fact she was the one who mixed the colors and wielded the brush. She slowly sank to her knees while her right hand, by its own volition, reached to her forehead to make the sign of the cross. Bowing her head, she offered a prayer of thanksgiving to the God she hadn't spoken to in years.

CHAPTER SEVEN

"Wow!" Crystal's voice emerged in an awed whisper as she stood staring at the finished painting. Turning to where Mary Elle hovered anxiously just beyond her shoulder, she confirmed incredulously, "You did this?"

Mary Elle's only response was to lift one shoulder in a slight shrug, bringing an amused smile to her friend's lips. Crystal turned her attention back to the painting adding, "The Virgin Mary. I didn't see her in the sketches you showed me."

"How do you know it's her?"

"Am I wrong?" Surprised, Crystal swung around to meet Mary Elle's anxious gaze.

"No. I'm just wondering how you knew."

Crystal shifted her focus back to the painting, and replicating Mary Elle's shrug of uncertainty, admitted, "I'm not sure. Probably because I felt the urge to genuflect the moment I saw the finished painting."

"Yes, I know what you mean. It's a little intimidating, isn't it? And strange. Very strange."

"Hm, no, not strange, more like compelling. And so amazing, Mary Elle! I can't believe you ever questioned the extent of your talent. This is incredible. What are you going to do with it?"

"What do you mean?"

"Well, you can't just leave this painting sitting propped up here on your old college easel."

Mary Elle understood what her friend meant. She was struggling with the same dilemma ever since she finished the painting. "What do you think I should do with her?"

Crystal paused to consider her question and then suggested, "I think you should have it appraised."

"Appraised?" Mary Elle echoed astonished. "You're joking right?" Seeing her friend was serious she protested, "No one bothers appraising paintings by unknown artists."

"I'm pretty sure you're not going to remain unknown for long. I think you should take it to the museum and have the acquisitions director give you his opinion."

"Why? So he can laugh me out of his office? No. No way." Mary Elle felt an inexplicable tide of panic rising in her chest. The opposite of the reaction she should be experiencing in the moment. What was wrong with her? What was she afraid of? Shouldn't she be thrilled her friend thought her work worthy of gaining the opinion of a true expert?

"Why don't you let me do a little research for you? There must be someone in the art world who would give you an honest assessment of the painting's worth."

At Mary Elle's half-hearted nod, Crystal persisted, "I'll just take a few photographs, send them out to a couple of art experts and see if any of them would be interested in consulting on the original painting."

"Consulting? I can't afford a consultant." Mary Elle felt control of the situation slipping away from her grasp. At the same time, her previous anxiety about the painting's fate was mounting so rapidly she was having trouble catching her breath.

"How much can it be? I'll lend you the money against the proceeds from the sale of the painting. You're going to be rich, Mary Elle. This painting is worth a lot of money."

Her friend's ridiculous assertion broke through the cloud of dread shadowing her. Mary Elle laughed, "You're delusional."

"So what if I am? It's my time and my dime."

When Mary Elle would have argued, Crystal held up one hand in an imperious gesture, effectively silencing her instinctive protest. "Let me do this. I was only teasing about the consulting fee. I'll just ask around at a few galleries to see if they're interested in displaying the painting, perhaps brokering the sale. Then we'll see. No commitment on either side. We'll just test the waters."

CHAPTER EIGHT

Crystal didn't have any intention of researching potential experts for their opinion of her friend's painting. It just so happened her uncle on her mother's side spent the past decade cozied up in their Parisian flat with the owner and operator of one of the most exclusive private galleries in Europe. Still, she didn't see any reason to confide as much to Mary Elle. It would only make her nervous.

With a little conspiratorial smile lifting the corners of her lips, Crystal transferred the photos she took of her friend's painting, composed an innocuous e-mail to accompany them with a little family chit chat thrown in to ease the pain of the favor she was asking, and pressed send. She didn't expect an immediate response. Her Uncle Drew was not a particularly time sensitive member of the clan, and she assumed it would take some wheedling on his part to convince Jean Paul to waste his valuable time assessing the work of an unknown American artist. She was therefore pleasantly surprised when a few days later, in the midst of closing down the store, her uncle's number flashed across the screen of her phone. As excited as if she was the one responsible for the painting, Crystal hurried to answer it. "Uncle Drew? Are you calling about the painting?"

"Yes."

"And?" She wasn't entirely successful in keeping the little sting of impatience from her voice.

"And, your friend's a fraud."

Crystal was so stunned by her uncle's blunt assessment, she didn't immediately respond. It took her a few seconds for her to catch up to her uncle's rambling, "Crystal? I'm sorry, sweetie, but it's true. Jean Paul is convinced your friend could not possibly be responsible for the painting you sent the photos of."

"No? Then who does he believe is responsible?"

"You're too young for sarcasm, niece of mine. Obviously it's impossible for him to definitively identify the artist from just looking at the photos, but he believes it's likely your friend discovered the painting in an attic somewhere or purchased it at auction from a seller who didn't comprehend its worth, and she is now trying to pass the painting off as her own work. He is also concerned she is attempting to drag you into her scheme."

"Her scheme?" Crystal was all but sputtering at her uncle's casual insult to Mary Elle's ethics.

"Yes, sweetie. How well do you know this friend, anyway? I don't recall you speaking about her before. Perhaps you should consider distancing yourself from this friendship."

"Uncle Drew, I'm hanging up now. I appreciate you doing this favor for me. Oh, and tell Monsieur Jean Paul he's a complete idiot. Perhaps you should consider distancing yourself from your relationship with *him*."

Crystal wished it was possible to slam the phone down like one could do in the old days, but she was forced to content herself with simply disconnecting the call. Still seething on her friend's behalf she slammed around the store picking up merchandise and tidying up the shelves. 'A fraud? Mary Elle? That was a good one.'

Still, she couldn't deny there was definitely something odd about the circumstances surrounding the painting's inspiration. She hoped her uncle's partner would instill a sense of normalcy into things. Nothing like a cynical Frenchman to bring one's head out of the clouds. Unfortunately, this particular Frenchman turned out to be more skeptical than she planned on. She debated her next step while she closed the shop and locked the door. She strode up the street to where her car was parked, and was nearly run over by a lunatic on a bike riding against the light when she stepped into the intersection.

Shaken by her close call, Crystal decided to set aside the problem of the painting until she was safely home. It was the end of a long work week. The staff usually handled Sundays and Mondays. In the meantime, she would do a little research on galleries interested in launching the careers of new artists and see what she came up with.

The following afternoon Crystal was curled up on her comfortable sofa, her attention focused on her laptop screen where she was taking down the information about a small gallery in the city whose owner was open to introducing the work of new artists to the Pittsburgh art scene, when her doorbell sounded. Her brows furrowing in irritation at the interruption, she debated whether or not to ignore the insistent summons.

She didn't get many unexpected visitors to her third floor apartment. Likely the person responsible for the persistent and extremely annoying buzzing was at the wrong door, but since whoever it was didn't appear about to give up anytime soon, she unwound her cross-legged position and crossed the narrow space to the door.

"Uncle Drew?" She exclaimed at the sight of her uncle. Then added in an almost awed whisper when she noticed his companion, "Jean Paul? What are you doing here?"

"Protecting you from yourself, sweetie," her uncle replied breezily. "Are you going to invite us in or are we relegated to camping out in your tiny entry?" He pushed passed her when she stepped back and barely paused for breath as he continued his typically forthright opinions of her life-style choices. "I can't imagine why you rent out the first two levels of this beautiful house. You're the owner. Let the tenants climb all of these dreadful stairs."

Crystal sighed and reminded herself not to be offended by her uncle's implied criticism as his reputation for speaking the first thing that popped into his head was well-deserved.

"I don't need all of that room. As you can see I have trouble keeping one floor in order."

"Yes, I noticed. You should consider a cleaning service."

Crystal bit back the instant retort springing to her lips about visitors showing up on a moment's notice and instead replied evenly, "Yes, I'll keep your suggestion in mind. I would offer you some wine, but I doubt you would be interested in anything I have in the wine department."

"Undoubtedly. Which is why we brought our own. We're here to see the painting by this so-called friend of yours."

"She's not a so-called friend and you can't honestly expect me to believe you flew four thousand miles to satisfy your curiosity about the painting."

Crystal followed her uncle into the kitchen where he was busy sorting through her kitchen drawers in search of a cork screw for the bottle of expensive French wine he was pulling from his leather carry-on.

"Well, the painting wasn't the only reason we flew four thousand miles, just the last few hundred. Jean Paul had business in New York, and since we were so close, I persuaded him to take a look at your friend's painting." When Crystal didn't respond, he turned to her with raised brows, "Gaining Jean Paul's opinion was the reason you sent the photos in the first place, wasn't it?"

"Yes, but that was before he called my friend a fraud."

"So, prove him wrong. Where's the painting?" He retrieved two wine glasses from her cabinet, lifted an inquiring brow in her direction, to which she nodded her less than gracious assent, and then waited in the doorway while he retrieved a third. "I assume it's all right if we stay with you tonight? Our flight doesn't leave until tomorrow afternoon, which gives us just enough time to catch up on the family gossip, get Jean Paul's opinion of your friend's painting, and then drive to the airport in time for our return flight."

Crystal was beginning to recall why it was so exhausting to spend any amount of time in her uncle's company. "I'll call

Mary Elle."

"I like your friend's name, anyway. Too bad she's a cheat."

"How can you possibly know anything about her?" Crystal demanded, frustrated by his obvious conviction.

"Oh, you're right, of course. I couldn't. I don't know a thing about art, but you will admit Jean Paul knows a great deal about it. He has a sixth sense for this sort of thing. He's never wrong. He's even consulted for the Louvre in regards to the validity of previously undiscovered works of famous, long-dead artists."

"Yes, I am aware of Jean Paul's qualifications, which is why I sought his opinion in the first place."

"Well, then let's get it. You call your friend, tell her you found an expert to examine her painting and ask if we could stop by to see it. After dinner. Is there a decent restaurant in this town?"

Sighing, defeated, Crystal didn't bother to bite her tongue. "Sometimes, Uncle Drew, you are such a snob."

"Of course, honey. Why do you think I moved to Paris?"

It was dusk by the time they pulled into the long, mostly gravel drive leading to Mary Elle's unusual home. "Your friend lives in a church?" Drew asked, eyeing the serene surroundings with surprise.

"Yes, she believes it's the perfect cover for her illegal activities," Crystal bit back, not bothering to hide her sarcasm.

"Hm, she has a point." Her uncle agreed amicably, and then slid his arm through hers as Jean Paul climbed out of the back seat of the car. Dinner was a rather stilted affair, what with her uncle's partner making snide comments about Mary Elle's integrity and Crystal honor bound to defend her friend. "Come on, let's get this over with. You can thank Jean Paul later," Drew added in pointed reference to her failure to express her appreciation to his partner.

Crystal leaned around her uncle and offered miserly, "Thank you, Jean Paul. I realize this was a great imposition. I hope after you see the painting you won't feel your time was thoroughly wasted."

Jean Paul nodded stiffly. "I have no great hope of that, but if our visit serves to separate you from an unhealthy friendship, I will not consider my time wasted."

Crystal's only response was to roll her eyes in her uncle's direction, and then set off with a purposeful stride towards the front door. Mary Elle pulled it open before Crystal could knock. Their eyes met. Crystal completed the introductions before stepping aside to allow her friend to charm her uncle and his admittedly art-expert partner.

"Please come in. This is so kind of you. I'm certain your visit is a total waste of your valuable time but, well, Crystal seemed to think otherwise, and this whole experience has bordered on the bizarre. Can I offer you anything? A drink? Wine, perhaps?"

Sensing Mary Elle's anxiety, Crystal wasn't surprised when her uncle stepped in to fill the awkward breach. "No, thank you, we just finished dinner. Mary Elle, what an unusual name. Perhaps you could show us the painting and then we can all be comfortable while we hear Jean Paul's opinion. I, for one, would like to know why you live in a church."

"Yes, yes, of course. The painting's upstairs in the tower. I can get it for you."

When Mary Elle would have hurried up the stairs, Crystal noticed her uncle exchange a meaningful glance with Jean Paul, who shook his head. "No, why don't we just follow you up. To the tower, did you say?" Drew kept up his innocuous chatter all the way up the two flights of stairs until the four of them were squeezed into the dim, tight space of the converted bell tower where the lingering odor of paint hung in the air.

"Sorry, it's a little cramped. I never come up here except to paint," Mary Elle apologized.

"Is this the painting?" Jean Paul asked, pointing in the direction of the easel.

"Yes." Mary Elle exchanged a nervous glance with Crystal. She was beginning to regret allowing her friend to talk her into this. She wasn't certain how she would react if her friend's fastidious expert called her painting amateurish and pedestrian. She only just finished piecing together the tiny fragments of her splintered heart.

Jean Paul looked around, "Is there a light switch somewhere?"

Blushing at his obvious disdain, Mary Elle reached for the lantern. "No, I'm sorry. There's no electricity up here. I use the lantern."

His haughty brows arched over his piercing light eyes at her stilted explanation, but he accepted the lit lantern from her outstretched hand and carried it with him to the center of the room. Mary Elle suppressed the sudden, inexplicable urge to jump in front of the easel to protect the subject of her painting from the scathing attack she was certain was about to be unleashed upon her innocent head. She exchanged an 'I told you so glance' with Crystal, who responded with an apologetic but encouraging shrug. The three of them stood huddled together near the door in uncomfortable silence awaiting Jean Paul's pronouncement.

After what seemed like hours, but Mary Elle realized was actually no more than a few silent minutes, Jean Paul turned his intent focus in her direction. "You painted this?"

"Yes," Mary Elle whispered, then confirmed with greater conviction."Yes."

"Do you have other works I could examine for comparison purposes?"

"None like this. I haven't painted in years. All of my art professors told me I should strongly consider another career choice."

At her admission, one perfectly shaped brow arched in surprise. "What made you decide to begin painting again?"

Mary Elle couldn't hold his probing glance for long. "She did."

"Who is she?"

Mary Elle stepped towards him and stood by his side

staring at the young girl's face in the painting. "She did," she pointed to her. "I dreamed about her."

She blushed at the blatant disbelief in his expression and thrust a nervous hand through her hair. "I know. I know it sounds crazy. I told Crystal this was a bad idea, but it seemed wrong to just leave her up here all alone."

He turned back to the painting. "Are there any preliminary sketches for me to look at or did you just go out and purchase a canvas and oil paints and begin expressing yourself?"

Mary Elle felt her already high color deepen at his derisive tone. She pointed to the corner where her sketch pads were stacked up. He carried the lantern over and retrieved the first one. Hanging the lantern on a nearby hook, he opened the cover and slowly leafed through the first tablet before bending down to reach for another and then another. "You did these?"

"Yes."

"Would you mind doing a sketch of the girl for me now?"

"You don't believe I painted her." Mary Elle felt compelled to state the obvious.

"No, I do not. Would you care to prove me wrong?"

Shrugging, Mary Elle stepped forward and took the pad he opened to a fresh page. She sank down to the floor and retrieved an unused charcoal and then propped the pad on her bent knees. Without glancing at the completed painting, and trying to ignore the suspicion hovering around her in the form of her best friend's art expert, she began re-creating her unusual visitor's face. The young girl's features were just taking shape on the page when Jean Paul commanded abruptly, "That's enough."

Mary Elle nodded and closed the pad, surprised when he reached down to assist her to her feet. "Your art professors were fools," he announced.

Mary Elle quickly protested his welcome conclusion. "No, no they weren't. They were right. I couldn't do this before. I've never done anything like this. I don't know where it came from. I don't know where *she* came from."

Smiling, a new gentleness in his expression, Jean Paul told her, "I believe we'll enjoy your offer of wine now."

CHAPTER NINE

Not quite a month later, Mary Elle stared back at her decidedly unfamiliar reflection in the antique Cheval mirror in the bedroom of her boutique Paris hotel. Unfamiliar because her designer gown and high-heeled evening sandals were not exactly daily fare at St Mary's. Her waist length, mahogany-colored hair was braided and twisted into a complicated chignon anchored at the base of her neck. Her grey-blue eyes appeared huge in her pale face, thanks to a strategic sweep of violet across her lids and expertly applied eyeliner and mascara. Her borrowed jewelry was understated but excellent quality. The view outside her window was of the magical Paris skyline.

She reached out to brush one manicured finger across her reflection in the glass just to assure herself it was her own face staring back at her and she wasn't immersed in yet another bizarre dream. Even when her hand encountered glass, she wasn't convinced it was her eyes she met within its depths. Clearly she must still be dreaming. What other explanation could there possibly be for her to be standing in a gown she suspected cost more than her annual salary, preparing for the painting she wasn't entirely certain she could claim authorship of to be auctioned off in arguably one of Europe's most exclusive private galleries?

Memories of the past frantic weeks circled through her thoughts. Her giddy excitement over Jean Paul's offer to represent her in the sale of the painting competed with her odd reaction at the possibility of having to bid farewell to the girl who invaded her dreams. She was torn between excitement at the prospect of launching her new career as an artist and fear and sadness over the thought of having to let go of the one responsible. There were other dreams in the intervening weeks. Dreams Mary Elle did her best to ignore.

In them the young girl was growing up, approaching womanhood, both fearful and excited at the future awaiting her beyond the quiet life the temple afforded her during her formative years. Mary Elle sympathized with the girl's confusion. Wasn't she both fearful and excited about the step she was about to take? Was she doing the right thing? Was she supposed to sell her? Is that what *she* wanted?

"Mary Elle, according to Jean Paul's exacting schedule, it's time for the newly discovered artist to make her dramatic entrance at the gallery."

Uncle Drew's pronouncement was enough to chase away her conclusion she was somehow still dreaming. He was Uncle Drew to her too now, at his own insistence. Crystal confided in her Jean Paul's original conclusion she was trying to pass off some famous artist's work as her own. While Crystal was still indignant about the insult to her integrity, Mary Elle didn't blame him. Part of her still believed she deserved the charge of fraud he labeled her with.

"Mary Elle?"

She felt sick. She couldn't do this. Why did she need to be there anyway? She wasn't being auctioned off. Her painting was. As far as Mary Elle was concerned her presence at the event could only diminish the painting's value in the eyes of potential collectors. Let the subject speak for herself. Her choice of artists to depict her was not cut out for the sophisticated, private gallery scene. The only small point she could conjure in her favor was her fluency in French.

She doubted Jean Paul would mention his young, newly discovered artist was American. Such a confession would be bound to instantly diminish the painting's value. To the French, the very idea of American art, particularly given the decidedly Renaissance flair of the subject matter, was an oxymoron.

"Mary Elle? Do you need help?"

"No, I'm coming," she whispered, her eyes still glued to her reflection in the mirror. Then at the feeling she was no longer alone, she turned to regard Crystal's uncle, who now stood framed in the doorway. Her lips curved in instant appreciation of the figure he cut in his elegant tuxedo. "You look amazing."

Surprised and delighted at her spontaneous compliment he grinned back at her. He crossed the room and came to stand by her side in front of the mirror. With his hands on her shoulders he gently turned her back to face their joint reflections. His tall, lean, elegantly clad form would blend in perfectly with the crowd he assured her would be in attendance at the auction.

The woman by his side looked as if she belonged at such an event too, but Mary Elle recognized Drew would fit in with the attendees from the inside out. She might give the impression of belonging tonight in her borrowed finery, but this was not her world and she was so nervous at the prospect of stepping outside her carefully drawn comfort zone her hands were shaking.

Their reflected gazes met, and catching a sense of her anxiety, Drew gave her shoulders a reassuring squeeze. "You are the one who looks amazing. Stunning. Your presence at the auction tonight will drive up the value of the painting by thousands of euros." At her disbelieving expression, he shook his head and added, "You'll be a complete mystery to them. Exquisite...talented...and so young, with an aura of innocence presenting a challenge to every man in the room." After a slight pause for effect, he added with an amused grin, "Well, at least every straight man in the room."

Mary Elle met his amused glance in the mirror and grinned back. Drawing a cleansing breath, she announced, "All right, I'm ready. Thanks."

He nodded his smiling acknowledgment, and Mary Elle turned from the mirror and reached for his hand. "No, really, thank you for everything you're doing for me. I don't understand why you and Jean Paul would go to so much trouble for a complete stranger, but I want you to know how much I appreciate it. No matter what happens tonight."

Drew held onto one hand while he drew her from the room and predicted confidently, "What happens tonight is going to change your life."

Mary Elle wasn't sure what to expect when they approached the gallery's well-lit entrance. She was awed by her initial visit to Jean Paul's gallery on the Rue de Seine but that was in the morning, before most Parisians were up and about and after a long, exhausting day and overnight flight from Pittsburgh through a layover in New York. At night, beneath the city lights and a full moon, with the whisper of spring on the fragrant air, the small gallery glittered like a diamond embraced by its perfect setting.

"What if no one comes?" Mary Elle anxiously gave voice to her worst fears.

Drew laughed at what he obviously considered the absurdity of her question.

They passed through the double, etched glass doors and found Jean Paul's establishment gratifyingly filled with elegantly clad, and Drew assured her, wealthy and carefully selected art collectors. Apparently, the auction tonight was limited to an intimate group of Jean Paul's clients. Mary Elle was able to relax somewhat when their entrance into the jeweled and tuxedoed crowd caused barely a ripple of interest among the other attendees.

Drew led her to the largest salon where a single pedestal was set up in the center. She noticed all of the other art on the walls and behind the exhibit glasses displayed on her initial visit had been removed. Her painting, unframed to both emphasize and complement the simplicity and innocence of its subject, was propped on a primitive wooden easel not so very different from the one it rested upon in the tower room where it was painted.

"I just have to check on her," Mary Elle explained softly then made her way as unobtrusively as possible towards the painting. There were a few people standing in front of it, so she waited until they were finished with their discussion and tried not to be hurt by their comments about its lack of depth and its obvious representation of the girl's rite of passage from the comfort of her family home to womanhood.

Mary Elle was flabbergasted by the depths of their misconception and thought to correct them, but managed to bite her tongue in time. Art was subjective. That was both its promise and its fulfillment. Art was whatever the beholder saw in it. When the pair stepped away, she took a little step forward.

"Are you sure about this?" She whispered half to herself and half to her subject.

She wasn't really expecting a reply from the subject of her painting and wasn't surprised when none was forthcoming. It scared her a little to think after tonight she would no longer belong to her. What if the collector who purchased the painting tucked her away in some dusty little-used hallway where no one would ever see her? She turned when Jean Paul came to stand beside her. "I think I made a mistake. What if whoever buys her doesn't appreciate her? What if he or she doesn't take proper care of her?"

He didn't laugh in her face as she was half expecting, but instead gently squeezed her arm and assured her, "Trust me. I will not let her go to anyone who lacks the ability to appreciate her."

"Do you promise?"

"Yes, I promise." The glance holding hers was filled with amused understanding.

"All right. I trust you." It wasn't as though at this point she had much choice in the matter.

"Wise choice." He waited for her to smile at his teasing and then added, "Are you ready?"

"Are you certain this is necessary?"

"Necessary, no, but how are they to know her if you don't tell them about her?" He made a sweeping gesture to encompass the crowd.

Mary Elle reluctantly nodded. "You're right. She deserves that much."

Jean Paul stepped in front of the portrait and announced, "*Mesdames and Messieurs*, if I may have your attention, S'*il vous plait*. I am certain everyone is anxious to proceed with the purpose of the evening, but first I wanted to introduce you to the artist, Mademoiselle Mary Elle McGann." Polite applause greeted his announcement and Mary Elle tried not to look as nervous as she felt. She nodded in acknowledgment and stepped to Jean Paul's side when he continued, "I'm certain Mlle McGann would be happy to answer your questions."

With somewhat bored but mostly polite expressions on their faces, the crowd gathered into the salon and moved closer to form a semi-circle around her. From somewhere in the crowd, Mary Elle heard a male voice ask if the subject was someone she knew.

Mary Elle suppressed the urge to laugh. "No, I wish I did." At the expectant silence that followed her response, she added, "She's the Virgin Mary on the morning she said goodbye to her former life with her parents and entered the temple."

She felt a ripple of renewed interest flow through the crowd at her explanation, as they tried to envision the scene she described. Mary Elle recognized not everyone in the gathering was familiar with the passage depicted in the painting. Before she recreated it, she wasn't either. The stained glass scenes in the bell tower gave her a hint, but after she finished the painting, she conducted more detailed research into the early life of the young virgin who would become the mother of Christ. There were scant offerings to be found, but she did locate a few references to a young Mary entering the temple to devote herself to prayer and study in order to fulfill St. Ann's promise to the Almighty when she prayed for a child.

"Who's holding her hand?" A male voice called out.

"The Archangel Gabriel."

"No, that's not right. There's no scripture passage suggesting Gabriel appeared to the virgin prior to the Annunciation."

Mary Elle sought and found the slightly derisive glance of the protestor who no doubt thought to mock her obvious mistake and impress the gathering with his knowledge of both art and scripture. She didn't want him to purchase the painting. Panic filled her at the very real possibility she would not have a say in the matter once the auction commenced. She turned back to where Jean Paul stood slightly behind and to her left keeping a careful eye on the proceedings. "I changed my mind. I don't want to go through with this."

Jean Paul leaned towards her in response to her fierce whisper and reassured her softly, "He's an arrogant fool. I would not allow her to go to him."

Mary Elle wasn't satisfied with his reassurance. "I want the final say. I want to reserve the right to reject the highest bid."

Jean Paul eyed her with a combination of both admiration and speculation and then cautioned, "What you are suggesting is an all or nothing proposition. You can only reject the highest bid if you decline to sell the painting completely."

Mary Elle nodded. "I'm all right with the condition."

"We're speaking about a considerable amount of money," he reminded her.

"It doesn't matter."

"The minimum opening bid is set at two hundred and fifty thousand euros."

Mary Elle gasped. "You're joking. No one is going to pay

that much for a painting by an unknown artist. They don't even know who she is."

"I've already received more than one offer in excess of the minimum."

"Oh, my God!" The words escaped her lips in a hushed whisper. This was really happening. She was going to have to let her go. Tears stung her eyes at the thought. She quickly brushed them aside when Jean Paul pressed her.

"Do you still insist on having the final say? I could take care of the process for you and you would never need to know who purchased her."

Never know where she was or who she was entrusted to? No, that was entirely unacceptable to her. Maybe she completely misread the situation. Maybe she wasn't supposed to sell her. Maybe she was supposed to keep her safe with her forever. As tempted as she was to grab her painting and run off into the Paris night, her heart told her such an outcome was not what *she* would want. "Yes, I need to have the last say."

"It would be unethical of you to sell the painting at a later date, and to do so would destroy my reputation."

Mary Elle nodded, her stomach in knots, but she assured him sincerely, "I would never do that, especially after all you've done for me."

Seeing she would not be swayed, Jean Paul regarded her with new respect and a slightly amused smile at this latest twist. "As you wish." He returned his attention to the now restless crowd.

"*Mesdames* and *Messieurs*, thank you for your patience. There's been a slight accommodation in the auction guidelines. Mlle McGann has elected to reserve the right to refuse the sale of the painting to the highest bidder and retain the painting for her personal collection. My apologies. I accept this is a rather unusual stipulation at this late hour and I certainly understand if anyone wishes to remove him or herself from the bidding process at this time."

No one left. Mary Elle could tell they were not happy about

the change in the terms for the evening. From the cynical looks cast in her direction, she concluded the majority of the attendees believed she was grandstanding in such a dramatic fashion in order to make the most of her moment of fame. Perhaps even to drive up their interest and therefore the price of the painting, but she didn't care what they thought. Relief flooded her knowing she would be able to assure herself she performed her duty to her subject and found her the best possible new home.

Her inner musings were interrupted by a cultured male voice calling out from the back of the crowd. "If we could continue, M. Girard. I have no objection to proceeding under the new conditions. Frankly, I respect the artist's judgment. She alone is in a position to judge the painting's true worth. If she would be willing to share her vision, we too will be in a position to make our own judgments as to the painting's value for each of us."

There were affirmative nods and echoes of agreement from the man's fellow bidders, and Mary Elle nodded her assent. With a nod in the direction of the collector who announced her depiction was incorrect, the stranger in the crowd added with an amused smile, "I am not particularly interested in whether or not there is historical validation for the artist's vision. Art does not require proof. It exists simply to be appreciated or not, depending on the vision of the beholder."

Mary Elle's glance briefly met the dark eyes of the speaker's. He understood. It comforted her to know there was at least one potential bidder in the salon who did. When the gathered crowd fell silent, she did her best to still the butterflies in her stomach. In order to gather her composure, she turned her back to the expectant crowd and faced her painting. She clasped her hands together in front of her to disguise their trembling. Determined to do her best for the young girl who changed her life, she turned back to her audience.

"She was just a little girl, excited to be chosen for such an honor. Her parents were proud of her and she was happy to make them so. She was anxious too, about leaving her home, her mother and father. Even though they tried to explain to her about her new life, and how she would be serving God, Mary didn't really understand the finality of the goodbye she was facing. How could she? She was so young. There were other little girls there, too. She noticed there were tears in some of their eyes, but she was determined not to shame her parents by weeping."

"Her mother impressed upon her again and again the need for her to be strong, and everything would be all right. It was God's will leading her to this moment. She was trying very hard to be brave. The temple where she would be living was huge. The bearded faces of the priests were intimidating, but *he* was there, she reminded herself. He held her hand and kept reminding her not to be afraid. He knew she was afraid because she confessed her fears to him about leaving her home and her mother, and he patiently explained her heavenly Father would provide her with a new home."

"But I like my old one," the young Mary assured her protector."

"At her whispered protest, he smiled down at her and squeezed her hand. For a brief moment the veil was lifted from her child's eyes and she recognized him as one of God's holy ones. She was both awed and frightened by the knowledge, suspecting even with her limited youthful understanding the Lord did not easily part with his most precious companions for what even she comprehended was not the kind of momentous occasion to warrant such an intercession. Then in the time it takes to draw a single breath she was just a little girl again, glancing back over her shoulder to see her mother fighting tears at their parting, with her father's strong arm to support her. Their glances met. Mother and daughter. In that instant, both of them knew, both of them understood, neither of their lives would ever be the same again."

Mary Elle let her voice trail off and she brushed tears from her eyes before she lifted her gaze to the crowd. A hushed silence hung over the room. She avoided eye contact with anyone in the crowd, expecting to be greeted with amused derision, and no little affront at her arrogant claim to be able to reach inside the painting and perceive the thoughts of the young Madonna on so pivotal a morning. She turned to where Jean Paul still stood at her side.

"Is it all right if I leave now?" She inquired softly.

"Yes. Drew will see you back to your hotel."

"No, it's not far. I'd rather be alone." At his assenting nod, she added anxiously, "You'll keep your promise?"

"Yes. I will not allow her to leave until you approve the transaction."

"Thank you. I know I don't really have any right..." Her voice trailed off at his quick dismissive gesture.

"You have every right. She's yours. You created her."

"No, I didn't create her and she doesn't belong to me, but she came to me for a little while. I just wish I could be certain this is what she wants." Their glances met before she lowered hers and stepped around him and headed towards the exit. As she passed through the double glass doors leading onto the still bustling street, she heard Jean Paul's voice rising above the murmur of the crowd.

"Shall we begin? I believe the agreed upon minimum opening bid is set at two hundred and fifty thousand euros."

CHAPTER TEN

Luc Bordeaux watched surprised as the lovely young artist slipped away from what he perceived from the excitement simmering in the crowd was about to prove to be an evening of great professional triumph for her. He was one of the collectors who offered to purchase the painting prior to the auction. He intended to make the *Young Madonna* a gift to his grandmother, who would appreciate both the subject matter and his gesture of giving a struggling, unknown artist a little boost out of anonymity into the glaringly bright scrutiny of the art world. The artist herself, however, did not seem inclined to appreciate his generosity.

He was amused at her insistence of retaining the right to pull the painting from sale if she did not approve its final purchaser. Amused and admiring, considering even the minimum bid was a great deal of money for one so young. Perhaps she was not forced to make her own way in the world, and she could therefore afford to indulge her pique at the petty offense offered her vision by one of his competitors in the evening's festivities. Luc was quite certain M. Bacchus would not find himself the owner of the painting in the morning even if he outbid everyone else, a circumstance Luc could no longer allow.

The young artist recognized instantly Bacchus was unworthy of her efforts. Luc meant to see to it her admirable perception did not result in her being forced to sacrifice a large sale while at the same time offending an influential collector, particularly when the charming mademoiselle displayed the excellent taste of putting the pompous ass in his place.

Luc waited for his moment. The bidding was brisk in the opening rounds, and as expected, Bacchus was apparently set on having his little revenge against the beautiful Mlle McGann. The other potential purchasers began dropping out when the bidding flirted with five hundred thousand euros. Luc allowed Bacchus a moment to bask in his triumph. Then when the call came for the third and final time for any additional bids, he calmly offered his coup de grace into the breach, "One million euros."

Luc enjoyed the stunned aftermath of his little joke at Bacchus' expense. He never cared for the man. His grandmother would enjoy his retelling of his purchase of her gift as much as she would the offering itself. He met Jean Paul's slightly amused glance over the heads of the rest of the astonished crowd. The proprietor of the gallery was about to make a substantial commission on this night's single offering. He was no doubt praying fervently the young artist would not find Luc an unacceptable steward of her work. Perhaps, he should bring his grandmother along to the interview to reassure the lovely but skittish Mlle McGann of his worthiness. He nodded a little mockingly in Jean Paul's direction as the other man brought the gavel down and announced the sale to be final pending the artist's approval.

Later that night, across the street from the entrance to *The Gallerie*, on the roof of a shuttered shop, a man camouflaged in the shadows watched as the last of the guests exited the brightly lit salon. He could not prevent a regretful sigh from whispering passed his lips as he observed the fine jewels glittering around the necks and wrists of the female attendees, but he no longer peddled his services for such menial rewards. There was no challenge in simply obtaining easily replaced trinkets from their unsuspecting owners. No, he reached a point in his illustrious career when he could be more selective in the commissions he accepted.

His requirements grew increasingly stringent over the

years, step in step with the progressively more disagreeable consequences associated with failure. The life he created for himself on the proper side of the law was not an unpleasant one, particularly compared with the prospect of a long exile in a French prison.

His musings were interrupted at the sight of M. Girard appearing in the entrance and turning to lock the door of his exclusive gallery before setting off up the street to his well-appointed town home purchased some years earlier by his wealthy American partner. The man on the roof sighed and settled into waiting. A few hours should be sufficient. He always found the hours just before dawn to be those with the least inherent risk for his line of work. Even the most devoted night-owl sought his bed by four am.

Two hours later and under the cover and quiet of the deepest hours of night, Francis slipped silently away from his observation place at the edge of the roof and stood to shake out his limbs grown stiff from maintaining the same position for so long. With lithe grace for a man his age he descended the fire escape on the side of the building into the narrow alleyway separating the neighboring establishments. There was no one around. Few of the proprietors lived over their store fronts in this affluent section of the city.

He crossed the narrow street and made quick work of the admittedly challenging security system. Modern thieves excelled at hacking into secure networks. He was rather proud of his old-school approach. Despite the advantages of modern technology, the security system he couldn't disarm had yet to be invented. Safes and locks of any kind were child's play for him.

He did occasionally run up against a particularly well-designed system. At such times he was forced to weigh the enjoyment of the puzzle against the time it would tale to unravel it. There were one or two occasions when he decided the risk of getting caught was simply not worth the promised reward. To accommodate such contingencies, he included a provision in his agreements allowing him to return his employer's deposit and void their contractual arrangement solely at his discretion. It was all very civilized.

He foresaw little difficulty completing his assignment this evening. He was inside the dimly lit gallery in under a minute. He ignored the paintings displayed in the store front. The more valuable works would be in the more secure interior of the salon. He passed by the majority without a backward glance. Though he paused momentarily to consider the offering of an up and coming young Italian artist whose vibrant work was beginning to attract the attention of seasoned collectors. Then chiding himself for succumbing to the distraction he moved on.

He suspected he was only going to get a single opportunity to procure the target he was contracted for. Once it disappeared into the vast Bordeaux collection, he would have a better chance of success in attempting to steal the *Mona Lisa* from the Louvre.

One million euros. The painting of the young Madonna from the unknown American artist just became the most valuable offering in *The Gallerie*. He liked the name. Arrogant but understated. He thought it suited its proprietor perfectly. Conveniently enough he was among the crowd in attendance earlier in the evening, a recipient of a legitimate invitation to the event. In recent years he became a collector in his own right and was rather proud of the exquisite taste he displayed in each of his acquisitions, a few of which came from the very establishment he was about to rob.

He recognized immediately the innocence of both the subject of the painting and the artist responsible for its unveiling, but accepted almost as instantaneously he would not be the successful bidder at the evening's event.

He did well for himself over the years, but it took more than a single generation for a man born on the streets to compete with the kind of wealth acquired and tended to over the course of centuries.

So he refrained from bidding on *The Young Madonna*, thinking it best not to show any interest at all in acquiring the painting. When it was discovered the depiction of the young Madonna went missing overnight, the police would first focus their efforts on the unsuccessful bidders, and then regrettably, would no doubt turn their attention to the unknown artist, assuming she planned some elaborate fraud at the expense of the unsuspecting heads of the wealthy and influential Parisians in attendance that evening. Certainly their conclusion would sit more comfortably on the shoulders of their superiors than the prospect one of the attendees was an art thief.

Francis was not surprised when he made his way to the center salon to find the easel his target rested on earlier empty. Jean Paul was no fool. He would have locked the painting away in the gallery's safe. One million euros was not a sum to be dismissed with carelessness even by so successful a proprietor as M. Girard.

A few false leads and Francis located the owner's safe behind a large sea scape facing the antique desk in Girard's office. He shifted the heavy painting aside and with his ear pressed close to the tumblers, sought the subtle shifts that would reveal the safe's combination. The haughty Jean Paul was more cautious than he gave him credit for, but still Francis opened the safe in under ten minutes.

Sighing with telling relief, he pulled open the heavy door and peered into the surprisingly cavernous interior. He was stunned by what he discovered. If he was wearing one, Francis would tip his cap to the absent Jean Paul. The safe was empty. Either the proprietor of *The Gallerie* was tipped off or the man was psychic.

But where was the painting? Jean Paul left empty handed when he locked up the gallery, as did each of his guests, including M. Bordeaux, the successful bidder. Therefore, the obvious conclusion was the painting was still somewhere in the gallery. Unfortunately, despite his long, successful career as an art thief, Francis was no more skilled at looking for obvious, unsecured hiding places than the next man. Consequently, he was forced to conduct a thoroughly frustrating search for the object he sought.

After an hour spent rifling through the cluttered back store room, searching beneath every painting large enough to conceal the *Young Madonna*, behind cabinets, behind locked doors, even beneath every tapestry on the marble floors or hanging on the walls, Francis was forced to admit defeat. If the painting was still in the gallery he no longer had the time to locate it. The fragile light of dawn was beginning to pierce the shadows through the large store-front windows and Francis accepted regretfully he would be returning the very large deposit to the person who engaged his services for the evening.

So be it. He learned long ago in his excessively emotional youth surrendering to sometimes inevitable defeat was a far more satisfactory outcome than being caught. Still he was just irritated enough not to clean up the mess he made. Let the ever-composed M. Girard wonder how his high-priced security system was so easily by-passed and what the violator was after tonight. The man deserved a couple of sleepless nights over this evening's work. Francis knew it would cost him more than a few nights spent wondering if he was losing his touch. Perhaps it was time for him to retire after all.

CHAPTER ELEVEN

After a restless night filled with vivid dreams and agonizing indecision over whether she was doing the right thing in parting with her painting, Mary Elle returned to Jean Paul's gallery the following morning at the agreed upon time. At least her sleepless night accomplished one thing. In the light of dawn she knew what to do. She was going to demand Jean Paul keep his word and return the painting to her.

The entire weekend was a mistake. She wasn't selling her painting. She only hoped Jean Paul would understand. She felt guilty about putting him to so much trouble on her behalf and having him come away empty handed. Without the proceeds from the sale of the painting there was no way she could afford to compensate him for the commission he would forgo when she pulled the painting from the auction.

Flashing lights up ahead interrupted her inner dialogue. Her heart began racing in response. She chided herself for her instant presumption the lights had anything to do with her. The police car parked in front of Jean Paul's gallery was probably there for a completely different reason than her painting.

She wasn't doing a very good job convincing herself of her reasoning. Her breath was lodged in her throat and she quickened her steps until she was almost running towards the entrance. She was prevented from entering by the armed *policier* blocking the door.

"I'm sorry, Mademoiselle, you cannot go inside. The gallery is closed."

Mary Elle tried to peer around him for any sign of Jean

Paul, then seeing none, turned pleading eyes back to the policeman. "Is everyone all right? I'm supposed to be meeting the owner this morning. He asked me to come by at ten."

"You are Mlle McGann?" he confirmed.

"Yes, yes. May I please go inside?" Her heart was pounding. What if someone stole her painting? How would she get her back? She rebuked herself for putting her at risk even as the policeman guarding the door motioned for someone out of her line of sight to escort her inside.

There were far more valuable paintings than her own displayed in the gallery, she reminded herself. It was merely a coincidence the robbery attempt, if that was what occurred to explain the police presence, took place on the same night as the auction. Thoughts racing, she anxiously trailed the uniformed officer across the marble floor and into Jean Paul's private office. Her heart flooded with relief when she saw he was unharmed.

"Jean Paul, what happened? Is everyone all right?"

Seeing her anxiety, he came around the desk to take both her hands and give them a comforting squeeze. "Everyone is fine. There was a robbery attempt after the auction last night."

"Oh, I'm so sorry." Her heart racing, she couldn't keep herself from asking, "Is she all right? Tell me they didn't take her."

"No, the *Young Madonna* is quite all right. Drew took the painting home with him after the auction was complete."

"Oh, thank God," she whispered and felt her legs go weak with relief.

He pushed her into the nearest chair and performed the introductions to the other men in the room. "This is Detective Dubois and his associate, Detective Martin. They are investigating the robbery attempt. This is M. Luc Bordeaux. He was the successful bidder at the auction last night."

She nodded in response to the introductions and only then noticed their speculative expressions as they regarded her.

She turned a questioning look back in Jean Paul's direction. "What's wrong? Why are they looking at me like that? You said she was fine."

Sensing her rising panic Jean Paul returned to his desk to lift the painting from where it rested in the center of it. "As you can see, the *Young Madonna* is fine. These gentlemen would like to ask you a few questions."

Confused, Mary Elle turned her attention expectantly back to the policemen. "Yes, of course. What is it you wish to know?"

"Mlle McGann, M. Girard informs us you left the auction early?"

"Yes," she whispered, only just realizing these men considered her a suspect in whatever went on here last night.

"Would you mind explaining why?"

"Do I need a lawyer?" She was becoming genuinely frightened of the fact she was in a foreign country, and apparently suspected of a serious crime perpetuated against her only acquaintance in said country. She turned scared eyes to Jean Paul. "Do you believe I had something to do with this?"

"No, I do not. I already explained to the detectives that there was no reason for you to steal the painting. If you changed your mind about selling it you reserved the right to cancel the sale until you approved the transaction this morning." His voice held an impatient edge, and Mary Elle was relieved by it once she understood his impatience was on her behalf.

"Thank you. But I don't understand why anyone would jump to the conclusion it was my painting the thief was interested in. There are far more valuable paintings in the gallery than mine."

"According to M. Girard that is no longer true," Detective Dubois countered.

"I don't understand." Her eyes sought Jean Paul for an explanation.

Smiling, he informed her, "M. Bordeaux offered one million euros to acquire the *Young Madonna*."

Mary Elle felt the color drain from her face. She turned to regard the silent man leaning against the entrance to the hallway leading into the main salon, silently watching the exchange among the other occupants. She recognized him as the one who asked her to explain her vision of the painting... the one she believed understood about the painting and could appreciate it. "Have you lost your mind?"

A quick grin flashed across his lips at her hushed question. "I do not believe so. Apparently I am not alone in recognizing the painting's worth. I imagine one of the unsuccessful bidders from last evening decided to take matters into his or her own hands before I took possession of the painting. He was no doubt well aware for him to acquire it after the painting was in my possession would require considerably more effort."

"That's ridiculous." She turned back to the two policemen who were still regarding her with intent suspicion. "You cannot seriously credit M. Bordeaux's explanation. The painting has enormous sentimental value to me, but no one would attempt to steal her. There must be some mistake. Wouldn't it make more sense to concentrate on the paintings that were stolen rather than the one that wasn't?"

Detective Dubois deferred a response to her protest to Jean Paul. "Nothing was stolen."

Mary Elle looked at the policemen for confirmation, then again at the large empty safe across the room. "But your safe is empty."

"Yes, I rarely use it. Most transactions these days are conducted electronically. There is no need to keep a large amount of cash on the premises."

"But your paintings," Mary Elle protested.

"It would be impossible to lock them up each evening. I am well insured. I do not display anything worth being killed over in a robbery attempt. To be honest, the safe was installed by one of the gallery's prior owners and was no doubt quite useful before computers and wire transfers made its purpose obsolete. I don't even know the combination. I've never used it. When I acquired the gallery, I was told it would cost a fortune to remove, so I merely hung a painting over it and forgot about it."

"But your partner removed Mlle McGann's painting from the gallery after the auction."

"Yes, as I already explained, I was uncomfortable leaving such a valuable piece overnight in the gallery. Forgive me, my dear, but I never expected the painting to be sold for the price it garnered, nor did I expect the active bidding to reach the level it did. No, I am forced to acknowledge M. Bordeaux's conclusion as the most logical explanation. One of the unsuccessful bidders decided to steal the painting prior to him taking possession of it this morning. He obviously hoped M. Bordeaux would be open to similar negotiations with him, or he or she intended to keep the painting for his or her private collection."

Jean Paul turned towards Mary Elle and added pointedly, "Of course my presumption M. Bordeaux is about to take possession of the painting is subject to your approval." At Mary Elle's hesitation, he continued in a serious tone, "I appreciate how much the painting means to you, Mary Elle, but under the circumstances I think you have little choice but to part with it."

"I don't understand. You promised I could still change my mind," Mary Elle whispered, her scattered thoughts swirling in her head.

"Yes, and technically you still can, but we both know you have neither the means nor the expertise required to provide a secure environment in which to house the painting. I imagine it will not take long for word to get around in the unscrupulous world of art thieves you are keeping a painting worth a million euros in your little home back in the states. I am concerned for you, Mary Elle, for both of you," he added, gesturing towards the *Young Madonna*.

Mary Elle felt a shiver of unease slide up her spine at his warning. "I still don't understand why you believe my painting was the one the thief was interested in."

Jean Paul turned towards the detectives for assistance in convincing her. Detective Dubois cleared his throat, paused to glance down at the source of the morning's events, and then raised his gaze to meet Mary Elle's anxious one. "There is no other logical conclusion to be reached under the circumstances. Nothing was taken, but there was clearly a break-in. This was not the work of an amateur. M. Girard's security system is among the finest available on the market today and yet the thief was able to enter the establishment without setting off any alarms. He appears to have spent considerable time searching the gallery and even broke into a safe that hasn't been utilized in years. One must conclude he was searching for a particular item of interest. It is very likely he was engaged to steal a single piece. Since your painting is the only one M. Girard recently removed from the premises, it seems reasonable to conclude the target of the robbery was yours."

"But how could anyone engage a professional thief to steal a painting in a matter of hours? How would the bidder know in advance he or she was going to be unsuccessful in acquiring the painting?"

"She has a point, Gentlemen," Jean Paul conceded.

"How long has the painting been on display at the gallery?" The detective asked.

"A few weeks."

"And has anyone displayed an inordinate amount of interest in it?"

Jean Paul shrugged. "The painting has attracted a great deal of attention from the very first day, which was why I suggested the auction to Mlle McGann in the first place."

Mary Elle leaned back against her chair, suddenly feeling overwhelmed and exhausted. She closed her eyes for a moment, praying when she opened them again she would discover the events of the morning were some hideous nightmare she thankfully awakened from. Her eyes popped open moments later at the sound of M. Bordeaux's voice.

"If you have no objection, Detective, Mlle McGann and I have some unfinished business to conclude."

The other man nodded. Jean Paul gave Mary Elle an encouraging nod when she looked to him for guidance, and she reluctantly allowed M. Bordeaux to assist her from her chair. "Thank you," she said softly.

He nodded and led her towards the exit. Within minutes they were settled at a private booth in a small sidewalk café near the gallery. She ordered tea from the attentive waiter and then waited in silence for her companion to break it.

"You are American?"

"Yes."

"May I compliment you on your command of the French language? If I did not know otherwise, I would conclude you were a native speaker."

"Thank you."

She was looking down at the pattern in the booth top so she missed his amused smile at her abbreviated responses to his opening conversational leads.

"Are you going to allow me to purchase your work, Mary Elle?"

She met his intent glance at the sound of her name. "I don't know."

He nodded, already aware of her reluctance, and sat back in the booth. "Why do you hesitate?"

"I'm not sure it's the right thing to do."

"Then may I ask why you engaged Jean Paul's services in the first place?"

She sighed and tried to explain her reticence, "I know that appears to be a contradiction, but I couldn't just leave her collecting dust in my little tower room."

"I agree."

When no response to his gentle sarcasm was forthcoming,

he asked, "You insisted on the condition to approve the final purchaser after M. Bacchus insulted your vision?"

"That wasn't the reason," she protested.

"No, then what was the reason?"

She waited to respond to his question until the hovering waiter was finished delivering their orders. She steeped her tea, took a cautious sip, and then met her companion's curious expression and admitted honestly, "I know it sounds silly, but it was the first time I realized I might never see her again. What if she went into the hands of someone who didn't appreciate her, someone who wouldn't care for her?"

"You do realize you refer to the painting as her, rather than it?"

"Yes," she admitted softly, feeling the embarrassed blush staining her cheeks.

"You have become very attached to …her." He inserted the feminine pronoun at the last moment.

"Yes."

"Then I will make you a promise."

"What is it?"

"I originally intended to make a gift of your painting to my grandmother, but I changed my mind. The painting will remain in my private collection."

"How extensive is your private collection?"

"Quite extensive."

"Then how do I know you won't lose interest in her and hang her in some forgotten hallway where she'll be all alone?"

Luc's lips twitched at her absurd question. He considered reminding his young adversary he was about to pay dearly for the privilege of doing whatever he wished with her painting, but suspected such a reminder would not bring him to the outcome he sought. "I give you my word should I lose interest in her and be tempted to relegate her to a forgotten hallway, I will return her to you."

"You will?" Mary Elle wasn't sure she could trust him to keep his word.

Not a little bit irritated by her obvious lack of faith in his very generous promise, Luc sighed audibly and asked, "Would you feel more comfortable if you could see where I intend to display her?"

"Yes," Mary Elle exhaled a sigh of relief. "I realize I don't have any right to make such a request of you, but it would help me to let her go if I knew she would be well cared for."

Shaking his head, Luc admitted smiling, "I believe this is the most bizarre conversation I have ever engaged in."

"Get used to it," Mary Elle muttered under her breath, then quickly reached for her tea.

Mary Elle hesitated only briefly when her companion's uniformed driver pulled up in a Mercedes limousine and held the door open for her to precede his employer into the back seat. The entire weekend just kept getting stranger and stranger.

Since she was the one who expressed an interest in seeing his plans for her painting, she could hardly decline to accompany him now. Besides, Jean Paul seemed perfectly comfortable with the notion of her going off with M. Bordeaux. She nodded her thanks in the driver's direction and climbed into the back seat, her lips curving as she slid across to the other side so her companion could join her.

"Something amusing?" he asked, seeing the smile on her face and the sparkle in her eyes.

"Yes," Mary Elle admitted with a half-laugh. "Though perhaps more surreal than amusing."

"In what way?"

"Oh, please. I'm riding around Paris in the company of a presumably wealthy Frenchman who purchased my one and only painting for a million euros, and on my way to God only knows where."

"My office," he supplied, apparently amused by her recitation.

"You're going to hang her in your office?"

"Yes. There I will be able to see her almost daily and assure myself she is safe."

"Oh." Mary Elle was overwhelmed by his commitment. She realized he could be lying to her in order to get his hands on her painting but as she couldn't come up with a single reason why he would, she decided to trust him. "You'll take good care of her?"

He nodded and added with a smile, "Yes. I should not wish when the time comes to be forced to explain to Allah my failure to do so."

"You're Muslim?"

"Yes, though the more devout of my brothers in faith would contest my claim. I was raised in both the faiths of my grandparents. Is my faith a problem for you?"

"No," Mary Elle hastened to assure him, "but I admit your interest in the painting surprises me."

"The Virgin Mary is highly revered in Islam."

"I didn't know that."

"You are Catholic?"

"Yes, raised Catholic anyway, but not particularly devout either," she admitted reluctantly.

He seemed amused by her confession. "No? And yet you chose a decidedly religious subject to paint."

"I'm not sure who chose who," Mary Elle retorted without thinking.

"What do you mean?"

She shook her head, denying his curiosity. "Never mind. You couldn't possibly be interested in my extremely boring history," she disclaimed, and then seeing they were pulling to a stop in front of a modern skyscraper in what appeared to be the financial district of the city, she added quickly, "Oh, is this your office?"

Luc raised his brows at her obvious attempt to change the direction of their conversation, but merely confirmed her assumption, "Yes."

They fell silent as his driver pulled the car to a stop in

front of the entrance, cut the engine and then climbed out of the driver's seat to open the rear door for them to exit. Mary Elle thanked him softly then joined her escort where he waited for her on the sidewalk. He led her into the building, passed security, then up to the private floors where it was necessary for him to swipe his access card to reach the floor he wished to ascend to.

He returned the greetings of his skeleton, weekend staff while Mary Elle tried to ignore their curious looks in her direction. Her host led her through another set of closed double doors into what she assumed must be his private office. Her companion politely waited for her to stop drooling over his unobstructed view of the Paris skyline from his floor to ceiling windows. Then he crossed the distance between the front of his desk and the wall opposite it and indicated the blank wall. "I will hang her here where I may see her each morning when I begin my day, and bid her *adieu* each evening when I end it."

Mary Elle nodded, comforted by his promise. She met his direct gaze, knew she wouldn't be able to tell if he was lying to her or not, and decided to take him at his word. "Thank you."

"Then you will allow me to complete our transaction?"

She blushed at his gentle mockery. "Yes, thank you."

For a moment their glances locked and Mary Elle wondered why she was only just now noticing how attractive he was and then quickly chided herself for the direction of her thoughts. "Forgive me for taking up so much of your time. I'll just see myself out now." She dropped her gaze from his slightly amused one and turned hurriedly towards the exit.

"Mary Elle?"

His voice stopped her just as she would have passed through his threshold. She turned to face him, noticed his intent gaze watching her. "Yes?"

"How long will you be in the city?"

"Just for today. My flight leaves tomorrow afternoon. I have to get back to school."

His brows arched in surprise. "You are a student?"

"No, a teacher." At the fresh surprise in his eyes at her disclosure, Mary Elle explained, "I teach Romance languages at an inner city Catholic school in Pittsburgh."

His lips curved as he reminded her of her earlier claim. "Yet you are not devout?"

"No, more desperate than devout. At the time I was hired the sisters were as desperate for a language teacher as I was for a job, so they overlooked the fact I didn't have a teaching certificate. Plus, there was the added bonus that they could hire a single instructor for several languages, and of course, Latin."

"You are a constant surprise. I would not have thought there was much demand in an inner city school for the Romance languages."

"Well admittedly, the language curriculum outside of Spanish is a luxury in such an environment, but the sisters are very traditional."

He nodded and changed the subject, "Will you allow me to show you Paris?"

"Why?" She asked. Then seeing the laughter in his eyes at her challenge, added quickly, "I mean you don't need to entertain me. I've already agreed to sell you the painting. I won't change my mind."

"I believe the business portion of the morning has been concluded. As to why I wish to share the afternoon with you, I should think it's obvious. You are a lovely, charming woman with a talent that intrigues me. I would like to become better acquainted with you, and since you will only be in Paris for a single day, it appears this is my only opportunity to do so. Is there a man waiting for you at home who would object to you spending the afternoon in my company?"

"No," she admitted baldly.

"Then there is no reason for us not to spend the day together?"

"No, I suppose not."

His lips settled into a satisfied smile. The shiny limousine and his scrupulously polite driver awaited them in the bright morning sunshine. When half an hour later they pulled up in front of the *Louvre* Mary Elle couldn't contain her excitement.

"You approve?" Luc asked.

"Yes, thank you. I was planning on visiting this afternoon. I couldn't leave Paris without at least spending some time here."

"Agreed."

Mary Elle couldn't help but notice they didn't stand in line for an admission ticket, nor did the very visible guards stationed prominently throughout the museum make any move to stop them when her companion led her through private salons secured with red velvet ropes. She cast a sidelong glance in his direction, wondering for the first time exactly who Luc was. When he merely returned her curiosity with his direct gaze, Mary Elle sighed and then nodded her assent when he inquired, "The *Mona Lisa*?"

Another line was waiting for them at the entrance to the salon where arguably Leonardo Da Vinci's most famous painting was displayed. Mary Elle was forced to suppress a grin when they were immediately escorted inside and the line was halted while they looked their fill. Apparently aware of her hastily suppressed surprise, Luc bent and whispered in her ear, "Your American sense of fair play is offended?"

Grinning she turned to meet his amused glance. "You're right, it doesn't seem fair. All of these people must have been waiting such a long time for their turn, but I have to admit it's a nice change of pace."

He returned her delighted smile. Then he nodded in the direction of the painting. "So, what is your opinion of Da Vinci's subject?"

"Personally or artistically?"

"Oh, definitely personally," he teased.

Sighing, Mary Elle admitted, "She seems a little grim to me, even though she has that secret little smirk on her face. Sacrilege, I know, but the truth is I've always preferred Michelangelo's work. One day I'm going to travel to Rome and spend the entire day in the Sistine Chapel staring up at the ceiling."

"And still you claim not to be religious," he reminded her.

She shrugged, considering his point. "I admit I've given the whole subject matter considerably more thought lately."

The rest of the afternoon soared by in a haze of happy disbelief for Mary Elle. Luc took her to see the *Musee' D'Orsay* where they viewed the Edgar Degas collection, Claude Monet's *Women in the Garden* and Vincent Van Gogh's self-portrait. They enjoyed cappuccino and chocolate croissants at a sidewalk café near the *Arc de Triomphe* and took in the Eiffel tower from the back of his limo.

"Do you wish to ride to the top?" Luc inquired, managing to maintain an admirably straight face when he made the offer.

Mary Elle was half-tempted to pretend she wouldn't consider her visit to the city complete unless she did so, recognizing Luc was polite enough to oblige her, but then decided not to tease him, considering he played the gallant host to her all day. "No, thank you." It was already early evening and she was quite certain Luc had other plans for the day than to show a first-time visitor around Paris.

Feeling both guilty at the way she monopolized his time and so grateful for the day in his company, she turned to him, "You don't have to do this. I'm certain you had other plans for the day. My hotel isn't far from here."

He eyed her curiously and suggested, "I thought we would enjoy dinner together, but if you are bored with the company..."

Mary Elle broke in, "You're joking, right? Today has been like a dream. I spent most of it pinching myself when you weren't looking. I feel like Cinderella at the ball, but even fairy tale princesses have to bow to the inevitable chime of midnight and its accompanying end to their dreams."

Grinning at her analogy Luc leaned in close and brushed

his lips across hers. "It's not yet midnight, Mary Elle."

Who was she kidding? She allowed herself to be persuaded. In truth, she didn't try very hard to protest his plans. They dined on the stone patio of his centuries old mansion on the bank of the River Seine.

"What will you do now?" he asked.

"What do you mean?"

"You are a famous artist who is no longer desperate for a job. You can afford to paint full-time if that is your wish."

Mary Elle deliberately avoided thinking about what her life would be like beyond the weekend. She was a little irritated with Luc for forcing her to face reality when she was desperate to hold it at bay until the last possible moment. "I'm not certain becoming a full-time artist is in the cards for me."

"Why not?"

"It's complicated."

Mary Elle felt his intent gaze probing her face, seeking the answers she was reluctant to share with him. "You do not wish to paint?"

"It's all I've ever wanted to do," Mary Elle admitted in a reluctant whisper.

"Then what's complicated about it? I'm certain the good sisters will understand your desire to follow your dream."

"Yes, they would, but I'm afraid this was a one-time deal for me...*she* was a one-time deal."

"Why? I can understand you fear not being able to replicate the success you enjoyed with the *Young Madonna* but the talent to create her is still there, inside you. It will be there to guide you through your next project."

"I'm not certain that's true."

"Why would you doubt it?"

"I've never done anything like her before. Before iI paint the *Young Madonna* it was years since I picked up a paint brush. Not since my art professors in college suggested I change my major to something more suitable to my skill-set." Her lips curved slightly at the confusion in Luc's expression. She really shouldn't drag him any deeper into whatever it was she fell into the middle of, but now she started, she discovered she wanted to confide in him. There was a solid air about Luc. He gave the impression he could listen to her incredible story and make perfect, rational sense out of everything she experienced the past few months. "I dreamed about her. She kept calling my name." Mary Elle decided to leave out the part about the little girl's claim of her being the chosen one. Luc might be a little too solid and rational for that confession. "It was almost as if I was compelled to draw her. I hoped if I could capture my dreams on paper they would go away and she would stop bothering me."

He leaned back in his chair, eyeing her closely. "They?"

Her voice dropped to a whisper, "You know…him."

"There's a him too?"

"Ha, ha."

"You refer to Gabriel?"

"Yes. He didn't like it when I finished her and he was still in the dark, so to speak. It was almost as if he was worried about her being here, alone in this world. He kept nudging me to get on with things and paint him in so she wouldn't be alone." At the lengthy silence greeting her admission, Mary Elle realized she made a mistake confiding in Luc. "If you want to cancel the sale, I understand. I shouldn't have said anything." When he didn't respond to her anxious offer, but simply sat regarding her with a look of not quite disbelief, but one suggesting she was stretching his ability to accept her account to the very limits, Mary Elle dropped her gaze beneath his probing one and wrung her hands together in her lap.

"If you shared this part of the story last night, the painting would have generated considerably more interest, and you would have likely found yourself an even wealthier woman than you are this evening."

"And I also likely would have been labeled a public nut-case."

He grinned and reached over to refill her wine goblet.

"Please continue. I admit I'm fascinated by your account even if you do turn out to be a public nut-case."

Mary Elle shrugged. "There's not much else to tell. I showed the sketches to my friend, Crystal. She encouraged me to paint her. I laughed and reminded her I didn't possess the talent to paint her."

"Apparently you were wrong in your assumption."

"I'm not as certain of that as everyone else seems to be."

"Have you put your presumption to the test?" He wondered.

"No, partly because there hasn't been time. This whole experience was a whirlwind."

"How did you convince Jean Paul to become involved?"

"Crystal's uncle is acquainted with him. She sent her uncle photos of the painting and asked if Jean Paul would be willing to give his opinion on the original. A few days later, they showed up on her doorstep in Pittsburgh and then the three of them showed up on mine. That was three weeks ago. And here I am with you. It's all been more than a bit surreal."

"I can imagine. You said you haven't tested your presumption of your lack of talent partly because you didn't have the time. What is the other reason?"

She glanced down at her hands clasped together in her lap and admitted softly, "I'm afraid to learn the truth. My entire life all I ever longed to do was paint. It was devastating to be forced to admit I would never be any good at it. So I packed away my dreams along with my brushes and canvases and tried to make a life for myself. It was hard...the hardest thing I've ever done. I'm not sure I can go through that again. I barely managed to get myself together enough to acquire the rhythm of a normal life...a job, an apartment, rent, utilities, a car payment. I'm holding my own now. She gave me a wonderful gift. For a few months I was able to hold my most cherished dreams clutched close to my heart. That's more than most people get. It would be greedy of me to want more...to ask for anymore."

He reached over and brushed away the tears threatening to fall from where they clung to her lashes. "Every time I think I know what you're going to say, you surprise me."

He reached down to clasp one of her hands between both of his. Then lifted hers to brush his lips across her fingertips. Their eyes met across the small distance separating them. Mary Elle's breath suddenly deserted her. He tugged on her hand and she leaned towards him. When it came, his kiss was more than she'd caught herself dreaming it would be. One of his hands released the one he was holding between them and his fingers trailed up her arm to clasp the back of her head and hold her close to him. When he leaned away he urged, "Stay with me, Mary Elle. Be with me."

"Yes." Her agreement slipped from between her lips with no thought of resistance. She didn't want to think about the consequences. She just wanted to let herself be, and to be with Luc.

He rose from his chair and pulled her up from hers and into his arms. He whispered erotic promises in French as he slid his lips along her throat. Mary Elle let herself be seduced by him, by the scent of Wisteria vines growing up the terrace posts and the whisper of a lover's promises along the air of the still Paris night.

He led her into his house and up the curving, marble staircase, down another long hallway and through the double hardwood doors leading to his suite of rooms. He closed the doors behind them and turned to her then, nudging her up against the closed door. Their glances locked and he reached up to remove the pins holding her hair in a tight knot anchored at the base of her neck. He drew in a sharp breath as the long strands cascaded in silk waves over his hand and fell to her waist.

He fisted one hand around the soft curls and with the other lifted tilted her face to his. Mary Elle leaned back against the steady surface of the thick, hardwood door and tilted her head back so his lips could explore her flesh. She felt his hands roaming over her, seeking the zipper securing her dress. Then she was aware of its slow descent, oddly reminiscent of her own fall into the dark well of passion he was stirring within her.

In a daze, she felt her dress fall away from her heated flesh and land in a soft whoosh at her feet. He barely touched her and her knees already felt weak. Fortunately Luc seemed aware of her difficulty remaining upright. Sensing her surrender, he swept her into his arms. Then he carried her across the oriental carpet covering his highly polished hardwood floor, coming to a stop at the side of his hand-carved antique bed.

For a moment he stood staring intently down at her. "You're beautiful."

"You make me feel beautiful," she confessed, so happy she gave herself permission to allow herself the joy of sharing herself with this man. A virtual stranger to her, but his hands, his lips were making her feel as if she was the most desirable woman in the world, as if he considered her a precious treasure.

He seduced her slowly and she glorified in his seduction. Wasn't the entire day one continuous slide into this culmination? The fine wine and meal, the luxury of being driven around the city in the back of his limousine? His indulgence in showing her Paris and playing tour guide to her eager questions. As she watched him watching her she thought it would be impossible for her to ever regret this night.

Wasn't she always the careful one? The one who planned out every moment? Who worried about the future so much she let the present slip through her fingers? Not tonight.

"You're very good at this." Mary Elle didn't realize she whispered the compliment out loud until Luc's shoulders began shaking with laughter. He grinned at her compliment. Charmed, Luc brushed his thumb across her lips. Her hands framed his face, thinking to tell him how grateful she was for the day he gave her, but somehow the words got all tangled up in the intense expression in his dark eyes probing hers. He lowered his head and kissed her then tugged on her hand leading her to his bed.

When morning came, Mary Elle woke naked in a near stranger's bed without a specter of the remorse she feared she might feel over her rash decision of the previous evening. The scent of strong coffee and early spring greeted her as her lids fluttered open and she returned to a sense of where she was. She realized she was alone, but with a little effort on her part, she rolled over seeking the source of the light in the room and saw Luc enjoying his morning coffee and paper on the balcony overlooking the river.

Since his back was to her she thought it safe to allow her lips to curve in a wide grin and let a satisfied sigh escape from between them as she rolled over on her back, her arms and legs spread-eagled. She lay there for a long minute or two or five staring up at the ornate ceiling. She couldn't remember ever feeling this wonderful before.

After a few minutes spent luxuriating in Luc's sumptuous bed with his million thread count sheets, Mary Elle sighed with regret at the approaching end of her fantasy weekend, and rolled over again, wrapping the sheet around her as she gained her feet. The subtle movement attracted Luc's attention and he turned, pinning her where she stood at the edge of his bed, with his admiring dark eyes roaming appreciatively over her bare skin, her sex and sleep rustled hair falling in tangled waves to her waist, before returning to capture her glance. For some silly reason she felt herself blushing beneath his intent gaze, memories of the passion they shared making her skin flush and her heart race. He was already showered and dressed. Mary Elle wondered how she managed to sleep through that.

As if aware of her thoughts, Luc laid the paper down on the table and stood, his eyes never leaving hers as he approached where she stood with her feet rooted to the floor. His hand covered her slightly trembling one holding the sheet in place against her chest while his free hand tugged gently on the silk, causing it to drop unresisting to her feet. He let go of the sheet and let his hand glide along her bare skin, setting off all kinds of tingly little reactions where his fingers trailed. Her breath caught in her throat and his hand slid around her back and drew her into his arms.

"This is so crazy," she whispered against his lips as he pushed her back into his bed.

The sun crept higher along its daily course across the horizon when Mary Elle lifted her head from where it rested against Luc's chest listening to the rhythmic beating of his heart and enjoying the feel of his hands stroking her naked flesh.

"I have to go," she announced with a regretful sigh. "I can't miss my flight. It's time for Cinderella to ride her pumpkin coach back across the Atlantic to her little corner next to the hearth."

His dark eyes grinned along with his lips at her analogy. "I want to see you again."

Mary Elle squashed the instant longing in her heart urging her to jump at the chance he was offering her. "No, I don't think that would be a good idea."

"Why not?" He countered, reaching up a tender hand to brush a stray curl from her face. He let his fingers linger on her skin.

"Because it's not real," she told him softly. "You're not real."

"I'm not?" He was back to laughing at her.

She couldn't share in his amusement, recognizing she was already way too involved with him for her own good. "No, not for me."

"Mary Elle," he began, but she stopped him from continuing his protest with her fingertips on his lips.

"No, don't. Fairy tales aren't supposed to end with awkward explanations." She pulled away from his arms and sighed inwardly when he made no move to prevent her. That was how it should be. This was real life, not a fantasy, despite the evidence of the past few days and weeks to the contrary. It was time for her to say goodbye to her handsome prince and ride her modern coach back to her humble little life.

As she pulled free of Luc's arms to shower and dress, she could feel him watching her progress to the adjoining bath. Then he stood to pull his pants back on and return to his place at the table on his terrace.

CHAPTER TWELVE

As Mary Elle's jet taxied down the runway in anticipation of take-off for her flight home, Francis sat in the private office of one of his most loyal clients and regretfully confirmed his attempt to acquire the *Young Madonna* the previous evening was in vain.

"So I assumed, my friend, when I read about the unsuccessful robbery attempt at *The Gallerie* in this morning's paper. I presume Jean Paul removed the painting from his establishment prior to your arrival?"

"Yes, though it must have been directly after the completion of the auction, as I was in place to see the attendees, as well as M. Girard, exit the gallery later in the evening."

His client lifted one shoulder in a philosophical shrug. "Regrettable. As always, I appreciate your efforts on my behalf. Unfortunately I must conclude the *Young Madonna* is beyond my reach for the foreseeable future as Luc Bordeaux is anything but careless about his art. However I have high hopes Mlle McGann will prove a profitable and hopefully prolific new talent. Certainly there is no shortage of religious fanatics out there who would be willing to offer double what M. Bordeaux paid for the *Young Madonna.* Now her work has been validated by a respected collector, the value of Mlle McGann's next offering should escalate quite dramatically."

CHAPTER THIRTEEN

She was going to be late for class again. Mary Elle hated being late. She always arrived fifteen minutes early for everything, but for some reason her new yoga class was proving to be the exception. The class was part of her plan to restore a sense of normalcy to her existence after what she referred to as her fantasy weekend.

Unquestionably, teaching Latin to a class full of freshman high school students helped to hurry along her journey back to reality. One morning she was waking up in the arms and bed of a near stranger, and the next she was back at her responsible job, standing at the front of her classroom sporting her boring flats instead of the sky high heels she wore for the auction.

She supposed she could afford to buy her own fancy shoes now. Good to his word, Jean Paul wired the funds from the sale of the *Young Madonna* directly into her account. The money arrived home before she did. Two weeks later it was still sitting untouched in her checking account. She didn't know what she was supposed to do with it any more than she knew what she was supposed to do with the rest of her life.

The tower room remained firmly off limits to her fragile sense of self. She wasn't ready to discover if she sold her talent along with her painting. Until she summoned her courage and risked the climb up those narrow stairs, her life remained on hold. It was as if she pressed the pause button on the remote right in the middle of a biography about her life.

It was Crystal who suggested the yoga class. Of course, the suggestion came only after she recovered from her astonishment prompted by Mary Elle's revelations about her weekend in Paris. Her friend's incredulous expression during the course of her confessions brought home to Mary Elle the full extent of the merry-go-round she was riding on.

According to Crystal, yoga practice was supposed to help its practitioners find balance in their lives. Balance sounded exactly like what she needed right then, so Mary Elle signed up for a beginner's class a few days after her return from Paris. Today was only her third class. She meant to get there on time, which according to proper yogic etiquette was no less than ten minutes early so she could set aside any lingering stress from her daily routine and fix a clear intention for her practice. Since she was still finding her way she already decided her intention for the upcoming session was to get through the next ninety minutes without making a fool of herself. Her phone rang as she hurried in the direction of the studio, interrupting her musings.

"Damn," she cursed softly beneath her breath, while she shifted her yoga mat to her other arm so she could dig through her jacket pocket for her phone, belatedly remembering she was supposed to leave it behind in the car. Nothing like a ringing phone to disrupt one's communion with the universe. Juggling her water bottle and purse, she retrieved her phone and barely managed to answer it and raise it to her ear without dropping it.

"Hello?"

"Hello." It sounded different the way he said it. As if it was some intimate French endearment instead of a very ordinary American greeting.

"Luc?" She confirmed, just to be sure.

"Yes." She could hear the ready laughter in his voice at her astonishment.

"Is something wrong with the painting? Do you want your money back? I still have it. Well almost all of it. I don't know about Jean Paul's part. I'm not sure how that works. I mean if he gives refunds..." She was actually relieved when he cut through her incoherent ramblings.

"Mary Elle, I'm not calling to request a refund for the painting."

"Oh, is she all right?"

"Is who all right?"

"Never mind. I really have to go. I'm going to be late for class."

"Forgive me. I assumed you would be finished teaching for the day."

Now he was being so polite, she couldn't just blow him off. She slowed her step and took a deep breath and admitted, "I am finished teaching. I'm on my way to yoga class."

"I didn't realize you practiced yoga."

"I don't." Then she realized how silly her denial sounded and explained, "I mean, not really. I signed up for a beginner class. This is only my third one."

"What made you decide to sign up for a yoga class?"

"A friend suggested I might find balance in the practice. Oh, there's the warning gong. I'm supposed to be on my mat preparing for class and contemplating the oneness of all life."

"Mary Elle..."

God, how did he do that? Make her breath catch at the sound of her own name. "No, I can't. You can't call me anymore. You're not real."

"Here we go again."

No wonder he was laughing at her. She forced herself to stop rambling. "You know what I mean. You're part of my other life...my fantasy life... where I'm an artist and my one and only painting is auctioned off in an exclusive Parisian gallery to a wealthy Frenchman for a million euros. You drink expresso on the porch off your bedroom suite overlooking the river Seine in a mansion that's probably been in your family for centuries and sleep with undiscovered artists whose first and likely only painting you just acquired for a small fortune."

"I live in an abandoned chapel with stained glass windows that take my breath away when the light hits them just right." She closed her eyes against the tears stinging behind her lids and bent her head to stare at her hands. "I have chalk dusk beneath my fingernails. I can never quite wash all of it away. Most high schools have made the switch to white boards by now, but inner city schools still make do with the old fashioned kind."

The gong sounded again. She was really late now. So much for contemplating the oneness of all life and setting an intention for her practice. The story of her life. She was always trying to catch up to the person inside something told her she was supposed to be. "I'm late. I have to go. Please don't call me anymore. I realize how rude and churlish the request is considering all you've done for me, but I don't know how to play this game, Luc, and I don't think my heart would survive the time it would take for me to learn the rules."

An ocean away, Luc sat staring at the phone in his hand, realizing belatedly his young lover just hung up on him. He didn't recall a woman ever hanging up on him before. Not, he was quite certain, because he never deserved the insult, but he understood most women would think twice about hanging up on a man in his position. Yes, he was quite certain he warranted such a response to some previous misdeed on his part, but today he did nothing to deserve it. After all, he was only trying to invite Cinderella to the ball.

CHAPTER FOURTEEN

Mary Elle tossed restlessly in her sleep, unaware she kicked the heavy quilts she was wrapped in to the floor. The cold hovered over her, replacing the quilts, wrapping around her and drawing her deeper beneath the cover of her dream. Her rapid breaths escaped her lips in visible wisps and she moaned softly beneath the unrelenting grip of the visions assaulting her defenseless self. Part of her understood she was trapped in a dream. She both feared and welcomed the realization.

Maybe she came back. Maybe she wasn't angry with her for selling her. Wasn't the fear part of the reason she felt so ambivalent about doing anything with the money she received in return? It reminded her too closely of the thirty silver pieces Judas accepted to betray his friend and Lord. Did she betray *her*? Would Luc take his money back in exchange for the painting? Somehow she didn't think so.

It wasn't the little girl she remembered who claimed her attention now. Or maybe it was, but she was grown into a young woman. She sat on the roof outside her bedroom window with her arms wrapped around her knees staring up at the star-lit sky. Mary Elle thought it ironic like her, the young woman she dreamt of was too restless to sleep. Her thoughts rioted around in her head, refusing to settle.

She was to be married in a few months to a man she barely knew…a man much older than she was and one who was much older than she envisioned her future husband would be. He was a widower with sons already her age. How was she to be a mother to them? What did she know about being the wife of a carpenter? A man who made his living with his hands?

The other girls from the temple were all to be wed to young men from wealthy families, but she was to be given to the silent Joseph, with his rough laborer's hands and brooding eyes. It would be her duty to run his household. She didn't know how. Her mother promised to teach her. Mary thought perhaps her mother was a little disappointed with the way things turned out. Joseph was by no means a poor man, but nor was he the first born of a wealthy Jewish family.

Distracted, her lips split into a delighted smile when one of the stars in the black sky above separated from the others and began its descent from the heavens. A falling star. It was a portent. She wondered if one of the mighty ones displeased God and was exiled from heaven as it was said of the evil one who once stood among the great of heaven before he was banished. Now in his discontent he was reputed to tempt mortal souls to turn from the path of righteousness and join him for all eternity in the fiery torments of hell.

The girl's intent gaze followed the star's descent until it seemed to come to rest beside her on the roof. Frightened, she scooted back against the open window leading to her room.

"Do not be afraid, Mary." The star spoke to her, only he was no longer a star, but a man. No, not a man but something more. At the thought, a wispy restlessness stirred in her mind as if a long forgotten dream tugged at her memories.

"Who are you?" she whispered.

"I am Gabriel. I stand in the presence of God."

"Oh." For what else was she to say? She understood now. He was one of the holy ones of God. "Why are you here? Have I done something to displease our Lord?" Her head was cricked all the way back so she could see his face.

Seeing her discomfort he knelt in front of her and replied kindly, "No, Mary. You have found favor with the Almighty. You are to bear Him a son and he will be a great king among his people. He will be called the prince of peace and redeemer king, because he comes to save his people from their sins."

"But how can this be? I am unwed. I have never known a man." Mary protested, grasping somewhat desperately at the obvious contradiction to his incredulous proclamation.

"By the power of the Holy Spirit and the will of God this child will be conceived in your womb."

Mary met his unflinching gaze, her thoughts swirling chaotically about her head, as she sought purchase in her ordinary worries prior to the holy one's sudden arrival. What would Joseph say to all of this? What if it was true? It wasn't possible. She was being foolish. She looked up from where her incredulous gaze clung to her clasped hands wrapped around her knees, expecting to see only the night sky, but he was still there.

His face shone brighter than the stars and his eyes probed hers thinking to discern her answer in them. It was then she realized he was waiting for her agreement. Her Lord would not force this momentous honor upon her. She had a say. She didn't have to do this.

She quickly dropped her gaze beneath the Almighty's holy messenger, ashamed of her hesitation. She knew she should feel greatly honored by having been chosen for such a distinction, but what would happen to her when people discovered she was with child? They would stone her and call her an adulteress. She would shame her parents. They wouldn't believe her when she told them about the holy one and what he proclaimed to her...that she was to bear God's holy son. They would laugh at her and believe she became pretentious during her years she spent in the temple.

This couldn't be real. This couldn't be happening to her. She was a humble, obedient daughter of the Lord, but there was nothing special about her. How was it possible she could be chosen for such an honor? Clearly she was dreaming. In her dreams she was as pretentious as her neighbors would claim, but even if it was only a dream, she could not disobey God. It wasn't even a matter of disobedience. She loved Him. She could not bear the thought of being a disappointment to Him.

She raised her eyes and saw the one who called himself Gabriel still there, silently watching her, awaiting her answer. "I am the handmaid of the Lord. Let it be done unto me according to thy word."

Mary Elle woke shivering in the cold. In the space of a heartbeat she was unbearably hot. Beads of sweat pooled on her brow. Her hands were clammy. Her thoughts lingered on the visions she just experienced. Dreams not visions. It was just a dream...her mind's way of releasing the stress of the past strange months.

Despite her rationalizations the images replayed themselves in her head, colliding with each other in her confusion. Unlike the stained glass depiction of the famous scene portrayed in one of the windows in the tower room above where she lay, in her vision God's holy one did not have wings and a halo. He didn't stand over the virgin. He knelt before her, not as a sign of deference, for he was a great one of the Almighty, one of His firstborn and he knelt only before God.

But Mary was a very young woman, still more of a child in many ways, and she was afraid. Even trying not to frighten her, he was an intimidating presence, particularly to one so innocent. So he knelt and drew himself in so the sight of him would not blind her mortal eyes and he spoke to her in a gentle voice, for she was beloved of God.

Mary Elle clenched her eyes closed trying to wash her memories clean, but the vivid images wouldn't go away. It was as if they were burned into her mind's eye. What was happening to her?

Accepting there would be no answer forthcoming to her silent question she retrieved her sweatshirt from the bed post and pulled it over her head. A moment ago she was too hot, now she felt the cold. Maybe she was coming down with something. That could explain her hallucinations. She allowed the hopeful explanation to run through her thoughts even as she recognized it for what it was. Another excuse, a rationalization. A foolish attempt to explain the unexplainable. It was happening again. She couldn't escape it. Whatever it was. She wasn't even certain she wanted to.

Sighing, she climbed out of bed, crossed the room by the light of the nightlight she kept burning in the hall and climbed the narrow, winding stairs to the tower room. They were still there where she left them. Her paints, canvases, and sketchpads. She hadn't been up there since the last time. There was a blank canvas set up on the easel beneath the moonlight shining through the stained glass. She lit the lantern. She didn't remember setting up the canvas.

The last time she was in the cramped space was to remove the *Young Madonna* painting she sold to Luc. What was his part in all of this anyway? She wanted to call him, tell him what was happening. She thought maybe he could help her make sense of whatever it was, but she wouldn't reach out to him. School teachers from Pittsburgh, Pennsylvania did not call wealthy Frenchmen in their Parisian mansions. That line of communication was meant to work in only one direction.

She sank to her knees in front of the canvas, aware of the tubes of paint scattered at her feet, and was afraid. She couldn't do this. Not again. The canvas confronting her was too empty. It appeared an almost blinding white in the light of the lantern, but to Mary Elle it felt more like a darkness preparing to consume her.

It would be up to her to bring it to life... to bring *her* to life, no longer a child, but a young woman on the verge of changing the world. "I can't. I don't know how." She whispered the words out loud, sensing another presence in the tiny space with her. There were no answering words of reassurance, nor any demand for her obedience, just this huge weight of expectation hanging over her.

She thought it might crush her if she sat there much longer. She backed away from the blank canvas and crawled on her hands and knees to where the virgin sketchpads waited. They were empty now too. She tore out the sketches of the young Madonna and packed them away, deciding if she was going to sell her painting, she would keep her sketches as reminders to cling to in her old age. So she could unpack them when she needed to convince herself it was all real, she really did visit her, and for a brief few months, she was part of her life.

Mary Elle pulled the largest pad onto her lap, reached for a charcoal, and then closed her eyes to offer up a silent prayer before she set pencil to paper. Her hand flew across the blank page, as if it possessed a will of its own separate from her conscious mind, until page after page was filled with her impressions.

When her hand finally stilled, her fingers were stiff and cramping. She could no longer ignore the mounting pain so she stretched out her fingers and allowed the charcoal to slip from her hand and fall to the stone floor where it bounced first before rolling across the stone to come to rest against the wall. She didn't look.

Instead she brought her hands together, blindly closing the pad, not letting her eyes drop to her lap. She felt nauseous and empty at the same time, noting for the first time the bright light of day streaming through the windows casting colored shadows around the tiny space. The lantern burned itself out. How long was she up there?

In a daze she stood and set the pad aside. She avoided looking at the canvas propped up and silently waiting for her to bring it to life and instead crossed the room to carefully descend the stairs to the second floor. Back in her room, she perched on the edge of her bed and let her thoughts slowly return to the present. A dazed glance at the clock by her bed told her it was after eight. She was going to be late for school. Reaching for her phone to call her boss and let her know, she slid her thumb across the face to check the calendar, sighing with relief when she noted it was Saturday. She wouldn't be late after all.

Not that the prospect of losing her job instilled in her the same panic it would have a few short weeks ago, before Luc's incredible generosity, but the sisters took a chance on her. A scared young woman, fresh out of college, with little more than a gift for languages and a fierce desire to make her own way in the world and not be forced to go crawling back to her parents and admit they were right. To acknowledge once and for all she couldn't paint and she couldn't make a living with her fall-back degree in Romance languages and an unofficial minor in Renaissance art appreciation. She didn't want to disappoint them. She hated disappointing anyone.

She felt better after a shower. She spent some time putting her small home in order. Afterwards, she decided she would go into town, buy some groceries, window shop, maybe even stop by the nursery and purchase some spring pansies to spruce up her tiny yard. Maybe it would help to be outside. She would do some yard work, mulch her beds and wash her windows. Get away from herself and pretend her life wasn't careening out of control. She wasn't just a puppet dancing at the end of a string at the will of some unseen presence. Maybe getting out of her space would convince her she still had a life. She was still herself. She was still normal.

Halfway into town she changed her mind. She wanted company. She needed to interact with other living, breathing members of the human race. Crystal would be in her shop.

Fortunately, it was a slow day at *Witchy Wantya* and her friend's weekend help showed up on time. After one look at Mary Elle's glazed but serious expression, her friend elected to take an early lunch.

"Well?" Crystal demanded as soon as the waiter left them alone with their drinks where they sat on opposite benches of the booth in the second floor of the Mexican restaurant across the street from the shop.

"Well what?" Mary Elle hedged, not ready to jump immediately into her troubled morning.

Crystal was having none of it. "You didn't just stop by the shop unannounced to buy me lunch...not that I don't appreciate it. What's up?"

Mary Elle sighed, seeing no point in putting off the uncomfortable discussion. Isn't this what she came for? The chance to bare her troubled soul to a sympathetic ear. "I had a dream," Mary Elle began, her eyes downcast as she toyed with her glass and swirled the ice idly around with her straw to give her restless hands something to do.

"Do tell. Did your hot French lover play a starring role?" Crystal asked, dramatically gesturing with her expressive eyebrows.

"No."

"Oh, too bad," she replied instantly, her disappointment evident. Then she noticed the way Mary Elle's hands were shaking slightly where they played with her glass."Oooohhh, one of those dreams."

"Yes."

"Another one? The same one?"

"Same theme, a new topic, or more like a different time."

"Which one was it? Moses and the Ten commandments? Jonah and the whale? Did he really get swallowed up by a whale and spit out after three days?"

Laughing at her friend's excitement, Mary Elle protested, "I have no idea."

"No? Damn! Since you seem to have a direct line to that kind of thing, I was hoping to get some lingering questions answered from eight years of Catholic school."

"I don't have a direct line to that kind of thing, as you refer to it."

"No? So what was this dream about?"

Mary Elle hesitated and then reluctantly admitted, "The Annunciation."

"Which one was that?" When Mary Elle rolled her eyes, Crystal shrugged. "Sorry, I get the A ones mixed up. The Annunciation and the Assumption."

"The Annunciation is when the Archangel Gabriel appears to the Virgin Mary to tell her she's going to have God's son."

"Right, the virgin and the archangel. I see what you mean. Same theme. What do you think it means?"

"I have no idea," Mary Elle sighed heavily.

"Are you going to paint it?"

"I don't know."

Crystal sat back in the booth and eyed her curiously. "Well, you certainly can't complain about how the first one turned out."

"No."

"But?" Crystal persisted.

The word hung between them for a moment. Crystal was right. What right did she have to complain about the way the first painting turned out? Then her fear and frustration coalesced and poured out of her in a rush. "But, why me? Why is this happening to me? And contrary to your silly belief, I do not have a direct line to..." She spread her arms in frustration, and added, "... this kind of thing. I'm more confused than anyone."

"Maybe, but you're the one having the strange, religious dreams."

"I know. Do you think I'm losing my mind?"

Crystal dismissed her angst with an amused grin and a shake of her head. "Nope, don't think so. You're the sanest person I know."

"I'm not sure that's saying much," Mary Elle replied with reluctant, answering amusement.

Her friend laughed. "Point for you," she quipped, then reached over and squeezed her hand. "Honey, I think you need a break. Why don't you take a few days off? Isn't your spring break coming up? Take a trip and get away to some place warm and beachy, where they serve cocoanut drinks with those little swirly straws. You're surrounded by religion. You teach in a Catholic school, paint religious subjects, and even live in an old church. It's probably all just seeping into your subconscious and the dreams are your mind's way of relieving the pressure."

"I would very much like to believe your explanation except

you're forgetting one pertinent detail."

"What?"

"I can't paint."

"I believe the fact someone just paid a million euros for your creation disputes your assertion."

Mary Elle shook her head, dismissing her friend's conclusion. "Don't you see? Someone paying a million dollars for the painting is what's weird about all of this. How does a broke, twenty three year old, American high school teacher with limited artistic talent have her first and only painting auctioned off for a fortune by an exclusive Parisian gallery without some kind of mysterious intervention?"

"Given the subject matter I would guess we're talking about divine intervention here?"

"Do you have a better explanation?"

"No. Actually I'm inclined to agree with you," Crystal announced with the air of someone who was waiting for Mary Elle to come around to the obvious conclusion, and then added with conviction, "Which means you're the one who's supposed to do this."

"Do what?" Mary Elle countered, feeling the panic she so desperately tried to suppress earlier begin to rise in her chest.

"I have no idea, but the possibilities are fascinating, don't you think?"

"Insert disturbing for fascinating and I would agree with you."

"Disturbing? My life should take such a disturbing turn. A shitload of money and a passionate fling with a hot French billionaire."

"How do you know he's hot?" Mary Elle protested, grinning.

"I googled him. Ooh...la...la."

Mary Elle laughed.

"Why don't you take those few days off I suggested earlier and use some of your pot of gold to fly across the pond and hook up with the rich Monsieur Bordeaux?" At Mary Elle's answering grin, Crystal continued, "Actually I'm surprised you never heard from him. I mean common courtesy dictates at least a phone call." At the telling blush staining Mary Elle's cheeks, she pounced, "Ah ha! He did call, didn't he?"

"Yes."

"And you didn't tell me? What did he say? Did he offer to fly you to Paris for the weekend on his private, billionaire jet?"

"Not exactly."

"Come on, give. I want details."

"I didn't exactly give him a chance to explain the reason for his call," Mary Elle confessed guiltily.

"What do you mean?" Crystal demanded, her brows furrowed in confusion.

"I sort of hung up on him right after I told him not to call me anymore," Mary Elle admitted, cringing at the memory, and realizing for the first time in their friendship, she managed to render her outspoken friend speechless.

Crystal was sitting across from her in the booth staring at her with her mouth wide open, seemingly trying to make sense of Mary Elle's confession. "You hung up on him?" At Mary Elle's guilty confirming nod, Crystal added confused, "This is the first man you've shown the slightest interest in since you moved here. I thought you liked him."

"I did. I do," Mary Elle protested stammering.

"And I can't imagine he was a lousy lover."

Blushing, Mary Elle confirmed, "No, no he wasn't."

"Is it the religious thing? Does God have something against hot, sweaty sex with single, wealthy, hot Frenchman?"

Laughing at the absurd direction their conversation was taking, Mary Elle pointed out, "You used hot twice. And no, I don't think God has anything against sex, but I have no way of confirming my assumption."

"May I suggest, my very good friend, it is possible your standards are just a teensy bit too high," Crystal offered.

"Oh, come on, there's no possibility of a future between us."

"So what? Why do you have to worry about the future all the time? Can't you just enjoy the moment for once?"

Mary Elle fell silent, wondering if Crystal was right. Why did she have to know where every little twist and turn in her life would lead her? Would it kill her to live in the moment for once? Didn't she allow herself to live in the moment with Luc? And weren't those hours some of the best of her young life?

"Call him," Crystal prodded.

"No!!" Mary Elle instinctively protested, aghast at the thought.

"Why not?"

"He'll think I'm stalking him."

"I think a single phone call does not make a man conclude he is the victim of a psychotic female obsession, especially when he initiated the contact between you in the first place."

"No, I'm not going to call Luc," Mary Elle replied, thinking out loud, "but I think you might have a point. Maybe I should get away for a few days. Take a break from all of this."

Crystal shrugged, "Well you can try, but if you're not going to hook up with Luc, I'm not sure there's much point in leaving town for a few days."

"Why not? Getting away was your idea, remember?" Mary Elle was having difficulty following her friend's fresh line of reasoning.

"I've been thinking about what you said, about why you, and how you couldn't paint before, and all of a sudden you produce a masterpiece and hook up seemingly out of the blue with a wealthy, influential collector. Something's definitely at work here and it's not the kind of thing that goes away because you spend a few days sipping fruity drinks out of cocoanut shells."

"You're not helping," Mary Elle replied, her earlier unease making itself felt again.

"Well, think about it. There's a lot of stuff happening in the world we don't have an explanation for, right?"

"Agreed."

Crystal continued, "The odds must be astronomical about all of this being some kind of crazy coincidence. Did certain genes in your head just wake up at the ripe old age of twenty three, despite your years of study and striving and decide, hey, I think we should paint a masterpiece today? And the rest of you replied, 'Oh, what a great idea! What should we paint? How about the really weird dream from last night about God's mother and the archangel?' I hate to say this, I hate to even think it, but I'm beginning to believe whatever this is, it's not going away. It's like once you opened the door and took the first step, you started something."

Since her friend's unwelcome conclusion very nearly matched her own, Mary Elle asked anxiously, "What do you think I started?"

"I have no idea, but you're not playing back-up on the b-team here."

They both fell silent for a moment until Crystal reached across the table and squeezed Mary Elle's suddenly icy hand. "I'm worried about you. The Virgin Mary seems to travel with her own protection. Where's yours?"

Mary Elle shook her head and replied softly, "I don't know. I'm not sure I warrant any."

Crystal's voice took on a suddenly serious note, "Well, I have a feeling you're going to need it. You know the old adage, wherever's there's light, darkness is sure to follow. Angels...demons...good versus evil. At least you seem to be playing for the right side, but maybe you should ask the powers that be who has your back."

Mary Elle's voice dropped an octave, "I'm not sure such a question is allowed."

"Well, an archangel is a pretty big deal, right? I'm sure he won't mind keeping an eye on you. That's sort of their job, right? Protect the innocent and all."

Mary Elle wasn't reassured by her friend's bracing argument. "I'm not certain I can rely on his assistance."

"Why not?"

"I don't think he likes me very much."

Incredulous, Crystal protested, "What? Don't be silly. How can anyone not like you? You're the best person I know. If this Gabriel has something against you, what chance do the rest of us have?" Crystal paused, obviously anticipating Mary Elle's laughing rebuttal to what she likely assumed was a rhetorical question on her part. When none was forthcoming, she persisted, "Mary Elle? I asked you what chance the rest of us have? Ha ha."

Mary Elle raised her glance to meet her friend's no longer laughing eyes. "I don't know, but I think it's a pretty big presumption we have one."

Crystal's eyes widened, and for the first time Mary Elle thought her friend was beginning to get a sense of her own alarm. "You know you're beginning to freak me out here," Crystal protested.

"Yes well, you're not alone. I'm freaking myself out a little. And while we're on the subject I don't think you should toss his name around so casually."

"Who? Gabriel?" Crystal's previously laughing voice suddenly dropped to a whisper.

"Yes," Mary Elle's serious confirmation was uttered in equally soft tones.

"Why not? I thought he was one of the good guys."

"I would say that is an awesomely, laughable understatement."

"So, then what can he do to me?"

Mary Elle hesitated and then replied cautiously, "I don't think you want to find out."

"Mary Elle, what in the world have you gotten yourself into?"

Wasn't the question the very one she came here seeking an answer to? "I don't know, but whatever it is, I don't think it has only to do with this world."

CHAPTER FIFTEEN

Her meeting with the department head ran over. What was it about her yoga class the universe seemed determined to make certain she didn't arrive on time? No question about it, she was going to be late...again. Mary Elle performed the quick calculation after a final glance at the clock in her classroom, gathered her purse and tote containing her students' assignments she needed to grade over the weekend, and hurried out the door. The main hallway was nearly empty, providing evidence everyone else was as anxious for the start of the weekend as she was.

Trying to compensate for her anticipated delayed arrival at the studio, she passed through the main exit with her thoughts already busy setting an intention for her upcoming practice. Because her mind was occupied elsewhere she was only vaguely aware of the number of students gathered near the circular driveway in front of the school and their admiring, mostly male voices comparing the pros and cons of some car in the drive.

A slight smile curved her lips at their excitement. With boys it was always one of two things, cars or girls, interspersed occasionally with a bragging session about their latest prowess on the field of competition. So it was with an indulgent glance in his direction she paused long enough in her hurry to the teacher's parking lot to turn towards one of her students in response to his greeting. "Miss McGann, do you see that?"

Smiling, Mary Elle teased, "Do I see what, Patrick?"

"The limo. Looks like it's waiting for someone. Do you

think one of the kid's dad's a drug dealer?"

Mary Elle laughed and tugged on the brim of his cap. "No, I don't." Still she was curious enough to turn in the direction of his glance and take in the long black limousine parked in the circular entrance. "All right. It is an impressive sight," she conceded and Patrick grinned back at her.

"Who do you think it's here for?"

She could answer truthfully enough. "I have no idea."

"Ah come on, Miz McGann, you know, don't you?"

Students automatically assumed teachers knew everything going on in a school. "I wish I did. Give me the scoop on Monday. I need to run," Mary Elle replied and hurried in the direction of her car.

"See you Monday, Miz McGann," Patrick called to her retreating back.

Another buzz of excitement among the interested students made her turn her attention in the direction of the limousine where the driver emerged from behind the wheel and was holding open the back door for his passenger to emerge. There was something vaguely familiar about the driver, but it took a few seconds for her thoughts to catch up with her instincts.

"Oh, no!" The hushed words emerged from between her lips even as Luc enfolded his lean length from the back seat. He nodded in her direction. Sensing the avidly interested eyes of her students turning their astonished glances in her direction, she momentarily considered pretending she didn't see him and continuing on her way to her car. Then almost instantly acknowledged her incipient plan wouldn't do her any good.

Luc came all this way. She suspected he wouldn't be put off by her silly plan. Likely he would simply follow her in his fancy car until he ran her to ground. Sighing, thinking uncomfortably about having to face her students and fellow teachers on Monday, she changed direction and reluctantly approached where Luc leaned against the car with his arms crossed in front of him, waiting for her.

"What are you doing here?" Mary Elle asked in a half-appalled, half-excited at the prospect of seeing him again voice.

"You told me not to call you anymore," he reminded her with an amused smile.

"I didn't mean to imply you should pop in instead," she pointed out.

"My mistake."

"Ha ha. Seriously, what are you doing here?" Mary Elle repeated on a sigh.

"I need a date for an event I am committed to tomorrow evening in New York."

"And you're looking for a recommendation? Sorry, I don't know anyone in New York."

He grinned at her sarcasm. "I happen to have several acquaintances in New York."

"No doubt." She shooed him with her hands back in the direction of the car. "Don't let me keep you."

He laughed and reached for her hand and brought it to his lips. "Come with me, Mary Elle. Let me take you to the ball."

She snatched her hand away. "No. No. No. I can't go with you."

"Why not?"

"I already told you." She clutched her tote bag in front of her like a shield and to keep her hands away from his dangerous reach. "You're not real. You're part of my other life I boxed up and locked away when I returned home." At his amused grin, her protests suddenly changed direction. "How am I supposed to explain all of this?" One hand released the tote and swung out in a sweeping gesture encompassing him, his driver, and his ridiculous car. "You show up here in your limousine, in your expensive, hand-tailored suit, with your personal driver, bodyguard, whatever he is. My students think I'm dating a drug-dealer."

His lips twitched and his eyes fairly danced with laughter. He looked beyond her shoulder and conceded, "We do seem to be attracting a great deal of attention. Perhaps we should get in the car."

"No. I'm late for yoga," she protested weakly.

"Ah, yes, yoga. How are your classes coming along?"

"Slowly."

"I understand the practice requires patience."

"Are you implying I lack patience?"

"You do always seem to be rushing from one place to the next. What time is your class?"

"Three forty five," Mary Elle admitted with a forlorn sigh.

He glanced at his watch. "It appears you have already missed the start, so there's no reason you cannot join me for a few minutes, perhaps show me where you live and give me a tour of your city."

Mary Elle couldn't think of a way to politely decline his suggestion, particularly when he was so gracious as to spend the day showing her Paris. Besides, who was she kidding? She wanted to be with him. "If I get in the car you're not going to take me to New York, are you?"

"Not without your permission," he replied, sensing he won their contest of will, and harbored very few doubts from the beginning as to the outcome of their little standoff.

"Fine," she conceded less than graciously and reached around him to pull the rear door of the limousine open before either his driver or Luc himself could perform the courtesy for her. She sensed Luc's amusement at her disgruntled display when he slid into the seat next to her, but neither commented on it.

Mary Elle couldn't help but notice Luc's driver didn't ask her for directions to where she lived. He just wove his way expertly through the winding, hilly streets out of town and up the interstate until they reached her exit. A silence, she suspected was only awkward on her part, prevailed during the short ride until they arrived at her unusual home. When she reached for the door handle to free herself from the close confines of the car, Luc restrained her with his hand on her arm. "Aman would prefer you allow him to do his job."

Mary Elle leaned back against the seat with a huff and turned to find Luc watching her with a wide grin. "Patience, remember? The practice will be good for your yoga."

"I suppose."

She waited for Aman to climb out of the driver's seat and hold the door open for her with what she concluded was ridiculous ceremony. He nodded when she thanked him, his dark eyes twinkling and echoing his boss's obvious amusement. She waited for Luc on the walk leading up to her door.

Looking around him curiously, Luc asked, "You actually live in a church? I didn't believe you."

"It's a little odd, I know. This place used to be a private family chapel on a large estate. Pittsburgh was once home to the robber barons of the industrial revolution. The family who owned this estate fell on hard times during the Great depression and the property was auctioned off. Since the property never belonged to a Carnegie or a Mellon there was no particular historical significance attached to it, so it wasn't protected by historical preservation laws.

"Back in the sixties it was parceled into housing lots, but apparently no one was quite sure what to do with the family chapel. The developer couldn't bring himself to tear it down, especially considering the graves in the family cemetery near the back boundary line, so he came up with the idea of converting the chapel into a private residence. Much to his surprise, there were no takers for his brainstorm, and in desperation he eventually donated the chapel-turned-residence to the Archdiocese in return for a generous tax deduction. The church wasn't quite certain what to do with it either, as it was too far from the city to be of much use to house priests, and the nearest parish church is five miles from here and already possessed a beautiful modern rectory attached to it. So the bishop, being a practical man, decided to rent it out."

"So you are not the first occupant?" Luc inserted.

"No, but we've been few and far between. Apparently it takes an unusual temperament to live in a church."

"Yes, I can understand that, but you are comfortable here?"

"For the most part. I didn't have much of a choice when I first moved here. It was all I could afford. Sister Connie recommended it when I accepted the job at the high school. The young family who was living here before me bought their own place."

"Who is Sister Connie?"

"My boss."

They went inside and she gave him a quick tour of the first floor. He looked curiously around. "Will you show me where you paint?"

"Why?" She countered suspiciously.

His lips curved and he shrugged. "I am a man with a great appreciation for art, but lack the ability to create it. I am fascinated by those who can."

"I suppose so, but it's a mess. I haven't done any painting since…"

"Since the painting you sold to me," he supplied when her voice trailed off.

"Yes."

"Why?"

Mary Elle pretended she didn't hear his question, and instead crossed the room to begin the climb to the tower room, aware of Luc following silently behind. It was late afternoon, so the sunlight was shadowed by the mature trees lining the boundaries of the property, leaving the space dimly lit. Luc looked curiously around. "There's no electricity up here?"

"No."

He seemed amused by her brief responses to his queries, but undeterred. "You use the lanterns when you work in the evenings?"

"Yes."

"There is a blank canvas waiting for you," he reminded

her, turning to face her so she couldn't elude his probing glance.

"I know," she admitted, eyeing the canvas set up in the center of the space. "It's intimidating."

He noticed her sketch pad propped up against the far wall. "May I?"

Sighing, she nodded reluctantly, "I suppose."

He crossed the distance to the far wall and bent to retrieve the pad. He leafed through it, slowly, his eyes intently examining each haunting image. "The Annunciation."

His statement wasn't a question, but still Mary Elle felt compelled to respond to it. "Yes."

"You're going to paint this." Again it was a statement of fact, not a question requiring an answer on her part. Again she felt compelled to respond, but this time it was to contest the surety of his assumption.

"Maybe."

He bent to return the pad to its original resting place against the wall, then holding her glance, silently closed the distance between them. His hands descended on her shoulders and pulled her unresistingly towards him. "Why is the canvas still blank? What is the reason behind your hesitation? Surely you no longer doubt the depths of your talent."

"I'm not sure it's mine," Mary Elle admitted in a whisper, bringing a smile to Luc's lips.

"I don't understand."

Mary Elle tried to explain. She wanted him to understand. "It's like a dream trapped inside me. I have to figure out a way to help her escape."

He reached up a gentle hand to cup her chin. "You are the only one who can."

"I know. It's why the blank canvas sitting there, waiting, is so intimidating. It's like she's sitting there too, trapped in the darkness and waiting for me to free her." Their eyes met and she added in a soft voice, "Do you think I'm crazy?"

"No."

She sighed, relieved at his instant response. "Really?"

"You're an artist, Mary Elle. You have the soul of an artist."

"That's a really lovely way of saying you think I'm strange."

"Not strange. Extraordinary," he corrected with a gentle smile.

She held his glance and then confessed in a whisper, "I like being with you."

"Despite your repeated attempts to avoid doing so?"

She laughed at his teasing and with a last uncertain glance at the waiting canvas, reached for his hand to lead him back downstairs. He forestalled her and instead, led her back to the corner where her sketches waited for her to bring them to life. He bent down and retrieved the tablet with the images of the Annunciation from her dream.

"Tell me about her, about that night. These images when she's alone, are they before or after Gabriel's visit?"

She gazed down at the page he held open for her. "Before," she whispered.

"Tell me. Share your vision with me," he urged.

Conscious of both a feeling of reluctance and inevitability, Mary Elle concentrated on the images and picked up the story at the place depicted in the scene in front of her.

"She couldn't sleep, so she climbed out on the roof, seeking relief from the heat of the night in the breeze rustling the window coverings. She was worried about her engagement to Joseph, about being a good wife to him. She was afraid she wouldn't fit in. She feared she didn't fit in anywhere anymore. Then suddenly *he* was there. She was frightened of course, but part of her remembered him from before and what happened the last time he showed up in her life. He took her from everything familiar to her. He was the reason she didn't fit in anymore with the life she should have led. She wondered what he wanted from her this time."

"It doesn't sound as though she was particularly happy to

see him again," Luc pointed out.

"No, more like resigned, as if she always suspected she hadn't seen the last of him."

When Luc didn't respond, she raised her gaze to find him grinning down at her. "Easy for you to laugh," she muttered beneath her breath, causing the laughter to fairly leap in his eyes. At her disgusted expression he managed to regain control of his amusement. "I apologize for my amusement at the virgin's expense. Take me there," he implored.

Shrugging, Mary Elle returned her attention to the images on the page and continued, "She kept her eyes downcast. She might not know what he was doing there, but she was fairly certain she wasn't going to like it. I imagine he was surprised by her lack of enthusiasm. She was just a young girl after all- a simple daughter of Eve. He didn't have a lot of experience interacting with one so young, particularly a daughter of Eve, and he assumed, only partially correctly, it was terror stilling her tongue, so he thought to put her at ease by telling her, 'Do not be afraid, Mary. You have found favor with God.'"

"Maybe Mary wasn't certain what she was expecting by way of a greeting, but his announcement she found favor with the Lord wasn't it. If anything the fear he thought to dispel with his reassurance only spiked in response to his strange greeting. She was happy, of course, to learn her Lord was pleased with her, but she found the prospect she was a topic of discussion between God and one of his great ones more than a little disconcerting. It didn't take any great reasoning ability for her to recognize if such a discussion did indeed transpire it did not bode well for the rather anonymous, unspectacular future she envisioned for herself. As much as she was worried about being a good wife to Joseph, she was actually somewhat relieved to learn her future would not be unlike her mother's or the other girls her age."

"She suspected she was destined for great things?" Luc queried.

Mary Elle lifted one shoulder in a slight shrug. "She was

afraid to set her heart too firmly on the future seemingly laid out before her and now she understood the reason for her premonitions. She was fairly certain God did not send one of his great ones to simply inform her He was pleased with her. So, she waited silently staring down at the roof she rested on, bracing herself for the other shoe to drop, so to speak. Her angelic visitor wasn't quite certain what to do with her silence. She obviously had no conception of the great honor about to be bestowed upon her. 'Do you know who I am?' He asked her."

"Mary shook her head, keeping her eyes downcast, wondering at the same time if the light surrounding him would attract the attention of their neighbors and if it did how she was going to explain his presence to her parents. Her visitor was oblivious to her mundane concerns, however, and announced proudly, "I am Gabriel. I stand in the presence of God."

"Oh." It was the best she could do in the way of a response. She imagined even in heaven, there were not many who stood in the presence of the Lord. The way her angelic visitor announced the fact, as if it explained everything she needed to know about him, only confirmed her supposition. Hoping maybe she was going to get off easy, she gathered her courage and raised her glance to his and dared ask, 'Is that what you came to tell me?'

His glance pierced hers for an instant, as if he suspected her of mocking him, but then satisfied by what he read in her thoughts, he informed her, 'No, as I told you earlier, Mary, you have found favor with the Almighty. You are to bear him a son."

"Mary was too astonished to respond at first, and then she was suddenly filled with an overwhelming sense of relief. This holy one who stood in the presence of God obviously made a mistake and showed up on the wrong rooftop. She didn't think he would appreciate her informing him of his error, so she merely pointed out the inconsistency in his reasoning, hoping he would realize it on his own and go away and leave her alone,

'How can that be? I have never known a man.'"

"But he was obviously unimpressed with her reasoning and waved away her protest with a sweeping motion of his powerful arm. 'The force of the Holy Spirit will overshadow you and you will conceive a son.'"

"The relief she felt just moments earlier faded rapidly in the face of his conviction. 'Oh.' She couldn't think of anything else to say in response to his stunning announcement."

"A new, heavier silence fell between them. Mary wasn't certain what was expected of her. The holy messenger stood there as if waiting for something, but she wouldn't ask him for answers to the questions chasing themselves around in her head. She was still reeling from the rather blasé way he just announced she was going to bear God a son. How was that even possible? Surely he was joking, or mistaken, or perhaps he was unfamiliar with the mechanics of human conception. The uncomfortable silence between them was like a weight pressing down on her. It took her a while to realize he was waiting for her answer."

"All of a sudden she was struck by two conflicting, but awesome thoughts. Number one, he was serious about her bearing God a son, and second, the Almighty would not force his will upon her. She could say no. His messenger was waiting for her response to carry back to the Lord."

"Have you noticed you avoid saying his name?" Luc wondered.

Mary Elle nodded.

"Why?"

She shrugged and replied in a whisper, "Two reasons. I don't think he likes me very much."

Luc smiled at her forlorn confession. "No? Have you spoken to him as well?"

"No, not spoken to, but I can feel his presence. He thinks I'm inadequate for the task at hand."

"What task?"

At his question, Mary Elle sighed and shook off the

memories of her dreams and returned to the present. Releasing an audible sigh, she responded to Luc's curiosity, "I wish I knew."

He waited for her to continue, and when she remained silent, he prompted, "And the other reason you avoid saying his name out loud?"

"He's not the kind of person, (for lack of a better word), whose name should be bandied about. Besides...."

"Besides?" Luc prompted when her voice trailed off.

Mary Elle looked down again at the images she drew and was struck by a forceful reluctance to continue. "I don't want to talk about that night any more. I'm not sure it's allowed."

Silence fell between them at her stark confession, until Luc reached over to close the pad she held in her hands and return it to its resting place in the corner. He took her hand and led her towards the stairs, then encouraged her to descend the steep steps in front of him. When she would have continued around to the first floor, his arms circled her waist, preventing her, and he bent to plead softly in her ear, "Have dinner with me, Mary Elle. Show me your city. Be with me tonight. Accompany me to New York tomorrow."

"What's in New York?" Mary Elle asked.

"An event at the Metropolitan Museum of Art. The family foundation is a supporter. My grandmother was to have made the trip but she asked me to represent the family in her stead."

"I don't really have anything appropriate to wear."

He easily brushed aside her weak protest, "I doubt anyone from the auction will be in attendance. You still have the gown you wore in Paris."

"Yes." The package arrived on her doorstep just after she arrived home, accompanied with a lovely note from Jean Paul. He made a gift to her of the gown and jewelry, even the shoes she wore the night of the auction. Who was she kidding? She wanted to have dinner with Luc, to show him Pittsburgh and go to New York and get all dressed up to be his date at the Met. She decided to take Crystal's advice and live in the moment.

CHAPTER SIXTEEN

They dined at one of the most sought after restaurant in the city. On a whim, she turned to him as they drove into town. "Do you mind if we stop somewhere? I want to introduce you to a friend of mine."

"Of course. I would be pleased to meet your friend."

She gave Aman directions to Crystal's shop in Shadyside. Minutes later he pulled the car to a stop at the curb in front of the shop and let them out. Mary Elle tried not to look around to see if anyone she knew was witnessing their little side show, but she decided the momentary twinge of discomfort at the potential consequences of being recognized was worth the risk when she saw Crystal's expression through the window of her storefront.

"*Witchy, Wantya*?" Luc read the fanciful lettering out loud. "Cute," he commented then held the door open for Mary Elle to precede him into the shop. Crystal was busy with the Friday evening rush, but her eyes kept straying over to them until she finally held up one finger in a desperate gesture promising them she would only be a few more minutes.

"Your friend has eclectic tastes."

"Yes," Mary Elle agreed, grinning at the love potion Luc was holding up for her consideration.

"Perhaps I should purchase this for later."

"I don't think you have anything to worry about," Mary Elle replied, getting into the spirit of his teasing.

"You relieve my mind." Mary Elle grinned and he added curious, "Your friend is the proprietor?"

"Yes."

"Then we must purchase something."

"A memento of your trip to our little town?" Mary Elle suggested.

"I shall be guided by your tastes," Luc responded with a smile.

Mary Elle was fairly certain his tastes didn't run parallel to the products in her friend's shop, so she browsed around and then was delighted to discover the perfect token: a little statue of Cinderella, with her godmother preparing to turn her tattered dress into a beautiful gown for her night at the ball. A fat, round pumpkin surrounded by waiting mice rested nearby. She lifted the set up for Luc's inspection. "This, I think."

Laughing, Luc accepted the offering from her hands. "Yes, I believe you are correct."

When it came time to ring up the sale Mary Elle would make certain Crystal charged her for it. She wanted to present Luc with the small gift to remember their time together.

"You were very quiet on the way back from the restaurant." Luc commented as they passed through her front door. His hands dropped to her shoulders then slid down her arms to clasp her hands from behind, tugging on them to pull her back against him.

Mary Elle wasn't sure how to respond. She didn't know how to play the game they were engaged in. Since the moment she climbed into the back seat of his car in the school parking lot, they both understood where this evening would end. Everything leading up to this moment was simply foreplay... the way their hands brushed across the table at dinner, how their glances meshed every now and then in a sensual dance of anticipation. Now the time to fulfill those silent promises was upon her and she didn't know what she was supposed to do.

As things turned out, her worries were unfounded. They never made it to her room. After, still in the entry, leaning against her own front door, Mary Elle leaned into Luc, and suggested, "Let's just sleep here tonight."

He laughed, but raised no objection to her plan and tugged her down to the floor where he sat holding her in his arms, trailing his fingers up and down her back in a soothing caress. She fell asleep in his arms, with his back leaning against her front door. At some point Luc carried her to bed, because when she woke later in the deepest part of the night, she was tangled up in him seeking his warmth as a defense against the cold. She felt his lips brush the top of her head, heard his whispered reassurance and sighing softly in the stillness, snuggled closer against him and fell back asleep.

They flew to New York the following morning on Luc's private jet. She stepped through the entry and into the plush cabin where a steward was waiting to greet them and see to their needs during the short flight. For one shining moment of sanity Mary Elle considered turning around and fleeing in the opposite direction, but the moment quickly passed and she meekly took the wide leather seat Luc indicated. Besides, it was too late to escape, to rewind the past twenty four hours and send Luc on his way while she still had the chance...while she could still pretend she wasn't already falling in love with him. The truth was she in so far over her head she couldn't envision any ending to their budding relationship that didn't entail broken-hearted disaster, at least for her.

The event was perfect, like watching a daydream come to life before her very eyes. Standing in the imposing entrance, she drank in every detail of the gorgeous view, feeling as if she had been sprinkled with fairy dust. She couldn't help but notice Luc's presence caused a noticeable stir, as an older tuxedoed gentleman, catching sight of him, hurried across the room to greet them at their entrance.

"May I introduce my guest, Miss Mary Elle McGann?"

Mary Elle held out her hand, which the older man accepted

with a slightly distracted air. "A pleasure, Miss McGann." Then it was as if a light bulb flicked on in his head, illuminating the reason for his distraction. "Miss McGann? You would not by any chance be the artist responsible for the *Young Madonna* painting Mr. Bordeaux recently acquired?"

Mary Elle wasn't certain how to respond. Something in the way the man was regarding her made her blush with embarrassment, as if he was implying Luc purchased her along with her painting. "Yes," she finally confirmed shortly, glad when Luc, sensing her discomfort, made their excuses.

"Mary Elle, you are going to have to get used to the fact that in certain circles you are now famous."

"I am not your latest acquisition," she muttered indignantly.

Luc grinned. "So you picked up on his implication?"

"The man wasn't particularly subtle."

He bent to brush his lips across hers. "Do not allow his poor manners to spoil your enjoyment of the evening."

"Easy for you to say," she pointed out with an outraged toss of her head. "You're not the one who comes across as the opportunistic bimbo making the most of her wealthy benefactor's generosity."

"He hasn't seen the painting," he reminded her, then added after a moment's consideration. "Besides, I imagine he is somewhat annoyed by your decision to auction off your work in Europe rather than giving him the chance to be the one to discover the next, great American artist."

"That's ridiculous!"

His lips curved at her fierce protest. "I cannot decide if your humility in regards to your talent is simply a charming, indelible part of who you are, or if you truly have no conception as to the depths of your gift."

When he said things like that it was impossible for her to cling to her annoyance. With an effort she set it aside and reminded herself how limited their time together was. Only a fool would waste it.

Despite her protests, Luc insisted on flying with her to Pittsburgh and driving her back to her home. The ride from the airport was strangely quiet and Mary Elle got the impression the broken-hearted disaster she foretold the previous morning was about to break over her unsuspecting head. She suspected the inconvenience of a cross-Atlantic affair was already making Luc regret his impulsive whim to stop in Pittsburgh on his way to New York.

She didn't blame him. He was a busy man. He made no secret of the fact he was attracted to her because of her talent. Unwilling to break the heavy silence between them, Mary Elle stared out the window as they turned into her driveway. She waited for Aman to stop the car and open the rear door for them to exit, accepting the hand Luc held out to her, but avoiding his glance. She was determined to be carefree and sophisticated about the whole thing. It was a brief fling. They both knew that going in.

He turned her towards him when they reached her front door. She bravely lifted her glance to his, a bright smile, she hoped he couldn't tell was blatantly false, curving her lips. "Thank you. I had a really nice time."

"As did I," he confirmed, a slight smile appearing at her formality.

"Well, I guess this is goodbye. Safe flight," she whispered and turned to insert her key into the lock with a hand that shook noticeably. She felt his larger hand close over hers and help her fit the key into the lock. Then he pushed the door open. When she would have escaped inside, his hands on her shoulders prevented her.

"Mary Elle…" he began, but she swiftly turned back to face him.

Blinking away her betraying tears, she silenced him with an imperious gesture. "Don't…don't spoil it. We both knew this was coming." When he would have interrupted her, she shook her head, "You don't have to say anything, Luc. No excuses or explanations necessary. I'm not so naïve I ever envisioned a fairy tale ending for us. Goodbye, Luc. I'm so glad I met you."

Mary Elle slipped from beneath his restraining hold and quickly passed through the door, shutting it firmly behind her. She used one trembling hand to silence the broken sob that wanted to escape her lips, unsure if Luc already left, or if he was still standing on the opposite side of the door. She rested her back against it, fighting to catch her breath, chiding herself for being such a fool.

She knew this was coming. They only spent a few days in each other's company. It was nothing. Get over it. The harder she attempted to convince herself Luc meant nothing to her, the more her spirit rebelled. Finally abandoning the effort to hold them in, she let the sobs escape and slid to the floor where she sat, doubled over, with her arms wrapped around her middle, crying as if her heart could truly break.

Hearing Mary Elle's desolation, Luc hesitated on the other side of the door. An unfamiliar pang of guilt struck him at the evidence of Mary Elle's distress, but even that did not prevent him from turning on his heel and striding in the direction of the waiting car.

He was surprised by her insight this weekend would be the last they would share with each other. He was even more surprised, and admiring, by her acceptance of the abrupt end to their brief affair. There were no tears, except the ones she tried so desperately to hide from him, no recriminations, no demands.

Contrarily, he felt almost slighted by the ease with which she sent him on his way. It wasn't as though he didn't enjoy his time with her, quite the opposite, but as much as he laughed off her insistence they were impossible, he was forced to acknowledge her point.

He recognized it was dangerous to pursue a relationship with Mary Elle, no matter how casual, when thoughts of her and memories of their time together began to consume him. He would look up from his desk and be confronted with the

Young Madonna and fall victim to his own fascination with its creator all over again. He couldn't be certain if his impulsive detour to Pittsburgh was his way of ending things between them in person before his carefully crafted plans for his future lay in shattered pieces around him, or if he simply couldn't resist the opportunity to spend another night with her.

In another man, he would label his interest in Mary Elle McGann for what it was...an incipient but growing obsession. If Mary Elle was more like his usual feminine companions he would have enjoyed continuing their association, but he recognized as soon as he saw the light in her eyes when she saw him outside the school where she taught he was not the only one in the throes of an unhealthy attraction. No, it was best for both of them, but especially for Mary Elle, for them to say their goodbyes before they became any more entangled with each other.

He did not make a habit of associating with women who needed to be protected from themselves. It was a pity Mary Elle was too naïve to appreciate his act of chivalry for what it was.

CHAPTER SEVENTEEN

The dreams were back. This time though it wasn't the young virgin's fears tugging at her spirit. No, this night Mary Elle sat on a wooden bench staring down into the eyes of her young daughter who knelt at her feet, clasping her icy hands between her own and staring pleadingly up into her shocked face. Tears filled both of their eyes but she brushed her own away, determined not to lose her battle with a woman's weakness.

The Lord only knew there was no time for tears now. She needed to get her daughter away. Fear robbed her of the ability to offer the comfort her daughter so desperately sought from her. Stark terror for what they would do to her beloved Mary dazed her reason and crowded her power to order her thoughts. She did not for a moment doubt her daughter's story of the holy one's visit, but the others would never believe her.

Hadn't they always resented her Mary's pious innocence, her luminescent beauty, and her steadfast devotion to the Lord? No, they would leap at the chance to tear her precious daughter apart. And here she knelt at her feet, regarding her with such innocent faith, as if she could stop them, as if she could protect her from the evil lurking in the hearts of men.

What was she going to do? What would Joachim say to this? She needed time to think, to plan their escape from Nazareth. In the meantime no one must know, no one must suspect. She would send Mary away to Elizabeth. She would be safe in her home until Ann could come up with a plan...

Mary Elle woke with a start, her heart pounding, sheer terror pulsing through her. As much as she was grateful for the gift she was given, despite her heartbreak over Luc, she couldn't know at what price it was purchased. She understood there would be a price. She only hoped when the time came she could afford to pay it.

Maybe it was time she tried to gain a step on the direction of the journey she was immersed in rather than being pulled along by its swift current, desperately trying to keep her head above water.

Jerusalem.

The name popped into her head unbidden, but Mary Elle immediately rejected it. Not Jerusalem. Not yet. She would travel instead to Nazareth, where two millennia ago an archangel visited a young virgin and changed the course of history.

CHAPTER EIGHTEEN

Israel was a country of contradictions. From modern Tel Aviv to the Sea of Galilee where it was reputed Jesus fed five thousand with a few fish and a couple of loaves of bread. Mary Elle was surprised to learn how small an area the country encompassed. It was comparable in size to the state of New Jersey. She assumed the stories from the bible would demand a grander setting.

On landing at the airport, she was astonished at the sight of the young men and women, some who appeared no older than her own students, carrying automatic weapons strapped to their shoulders. They wore them as casually as if they were another appendage. The tour guide informed them that every eighteen year old, man or woman was required to serve in the Army in defense of their country. Religion was the national past-time, though for many of the small country's citizens their Jewish heritage was more secular than devotional in nature, resembling more of a cultural tradition passed down through the generations than one rooted in religious fervor.

Much to her surprise Mary Elle learned several areas of the country hosted majority Arab populations, most of them centered in the occupied territories from the Six Day War in 1967. Everywhere they visited, Mary Elle was aware of the religious tension permeating the dry air. It reminded her of the racial tensions still lingering in America's Deep South.

Despite its modern cities and economy, Israel itself was all but synonymous with the ancient city of Jerusalem. The much-contested and fought over city claimed a starring role in the histories of three of the world's major faiths, Jews,

Christians and Muslims. It was in the Holy of Holies in the Temple of Solomon where Jews believed the Ark of the Covenant containing the Ten Commandments was housed. On that same site, from the Temple Mount, Muslims believe the Prophet Muhammed ascended to heaven to converse with God, and just blocks away was the site where Christians believe the son of God was condemned to death by the Roman governor Pontius Pilate and was crucified.

Such a tiny area, yet the events that took place within its boundaries shaped much of mankind's history. To current day it continued to challenge man's ability to carve out the peaceful existence all professed to seek. Jerusalem, the city God claimed as his dwelling place on earth, remained divided among several of the world's major religions and contested over like siblings arguing over a favorite toy shouting at each other their father loved them more than the others.

Mary Elle found all the squabbling rather depressing, to think man changed so little over the course of his violent, self-righteous history. She couldn't help but wonder if God ever got depressed too at the thought of how little progress mankind made towards peaceful coexistence.

She stared out the window as the tour bus climbed the steep, curving hill along the narrow streets of Nazareth on its way to the Church of the Annunciation. Nazareth was a majority Arab city and most of the signs were written in Arabic. Even the entrance to the church itself was a spot of contention between the world's major religions, where the tour guide pointed to a sign proclaiming in awkward English Islam was the one true religion and all others would find themselves the losers in eternity.

The Church of the Annunciation was believed to be built on the very site of Mary's childhood home, where the actual events Mary Elle dreamed about took place. When the bus drew to a stop, she checked to make sure her sketch pad and charcoals were safely stowed in her small bag before filing out of the bus behind her fellow tour group members.

She stood at the rear of the group listening to the tour guide provide a brief history of the church before releasing them to wander through the basilica on their own. The first shrine on the site was believed to date back to the middle of the fourth century. The current structure was consecrated in 1969 above the remains of earlier churches.

Mary Elle passed through the entrance with a sense of anticipation absent at the other sites they visited. She stared in awe at the mosaics of the virgin donated by communities from around the world decorating the upper church, and then explored the Grotto of the lower church where the actual angelic visit was believed to have occurred.

She grew increasingly anxious as their time at the church grew short and she realized whatever she hoped would be revealed to her at the holy site remained frustratingly elusive. Deflated and disappointed, she exited the church ahead of most of the group and sought refuge in the courtyard near a statute of the virgin while she waited for the other members of the group to catch up.

She turned her attention to the statue and asked silently, "Why did you bring me here? I don't know what I'm supposed to do."

There was no answer to her query. Defeated, Mary Elle perched on the edge of a nearby bench waiting for the rest of the tour group to exit the church. She was tired from the tension of being among strangers alone in a foreign country, eating unfamiliar food and packing up every few days as the tour moved on. More discouraging than her feelings of exhaustion, was her disappointment at the possibility of having travelled six thousand miles for nothing.

A movement to her left caught her attention and she looked up, her focus captured by the statue of the virgin, her arms outstretched, but it was her face attracting Mary Elle's gaze. The eyes of the statue seemed to stare back at her, beckoning her forward, so they could speak privately, away from the conversations going on around them as visitors exited the church and gathered in the courtyard.

Mary Elle was only half conscious of pulling her sketchpad and charcoals from her bag, before she sank to her knees and crawled towards the statue, her eyes never leaving the virgin's face. If this was why she was brought here she didn't want to risk breaking the connection between them. When she was directly in front of the statue she sat back on her heels and retrieved a fresh charcoal from the box.

The inspiration she felt the lack of so acutely just moments earlier struck with overwhelming force. Her hand flew across the blank pages recreating in charcoal the images playing out across the canvas of her thoughts. Visions of a young girl on the brink of womanhood, uncertain at first of what her future would hold, then disbelieving of the angel's promise and even more concerned about her future after his visitation. She gave her assent to God's holy messenger, but afterwards she wondered if she could take it back. She didn't want to be singled out again.

Her mother's friends and family, their neighbors, considered her odd, uppity, unlike most girls her age. She could not embrace their frivolous concerns. Their lives seemed empty to her, with little room for true devotion to the Lord. They observed the law and were all proper Jews but it seemed to Mary their faith was something they pulled out each week and packed away again at the end of the Sabbath. She realized they didn't have the privilege of being raised in the temple where every breath was steeped in Him, but she couldn't imagine ever fitting into a world so devoid of true fidelity to their heavenly Father.

She thought they would be both appalled and secretly thrilled by the staggering depths of her fall from grace when they learned she was carrying a child. She would become the object of gossip and condemnation, even stoned for adultery. Would Joseph believe her or would he shake his head in disgust at her tale of the Lord Gabriel's appearance before her?

Was her life then to be the price of this new great honor he promised was about to be bestowed upon her? Was the Lord testing the love she professed to feel for Him as he did their father in faith, Abraham? Would He change his mind at the final, pivotal moment once she proved her love...once she agreed to sacrifice her very life at the hands of merciless men if such a sacrifice was His holy will?

Tears filled her eyes and fell silently down her cheeks. She sat on the roof outside her bedroom window as she did the night not so long ago, but the holy one did not separate himself from the other stars shining so brightly above her. Perhaps all her fears and anxious wondering were a wasted effort by now. Maybe she already carried the child the holy one spoke of. Would she know if she did? Was she even now carrying the son of God in her womb?

When a damp tear dropped on the page beneath her hand and smudged one of the charcoal images, Mary Elle reached up to brush away the rest before they could fall and obscure the other images on the page. She didn't question the source of her tears and saw them reflected in the agonized indecision on the face of the young woman staring back at her from the no longer blank pages beneath her hand. Empty, she let the stubby pencil fall from her fingers. There was nothing left inside of her clambering to escape. She glanced up to confirm her supposition but it was just the vacant gaze of a stone statue staring back at her. *She* was gone.

Her shoulders relaxed, releasing the tension she carried to this holy place, knowing her purpose there was fulfilled. It was time for her to return home and translate what she was given onto canvas. Clasping the pad against her chest and retrieving the unused pencils with her free hand, she struggled shakily to her feet, grateful for the strong hand reaching down to assist her.

When she turned to offer her gratitude, her eyes met those of a young priest, who she guessed was assigned to the church. Behind him stood the majority of the members of her tour group along with their guide. She was so focused on her drawing she was unaware of the passage of time. She wasn't certain if it was minutes or hours since she entered the courtyard.

Blushing slightly at the realization she was the focus of attention of the small crowd gathered behind the young priest, she instinctively retreated a step. "Thank you," she whispered, recognizing she owed him her gratitude for not only his assistance in helping her to her feet, but also she suspected for keeping the crowd from pressing too closely in on her while she worked.

"You are welcome," he replied in formal English, giving her the impression it was not his first language. "May I?" he added, gesturing to the pad she clutched close to her chest.

Sighing, aware of her reluctance to share what she was given, even with a priest, she passed him the pad, "Yes, of course."

He leafed through it in silence, an intent expression on his face, and then just as silently handed the tablet back to her. "You were given a great gift. Thank you for sharing it with me."

Mary Elle nodded. "Thank you, Father. I need to go now."

He nodded, his lips curving in a slight smile at her obvious discomfort. Her eyes quickly sought out the tour guide. "I'm sorry for keeping everyone waiting."

He was regarding her with a strange expression on his face that only served to make her feel even more self-conscious. She suspected over the past days and evenings spent in his company the confident and affable guide, who appeared to know so much about his country's long history, was never personally touched by the divine aura hovering over it.

After a brief, uncomfortable silence following her apology, he merely nodded and announced to the members of their group it was time to reboard the bus. Mary Elle kept her eyes downcast as she trailed the rest of the group, keeping her precious sketches wrapped close in her arms. When her phone rang she was grateful for the distraction if only because it provided her an excuse not to have to respond to the silent questions being cast in her direction by her tour companions.

"Hello?"

"Mary Elle?"

"Luc." She exhaled his name as though it was a lifeline in her suddenly careening world.

"Are you all right?" He inserted swiftly at her obvious relief.

"Yes, yes of course."

"Where are you?"

She debated whether or not to admit the truth and then because she couldn't think of any reason to lie, admitted, "I'm in Nazareth."

"Excuse me?" he echoed.

"Nazareth. You know, in Israel."

"I am aware of its location, but I cannot imagine what you are doing there."

Mary Elle lowered her voice to a whisper and dropped back a little so the others wouldn't overhear her side of their conversation. "I'm on a tour group. I needed to come here. I needed to see it."

"Why did you need to go to Nazareth?"

"How can you ask me that?"

"The Annunciation."

"Yes," she breathed, then looking up ahead to where her tour companions were already boarding the bus, she added swiftly, "I'm sorry. I need to go now. The bus is leaving and we're not supposed to speak on the phone once we board the bus."

Two thousand miles away, Luc stared at the now silent phone in his hand, shaking his head in disbelief. She hung up on him, again. This was getting to be a habit. He stood up from behind his desk and crossed to the wall of windows looking out on the bustling city beneath him. His mind grappled with the repercussions of his young lover in the holy lands and the shiver of unease at the thought.

He resisted the urge to call her for the past long weeks since he so abruptly ended their relationship. Rather than time and distance making her memory fade from his thoughts, the more he suppressed his memories, the more urgently they assailed him. During his waking hours his will was still strong enough to resist her appeal for him, but at night when he was asleep, thoughts of her invaded his dreams, just as she claimed the virgin had invaded hers.

CHAPTER NINETEEN

Mary Elle was so anxious to return home she skipped the rest of the tour. Back in the hotel, she changed her flight to the following afternoon, contacted the tour guide and lied to him about there being a slight emergency back home requiring her immediate attention. After speaking to the tour guide she called the front desk to arrange for transportation to the airport. It took her a full day to get home. Once she arrived, she was too exhausted to do anything but dump her luggage by the front door, take a quick, semi-conscious, thankfully warm shower and fall exhausted into bed.

Sleep eluded her. From the safety of her own bed, she could admit the real reason she cut her trip short so abruptly. Though it was true she was anxious to get back and begin work on the painting, she recognized it wasn't the only reason she was so anxious to leave Israel. After leaving Nazareth the bus drove directly to the tour's next stop: Jerusalem.

As they approached the holy city her sense of panic became more pronounced. She didn't want to go there. As a child, attending the Stations of the Cross during the Lenten season made her nauseous. She didn't know what her reaction would be to strolling along the Via Dolorosa in the company of strangers, but she knew she wasn't ready to find out.

Whether the dark fear settling over her as they approached the city was simply a lingering foolishness from childhood or something connected to her recent visions she couldn't be certain. The fear itself was enough to convince her to run in the opposite direction. She figured Pittsburgh was pretty much as far away from Jerusalem as she could get.

Happy and genuinely relieved to be back home in her own bed with her familiar things around her, Mary Elle rolled over and closed her eyes, assuming, given her exhausted state, she would slide effortlessly into a long, healing sleep. Her assumption proved only partially accurate. Whether it was the change in time zones or the long hours in flight, the sleep she longed for came only in restless fits. After a few, too-short hours, it eluded her completely.

"You're not going to stop are you?" She asked out loud into the dark. "You won't leave me alone until I paint you out of there."

Silence was the only response she received to her frustrated query. Accepting it was useless to fight her inevitable capitulation to the compulsion within her, and knowing continuing to attempt to do battle against it would only drain her of much needed energy for the task at hand, Mary Elle threw back the quilts and climbed out of bed.

Ascending the stairs, she hesitated at the entrance to the bell tower, reaching for a lantern and lighting it so she could see what awaited her in the cramped space. The blank canvas was still there propped up on her college easel. The last time she was there was during Luc's brief visit. She immediately shut off the emotions the memory resurrected and focused instead on the canvas. It too seemed to be waiting for her. Mary Elle sensed its grudging welcome, as if it was relieved to see her again, but at the same time was irritated it took her so long to get on with things.

Thrusting a hand through her long hair to push it away from her face, wishing she thought to retrieve a hair tie before ascending the narrow steps, Mary Elle crossed the distance to the waiting canvas. Kneeling before it she confronted its vacant gaze then closed her eyes to avoid the accusation she imagined she read there.

Suddenly anxious to get started, she jumped to her feet to organize her supplies and to make a few additional preliminary sketches before she put paint to canvas. The uncertain light of early morning filtering softly through the stained glass windows added an eerie, supernatural feel to the light cast by the two oil lanterns hanging on the hooks above her. No, not an eerie feel, she quickly corrected herself, a sacred one, as if both her hand and vision skipped along the edges of the divine.

As with the first painting, she focused her initial efforts on the young woman who was only just beginning to emerge from the innocence of girlhood. She figured an archangel didn't need her assistance to bring him to life, and would likely take affront at any presumption on her part he did. So it was the young virgin's delicate features she recreated beneath her brush, the eyes both fearful and excited at once, both proud and frightened to reach out and grasp the exalted place in history her Lord's messenger was offering her.

She led a sheltered life, one of prayer and seclusion in the safety of the temple, with no real experience of the outside world or of the evils of men. But she was not so innocent she did not know evil existed. And despite the years she spent isolated in the temple, she learned enough to fear it.

Long, silent hours later, Mary Elle laid aside her paintbrush and drifted down towards the floor. She fell asleep with her head pillowed on her bent arm and the virgin's watchful eyes upon her. When she woke, it was to the confusion of colored lights flickering over her face as the sun rose higher in the sky and finally managed to rouse her from her dreams. Stiff from lying on the stone floor for so long, Mary Elle groaned and shifted awkwardly into a seated position.

Pushing aside the long weight of her hair from her face, she raised her anxious glance to the painting she barely recalled coming off her brush. She blinked away the tears filling her eyes, reaching out a hand, then stopping just short of brushing her fingers across the virgin's lovely face, unwilling to risk smearing the still drying paint.

"You're here. I'm so happy to see you," she whispered in an

awed voice.

There was no answering greeting from the subject of her painting, but Mary Elle wasn't really expecting one. She was so thankful to be given this precious gift for just a little while longer she didn't mind. She thought maybe she would go to yoga class. It would help work the stiffness from her fingers and limbs. Smiling to herself, she rose to her feet, paused to retrieve her phone, and saw a message from Crystal waiting for her.

Skipping down the stairs, she hit send on the face of her phone to return Crystal's call. A few moments later her friend's greeting came over the line. "Welcome home. You are home, right? I thought you weren't getting back until Tuesday, but I must have gotten my dates wrong."

Rather than admit she left the tour early, Mary Elle simply confirmed, "Yes, I'm home. Did I miss anything?"

"Nope, nothing exciting. How was the trip? Did you hook up with Monsieur hottie?"

Mary Elle laughingly denied any hottie hook-ups and Crystal continued unchecked, "Well something's going on with you. You're fairly bursting with news."

"How do you know?"

"Psychic, remember? It's in the genes."

"Well, this time you're right. I want to show you something."

"You painted it, didn't you? The Annunciation?"

"How did you guess? But yes, you're right, part of it, anyway. I painted her. I want to show you. To see what you think."

"I thought your Luc was the expert."

"He's not my Luc, and yes, he is, but he's a collector. I'm not concerned about her monetary value. I just want to share her with my friend," Mary Elle explained.

"You do realize you do that, don't you?" Crystal asked.

"Do what?"

"You refer to your paintings as her, not it."

Mary Elle hesitated and then admitted softly, "Yes. That's the way it is for me...the way *she* is to me."

"Well then, I guess you better introduce us. If it's slow this afternoon, I'll be over once my evening help arrives. How about I stop and pick up a pizza and some wine to celebrate your return from far, exotic places to our humble town?"

Laughing, Mary Elle replied, "Pizza sounds fabulous. My stomach's experienced enough of far and exotic food for a while."

Mary Elle avoided returning to the tower room until Crystal arrived. She knew if she returned upstairs she wouldn't be able to stop herself from diving back in to work on the painting. So, though she could almost feel its long pull reaching out and whispering through her thoughts whenever she allowed them to drift from her unpacking and the setting of her life to rights after being away, Mary Elle stood firm and resisted the urge to ascend the narrow stairs.

After pizza and much reminiscing about her trip, Crystal eyed her with a considering look. "Did you change your mind about introducing me to your unusual visitor?"

Blushing, Mary Elle shook her head. "No, of course not."

"Well then?"

"Right, let's go. Remember, I don't want you to be nice. I want your honest opinion."

Crystal's expression went from considering to incredulous. "You're joking, right? Do I need to remind you Monsieur hottie paid a million euros for your first painting?"

Laughing, Mary Elle protested, "Would you stop calling him that?"

"If the shoe fits..."

Mary Elle threw up her hands in surrender, then reaching for her friend's hand led the way up the stairs.

Mary Elle lit the lanterns and waited anxiously near the entrance while Crystal crossed to the easel and for long, silent moments stared intently at the image on the canvas.

Finally, she exhaled audibly and breathed in a near whisper, "Wow!"

Relieved, grinning, Mary Elle responded, "That's pretty much the way I feel about her too."

Crystal threw an amused look over her shoulder then switched her focus back to the painting. "What about him?"

Shrugging, Mary Elle admitted, "I'm working my way in his direction."

Crystal eyes sparkled with laughter at her obvious reluctance. "You really think he doesn't like you?"

Mary Elle shrugged. "I'm not sure it's anything personal. I just get the impression he doesn't think too much of us in general."

"Us?"

"You know, mankind… the human race."

"Oh, sure, well at least it's not personal," Crystal quipped and added, "The Annunciation. I seem to remember that's one of the mysteries of the rosary, isn't it?"

"Yes. It's the first of the Joyful mysteries." Mary Elle supplied automatically, then as the thought struck her, she turned her gaze to the painting, "Or not," she added in a whisper.

"What do you mean?"

"I don't think it's the first. I think they have it wrong."

"Who has it wrong?"

"The church."

"The church is wrong? The Catholic Church?" Crystal echoed incredulously.

Mary Elle ignored her friend's teasing.

Crystal whistled softly as the conclusion came to her. "The first painting, the one with the little girl and the angel. You think that's supposed to be the first mystery, right? You're thinking that's what she came to tell you?"

"I don't know," Mary Elle hedged.

"Seems to me a lot of trouble to go to for such a little

detail."

"Maybe it's not such a little detail to her."

"So are you going to call the pope and tell him he has it wrong?" Crystal prompted, obviously awed at the prospect of her friend's daring.

"No. I'm not going to call anyone. I have a feeling she's going to tell everyone," Mary Elle replied, pointing at the canvas.

"Oh, wow. This is so cool. Are you going to call Jean Paul?"

"No."

"Why not? I thought you liked him," Crystal countered, confused.

"I do, but I don't need his services this time because I'm not going to sell her."

"You mean the painting, right? I have to tell you Mary Elle it's a little spooky the way you keep referring to it as her."

Later that night after a satisfying and normal evening spent in the company of her best friend, Mary Elle sat on the stone floor of the bell tower staring up at the subject of her painting. The glow of the moon and the lanterns she lit provided enough light for her to paint by. Still she hesitated while she worked herself up to put oil to canvas to begin work on the rest of the scene. The young virgin looked lonely sitting there by herself.

At the same time, Mary Elle got the impression her angelic protector didn't like the idea of her being alone, perched on the roof in such a vulnerable way. There was no less evil in the world today than there was in biblical times and an innocent young woman needed to be careful to be on her guard against it.

Mary Elle could feel his much stronger will pressing against hers, urging her to get on with things and paint him into the scene so he would be there to defend her. It occurred to her he wasn't sent to just deliver a message to the virgin. If so, what was he doing in the first painting? Of course there was no record of the angel escorting Mary to the temple when she was a child. She was the one who painted him there. No, it wasn't her idea. It was Mary's. She was the one who wanted to set the record straight.

Mary Elle was fairly certain an archangel didn't particularly care about whether the human race got his part in God's plan right or not. She sighed and met the gaze of the woman staring out of the painting. "You know it would be a lot easier if you would just tell me where all of this is leading and what you want me to do for you." Silence greeted her hopeful suggestion. No new inspiration struck. "One step at a time, Mary Elle," she chided herself. "Live in the moment. She can't bring you up to speed until you finish the task at hand." It was time to bring an archangel to life.

Unlike her young subject who simply waited patiently for Mary Elle to recreate her image on canvas, the virgin's protective companion bristled with impatience at her procrastination. Every little pause on her part would bring the echo of a frustrated sigh through her thoughts. She would swear she could feel her hair lifting from the nape of her neck whenever she took a break to use the bathroom or grab a bite to eat.

The last time she descended the steep stairs towards the kitchen, she tripped over some unseen obstacle in her path, causing her panicked grip to tighten frantically around the railing to prevent a nasty fall. She couldn't help but wonder if her impatient subject was responsible for her near disaster. Though she instantly rebuked herself for her fanciful conclusion she remained unconvinced her supposition wasn't the correct one.

After she descended the stairs she decided to break for the night. It was an unseasonably warm night for spring. She made herself a cup of tea and carried it outside. The cool breeze felt good against her skin as she raised her gaze to the stars blanketed across the dark sky and wondered if *she* was up there, watching her from heaven. She smiled, remembering Crystal's question about whether she was going to call the pope about the discrepancy in the mysteries of the rosary. The reminder started her wondering. As she recalled there were five Joyful mysteries. What was the next one? The little puzzle bothered her enough to send her back inside to research the answer.

The response to her small mystery presented itself readily enough. The Joyful mysteries of the rosary were in order: the Annunciation, the Visitation, the Nativity, the Presentation of the infant Jesus in the temple, and the Finding of a young Jesus teaching in the temple. So far, she dreamt of only one, so maybe she was off base in her speculations there was any connection to the inspiration for her paintings and the mysteries at all.

The truth was she was grasping at straws, trying to make sense of the incomprehensible. Deciding she'd done as much as she could for one day, she finished her tea and headed for bed, resolving to finish the painting and see where it led her.

CHAPTER TWENTY

Jerusalem. The ancient city hung like a heavy weight around her neck, pulling her back to a place she'd never been. Impossible memories of its narrow streets, busy marketplaces and the imposing temple no longer standing haunted her dreams and began to seep into her waking hours. In unguarded moments she would catch herself brushing aside the scent of pungent spices mixed with the strong odor of horses and other livestock along with the sweat of unwashed flesh. She would hear the echo of voices crying out in unfamiliar tongues. Sometimes it seemed as if they hailed her from afar in an attempt to capture her attention.

Most of the time she managed to shake off the strange encounters and go about her day as if nothing was amiss. At night though, when she slept and her defenses were at their weakest, the city came to life in her dreams. She was there, one of them, hurrying passed the stern Roman soldiers with her head bowed so as not to draw attention to herself. Surrounding her, almost choking her as she drew in every breath was the resentment of the occupied simmering close beneath the surface of the native population, lying in wait for a spark to provide the catalyst for a full-scale rebellion against their homeland's invaders.

The temple stood, regal and silent, at the center of Jewish life. In her dreams Mary Elle watched fascinated as the vanquished citizens of the even then ancient city practiced their daily devotion to a God who delivered them to their conquerors. Amidst their religious constancy there were taxes to be paid and collected, meals to prepare, livestock to tend, criminals to judge and condemn, and always, commerce to be conducted. She was not a resident of the city, but nor was she a stranger to its daily rhythm.

The city itself stood unchallenged and untroubled by the angst within the hearts and souls of her residents, both native sons, and those who found themselves temporarily dwelling within her boundaries at the order of their Caesar. She was occupied before and would be again long after the current residents of the city were but dust and ashes mingled with the gritty desert sand lining her streets.

To Mary Elle it seemed as if the city waited, awash in expectation and anticipation its residents were not yet cognizant of. As if it knew what the God who claimed her for his own dwelling place on earth was planning. The city both mourned and rejoiced at the great events that would unfold within her gates, even as its foundations trembled beneath the will of the Almighty who would tear her asunder once those events reached their final consummation.

More often than not Mary Elle woke with tears in her eyes and her heart wrenched wide open. A grief she never experienced before and one for which there was no earthly explanation tore at her soul until she dreaded the setting of the sun, anticipating the agony awaiting her before the dawn of a new day freed her from its relentless grip.

This morning was no different. Hands trembling, she reached up to brush the familiar tears from her eyes. She took several calming breaths, the ones she learned in her yoga class, and closed her eyes in an attempt to settle herself back into the present day. It was happening again. She was being drawn back to the place where it was destined to end and where the blood of a prophet mingled with the spilled blood of God's earlier messengers in the sunbaked dust of his holy city.

She suspected her resistance to its call was futile. For now though, she was willing to acknowledge another trip was in her future. She would go back, but not to Jerusalem. Not yet. It wasn't her time and the painting of the Annunciation wasn't finished yet. She delayed its completion, putting it aside after she brought an archangel to life. There was more work to be done, but she dawdled over it, knowing once the painting was finished she would no longer have an excuse to evade the will urging her to return and take the next step on the odd journey she'd begun.

For what purpose it urged her, she was ignorant of and she was unwilling to ask, afraid to question too deeply where it was leading and what the price of the journey would be to her. She negotiated with His will once before when she was a young girl and was not pleased with the outcome. She understood the stakes were higher now, even though she refused to speculate on exactly what they were.

Mary Elle rose on trembling legs and padded silently across her dimly lit room, heading for the narrow stairs leading to where the almost finished canvas sat waiting for her, impervious to her delaying tactics and her indecision as she knelt before it. Her eyes met those of the young virgin. Unlike the disapproving glance she could feel beating down on her from her angelic companion, the gaze of the young Madonna was watchful and filled with compassion, as if she was aware of Mary Elle's struggles and was sympathetic to her plight.

Mary Elle felt the odd bond between them strengthening with each improbable encounter they shared. Belatedly she realized whatever was going on between them required both of their consents. Mary Elle very much feared she was destined to disappoint the younger woman who she brought to life beneath her paintbrush.

She reached for it now, where it lay at her feet, as if it too waited, ready, prepared to do its part and she was the one solely responsible for the delay. Muttering a silent apology to everyone involved, she picked up the brush, mixed the colors and began again, losing herself in the scene of a clear night over biblical Nazareth, with angels appearing as stars in the black sky, standing watch over the simple house where a young woman sat and conversed with one of their brothers.

CHAPTER
TWENTY-ONE

She was going back, but not yet, not right away. She would wait until the end of the school year. Her capitulation seemingly assured, the powers that be adopted a fresh waiting posture, but Mary Elle's doubts were not so easily appeased. Throughout the remaining weeks of the school calendar, she told herself she was crazy. There was no reason for her to go back, but she accepted in the end she would do as she was told. The compulsion to return took hold of her and grew until it was part of her every thought. The more she resisted the more it impelled her, until she finally surrendered and booked her place on another tour ...but not to Jerusalem. Not yet. She would go instead to Bethlehem, the birthplace of Jesus.

As the final days of the term wound down, and aware of Crystal's watchful concern, Mary Elle quietly began to make more concrete plans for her upcoming trip. There was only one final detail for her to arrange. The painting of the Annunciation was complete and rested serenely on her easel in the tower room, surrounded by other stained glass depictions of pivotal moments of Christ's life. Mary Elle couldn't bring her along on the trip and she was even more loathe to leave her alone while she was gone, even if she could convince Crystal to swing by and check on her. Her friend would agree because she asked her to, but she wouldn't understand the need and Mary Elle suspected Crystal would neglect her promised stewardship.

There was someone who she thought understood, and who could be trusted to act as the painting's guardian while she was away. She thought she could convince Jean Paul to watch over the painting. As much as she longed to call Luc and hear his voice she thought it best if she avoided dragging him any deeper into whatever was happening to her. Besides, part of her worried once he saw the painting, he would somehow convince her to sell it to him, and she was determined not to succumb to any pressure to part with it.

Jean Paul answered on the first ring. "Jean Paul, it's Mary Elle."

"Yes, I recognized your number. How are you?"

"Fine." She wasn't certain how to broach the favor she called about until he finally prompted her.

"I am fine as well, but I suspect you did not call me merely to exchange pleasantries."

Even when he wasn't trying to, Jean Paul had a way of making her feel stupid. Just get it done, Mary Elle, she chided herself, he's a busy man. "I was hoping I could ask a favor of you."

"Of course. How may I be of service?"

She was suddenly feeling inexplicably guilty she wasn't going to let him sell the new painting. Maybe it was unreasonable to ask him to simpy watch over the painting while she was away. Maybe she should offer to pay him.

"Mary Elle?"

"Sorry. There's another one. I mean, I painted another one and I'm going on a trip and I don't want to leave her alone. Will you watch over her while I'm gone?"

"There's another painting?" His voice dropped an octave.

"She's not for sale this time."

"Understood. I would be honored to act as the virgin's guardian in your stead. Will you send her to me? Or would you like me to arrange for transport?"

"No, thank you. I'll bring her myself. It's sort of on the way."

"Oh, where are you travelling to?" He asked.

"Bethlehem," she admitted reluctantly.

"The birthplace of Christ."

"Yes."

"May I inquire as to the subject of the painting you are entrusting to me?"

"The Annunciation."

After a moment's silence, Jean Paul added, "Give me your flight information and I'll meet you at the airport."

"Thank you. I haven't booked my flights yet. I wanted to make sure you would watch over her for me. I'll forward the information once I book my flights."

"Are you shipping the painting?"

"No, I'm keeping," she paused and made a conscious effort to insert the impersonal pronoun in place of her, "*it* with me. If I have to I can purchase another seat on the flight."

Fortunately she wasn't asked to purchase a separate ticket. The flight wasn't full so they let her use the middle seat next to her for the painting. It was securely wrapped and stowed in a wood case so it wouldn't be damaged in transport.

Jean Paul was waiting for her as she passed through customs, where she was required to open the box and show the official the painting. He couldn't have been less interested. She closed the case and passed through the customs exit to where Jean Paul was waiting for her.

He looked as though he would offer to carry the painting for her, then anticipating Mary Elle's discomfort with such an offer, he refrained.

"Are you certain you would not be interested in selling? I've fielded numerous inquiries as to whether any more of your work has come on the market and when your next painting could be expected to. I could get double what the first painting brought," he announced confidently.

"Double?" Mary Elle echoed awed.

"Yes, my clients are all convinced M. Bordeaux got a bargain. Hardly surprisingly given the family's reputation for discovering unknown talent."

"She's not for sale," Mary Elle reiterated firmly.

"As you wish," Jean Paul replied, and then added, "May I display her in the gallery while you're away?"

"I suppose so." Mary Elle thought it would give her a little company while she was away.

Mary Elle arranged for an overnight layover in Paris for her trip back to the Middle East. She spent the night with Jean Paul and Drew and the following morning boarded the next leg of her flight to Tel Aviv.

While Crystal's uncle was waving a smiling goodbye at the security line, Jean Paul was behind his desk at *The Gallerie*, his phone in hand.

"Yes, please inform M. Bordeaux I have another painting by the same artist he recently acquired from the gallery. I thought he might be interested in viewing it."

Luc stared at the message in his hand. She painted it. She didn't call him. He was uncertain which realization surprised him more. His rational side told him he was being unreasonable. They spent a few days and nights in each other's company. It was more than two months since they shared their weekend together in New York. Was she still in Paris? He would bet on it. He couldn't imagine Mary Elle shipping her work. No she would accompany it personally. Of course he was only assuming the painting Jean Paul called about was the finished product of the preliminary sketches he saw in her studio in Pittsburgh. No, his mind rejected his caution. He felt confident the painting Jean Paul invited him to see was the Annunciation.

He could regret Mary Elle had not seen fit to issue the invitation herself, but he did not blame her. He was less than gentle with her youth and innocence when he ended their relationship so abruptly. The depth of his regret was brought home to him when he greeted her benefactress each morning and bid her *Bonne soiree* each night. He lifted his glance now to the *Young Madonna,* and calling himself all kinds of fool, he instructed his assistant to clear his schedule for the next few hours and summoned his car. Half an hour later he strode imperiously into Jean Paul's office at *The Gallerie.* Dispensing with the formalities, he demanded, "Where is it?"

Even though Luc saw the preliminary sketches, he was still stunned by the impact of the finished painting. The scene was similar to the images he remembered, but the flat, two dimensional sketches could not bring to life the virgin's uncertainty, or her vulnerability and indecision over the awesome responsibility about to be thrust upon her young shoulders.

There were not many sketches of the Archangel Gabriel. There was more of him this time, but his face remained hidden from view. He appeared more as a man than the traditional depiction of angels in religious art, but there was a barely contained power in him he was obviously struggling to hold in check so as not to frighten the girl any further than she clearly was.

It was magnificent, and though he did not toss the word around lightly, a masterpiece, created by a staggering talent only just beginning to discover itself. He met Jean Paul's gaze over the width of the desk where the painting rested.

"The painting is on loan only. It is not for sale," Jean Paul informed him regretfully.

"Good. Where is the artist by the way?"

Jean Paul hesitated then admitted, "On her way to Bethlehem. Drew dropped her off at the airport this morning."

Sighing, Luc concluded, "The Nativity."

"Yes, I believe so."

Luc thrust a telling hand through his hair. Neither man offered their opinions as to the wisdom of Mary Elle's impulsive and potentially naive trek into a country constantly on the brink of, if not actively engaged in, hostilities with its Arab neighbors.

CHAPTER TWENTY-TWO

The birthplace of Christ, Mary Elle learned from the tour guide, was the least disputed site of the often conflicting historical evidence attempting to trace the footsteps of his earthly incarnation. Mary Elle knelt and stretched inside the opening in the Grotto of the Nativity beneath the basilica to brush her fingertips across the fourteen pointed star set in the marble floor marking the presumed spot where God's son was born a man. The visions struck instantly, and with such force, she reeled back on her heels and would have fallen if not for a fellow tour member who reached out to steady her.

"Thank you," she whispered and moved aside to allow those behind her the privilege of sharing in the experience. She doubted, though, even after their fingers brushed against the divine, they would find themselves struggling to catch their breaths and to close off the vivid, striking images assaulting her senses.

She retreated back to the surface and collapsed on one of the vacant pews in the church, dropping her head into her hands, fighting against the pain and the tears from the flashbacks. Not her own, but *hers* of that night, the pain, the stark terror of giving birth without her mother, without anyone but her husband present. A husband she could tell was just about at the end of his rope with the Roman demand they return to Bethlehem to be counted in their emperor's census.

"Miss McGann, are you ill?"

Mary Elle thought she might throw up on the tour guide's worn leather Loafers, but she raised her head, pasted a wan, hopefully reassuring smile on her face and responded, "No, I'm fine, thank you, just a little overwhelmed."

He nodded his understanding. "Yes, this place often has an overwhelming effect on visitors."

Mary Elle nodded weakly, and then tried to hold it together while she waited for the others to look their fill. She was relieved when the tour guide reminded them of their tight schedule and asked everyone to meet back at the bus. The group was scheduled to cross into Jordan on its way to visit the ancient World Heritage site of Petra.

Their bus was waiting at the check-point to enter Jordan when Mary Elle heard the insistent buzzing of her phone. She was so happy to see Luc's number flash across the screen, she risked the irritation of her fellow group members and answered her phone in a whisper.

"Luc?"

"Where are you?"

"I'm on the bus. We're not supposed to talk on our phones."

"Yes, I remember. At the moment, I am not particularly concerned about the rules of etiquette on your tour bus." He sounded annoyed and she wondered why he was calling. He didn't wait long to enlighten her. "You finished the painting."

"Yes."

"It's magnificent."

The way he said it, so bluntly and with more than a little irritation in his voice, washed away any doubts she might have harbored he was just being nice in his assessment. "Thank you. Is she all right?"

"Yes. Jean Paul is taking good care of her. Where exactly is this bus you're not supposed to be speaking to me on?"

"At a checkpoint in Jordan. Uh oh, I better hang up now. There are uniformed men with guns boarding the bus. Bye."

"Bye! Bye??" Luc pressed re-dial. She ignored him. He

suspected she turned her phone off. He cursed vividly and reached for the intercom on his desk, stabbing at it viciously.

Later the same afternoon, Mary Elle leaned back against the hard wooden bench, squirming in a futile attempt to find a more comfortable position on its unyielding surface. They spent hours waiting in the check-in center for their entry into Jordan. Though there didn't appear to be anyone else awaiting entry into the country, they didn't seem to be making any progress. She closed her eyes and raised her hands to massage her temples. The visions she experienced at the Church of the Nativity had subsided, but in their wake they left her head pounding.

Sensing movement in front of her she opened her eyes. Her startled glance fell on the tips of a pair of expensive leather men's shoes standing directly in front of her. The shoes peeked out from the end of dark, finely tailored pants. Cringing slightly as her mind leapt to the obvious but incomprehensible conclusion, her glance trailed up along the legs the pants encased to an exquisitely tailored jacket and crisp white shirt knotted by a dark tie, until her hesitant gaze finally clashed with Luc's furious one, staring down into her astonished face.

"What are you doing here?" she whispered stunned. Part of her was aware of the sudden hush in the room, as if everyone was vastly interested in their conversation. More likely, they were just happy to have something to relieve the tedium of waiting to be on their way again. Out of the corner of her eye, she saw Aman speaking with one of the uniformed Jordanians.

Rather than answer her verbally, Luc gave voice to his annoyance by reaching down and pulling her to her feet. With a hand in the small of her back he steered her towards the exit. She was so happy to see the limousine waiting for them outside in the oppressive heat she didn't raise any objection to his high-handed tactics and merely asked hesitantly, "Are we allowed to just leave like this?"

Luc ignored her hopeful query and directed her with no hint of his usual courtesy into the back seat of the waiting car.

"Why didn't you call me?" He demanded as he settled down beside her and Aman slid behind the wheel.

"About what?"

"About the painting, about this trip of yours."

"Why would I?"

At her obvious confusion, Luc threaded one hand through his perfectly styled hair. He managed to explain in an even tone, "If you wanted to travel to Bethlehem, I would have made the necessary arrangements for you."

"Why?"

His response was to reach out and pull her against him. "I have no idea," he replied and kissed her.

Perhaps she should have resisted given the finality of their last parting, but Mary Elle was so happy to see him, so relieved to be away from strangers and held close in Luc's arms, she offered no protest. Instead she moved closer, gripping his shoulders in the tight confines of the car and pouring out her joy at seeing him again in her response to his kiss. Feeling her soften against him, Luc lifted his head and smiled down into her flushed face and dazed expression.

"What am I going to do with you?" He asked and since Mary Elle wasn't completely certain his question required an answer, she remained silent and burrowed closer into his arms and laid her cheek against his chest. He smelled good. The foolish conclusion brought a smile to her lips.

"You are amused at making me chase across the continent for you?"

Mary Elle raised her head at his question, relieved when she saw he was teasing her. "No, not amused," she replied seriously, "but really relieved you're here, and so happy to see you."

"If that is true, why didn't you tell me about this trip you were planning?"

"Why would I?" When his expression darkened again,

Mary Elle quickly added, "How could I? There's nothing between us, Luc, but a brief history. You purchased my painting. We shared a few incredibly, amazing weekends together. I have no right to ask for your help with any of this. What are you doing here? How did you know where to find me? I'm trying to keep a safe, responsible distance and you keep popping in when and where I least expect you. I don't have time to recover and fortify my defenses. It's not fair."

Luc's lips twitched at her disgruntled tone and he reached out to gently thread his fingers through the strands of her hair escaping the confines of the long pony tail she used to keep it off her neck in the heat, and brushed it away from her face. His tenderness brought fresh tears to her eyes. "All's fair..." he reminded her and she jerked away from him.

"No, it's not. That's just a stupid cliché. It doesn't apply in real life."

She was saved from continuing their ridiculous conversation when the limo pulled into a private airstrip. Aman stopped the car near a sleek, private jet emblazoned with the Bordeaux name and logo. Another private jet. A smaller one this time. Were there different sizes for when one was flying across a continent versus an ocean? She was in so far over her head she could no longer tell which way was up and which way was down.

Making no attempt to break the silence between them, Luc led her across the tarmac towards the waiting plane. At his prompting she ascended the stairs before him and entered the spacious interior, mentally shaking her head at the stark contrast to the commercial flight she'd taken from New York. She nodded in the direction of the waiting steward and hesitantly proceeded to claim one of the wide leather seats near the front of the plane. She could feel Luc's questioning glance, searching her face as he took the seat next to her.

Taking in her trembling hands and pale complexion, he demanded quietly, "When did you last eat?"

Mary Elle kept her eyes averted when she admitted, "I

don't remember. I was too nervous to eat breakfast this morning."

"Why? What happened this morning?"

Reluctantly, she turned back to meet his glance. "We went to the Church of the Nativity in Bethlehem. Have you ever been there?" When he shook his head, she added in a whisper, "There's a star in a small cave beneath the floor. If you kneel down, you can reach in and touch the spot where it's believed he was born. It's overwhelming. When I touched it..." She let her voice trail off.

"When you touched it?" Luc prompted.

"I could see her. I could feel all these emotions from the night when he was born. The images were so strong they made me dizzy. I couldn't stay there. I had to get away. My head's still throbbing. I don't think I'm the type of person who's cut out for this sort of thing."

His lips tilted up at the corners. "I think the virgin disagrees or she would not keep coming to you. Perhaps you will feel better after you have eaten something."

She rolled her eyes at his suggestion, "Yes of course, like a cup of tea and a sandwich is going to turn back the clock and make everything normal again."

He grinned at her sarcasm and asked curiously, "Do you wish it was possible to turn back the clock and return to your life before she appeared to you?"

Mary Elle barely hesitated, "No, no, I can't wish that, even if I don't understand where all of this is headed and why she chose me." At the reminder of the first time, she tacked on guiltily, "I never told you this before, but the first night when I was trying to explain to her she must have gotten me mixed up with someone else, how I couldn't paint and she needed to find someone else, she told me, 'You are the chosen one. If you will not help me, there is no one else.' I couldn't walk away then. I can't walk away now, but that doesn't give me the right to drag you into all of this."

"I don't recall being dragged anywhere, or you attempting

to persuade me to involve myself. Quite the opposite in fact."

"You don't think I'm crazy?"

He held her worried glance, refusing to release her. "I've seen your work, Mary Elle. I've witnessed the effect it has on everyone who comes into contact with it. No, I don't think you're crazy. I don't believe the virgin would choose an unbalanced steward for her message."

"I'm not convinced she was the one who did the choosing."

Mary Elle didn't realize she spoke the words out loud until she saw Luc's reaction. Fortunately she was saved further explanation for the moment by the arrival of her lunch. The sight of the fine porcelain tea cup and the offering of finger sandwiches and sweets brought a delighted smile to her lips and an appreciative smile for the steward who delivered them.

Luc didn't pester her with questions while she ate and she was grateful for his forbearance. She took the opportunity to re-fortify her shaky defenses against him. She wasn't certain how he did it, but somehow he always managed to sneak behind the wall she erected in her mind and made her reveal to him more than she intended.

Feeling somewhat normal again after her meal she took in her surroundings and spoke out loud the first thought that popped into her reeling brain. "It must be nice to live like this all the time."

Luc's lips kicked up and his shoulders shook in silent amusement.Regaining control, he urged, "Tell me about the Nativity."

Mary Elle shook her head. "I can't. It's all jumbled up in my head."

"Then tell me more about the Annunciation. You didn't finish the story the last time. Tell me about him."

"You mean Gabriel?" Her voice dropped to a whisper.

"Yes, is he in love with her?"

Mary Elle shook her head. "No, it's not like that. He knows she belongs to our Lord. It's just he never expected to become so attached. She is human, after all. I don't think he likes us very much, women especially. You know, after what happened with Eve."

She cast him a disgruntled look at the amused chuckle escaping his lips. "Don't laugh. He's not such a fan of men either."

"What did we do to displease him?"

"You mean besides mankind's inherent violence, lack of faith and disregard for anyone or anything outside his own narrow self-interest?"

He grinned. "Yes, besides all of that."

Shrugging, Mary Elle explained, "He thinks Adam was weak. He blames him as much as Eve for getting themselves tossed out of Eden and starting mankind's descent into...well, into the way things stand now."

Curious, Luc asked, "But he likes Mary?"

"Yes. It's quite inexplicable to him. Of course he intended to deliver God's message, to carry out His will where the girl was concerned, but somehow he got all twisted up in her and in her story, and he's not particularly pleased about it."

"How do you know these things?"

Mary Elle lifted one shoulder in a slight shrug. "It's hard to explain, but when I'm painting them it's almost like they're in the room with me, telling me no, that's not right, or why is this taking you so long, and sometimes even, that's enough for today. Sometimes other things slip through too, though I don't think they're always intentional. Just impressions really."

"Does she speak to you?"

Mary Elle hesitated, and then admitted softly, "Sometimes, but she speaks to me as if she's still the person in the painting. So with the first painting it was a child's voice and a child's thoughts she shared. With the Annunciation she's a very young, scared woman who's just been told she's going to have God's son."

"Did she believe him?"

"Ah, he's not exactly someone you would disbelieve, if

you get my meaning. He's overwhelming and awesome and intimidating all at the same time, but certainly she doubted if what he predicted turned out to be true, she would live long enough to actually deliver the child he told her she would conceive."

"What did she think when she realized she was pregnant?"

"I have no idea. I only get a sense of the scene depicted in the painting. It's very frustrating."

"Who chooses how the final painting turns out?"

"What do you mean?"

"*The Annunciation* is different from the preliminary sketches I saw. I'm missing part of the story and I can't quite figure out what it is. I understand the angel was sent to deliver the message the virgin would bear God's son, but there's something else I can't quite put my finger on."

"No, he wasn't sent with a message, as if the events that followed were a foregone conclusion. He was sent to make a request."

"A request?" Luc echoed.

"Yes, that's the missing piece. It wasn't a demand. There was no inevitability attached to the moment. She could have said no. It's surprising she didn't when you think about it. Look what she was facing, being accused of being an adulteress, stoned to death, becoming subject to the law of the times. She was so young, still more of a girl than a woman. She was so afraid and trying to convince herself it was all a dream, but in the end she knew it wasn't. She knew it was real and God was waiting for her answer."

"And she said yes," Luc supplied, but Mary Elle shook her head, denying his obvious conclusion.

"Not in the painting ...not yet...she was still considering her options."

"Ah. Of course, that's what draws the viewer in...the moment of indecision. The fact there is no inevitability about her answer. Her doubt is there in her eyes, hovering over her. She knows what she should do, but she's not sure she has the courage to face the consequences."

"Yes, exactly. And don't we all face the same moment of truth? Don't we all hope and pray when our moment comes, we'll have the courage to overcome our fears and say yes. Because if we don't, just like Mary, we can't see the repercussions of our refusal. That's the other missing piece lost in history. If Mary said no, there was no one else. Christ would not have come and man would have fallen even further into evil. As difficult as it is to believe we might be even worse off than we are now. If she said no, if each of us says no when it's our turn, we don't get to see the fall-out from our refusal."

"You don't have to worry," Luc reminded her. "You said yes."

"It doesn't work that way."

"What do you mean?"

Mary Elle ignored the amusement she saw lurking behind his question at her adamant conviction. She pushed passed it because she needed to make him understand. "It's like Crystal said. When I opened the door the first night something was put in motion. I still don't know what it is. I just know the first painting was only the beginning. It was the first test, but there will be others and each one will demand more, each one will mean more."

Suddenly overwhelmed by it all, she evaded his searching glance and asked, "How long before we land?"

"A few hours."

"Is it all right if I take a nap?"

"Of course."

Exhausted, Mary Elle scooted closer to the window, leaned her head against it, and closed her eyes. She heard Luc's frustrated sigh at the distance she felt compelled to insert between them. Then he tugged on her arm and drew her up against his side, with his arm around her shoulder. Sighing, unable to resist the temptation, she let herself lean into his side before cautioning him in a whisper, "I don't think you should become anymore involved with me."

"Why not?"

"Because I don't understand what's happening to me and where it's all going to end. Are you familiar with the story of Jonah and the whale?"

"Yes. God commanded the prophet to warn the residents of the city of Nineveh to repent their evil-doing. Jonah tried to evade God's will by boarding a ship and sailing off in the opposite direction. The ship was threatened by a storm and Jonah was thrown into the sea where he spent three days in the belly of a whale before being spit out again after he prays to God and commits to follow his demand to travel to Nineveh."

"Right. I really don't want to end up in the belly of a whale, Luc, and it doesn't seem fair if you end up there with me just because you were trying to be nice."

"Is that what you think? Our time together has meant nothing to me and I pursue you across oceans and continents just to be nice? You give me too much credit."

Mary Elle was too tired to puzzle out his cryptic remark, and instead snuggled closer and closed her eyes, sighing contentedly as she felt Luc's arm tighten around her and his hand smooth aside the stray tendrils of her hair from her face.

She woke as the plane began its descent into Paris. Stirring in Luc's arms, a little embarrassed at her lengthy nap, she pulled away from him to straighten her hair and stare out the window. A great sadness filled her as she saw the City of Light sprawled beneath her in all of its grandeur. She couldn't account for the origin of her desolation, especially because she was relieved to be one step closer to home.

If she caught a flight back to the states tonight, she could be home by morning and painting by noon. A great urgency pricked at her to capture the images from the pivotal night on canvas before they faded from her memory...not just the images, but the emotions...*her* emotions. She was reluctant to share them with Luc earlier...he was a son of Adam, after all. How could he possibly comprehend the terror consuming her?

Staring back out at the city coming into closer view

beneath her, she commented softly, "She doesn't understand why they turned from her."

"What do you mean?"

Mary Elle looked back over her shoulder and met his curious gaze. "The churches, the beautiful cathedrals they built in her honor...they're mostly empty. And cold. It's so cold here now." Mary Elle instinctively wrapped her arms around her middle to ward off the sudden chill. "Do you think I can catch a flight home tonight?"

"No."

"Oh." She raised her eyes to meet Luc's intent gaze. "I was hoping I would be home by tomorrow morning. I need to work."

"You mean you need to paint?"

"Yes, before I forget."

CHAPTER TWENTY-THREE

Mary Elle stared at her reflection in the mirror as she prepared for bed...Luc's bed. She didn't understand how she kept ending up there. She wasn't in his home out of some misplaced sense of gratitude or obligation to him for rescuing her. No, her reasons were much less complicated than that. She wanted to be there. She wanted to be with him. Tomorrow, or the next day, she would fly back to Pittsburgh and begin work on the Nativity. For now she would allow herself this indulgence. For tonight she would not look any further than the dawn.

The woman staring back at her from inside the mirror was not the same innocent of just months earlier. It was less fear than anticipation at the thought of sharing Luc's bed with him. A sudden movement behind her caught her attention and she looked beyond her shoulder and met Luc's dark eyes in the mirror. The questions from that first night were largely answered for both of them. Now their glances held queries not so easily put to rest. Fortunately for Mary Elle's peace of mind neither seemed inclined to explore them that night.

"Come to bed, Mary Elle."

She nodded and turned to face him. She stepped towards him and then stopped before him where he stood in the doorway waiting for her. He lifted one hand to cup her chin, his thumb brushing across her lips, while his other arm reached out to circle her waist and draw her close against him. "I've missed you," he told her and she dropped her gaze beneath his intent one. Sensing her withdrawal he added, "You do not believe me?"

Mary Elle raised her glance to meet his. "I doubt there's been any shortage of woman willing to take my place in your bed."

"Perhaps," he conceded, and then feeling her stiffen in his arms, added, "but none who appeal to me as you do."

Her head shot up, her gaze searching his, trying to discern the truth of his claim. "I've missed you," he repeated and Mary Elle felt the hard knot around her heart begin to dissolve.

She leaned towards him, and lifted her arms to close around his neck. "I've missed you too. Thank you for coming for me today."

Smiling, he lifted her off her feet and into his arms and turned back towards his bed. "You are welcome," he teased.

The following morning, Mary Elle slipped naked from Luc's bed and slid into his discarded shirt before joining him on the terrace outside his suite. He looked up as she shyly took the chair opposite him at the round table.

"Tea?" he offered.

"Yes, please."

While they waited for her tea to arrive, Mary Elle asked, "What day of the week is it? I've lost track of the days since I left home."

"Sunday."

"I need to attend Mass.""All right. I'll have Aman drive you."

"That's not necessary. I can take a cab," Mary Elle protested instinctively.

"I would prefer Aman to drive you."Mary Elle grimaced at his implacable tone, but she didn't raise any further protest about her mode of transportation.

"After Mass I need to stop by The Gallerie to see her and make sure she's all right."

"As you wish."

Mary Elle was surprised when after attending morning Mass she arrived at the entrance to The Gallerie to find a long line snaking along the busy sidewalk leading up to Jean Paul's door. She imagined Jean Paul's was not the kind of establishment that held clearance sales on its merchandise, so she was having difficulty puzzling out the purpose of those waiting to gain entrance.

Because of the crowd seeking entry into the gallery, she found herself actually grateful for Luc's insistence that Aman drive her. Especially when Luc's driver simply ignored the line at the door with a breathtaking arrogance she found awe-inspiring, merely nodding to the guard stationed at the entrance as they breezed by. They followed the line of onlookers into the main salon where Jean Paul was just exiting his office with another gentleman who looked far more at home in the exclusive salon than the people in line at the door.

"Mary Elle," Jean Paul hailed her, a wide smile splitting his lips. "I didn't realize you were back. How was your trip?"

Mary Elle exchanged the double cheek greeting of the French and replied, "It was fine, Jean Paul. I stopped by to see her. Do you have a special exhibit going on? There's a line half way down the block leading to your front door."

An amused smile curved his lips at her confusion. "Come, I will show you my special exhibit, but first you must allow me to introduce you to M. Bernard Jacques. He is in charge of the new special exhibit opening at the *Louvre* this fall. M. Jacques, may I present Mademoiselle Mary Elle McGann?"

Mary Elle held out her hand. The other man took it in his and raised it to his lips in a gallant gesture that was purely French. "Enchante'."

Despite her recent experience Mary Elle had yet to learn how to respond to the extravagant nature of the typical Frenchman without becoming flustered, so she was unable to contain the blush creeping up her cheeks at M. Jacques frankly admiring glance.

Amused by her reaction Jean Paul reached for her arm to

lead her in the direction of the main salon. "May I present my special exhibit," he announced dramatically, his hand arcing in a sweeping motion.

Mary Elle glanced curiously around the salon, her brows drawing together in confusion, even as a sense of deja vu assaulted her. In the middle of the main salon a single easel was set up with a solitary painting gracing it. Puzzled and uncertain at the implication of the similarities in the display from the night of the auction, she turned back to where Jean Paul stood at her side, watching her reaction.

"You gave your permission for me to display your latest painting," he reminded her.

Mary Elle raised astonished eyes to his, seeking confirmation all of these people were waiting in line to see The Annunciation. "I don't understand," she whispered, shaking her head.

He took her hand, and avoiding the line, led her around the rear of the easel to bring her face to face with her own painting. "As you can see, she is quite all right. Certainly she has not been lonely while you were away."

Nodding distractedly, Mary Elle's focus was instantly captured by the subject of her painting. Unaware of Jean Paul's motion to halt the progress of the line of people waiting for their chance to view it, Mary Elle stepped in front of the canvas and sank down to the floor, leaning back on her heels as she often did when she painted. A contented smile curved her lips as her eyes met those of the young woman adorning the canvas. A hush fell over the crowded salon, but Mary Elle ignored it.

She seemed happy in Jean Paul's salon and glad to be receiving so many visitors. Mary Elle decided she did the right thing entrusting her to him. With a relieved sigh she reached out to brush her hand across her sweet lips.

"The Nativity, right? That's where we're heading next?" she whispered in her mind though no words left her mouth. "That must have been awful for you...and wonderful, of course. I wouldn't really know. I've never been a mother. Are you sure you want me to be the one to walk with you through this next part? You're growing up and passing me by. I'm not certain I can keep up."

"You are the chosen one. There is no one else."

The words echoed in Mary Elle's thoughts as clearly as they had that night, but it was no longer a child's voice framing them, but a young woman's, still younger than Mary Elle was now, but soon their positions would be reversed. The child would become a mother of an infant, then the mother of a growing child, then the mother of a man and then... Mary Elle didn't want to dwell on what happened next. They seemed to be working their way through the Joyful mysteries.

Maybe the sorrowful ones weren't for her. She raised her eyes again to meet those of the young Madonna. There was compassion reflected within their depths, as if she read Mary Elle's thoughts and already knew her hope would prove a futile one. Mary Elle drew a deep, steadying breath at the thought and then nodded slightly. So be it. They would walk this road together, wherever it led them. She was committed now. There would be no more denials, no more trying to convince herself she was imagining things, no more excuses or rationalizations. For her, there was no longer any turning back.

"All right, I'm in. Tell me what you want me to do."

But of course she didn't. She just gazed out at her from the painting, her expression reflecting Mary Elle's own fear and uncertainty at this early, but pivotal stage of things.

Sighing, resigned, Mary Elle struggled to her feet and met Jean Paul's measuring glance. "Thank you for taking such good care of her. She's content here."

He nodded and smiling replied, "You relieve my mind. Come let us return to my office. M. Jacques has a request to put to you."

Startled, Mary Elle met the other man's speculative glance, surprised to discover he followed them into the salon. She lowered her gaze from the curiosity she read in his and nodded in Jean Paul's direction, allowing herself to be led back to the privacy of his office.

Uncomfortable with the silence that fell over the confined space once they each took their respective seats, Mary Elle turned to M. Jacques. "What was it you wanted to ask me?"

Seemingly not quite comfortable with her typically American directness, the older man's lips curved in a slightly amused smile when he explained his request. "The museum is hosting a special exhibit focusing on the art of the Madonna at various stages of her life. We would very much like to include your paintings of the *Young Madonna* along with *The Annunciation* in the exhibit."

Mary Elle almost fell out of her chair. If the man suddenly grew wings and began flying around the room she wouldn't have been more stunned. "You can't be serious. This is a joke, right?" Mary Elle turned her astonished gaze in Jean Paul's direction. He was regarding her with a mixture of amusement at her reaction and pride at the great honor being bestowed on her, as if he was the one responsible for her meteoric rise in the art world, which she supposed was no less than the truth.

"No, Mlle McGann I am not joking. Surely you can see how people respond to your work. Thousands have lined up outside M. Girard's gallery each morning for their opportunity to view *The Annunciation*. His salon is not geared to accommodate such large amounts of traffic, but the museum is."

He left unsaid the implication that having *The Annunciation* displayed in Jean Paul's private gallery was at best an inconvenience and at worst a major disruption of his business. Mary Elle turned aghast eyes in Jean Paul's direction. He immediately waved off her concern. "Please, my dear, there is no reason for your distress. It has been both my honor and pleasure to offer this small service to the virgin. But M. Jacques is correct when he points out she deserves a grander setting than my small gallery can provide."

Mary Elle choked back the swell of emotion blocking her

throat and took refuge in the first obstacle that popped into her reeling thoughts. "I can't give you permission to display the *Young Madonna*. She no longer belongs to me."

"M. Bordeaux already agreed to loan the *Young Madonna* for the length of the exhibit," M. Jacques informed her, brushing aside her first challenge to his preposterous plan without breaking a sweat.

"I see." Though she didn't really. Why didn't Luc say anything to her about all of this? It would have been nice to be prepared. All she wanted was to take her home and begin work on the Nativity. She couldn't if she left her behind in France for the exhibit. She didn't want her to be an ocean away where she couldn't check on her. "I have to think about this," she told them, bringing a look of astonishment to M. Jacques angular face. Mary Elle turned to Jean Paul, her eyes pleading for his understanding. "I need to return home to paint. I don't think I can leave her behind."

He rose from his desk and came to stand in front of her. He reached down to clasp her cold hands between his. "I understand. Perhaps you would consider returning to Paris when the exhibit opens. You could bring her back with you and loan her to the exhibit for a short time, at least for the length of your stay."

Mary Elle released a relieved sigh. "Yes, all right. Maybe I can do that. The exhibit opens in the fall? I don't know...it's at the start of the school year. I'm not sure I can ask for time off from my job so soon after the summer break. I'm a teacher," she tacked on, turning apologetically to M. Jacques who appeared stunned by her reluctance to jump at his undeniably magnanimous offer.

"You are an artist," Jean Paul corrected and Mary Elle swung back to meet his serious expression.

Wasn't that the root of the issue for her? She was surprised this virtual stranger recognized it before she did. Her old life was fading away and was being replaced by this fantastic, impossible new life, she wanted desperately to believe was real, but part of her still resisted letting go of the life she so painstakingly built for herself in Pittsburgh. What if this new life turned out to be a dream after all? How would she ever go back and find her way again?

Gathering her resolve, she turned back to M. Jacques. "I'm incredibly honored by your frankly, stunning offer, but everything is happening so quickly, I need time to consider the consequences of such a step. I'm not certain it's right for me."

M. Jacques nodded, his glance now tinged with a new respect accompanying his astonishment. "I understand, Mademoiselle, but I hope you will also consider what is right for our lady. Would she not be pleased by the evidence she has not been forgotten in this world of men by those who daily line up to pay her tribute?"

"That was a low blow," Mary Elle retorted. And an effective one, she admitted silently.

"Unintentional, I assure you. But surely you can see the impact your work has on all those who've had an opportunity to view it. The *Young Madonna* was seen by only a few before M. Bordeaux acquired it. While we are grateful for his willingness to loan your earlier painting for the length of the exhibit, once the exhibit closes, she will be returned to his private collection. Art is meant to be enjoyed by all, not merely a select few. Art such as yours, Mlle McGann, that touches the hearts of so many, should not be reserved only for those who can afford to pay an enormous sum for it."

Mary Elle sat staring at her hands clasped in her lap while he berated her...gently perhaps, but she recognized a rebuke when she heard one. He stood and approached where she sat. Her eyes were focused on the tips of his polished shoes.

"It was not my intent to distress you, Mlle McGann. Quite the opposite, I assure you. I am a great admirer of your work. Having met you, I find myself an even greater admirer of the artist who created it."

Mary Elle lifted her glance to meet his now gentle one. "Thank you. Is it all right if I let Jean Paul know my decision in a few weeks? If you can't wait, I understand…"

He cut off her rambling with a quick gesture of his manicured hand. "We will wait, Mademoiselle, until you make your decision. We will welcome the virgin for even a single day if a single day is all you are comfortable with."

"Thank you," she repeated, then stood on shaky legs and offered him her hand.

Smiling, he took it and raised it to his lips.

Blushing, flustered, Mary Elle retrieved her hand and fairly raced for the exit.

Aman was waiting for her outside the entrance to the gallery. For once she was relieved to see him standing there holding the rear door of the limo open for her. She ignored the curious stares of those waiting in line to see *The Annunciation*, and offered her sincere gratitude to Luc's driver in a soft voice. He nodded his head in acknowledgement, asked if she was finished with her errands, and at her confirming nod, closed the door and climbed behind the wheel.

Not long minutes later they pulled into the gated entrance of Luc's ancestral home. For a moment she sat staring at the grand façade, the solidness seemed to pronounce, 'I have stood for much longer than the brief, aborted lives of men and I will still be standing here long after you are gone.' Its surety of purpose made Mary Elle question her own.

Now she was being given the opportunity to change the trajectory of her life. She need only cross the threshold of the door being held open for her. It didn't matter if she was ready or not, or even if she knew ultimately where her journey was leading her. She sensed her life suddenly and inexplicably took on a meaning far beyond her worth. She wished she could be more certain she could summon the necessary courage to see it through.

Mary Elle looked passed where Aman stood holding the rear door open to where Luc waited for her at his front door. What would it be like to be able to come home to him like this every day? She immediately dismissed the impossible fantasy before it had a chance to take root in her heart. It was time for her to leave. She needed normal.

Luc admitted to her once he was fascinated by her talent, but such intense obsessions had a way of burning out just as quickly as they arose. She was a novelty to his otherwise, she suspected, very ordered life. More often than not, novelties wore off and were cast aside without a backward glance by those in the throes of them.

Belatedly realizing Aman was still holding the door for her while she was distracted by her daydreams she dropped her gaze from where it was locked with Luc's probing one. Offering his driver a quiet apology for keeping him waiting, she climbed out of the car.

"Were you able to assure yourself all is well with the virgin?" Luc asked innocently as he took her arm and led her into the house.

"Why didn't you tell me?" She demanded, ignoring his polite inquiry.

"Tell you what?"

He seemed genuinely puzzled by her query and Mary Elle enlightened him less than graciously. "M. Jacques and the special Madonna exhibit opening in the fall? He said you already agreed to loan the *Young Madonna* to the museum for the length of the exhibit."

"Yes. I did so over a month ago, when M. Jacques made his request."

"Oh." Now she felt like a fool for her suspicions he was somehow conspiring with M. Jacques to get her to agree to loan *The Annunciation* painting to the exhibit. She recognized the signs. She was on the brink of losing it. "Sorry."

His lips curved upward in an amused grin at her embarrassed apology. "May I presume M. Jacques has somehow managed to catch up with you between morning Mass and your stop at *The Gallerie* and has made a similar request of you in regards to *The Annunciation*?"

"Yes. He was in Jean Paul's office when I arrived. Just my luck I guess," she added self-mockingly.

His brows lifted in surprise. "You are not pleased at the prospect of having your work displayed in the museum? I would think such a request by M. Jacques would put to rest once and for all your unfathomable insecurity in regards to your talent."

Mary Elle shrugged guiltily. "I realize it's an astonishing honor…"

"But?'

"But, the exhibit's in the fall and I'll be back in school and I'm not sure I can let her go for that long and be so far away from her. What if she needs me? How would I know?"

With his hands on her shoulders he turned her to face him and lifted her chin so she was forced to meet his tender scrutiny even as she continued her rambling explanation, "I know how it sounds. I should be on my knees kissing M. Jacques hand stitched leather shoes for such an opportunity, but I'm not ready to let her go."

He bent to brush her lips with his. "She would be on loan only. You are not letting her go," he reminded her.

"I know, but then once she became famous Jean Paul would argue how I don't have the resources to keep her safe back in my humble little home in Pittsburgh, and I know he's right, and I would have to say goodbye to her all over again." His eyes roamed her face bringing a deeper flush to her cheeks, but she continued to pour out her confusion to him undeterred, "M. Jacques claimed art was not meant to be reserved for the select few who could afford to pay enormous sums to possess it. He said art like mine, that touched the hearts of so many, should be available for everyone to see."

Luc grinned. "Apparently M. Jacques was not shy about using every manipulative trigger at his disposal to coerce your agreement."

"No, he wasn't," Mary Elle agreed in a disgruntled tone, leaning into his strength. "And it's working," she tacked on as she rested her cheek against his chest and his arms came up around her.

"You are seriously planning to return to teaching in the fall?" Luc inquired, pulling back to see her face and turning with her in the circle of his arm to lead her through the house to the terrace where they had dinner their first night together.

"Of course. I have to work," she replied, confused he felt the need to confirm her intent on such an obvious point.

"I am in a better position than anyone, I think, to know your previous financial constraints no longer apply," he reminded her gently. "Your new painting, the one you were so uncertain would replicate the success of your first, has hopefully put to rest your doubts about the depths of your talent. A talent I believe you have only just begun to explore. I don't understand why you would put your art career on hold so you might return to teaching. If teaching was all you ever dreamed of doing, I could accept your insistence, but you admitted to me all you ever longed to do was paint. Here is your opportunity to do so. Every obstacle has been removed from your path. You have realized almost inconceivable success at the very incipient stages of your career. Why do you hesitate to accept what has been given you?"

Ashamed at herself, Mary Elle dropped her glance beneath his intent one and admitted in a hushed whisper, "I'm scared."

"I imagine she was also scared."

"That's not fair," she protested weakly, raising her glance to his.

"I know, but clichéd as it sounds, sometimes life isn't fair."

He let the silence extend between them and then added, "Why don't we take a few days away? There is no reason for you to make a decision today, is there?"

Relieved at the chance of the easy escape he was offering her, Mary Elle shook her head and searched his eyes for any sign of regret. When she saw none, she replied, "You don't have to keep doing this, you know."

"Doing what?"

"Rescuing me."

He grinned. "I enjoy rescuing you. It is good for the chivalrous French half of my soul."

CHAPTER TWENTY-FOUR

True to his word they left the same afternoon for Luc's family estate in Bordeaux. Mary Elle was forced to make a concerted effort to keep her jaw from dropping open at the sight of the medieval castle sprawled across a maze of endless green. Trees lined the drive they turned into, their massive size and the width of their trunks leading her to the conclusion they were guarding the entrance to the chateau for generations. Flags, which she guessed bore Luc's family crest, flapped from the parapets in the brisk breeze.

She didn't ask. She wanted to, but she refrained. She thought if she confirmed any more details about the wide discrepancy between their respective social circles she would no longer be able to delude herself about where this relationship was headed. Since she was already dealing with enough emotional upheaval over her uncertainty in regards to her art and her future career as a teacher she wasn't ready to confront another hurdle just yet.

Deciding to take Crystal's advice, Mary Elle promised herself she would simply enjoy these precious moments with Luc without analyzing them to death. She turned to meet Luc's curious glance from where he sat beside her, watching her reaction to his country home. She grinned and threw up her hands in surrender. "You live in a castle? Does that make you lord of the manor?"

He grinned back. "I live in Paris. The castle is actually a

working vineyard, and no I am not a lord. If you recall the nobility was ah, shall we say...largely extinguished at the time of the French Revolution."

She rolled her eyes at his lecturing tone and teased, "A vineyard? How do you reconcile a vineyard with your Muslim faith?"

"As I previously confessed, my Islamic brothers in faith would likely take issue with the French side of my family's association with alcohol. I do my best to reconcile the two sides of my family without overly offending the other."

"Considering recent events and the current political environment in France I imagine those efforts are not always easy," she speculated.

"No, it is not."

And she suspected that was all he was going to offer on the subject. Maybe she should have followed Crystal's example and googled him. It wouldn't hurt to learn more about him. Luc was proving to be a far more complex man than she previously realized. Probably because she was so wrapped up in her own problems and so relieved for his assistance in resolving them, it never occurred to her he might have a few of his own.

The opportunity for further meaningful conversation was lost to them when Aman pulled the car to a stop in front of the imposing stone entrance. She wondered if Luc would mind if she snapped a quick photo to send back to Crystal, but quickly squelched her incipient plan. Just because she was a wide-eyed, gawking American tourist didn't mean she should bury herself in the part. So attaching a firm leash to her over-the-top excitement she meekly allowed Luc to lead her to the entrance, introduce her to his housekeeper and then respond with a dignified, 'Yes, very much,' when he asked if she would like a tour of the estate.

It was all surreal. The house, the exquisite art lining the seemingly endless hallways. They paused in front of what she assumed was a genuine Rembrandt, and she wondered out loud, "Is this where you originally planned to hang her?"

Luc turned to face her when he responded, "No. It was my original intention to make a gift of the *Young Madonna* to my grandmother, but the artist proved somewhat challenging and I worried I would be unable to convince her of my trustworthiness as a steward for her work. So I changed my mind and elected to retain her in my own collection. I must admit I am quite pleased with the way my decision played out. My grandmother, on the other hand, is quite upset to have been deprived of such a magnificent piece."

Mary Elle couldn't tell if he was teasing her or not. "Your grandmother has seen the *Young Madonna*?"

"Of course. She was quite curious after I relayed the story of my acquisition of her, and as I said, quite upset when she could not convince me to part with it."

Mary Elle was unsure how to respond to his banter, so she remained silent while they continued their tour of the estate. It wasn't until he led her across the grounds to the family chapel she couldn't suppress her delighted gasp.

"It looks just like mine," she exclaimed, then added quickly, "or vice versa."

Smiling, Luc held out his arm for her to precede him inside. "Oh my, it's fabulous!" The awed whisper escaped her lips as she took in the stained glass and the wooden pews, oiled and gleaming softly in the dim light. She suspected they adorned the little church for centuries. The altar beckoned and Mary Elle stepped further into the church. Genuflecting, she made the sign of the cross, aware of Luc watching her reaction from the door. She rose and turned back to him, brimming with excitement. "Is there a bell tower?"

Smiling at her excitement, he pointed towards the spiral staircase in the corner near the front of the church beside a small shrine to the virgin.

"May I?" Mary Elle thought it more polite to ask than to simply set off at a run up the aisle before seeking his permission.

He nodded, and without thinking Mary Elle reached for

his hand and began dragging him behind her. When they reached the bottom of the narrow staircase, Luc tugged on her hand and pulled her back into his arms, turning her to face him. Their eyes met, his wearing the slightly amused expression she was growing accustomed to when he regarded her, hers shining with pleasure at his surprise.

The atmosphere around them pressed in on them and Mary Elle was reminded they were in a sacred place. She wondered how many couples were married before this altar, how many babies baptized and how many funerals were presided over in this small house of God. "It's amazing, incredible, thank you so much for bringing me here."

"You are amazing..."he whispered and bent his head towards her, "incredible," he added brushing her lips with his, "thank you for letting me share my home with you." He held her glance while her eyes searched his, then released her from his arms but retained his hold on her hand, raising it to his lips. "Would you like to see the bell tower?"

Mary Elle dropped her glance beneath his and nodded. She swiftly turned and hurried up the narrow stairs, trying to pretend her hurry was not because she felt compelled to put some distance between them.

She needed to clear her head, to remind herself this wasn't forever. To Luc they were just a summer fling. It was okay to live in the moment, but it would be better for her to keep her feet solidly on the ground and her heart locked safely away while she was living in the moment.

As soon as she ascended to the entrance of the circular cupola encasing the huge iron bell hanging in the center of the small space, an eerie sense of *deja vu* crept over her. It was as though she stepped through some magical porthole sweeping her back across the sea to her unusual home in Pittsburgh. The scent of paint and turpentine whispered along the air. She half expected to see her easel resting near the center of the room with a blank canvas propped up on it awaiting her attention. She could paint here, she realized with growing excitement.

She wouldn't have to leave her behind in Paris.

Maybe Luc wouldn't mind if she converted his family chapel into an artist's studio for a little while. Given he was Muslim she doubted a Catholic Mass was offered very frequently before the altar downstairs. They drove through a small village on their way to the estate. She could probably find an apartment to rent, or even a hotel to stay in while she worked. Luc wouldn't be stuck having her as a semi-permanent guest in his home.

Lost in her musings she wasn't aware of Luc's eyes on her face or when he crossed the room to her. He wrapped his arms around her waist and drew her back against him, offering softly in her ear, "I thought you could paint here instead of returning to Pittsburgh."

Astonished at the similarity of their thoughts, she swung around to face him. "Really? Is that why you brought me here?"

"Yes. I should confess I've been conspiring to get you here since I visited your unique home. I recognized it immediately. It was rather disconcerting."

"To say the least," Mary Elle agreed.

"Well, will you stay?"

"I can't just move-in here. What if you get tired of having me around?It could get awkward, don't you think?"

"No, it will not become awkward. I will not grow tired of having you around. Besides, I spend most of my time in the city. You will be able to work undisturbed, and if it pleases you, we will spend our weekends together."

Mary Elle knew she should be careful about falling too easily into what appeared to be the ideal solution to her fear of leaving *The Annunciation* behind in Paris while she returned home to begin work on the Nativity. She suspected part of the reason she longed to say yes was because she would be able to delay her eventual parting with Luc for a little while longer. She could have the best of both worlds... her art, and Luc, at least for a little while. Didn't every woman deserve a forbidden summer to look back on and reminisce over in the autumn of her life?

"For the summer? Until I have to go back for the new school year," she quickly qualified.

He seemed amused by her reluctance to take him up on his admittedly generous offer.

"As you wish. For the summer, for now," he agreed.

CHAPTER
TWENTY-FIVE

Mary Elle sighed with relief when she was finally able to sink to her knees before the blank canvas in Luc's chapel. She wasn't sure why, but it felt right to bow her head and offer a small prayer for the success of her efforts before she dipped her brush into the newly mixed paint and set brush to canvas. It was a long time since she initiated a conversation with the Almighty. "Please God; don't let me screw this up." Not a particularly eloquent prayer, perhaps, but Mary Elle thought it expressed her feelings in the moment perfectly.

If she thought she detected an answering chuckle in her head, she quickly dismissed it as her imagination and settled into her work, aware of the joy bubbling up inside her at the chance to paint again.

Very early the following Saturday morning Luc ascended the stairs to the bell tower. He was glad to be at the end of a hellish week, and was surprised to discover how much he was looking forward to spending the evening with Mary Elle and hearing about the progress of her work on *The Nativity*. He was, however, not particularly surprised when she didn't appear for dinner. His housekeeper already informed him Mlle McGann kept rather odd hours and did not seem to be eating regular meals.

The odd hours Luc could tell were waved off with the French's indulgence of the artistic temperament. The skipping of regular meals on the other hand, warranted a completely different level of concern. His father's countrymen respected art, but for the French, food occupied a much higher place on the scale of life's necessities.

So because he was half French, he enjoyed his meticulously prepared meal and completed some lingering items from the week requiring his attention. By midnight he set off in search of his young lover. The evening air was pleasant. The scent of the ripening grapes from the vineyard danced along the uncertain breeze. His lawns were green and lush. He made a mental note to compliment his gardener. He arrived at the chapel entrance after following the illuminated path lights. Their recent installation was no doubt in response to, and for the benefit of, Mary Elle's erratic hours.

He paused a moment on the threshold, taking in the hushed quiet of the small church, bowing his head in the direction of the altar. A house of Allah was a holy place, regardless of the earthly faith of its intended worshipers. He couldn't detect any sound coming from the bell tower. Hardly surprising given painting by its nature was a silent and solitary endeavor. Still the complete stillness hovering over the space made him uneasy. With new purpose, he strode down the center aisle, bowed again before the altar then turned toward the circular staircase.

He ascended the stairs as silently as possible, hoping not to startle Mary Elle by his sudden appearance. They'd spoken a few times during the week, but their conversations were brief and largely unsatisfactory to Luc's mind. Mary Elle seemed both distracted by her work and uncomfortable with their relationship. He imagined if someone put the query to her she would deny they were even involved in a relationship.

Not wishing to disturb her if she was working, he paused at the top of the winding stairs. His lips curved in a smile at the sight greeting him. Mary Elle was sound asleep on the stone floor in front of the canvas, her head pillowed on her bent arm. The lanterns still burned on the iron hooks along the granite walls and the scent of paint hovered in the air. He couldn't see the front of the canvas from his vantage point.

Silently, he crossed the room to view what he missed in his absence. The prospect of being able to witness the progress of *The Nativity* as the painting unfolded on canvas appealed to him. Mary Elle didn't waste any time while he was away. The virgin's face appeared nearly complete. A slight smile curved her lips as she gazed down at what he presumed would become the face of her infant son. There was no sign yet of Joseph or the mysterious Archangel Gabriel. Luc was relatively certain the latter would be making his majestic appearance at some point. He wished he could be as convinced about Joseph's eventual arrival on the scene.

Ironically, Luc found himself cheering for the man Christians believed acted as the human father of God's son for his earthly incarnation. Luc felt a little sorry for Joseph. To his way of thinking he never received the credit he deserved in Christian liturgy. He hoped Christ's mortal father would at least warrant an appearance in Mary Elle's nativity scene.

Amused by the direction of his thoughts, he bent to lift Mary Elle into his arms. She stirred slightly, and then curled closer against his chest. Moved by her implicit trust in him, he bent to place a gentle kiss upon her brow and whispered softly so as not to disturb her, "Sleeping beauty. We do seem to be working our way through the fairytales."

CHAPTER TWENTY-SIX

Mary Elle's life settled into a blissful routine over the early months of summer. Just as she always dreamed of doing, she painted the long days away surrounded by the magnificent beauty of Luc's family home and spent the weekends in the arms of the man she was hopelessly in love with. Surprisingly she managed to refrain from berating herself too harshly for her susceptibility.

What woman in her right mind could resist such temptation? Given she was never before involved in a serious relationship she had no natural defenses built up against the devastation their inevitable parting would bring. The truth was, all of her attempts at maintaining a careful distance between them turned out to be futile. She never stood a chance.

Luc, for her, would always be the man she compared every other man to. He was her new standard...a gold standard admittedly, but it was too late for her to pack up her fledging heart and flee back to the safety of Pittsburgh. Since there was nothing she could do to prevent her eventual heartbreak she decided she might as well enjoy herself in anticipation of it. She refused to contemplate how swiftly time was passing, but she recognized July would soon be a memory. It wouldn't be long before she would have to begin making concrete plans to return home and to her job.

She set August first as her self-imposed cut-off date to

begin extricating herself from her fantasy life. Welcome or not, she could not remain indefinitely as a guest in Luc's home. Lately, the feeling was growing on her she was not destined to become a full-time artist. Even though she no longer needed the money as badly as she once did, she hoped the disciplined schedule of her teaching career would provide some solace for her loss. At least its demands would fill her days and give her something to do with her life besides mourn both the loss of her art and the loss of her love...the former, likely contributing to the latter.

The recognition her day of reckoning was fast approaching compelled her to set her unspoken August deadline. She could no longer deny the mounting evidence of the loss of her talent. She was forced to confront it every time she ascended the narrow spiral stairs to the bell tower where the partially completed painting awaited her. The painting wasn't going well. Surprising given the initial stages progressed quickly. Her technique was dramatically improved since college. Luc even suggested one evening M. Jacques might like to include the completed Nativity painting in the Madonna exhibit.

She resisted his hints, suspected even then her current offering would not prove worthy of such exalted company. He didn't press her and she kept silent about her doubts. Now she leaned back on her knees, resting her weight on her heels and contemplated the half-finished painting. When her eyes met those of the virgin's, she finally acknowledged the truth silently stalking her for weeks.

The reason the dark, almond shaped eyes on the too-young-to-about-to-become-a-mother's face appeared vacant was because there was nothing behind them but blank canvas. The rest of the painting was equally empty. There was nothing compelling about it. Without *her* presence the offering was ordinary, reminiscent of Mary Elle's efforts when her art professors criticized her lack of creativity.

Her angelic protector wasn't pestering her to paint him

into the scene because *she* wasn't there to protect. She could no longer deny the depressing truth. Whatever it was responsible for the genius of the first two paintings, it deserted her. She was back to being an incompetent hack. Tears filled her eyes and slid silently down her cheeks. She felt empty inside, as if when the virgin deserted her, she hollowed out her insides, leaving nothing behind but resigned acceptance to her fate.

There was no point in railing against fickle destiny. She had her moment. They were wonderful moments, but they were gone, stripped from her as easily and unexpectedly as they were bestowed in the first place. The first sob broke unheralded through the brittle wall of her defenses and was quickly followed by its sisters.

Devastated by her loss Mary Elle wrapped her arms around her middle and bent over double, protesting against the pain, rocking back and forth, mewling between sobs and gasps torn from the depths of her desolation. She remembered this feeling, but what she felt when she packed up her art supplies in college was nothing but a pre-emptive shadow of the devastation she now contended with.

Eventually the tears stopped of their own accord. Her breathing slowed to its normal rhythm. There were no tears left inside of her to spill. She was empty. Lost. Even knowing this day was not far off she didn't expect it to arrive so soon, right smack in the middle of her fairytale summer with Luc. Couldn't *she* have at least waited to desert her until after she was back in Pittsburgh?

How was she going to face Luc? How was she supposed to confront the look she knew would come into his eyes when she confessed she couldn't paint anymore? He would turn from her then. Not right away perhaps. He was too much of a gentleman to be so obvious about it.

He would take his time, be as gentle as possible in letting her know he lost interest. She suspected they would go along just as they were for a few more weeks, but there would be no insistence on his part when July folded into August she extend her stay. No suggestion she call the good sisters at St. Mary's and explain to them she wouldn't be coming back. Instead she was going to live forever with her lover in Paris and paint masterpieces, and be the toast of the City of Light. Dreams, Mary Elle…just foolish, naïve dreams.

Like every young woman in love, she was entitled to them, but she was determined not to allow their goodbyes to become awkward or dissolve into acrimony, or worse, indifference. What they shared, what Luc gave her was too precious to allow for its ending to mar the perfection of its beginning and its in-between.

No they would part as friends, and if possible, Luc would never know the true depths of her devastation. He was a good enough man to feel regret over hurting her, even when he was nothing but honest with her from the start. There were no promises attached to their time together. The first time he asked her out he admitted he was fascinated by her talent. It wasn't his fault she was fascinated by him.

Hands still shaking, she very deliberately unwound them from around her middle and straightened her back, giving herself a bracing lecture as she rose to her feet. 'Stop whining. Don't you remember how grateful you were for the gift you were given? Didn't you claim it didn't matter if it was only for a little while? Wasn't it you who said not everyone gets to hold their dreams in their hands and how blessed you were to do so longer than most? Get over yourself and start packing your bags. Pittsburgh, here we come.'

When merciful silence fell inside her head, Mary Elle stood staring at the half-finished painting, still hoping to detect some glimpse of the brilliance she was able to bring to life before. There was nothing, no sign, no redeeming quality she could deceive herself with. There wasn't the slightest hint of *her* presence in the painting. She wouldn't insult either of them by pretending otherwise and forcing Luc into the position of having to pretend *The Nativity* was equal to her initial offerings. At least she could save them both the awkwardness of that encounter.

With renewed purpose she reached down to retrieve the paintbrush where it rested in turpentine and after swiping it across the drop cloth to dry it, she slathered it with red paint. Not giving regret a chance to stop her, she struck quickly, slicing a thick red slash across the images she created with her brush. Rage and disappointment coalesced inside of her and erupted in a savage outburst she took out on the partially completed painting.

She didn't stop until the young mother staring back at her from the canvas appeared to have been the victim of an act of great violence. The red paint dripped from the canvas onto the drop cloth and surrounding stone like blood seeping out from the wounds Mary Elle inflicted. Equally appalled and satisfied with the completeness of her destruction, Mary Elle let the brush slide from her hand and drop to the floor. Without a second glance, she crossed the small space towards the exit.

CHAPTER TWENTY-SEVEN

Luc stepped through the front door of his family home in Bordeaux and almost stepped back out again, convinced Aman turned up the wrong drive. Since his was the only thousand year old castle in the vicinity, he dismissed the foolish thought and went in search of the source of his confusion. He didn't have long to search.

He stopped at the entrance to the conservatory where Mary Elle sat on the bench before his mother's grand piano, her posture erect. The ease with which her hands moved over the ivory keys revealed her comfort with the instrument. But it wasn't the sight of her that took his breath away, it was the music flowing from her hands and filling the space between them. Though his expertise with art did not extend to music, he was not so untutored he didn't recognize true skill when he heard it.

As if some sixth sense alerted her to his silent presence, Mary Elle glanced over her shoulder and caught him watching her. The beautiful music came to an abrupt, discordant halt. He could not mourn its loss too deeply when it was replaced with the delighted smile curving his lover's lips at his surprise return. He returned her smile and crossed the distance separating them, bending to brush his lips against hers and renew the connection he missed while he was away.

"Let me guess, another staggering talent was suddenly dropped from heaven upon your unsuspecting head."

Despite her moodiness over the loss of the other staggering talent he referred to, Mary Elle grinned in response to his teasing and explained, "No, actually I was a child prodigy. I was supposed to grow up and become a famous concert pianist."

She could tell from his answering smile he thought she was joking. He joined her on the bench, forcing her to scoot over to make room, and asked, "What happened?"

"I didn't."

He grinned and protested, "That is not an answer."

She shrugged aside his complaint, but expanded, "I always loved the visual interpretation of art more. Music could never fill the emptiness inside of me at what I lacked in terms of artistic ability."

"There is nothing you lack, Mary Elle," he told her, his voice taking on a new seriousness.

"You make me feel as though there isn't," she admitted. Then flustered at the way his intent gaze held her own, she quickly changed the subject. "Do you play?"

"My grandmother insisted I learn and both of my grandfathers supported her determination. When presented with a united front among them I learned at a very young age it wasn't worth the effort to argue. I'm told my mother was an accomplished pianist. I suppose they wanted to give me that connection with her."

The repercussions of Luc's admission hit her all at once. One did not go out and purchase a rare and expensive instrument for a young, seemingly indifferent boy to practice on. Which meant the piano she was amusing herself on to relieve her boredom at waiting for Luc's return very likely belonged to his dead mother. "This was your mother's piano, wasn't it?" she confirmed in stunned embarrassment.

"Yes," Luc confirmed. "It was a wedding gift from my father."

Mary Elle didn't think she could feel any worse. What an unforgiveable affront on her part. She tripped over herself trying to apologize for her poor manners, "Oh, Luc. I'm so sorry...I had no idea...I would never have intruded...I should have waited to ask your permission...or not, no of course not... I would never have dared to ask..."

The inarticulate flow of words thankfully stopped when he placed a gentle finger across her lips. "I'm not angry with you, Mary Elle. On the contrary, I enjoyed your playing immensely. I am quite certain my mother would also be delighted to hear the instrument played so lovingly and so competently. Her only son's prowess could never hope to equal yours."

"That's very generous of you," Mary Elle muttered guiltily.

He grinned at her discomfort and asked, "How old were you when you stopped playing?"

When she didn't respond to his curiosity, he prodded further, "I am curious about what your parents thought of your decision to abandon your childhood ambitions and focus on art instead. You don't speak of them. Are they no longer a part of your life?"

Accepting he wouldn't give up until she told him what he wanted to know, Mary Elle replied on a sigh, "Yes and no. We're not estranged or anything, just apart. My parents divorced when I was ten. They both remarried and started new families. I always felt like I was this embarrassing reminder of a mistake they made when they were young. They're busy with their younger children now. I don't see them very often."

"I cannot imagine your parents believe you were a mistake."

"Probably not. Even if they did, they love me too much to admit it out loud. Don't get me wrong. They were good parents. They always supported my decisions. Though there was some, ah... shall we say... loudly, expressed regret and consternation when I informed them I didn't want to play the piano anymore...instead I wanted to grow up and be a famous artist. I didn't blame them. They invested a fortune in successively more expensive pianos, music lessons, tutors. It wasn't like I ever displayed any artistic talent equal to even a fraction of my musical potential."

"How old were you when this conversation with your parents took place?"

Mary Elle thought back and admitted with a smile, "Oh, I couldn't have been more than seven or eight."

"Seven or eight? You are joking."

"No, I remember the day very clearly, because the events from the day before will forever remain imprinted on my memory."

"What happened the day before?"

She hesitated, already regretting bringing up the subject in the first place, and then acknowledging Luc was unlikely to let the matter drop, confessed in a resigned voice, "Well if you had any doubts as to my mental stability before, this should push you over the edge."

Grinning, Luc prompted her, "Tell me."

"I remember vividly every detail of the day. Like I said, I couldn't have been more than seven or eight. Actually I know I was still seven, because we just celebrated my First Holy Communion. I was secretly drawing pictures in my room at night when I was supposed to be sleeping. My schedule was pretty intense for someone my age. The lessons, the practices pretty much consumed all of my free time. I didn't have what you would consider a normal childhood. There weren't many friends my age. I was always too busy. Playdates were arranged around my practice schedule. Art, or my passion for it, kind of crept up on me slowly."

"I knew my parents wouldn't approve if they knew how much it meant to me. By this point they were as committed to my musical future as they believed I was. I didn't know how to tell them I didn't think I wanted to be a musical prodigy anymore. Besides, even at seven I could tell I wasn't as skilled at art as I was at music. So I decided to negotiate my terms with God."

Luc laughed, assuming she was joking, but when he

noticed her serious expression, his laughter quieted and only his eyes revealed his lingering amusement. "What exactly did this negotiation entail?"

"I informed the Almighty if He wasn't going to let me draw pretty pictures, I didn't want to play the piano anymore."

"And what was his response?"

"It was brief and to the point. He said, 'As you wish.' I thought He meant I would become a famous artist instead of a concert pianist. I couldn't wait to tell my parents so they could rush out and buy me new art supplies. Instead what he meant was, 'Fine, do whatever you want. No one's forcing you to play the piano.' Hence my rather pitiful decade-and-a-half long pursuit of artistic fame and fortune."

Smiling, Luc pointed out, "It would appear Allah has held up his side of your agreement."

Stunned by his conclusion, Mary Elle asked, "Do you think He remembers? Do you think that's what this is all about?"

"Only a foolish man speculates on the Almighty's motivation, but I have no doubt he remembers your request."

Sighing with regret, she admitted, "I wish my memory of our conversation reflected me in such a charitable light. It was actually more of a demand than a request."

"Well, either way, it appears he has answered your prayer."

"You're starting to sound like me," she warned him.

He laughed and pleaded, "Play for me."

She hesitated. "I suppose that would be all right."

"Is it not allowed?"

Mary Elle ignored the laughter in his voice and replied in all seriousness, "I don't know if it's allowed or not. I just sort of fell out of the habit of playing except when I was alone. My parents assumed I was just going through a phase; and I would change my mind and return to music. I didn't want to give them false hope, so I stopped playing at home. On those rare occasions when I did play, I'm not certain if I was trying to remind Him of our unfinished negotiation or if I just wanted to give Him something back, you know, to apologize for not really wanting to become a concert pianist when He was so generous as to bestow such a wonderful gift on my ungrateful head."

After a moment of considering silence Luc wondered, "Do you sing, too?"

"Sometimes." The admission escaped in an almost inaudible whisper Luc was forced to bend closer to hear.

"Sing for me, Mary Elle," he urged her.

It took considerable effort on her part to resist the force of his compelling charm, but she managed to shake her head, denying him. "No, I only sing for Him."

Like a physical caress she felt his glance probing her face again, though she refused to lift her gaze to his. After an extended silence between them, he leaned in to kiss her brow and reminded her, "And yet you cling to your claim you are not devout?" When she still refused to meet his gaze, he refrained from pushing her further. "As you wish, but I would still like you to play for me if you believe Allah would not object."

"I'm not sure I can. I only play when I'm alone now. I'm not really comfortable with an audience."

"Then I shall retreat to the entrance and you may pretend you are alone. Yes?"

"I suppose."

Luc rose and dropped a kiss on the top of her head before retreating back to the entrance of the salon. Mary Elle hesitated; fighting against her uncertainty, and then forcing herself to recall her earlier ease with an audience when she was a child, began playing again. Only this time it was different than when Luc surprised her with his appearance in the doorway. No, then she was merely whiling away the tedium of waiting for his return. Now she wanted him to understand, to at least give him a glimpse of the depths of her true talent...her *own* talent.

When long minutes later, her hands finally slowed and the haunting music gave way to a lingering silence she stood from the bench and turned to find Luc standing in the entrance regarding her with a look on his face she was unable to interpret. She was growing accustomed to being on the receiving end of the same expression when strangers saw her and made a quick, silent comparison between her and her art. She always felt as though she came out on the losing end of such comparisons.

It unnerved her now to see the same mental calculation reflected in Luc's probing glance, as if he was wondering whether she was attempting to deceive him the same way Jean Paul concluded when he first viewed the *Young Madonna*. She didn't blame Luc for his ambivalence towards her. How could she? Wasn't she more confused than anyone over what was happening to her?

She sensed Luc cherished his orderly, immaculate life. She was willing to bet getting involved with her was the most impulsive and least disciplined thing he ever did. They were destined to be a brief Paris fling.

She was prepared for just the fling, and returned home ready to resume her previous, uneventful life. But it didn't end there. Luc pursued her to Pittsburgh, and then followed her to the Middle East. All the while she was trying to keep her head and her heart. She kept telling herself not to become too involved, not to let herself begin to depend on him. Yet here she was in his home. She still wasn't quite certain how she ended up here.

Everything inside of her came to life when she was with him. How was she supposed to defend against her own undisciplined reaction to him? She could be grateful he was too distracted by her playing to ask about her progress on *The Nativity*. She cringed at the thought of his reaction when she revealed to him what she did. They said confession was good for the soul. She guessed she was about to find out.

Uncertain how to break the silence between them, she crossed the polished, hardwood floor to where he waited for her in the entrance. Their glances held when she stopped in front of him, but it fell on Luc to break the heavy silence. "I believe I understand the depths of your parents' regret when you gave up your music."

"Yes, me too. Back then it seemed like it was either or. It never occurred to me I could have both. Each of them is so all-consuming...so intense. I think if I tried to develop both it would have destroyed me and I would have ended up without either one, which is very nearly what happened, what would have happened, without her intervention."

"Since you brought it up, is it intrusive of me to inquire how *The Nativity* is progressing? I was frankly surprised to arrive home and discover you were not at the chapel. Did you perhaps finish the painting?"

Swallowing the desperate laughter trying to escape at his ridiculous conclusion Mary Elle shook her head. "I need to show you something."

"*The Nativity*?"

"Sort of."

"Sort of?" he echoed, the familiar amusement returning to his voice.

"It will be easier to explain after you've seen it."

"It?" He immediately pounced on her use of the impersonal pronoun.

She shrugged and stepped back, reaching for his hand. "How was your trip?" She asked, deliberately changing the subject as they passed through his impressive front entrance and into the bright summer sun.

Apparently willing to play along with her reluctance to talk about the painting Luc replied, "My trip went well. I accomplished the reason prompting it."

"That must be satisfying."

"Extremely," he agreed.

At his obvious amusement, Mary Elle regarded him curiously, but seemingly intent on copying her evasive manner he merely lifted his shoulders in a slight shrug and grinned back at her. "How did your parents react when you informed them of the success of your art?"

"I haven't."

One finely shaped brow arched in surprise. "Why not? I thought you said you were not estranged from them."

"No, the current state of our relationship is more a result of benign neglect. The truth is I can't figure out a way to tell them about the success of the *Young Madonna* without it coming out sounding like, 'I told you so.'"

He nodded, appreciating her dilemma. "I imagine it is a difficult impulse to resist considering the opposition to your insistence on pursuing a career in art you encountered from both your parents and your art professors."

"Yes and no. They weren't wrong, Luc. I know you believe otherwise, but it's true. I may be the one having the visions and wielding the paintbrush, but I wasn't solely responsible for the *Young Madonna* and *The Annunciation* paintings."

"And *The Nativity?*" Luc prompted at her obvious omission of her current project.

Mary Elle shrugged again. "I'll let you decide for yourself."

Silence fell between them as they continued across the expansive grounds to the old chapel. With each step closer to their destination Mary Elle felt the hard knot of suppressed anxiety rising in her chest in anticipation of Luc's reaction when he saw what she did to the partially finished painting.

The silence between them remained unbroken as they entered the dim chapel. When they ascended to the top of the narrow stairs to the bell tower, Mary Elle stepped aside for Luc to precede her into the small space. Curious, Luc gazed down into her averted face and then crossed the confined space to stand before the canvas. Mary Elle watched his expression turn from anticipation to astonishment and braced herself against his anticipated anger.

When he turned back to her, it was with one brow raised in query and familiar amusement lurking in his dark gaze. "May I assume you were unhappy with the way the painting was progressing?"

"This isn't funny," Mary Elle protested.

His shoulders began shaking and Mary Elle crossed the

room to stand next to him. For the first time since she defaced the painting she looked at the destruction she wrought and was surprised by the lack of guilt she felt. The truth was she didn't feel anything at all except perhaps a nagging sense of regret over the mess she made. She bent down to pick up the now dried brush and placed it back into the can of turpentine. When she retrieved a cloth and soaked it in turpentine to begin removing the paint blotches from the stone floor, Luc reached down to gently remove the rag from her hand and pull her back up to face him. When she refused to meet his eyes, he nudged her face up to his.

"Are you angry?" she whispered.

"What right do I have to be angry? Your art is yours to do with as you wish."

She sighed and leaned into his chest, burrowing closer when his arms came up around her, then laid her cheek against his chest.

"What prompted you to destroy the painting?"

"I had to. It wasn't right. I didn't want you to be forced to pretend it was like the others."

Her explanation was offered so softly he was forced to bend closer to hear it. "What was wrong with it?"

"She's not here. She never was and neither was he."

"Maybe because you hadn't painted him into the scene yet."

"No, that wasn't it. He didn't care if I painted him in or not because she wasn't here, and if she wasn't here, she didn't need his protection. It was too..." She searched for the right adjective, then finally settled on one, "... banal."

"Banal?" he echoed amused.

"You know what I mean. It's too ordinary. Too expected. It's like I painted her the way I was brought up to see her and that night. I'm missing something. I need to fix it, but I'm stuck. I don't know how."

When Luc remained silent, Mary Elle added in a hesitant whisper, "What if she's gone? What if she never comes back?"

"Is that what you fear?" She nodded against his chest.

After a long silence, Luc finally bent and asked into her ear, "Is this the part where I'm supposed to turn from you in disgust and inform you I am no longer interested in continuing our association? Then perhaps subtly encourage you to return to your teaching career and your home in Pittsburgh?"

Mary Elle shook her head, surprised by his insight. "No, you're too polite to kick me out right away."

"Ah, so I am to let you down gently. Maybe begin by spending more time away from the estate. Perhaps arrange for word to get back to you I have been seen in Paris frequenting the company of another woman."

Mary Elle was shocked at her pain at the thought of Luc with another woman. She wasn't sure why she never considered the possibility before now. She stiffened in his embrace and would have freed herself but he refused to release her. When she struggled against his restraint, he gripped her arms, drawing her up against him, impatience lacing his denial, "Mary Elle, I am not seeing another woman. There is no other woman whose company I enjoy as I do yours. I was only teasing you. It's obvious you believe our relationship, at least on my side, is contingent upon your artistic talent."

When she failed to respond to his blunt accusation, he added, frustrated, "Do you have any comprehension how insulting that is?"

"I'm sorry," she apologized against his chest, feeling miserable and confused.

He released his frustration in a resigned sigh, and forcing her to meet his glance, added, "But it is what you believe?"

"Yes."

"And how am I to convince you otherwise?" When she only shrugged in answer, he asked, "How would you feel if I believed you were only interested in me because of my wealth?"

Appalled, Mary Elle protested, "Is that what you think?"

His lips reluctantly curved at her obvious distress. "No, it is not. Unlike you, I have some experience with the type and you do not fit it. Actually, I'm hoping you allowed me to persuade you to remain in my home this summer for the same reason I asked you to stay."

"What is this reason?"

"I was hoping you chose to remain in France because you were falling in love with me."

"Luc..."

"The same way I was falling in love with you."

"What? What did you say?" Mary Elle protested, disbelieving.

"Mary Elle, you are the only woman who I have ever invited to live in my home."

Frowning, Mary Elle, denied, "But that was just..."

"Because you needed a studio to paint in? Why would it matter to me where you painted? You already made it clear you were not interested in selling any more of your work."

"Can we back up a few steps?" Mary Elle asked, waving her hand in front of her face to clear her confusion.

Smiling at her disoriented gesture, Luc asked, "How far back would you like to go?"

"Just to the part where you said you were falling in love with me."

"Ah, I'm afraid that is a little too far back." At her crestfallen expression, he gripped her shoulders and shook her gently. "I am no longer falling in love with you, Mary Elle, because I have already fallen completely."

Tears stung her eyes at his admission. "Oh, Luc, I'm so crazy in love with you, but you can't love me."

"I can't?"

"You know it's impossible. We're impossible."

Grinning, Luc replied, "Well, I suppose I should regard impossible as a step up from when you believed I was not real."

"It's the same thing," Mary Elle protested miserably.

"Why are we impossible?"

"I can't believe you need to ask me that."

Smiling, he turned her in his arms away from the defaced canvas and led her towards the stairs. "Why don't you explain it to me on the way back to the house?"

Without warning, she stopped moving her feet, forcing Luc to either stop with her or drag her down the stairs. "You really love me?" she confirmed, still unable to take it in.

"Yes, love." He framed her face between his hands. "Have I been so remiss in my displays of affection my feelings for you come as such a surprise?"

Blushing, Mary Elle, protested, "Displays of affection are not necessarily equated with falling in love."

Grinning at her ready blush he conceded, "True, but surely you could not have missed the other signs."

"Other signs?"

"Yes. Did I not pursue you across the Atlantic, across Europe and the Mediterranean to the Middle East? Until I finally grew so tired of chasing after you I was forced to come up with my devious plan to have you move in here with me."

"I didn't move in with you," Mary Elle protested.

"No? My mistake. I do seem to recall though falling asleep with you in my bed and coming home at night to find you waiting for me."

Mary Elle shook her head. "You're just trying to confuse me."

"On the contrary, the last thing I want is for you to be confused about your feelings towards me. Are you?"

"No. I've been fighting against them since that first day, but I've never been confused about them. Loving you is the only thing I've been completely clear on throughout all of this craziness."

Smiling at her confession, his glance held hers as he bent his head and kissed her. Sighing, relieved, anxious, disbelieving, she let herself stop resisting and simply slid into him. He was her fairytale. There would never be another Luc for her. A woman was entitled to have one in her lifetime. She was going to cling to hers for as long as fate allowed.

It took a moment for her fuzzy brain to clear when Luc raised his head to gaze down into her flushed face, but it didn't take long at all for reality to return.

"What are we going to do?" she whispered, hoping if she didn't say the words out loud, she wouldn't have to face the truth.

"Why don't we take a little time to get used to the idea of being in love?" Luc suggested, very reasonably, Mary Elle concluded.

"All right," she readily agreed and sighing, turned back to the painting. "What am I going to do about that?"

"Why don't we take a little time to get used to that as well? Perhaps, you need a break from divine intervention for a while. Why don't we return to the city and spend some time in perfectly normal, mortal endeavors, like going out for an evening or two? I would like to introduce you to my grandparents."

"Why?"

Grinning at her near-panicked expression, Luc teased, "Why do I want to enjoy an evening with you?"

Rolling her eyes at his teasing, Mary Elle protested, "I thought we were going to take some time to get used to the idea of just being in love. Introducing me to your grandparents is not taking time."

"All right, we will wait on the introductions for a while ."

CHAPTER TWENTY-EIGHT

They left for Paris the following morning. True to his word, Luc insisted they dine out the evening of their arrival. Mary Elle always suspected life was a completely different experience for the wealthy and connected, but prior to her time with Luc she didn't have any basis for comparison. After spending months in Luc's company, being driven around in a limousine, flown in private jets directly to their destination and being catered to in every conceivable circumstance, she now possessed plenty of evidence for comparison purposes.

Arriving at the restaurant they were immediately led to their solitary table on the private enclosed terrace in the rear of the restaurant.

"Oh, this is wonderful," she exclaimed at the sight of the walled space, with colorful, blooming annuals in pots and hanging planters crowding the corners of the mosaic tiled floor. Strands of tiny white lights hung along the top of the walls, reinforcing the fairy tale image already in her mind. Overhead the stars were just beginning to appear in the darkening sky and floating along the heavy summer air was the fragrance of flowers and French cuisine from the restaurant kitchen. She couldn't have conjured a more romantic setting if she tried.

"*Merci, Mademoiselle,*" the maître de replied as he held out her chair for her.

Moments later a bottle of wine bearing the Bordeaux label

was produced. The attentive steward must have been aware of Luc's abstention because it was to her he offered a sample for approval and at her nod, filled only the single glass in front of her place setting, before setting the bottle in the bucket prepared for it near the table.

"The wine wasn't necessary. I can't finish the entire bottle by myself," she protested when the sommelier left them alone.

"In France, wine is always a necessity. I certainly don't expect you to abstain in my presence. I take pleasure in your enjoyment of the product of my family's vineyards."

"Have you never even tasted it? Aren't you curious?"

"Well, as to my past misdeeds, perhaps we should leave those between myself and Allah," he demurred with an amused smile.

He never brought up *The Nativity* or what she planned to do about her painting. Because he didn't Mary Elle was able to forget about it, at least over dinner. After they left the restaurant, they strolled hand in hand along the cobblestone walkways in a nearby park. He kissed her in the moonlight with the outline of the Eifel tower imprinted on the horizon. She solved her anxiety over her mobility in her high heels by simply slipping them off and dangling them by the strap.

"Are you enjoying the evening?" Luc asked, as he slid in beside her in the back of the car where they caught up with Aman.

"Yes, so much. How am I supposed to keep my feet on the ground when you insist on sweeping me off of them whenever we're together?"

"You are the one who dazzles me, *Mon amour*. Everything about you is more than I ever believed I would find. It makes me regret my uncharitable thoughts towards my parents over the years."

"What do you mean?" She was curious but hesitant to intrude on painful memories. She read the scanty stories of his childhood on the Internet, but Luc never mentioned his parents. So she refrained from prying into his thoughts about his own, romantic, but decidedly tragic, history.

"You are no doubt familiar with some of the stories," Luc queried with a raised brow.

Blushing, Mary Elle admitted guiltily, "I researched you while you were away."

Chuckling Luc replied, "Yes, of course, the Internet, an unimpeachable source."

"Sorry," she muttered embarrassed.

He caught her chin and lifted her face to his so he could kiss her. "Don't be. I think I would be disappointed if you weren't at least a little curious. I admit you are the least inquisitive woman I've ever dated."

"It's none of my business," Mary Elle protested.

"Perhaps, perhaps not, but getting back to my earlier point, I've often resented my parents running away the way they did and then getting themselves killed in the accident in Switzerland. I never truly understood what drove them to take such a drastic step. I have a better understanding now."

His admission and the implication behind it momentarily robbed her of the ability to speak, but feeling the need to say something, she exclaimed, "Oh, Luc. I'm so sorry about what happened with your parents. It must have been awful for you growing up without them."

He shrugged off her sympathy. "How would I know? I never knew them, but I was loved and well-cared for by father's parents and my mother's father. I consider myself very fortunate my grandparents were willing to put aside their differences where I was concerned."

There was no further opportunity to learn more about Luc's formative years because Aman pulled the car to a stop at the entrance to the museum near where the enormous glass pyramid shimmered beneath the moonlight. Puzzled Mary Elle glanced out the window and then confused, turned back to Luc. "Why are we stopping here? The museum's closed."

"To the public, yes," Luc agreed, smiling at her astonishment before climbing out of the car and turning to assist her to alight beside him.

'Different galaxies completely,' Mary Elle muttered to herself, swiftly slipping back into her shoes before reaching for Luc's hand.

The guard at the door was apparently expecting them. Seeing their approach, he unlocked the main entrance and stepped aside for them to precede him into the hushed entry. Mary Elle looked around her in wonder. It was almost like being alone in a cathedral, the same reverent silence hovered over the air. She turned to Luc and asked in a whisper, unwilling to intrude too harshly upon the almost sacred aura of the near empty museum.

"How do you do this? Are you sure it's all right if we're here? We're not going to get arrested, are we?"

She saw Luc exchange an amused glance over her head with the nearby guard, and then he took her hand and led her through the entry, explaining, "I merely called the Director and requested a private viewing of a few of the exhibits we missed on our earlier visit. And no, I do not believe we are about to be arrested and thrown into, by all accounts, a very unpleasant French prison."

Excitement bubbled up inside her. Getting into the spirit of his surprise, Mary Elle hurried ahead, pulling on his hand, "Can we see the *Venus de Milo* and the *Psyche Revived by the Kiss of Love?*"

"Sculptures?" Luc inquired, surprise at her choice lifting his brow.

"Well, I wouldn't mind seeing Caravaggio's *Death of the Virgin*, but I've always been fascinated by sculpture. Someday I'm going to visit St. Peter's Basilica in Rome to see Michelangelo's *Pieta* in person. I can't imagine starting with a block of marble and chipping away the parts I didn't want. It's like everything's backwards. Did you know Michelangelo thought of his sculpting as freeing the human form trapped inside the stone?"

"Apparently I chose the correct venue with which to seduce an artist," Luc commented, his eyes flashing with amusement at her excitement.

"Is there a correct one?" Mary Elle quipped over her shoulder, smiling at his teasing, "I don't recall there being a venue that didn't work for us."

After they viewed the sculptures she requested, Luc led her to a gallery displaying the equivalent of England's crown jewels. There was a coronation crown of Louis XV and an emerald and diamond necklace and earrings worn by Empress Marie Louise. Mary Elle peered into the case containing the crown and the one containing the one hundred and forty carat Regent Diamond mounted on the crown for the king's coronation ceremony.

"Can you imagine wearing something like that? How much do you think all those jewels weigh? Do you think his neck got tired of holding them up?" Then when Luc didn't respond to any of her questions, she turned to face him and added doubtfully, "It's a bit ostentatious don't you think? I mean, even for a king."

Luc chuckled. "I believe ostentation was the point." Reaching for her hand, he added, "Come, there is another set I wish to show you."

Mary Elle allowed Luc to lead her to a smaller case in the rear of the salon containing a jeweled necklace and earrings made up of sapphires and diamonds. A matching solitaire ring with an enormous sapphire cut in an emerald shape and surrounded by square cut diamonds completed the ensemble. The set appeared medieval in design with its heavy silver setting gleaming softly beneath the subtle lighting in the display case. She didn't see a museum card explaining their significance, and curious she turned to Luc. "Whose were these? Aren't they beautiful? So much more tasteful and elegant than the king's foolish crown."

"Ssh, there are ears everywhere. You do not want to risk us being beheaded for blasphemy," he cautioned with a teasing smile, then added in a conspiratorial whisper, "But I happen to agree with you. Why don't we take a closer look?"

Mary Elle gasped audibly when Luc opened the glass case and reached inside. She quickly grabbed hold of his arm to pull it away from the interior of the compartment, protesting his daring in a panicked whisper, "Are you crazy? I don't think we're supposed to touch anything, even if you do know the Director. I'm sure they'll let *you* go with the proverbial slap on the wrist, but if you recall, I've already had one run-in with the Paris police. I'm certain Detective Dubois would be only too happy to arrest me for being a jewel thief."

Luc grinned at her fears but allowed her to pull his hand from the case. Mary Elle didn't notice it was no longer empty until he knelt before her and held up the sapphire solitaire for her inspection.

Belatedly realizing the significance of his kneeling before her with a priceless ring in his hand, and that he staged the entire evening around this pivotal moment, Mary Elle raised her hands to her cheeks. Shaking her head in instinctive denial, she met Luc's gentle gaze. "You can't...we can't," she protested, tears stinging her eyes even as she reached down in a futile attempt to force Luc to regain his feet.

"Hush, love, it's impolite to interrupt a man when he's preparing to make a marriage proposal."

She stopped trying to get him off his knees. The tears she tried to blink away streamed down her cheeks as he captured her hands in his and held her disbelieving glance with his own intent, but tender one. "Mary Elle McGann, even though I am not real and you consider us impossible, I have fallen desperately in love with you. Will you be my wife and share our impossible love and life with me?"

Shaking her head, Mary Elle responded with the first words penetrating her glazed disbelief, "Have you lost your mind?"

Luc merely grinned at her less than flattering response to his proposal. "If I recall, those are the very first words you ever spoke to me." At her confused look, he added, "In Jean Paul's office, when he informed you of the amount of the winning bid for the *Young Madonna*."

Distracted for a moment by the reminder, Mary Elle shook her head and asked perplexed, "How do you remember these things?"

His grin flashed again and he suggested gently, "Perhaps we could return to the moment at hand."

Fresh tears spilled from her eyes. "You can't, we can't, why are you doing this to me?"

"Do you love me, Mary Elle?"

"Yes," she whispered, dropping her gaze to her feet to avoid meeting his.

"Do you wish to marry me?"

"Yes."

He could barely hear her soft assent. Smiling he tugged on the hand she kept trying to free from his grasp and pulled her down onto his lap. He placed his free hand under her chin to force her to meet his gaze. "I love you, Mary Elle. You love me. What obstacles are there to us marrying?"

"Your family wouldn't approve."

His lips twitched. "Which one of my families are you referring to? And why wouldn't they approve?"

"Both, but especially your family in Egypt. I'm Catholic."

"Yes, I know."

Frustrated by his carefree attitude, Mary Elle protested, "This isn't funny. I told you I researched you while you were away."

"So you said. Enlighten me, if you please. What was it you discovered about me that was so objectionable it prevents you from agreeing to marry me?"

"Stop it. Stop teasing me. You don't know how hard this is for me, but one of us has to be the strong one...the rational one. I'm sorry I pried, but I found out about your parents running away to get married because they knew their parents wouldn't approve, and how you were sent to live here when you were eight years old after spending the first seven years of your life in Egypt while an international custody battle raged over your young head. Now there's all this speculation about whether you'll marry a European woman or one from the Middle East... a Christian or a Muslim. You never talk about them, but I can tell your heart remains with your family in Egypt. Despite the fact you live and work in France, the Middle East is the home of your heart. You wouldn't do anything to damage your relationship with your family there."

"That's very perceptive of you."

"I'm not a complete idiot," Mary Elle muttered under her breath.

"I never believed you were. Perhaps you will explain to me why you believe my family will object to our marriage."

"I just did!" Mary Elle exclaimed then struggled against his restraining arms to free herself from his lap. She couldn't be expected to remain strong forever, especially against the frantic urging of her own heart.

"Mary Elle, my love, look at me." He waited for her to comply, then held her gaze when he explained, "I lost my parents to the division between their families...my families. I will not allow my life and my heart to be torn apart again because we call Allah by a different name."

"Luc, don't you see? I can't be the cause of the division that tears you apart again. I won't be the cause of a breach between you and your family."

"You will not." When she would have protested, he added, "You are the only one who has the power to tear me apart."

"Your uncle has political ambitions." When no response was forthcoming to her announcement, she persisted, "There's speculation he'll run for president."

"So?"

"So?" She echoed flabbergasted. "He won't approve of you marrying outside your faith, let alone marrying an American."

"My uncle will not approve of my marriage to anyone outside of his select circle. Do you expect me to submit to the emotional blackmail I've been subjected to my entire life over the question of who I will wed?"

She'd touched a nerve, a painfully, raw one, apparently. At his fierce outburst, Mary Elle reached up to frame his face with her hands, realizing their relationship was already tearing him apart, but accepted Luc was right. No one had the right to tell him who he should or shouldn't spend his life with. "You're certain this is what you want?"

"I have never been more certain of anything in my life."

"Then ask me again," she urged.

At her request, the beginnings of a smile replaced his anguished frustration of moments earlier. "Mary Elle McGann, love of my life, you have captured my heart and hold my very soul in the palm of your hand. Will you marry me and share my life, raise our children with me and grow old by my side?"

Throwing caution, along with her fears of his families' reactions aside, she flung her arms around his neck and threw back her head, exclaiming, "Yes! Yes! Yes!"

Laughing at her enthusiasm, he hugged her close. The kiss they exchanged was more one of solemn promise than heated passion. When he raised his head, he reached for her left hand and slid the enormous sapphire onto her third finger.

Awed by its weight and the sight of the priceless ring gracing her left hand, Mary Elle raised an anxious glance to his face and saw immense satisfaction reflected there. "You're going to put it back, aren't you? This is just for show?"

He laughed off her anxiety and raised the hand bearing his ring to his lips. "Perhaps," he conceded and then rose to his feet with her in his arms. Mary Elle looped her own around his neck and continued pleading with him.

"But, Luc, what if I get paint on it? You know how careless I am. I want your family to like me. I don't think we'll get off to a very good start if I get paint spatters over your ancient, priceless family heirloom."

He grinned at her ridiculous protest, bent to kiss her again and then carried her towards the exit, ignoring the silent alarms flashing behind them as they passed into the hall.

CHAPTER TWENTY-NINE

Mary Elle woke the following morning with her head resting on Luc's shoulder. She reached up and stroked his chest with a playful hand before cautiously broaching the favor she wanted to ask him, "Can we keep this quiet for a little while?"

"You would like to inform your parents of our engagement before a public announcement is made?"

Mary Elle's mind boggled at the thought of her parents' reaction to the news she was going to marry a French zillionaire. "Eventually, I guess that's unavoidable, but I'd like to tell Crystal in person and I have to let the sisters know I'm not coming back to teach. I don't want to tell them over the phone. They've been really wonderful to me."

"As you wish. Aman will accompany you."

She was expecting his condition. Somehow he seemed to have trouble grasping the fact she managed to get herself from place to place without incident for the first twenty three years of her life. She raised her head off his chest so she could meet his glance. "No, I appreciate it, your concern for me, but I need to take this one trip home on my own." When he would have interrupted, she pressed her fingers against his lips and added, "I'll just book a commercial flight and Crystal can pick me up at the airport. I'll be fine. Maybe if I go back to Pittsburgh, to the place where this all began, I'll figure out what I did wrong to make *her* desert me."

"What do you mean?"

"Maybe I offended her somehow. Maybe that's why she left me. I have to try. I know I'm being greedy, and I promised myself I wouldn't be, but I can't just let it go and walk away without trying to get it back, to make things right between us. In order to do that, I need to be alone."

"As you wish."

She could tell she'd offended him, maybe even hurt him a little by her insistence on going back to Pittsburgh alone. "Don't," she whispered.

"Don't what?"

"Don't be hurt. I need to do this. I need to see this through, wherever it takes me. You know that. You've always known that."

Holding her anxious glance, he gripped her chin so there was no opportunity for her to evade his probing glance. "I admit I do not like the idea of you feeling the need to be so far away from me and your insistence on going alone, but I am willing to make allowances for the artistic temperament you deny you possess. As long as you promise you will not change your mind about becoming my wife while you are away, or allow your concerns about my families' reactions to persuade you it would be in my best interest if you ended our relationship and you remained behind in Pittsburgh. Before I let you go, I want your promise you will trust me to know what is best for me and your acceptance *you* are what is best for me."

Her eyes lit with a bemused smile at his commitment. How was it possible he believed her capable of denying her heart's longing even if she believed it was best for him in the end. "Yes, I promise. You are the one who gives me too much credit. I'm far more selfish than you seem to realize."

He smiled at her claim. When she would have attempted to convince him, she was distracted by the light flashing off her jeweled hand. "We're going to have to do something about this."

"About what?" he asked innocently.

She raised her hand for his inspection. The ring he slid on

her finger the night before dominated her entire hand. "This. It's beautiful. It's amazing and incredible, but it belongs in a museum. I can't wear it. If I tried to pass through security at the airport I'd be arrested for stealing a national treasure."

Luc's lips twitched. "I assure you the ring belongs to me, not France. It is perfectly legal and within my power for me to dispose of it as I see fit."

Mary Elle rolled her eyes at the laughter in his. "This is not a fitting way for you to dispose of it. Which by the way is a somewhat offensive term to use in reference to my engagement ring, but let's not get sidetracked by petty details here. I'll wear it when we exchange our vows. I'll even wear the entire matching set for the wedding if it makes you happy, but I can't walk around like this."

Delighted feminine laughter greeted Luc's retelling of his debate over her engagement ring with Mary Elle. His lips curved at the sight of his grandmother's amusement where she sat opposite him at a sidewalk café. Though he agreed to Mary Elle's request not to make a public announcement in regards to their engagement, he exempted his grandparents from his concession.

"Oh, Luc, I am so happy you have finally found someone. She sounds delightful, and frankly not at all like the kind of woman I assumed you would choose for your wife. Why haven't you brought her home to meet us? And why haven't I seen an engagement announcement in the papers?"

Luc smiled and protested gently, knowing the topic was still a sensitive one even after so much time. "Did you believe I would expect my grandparents to learn of my engagement by reading about it in the papers?"

"You've told your grandfather about your plans?"

Luc knew by her cautious tone he referred to his grandfather in Egypt. "Yes. He did not seem particularly surprised by my stunning announcement I was marrying an American Catholic ten years my junior. Or if he was, he hid it well. He was very supportive, and like you expressed his desire for me to bring Mary Elle to meet him and the rest of the family as soon as arrangements could be made."

"You are reluctant to introduce your fiancé to your family?"

"No, quite the contrary. I am anxious for both of my families to meet her. It is Mary Elle's reaction I'm concerned about. I am forced to approach the subject with her in a round-about manner."

Concerned his grandmother asked, "Why is that? Does she fear we won't welcome her? One could hardly blame her after what happened with your parents, but Luc, I swear we learned from our foolishness with your father, and we certainly paid the highest price for it. Surely you don't think..."

Seeing her distress, Luc reached over and covered her hand with his, squeezing it gently. "I never for a moment doubted you would welcome my future wife with open, loving arms. I have not the slightest misgivings about introducing you to Mary Elle. I am quite certain you will be unable to resist falling madly in love with her, just as I have. No, it is Mary Elle's reaction I am concerned about. She is not completely certain about her decision to marry me. I am forced to reel her in slowly. Otherwise she might slip from my grasp and I'll have to pursue her, not for the first time, across the width of the Atlantic Ocean."

Laughing his grandmother protested his analogy. "Really, Luc, I do not believe your Mary Elle would be flattered at being compared to a catch at the end of a fishing line. I must admit I am quite stunned to learn she is not jumping at the chance to marry you. I imagine it was not the kind of reaction you were expecting when you finally found a woman you wished to wed." "

Touché', Grand'Mere, but over the course of our brief courtship, I learned not to try to anticipate Mary Elle's reactions. She has proven quite unpredictable. I find her impulsiveness one of her greatest charms, even if it can be irritating at times."

CHAPTER THIRTY

Mary Elle heaved a relieved sigh as the wheels of the jet touched down in Pittsburgh. As much as she insisted she wanted to travel on a commercial flight, she was not so stubborn she couldn't admit to herself it was a far more exhausting journey than it would have been in Luc's luxurious private plane. Even though Luc bumped her up to first class without telling her ahead of time, she could only be grateful for his interference. There were no direct flights to Pittsburgh from Paris. Though the layover in New York was a blessedly brief one, she was glad to arrive at her final destination. At the reminder, she dutifully reached for her phone and texted Luc she landed safely.

Looking ahead, her lips curved in anticipation of Crystal's reaction to her stunning news. Her eyes dropped to her left hand. There was no sign of the huge sapphire, but only because she slid the ring around so only the silver band showed. Luc remained firm in his refusal to take the ring back. He said they could shop for an everyday replacement when she returned to Paris. Mary Elle suspected he was using the ring as leverage to make certain she returned to him, though how he could possibly believe she could resist the chance to be with him, she couldn't comprehend.

Guiltily she turned her hand over and stole a peek at the sapphire solitaire and glittering diamonds surrounding it, offering up a little prayer nothing happened to it during her visit. The jet reached the gate and the pilot announced their arrival in Pittsburgh. Mary Elle gathered up her belongings and gratefully headed for the exit. She agreed to meet Crystal in baggage claim, as she was not one of those experienced travelers who could pack several days' worth of outfits in a carryon. Since she already passed through customs in New York, she headed straight to the baggage claim area.

Crystal was waiting for her at the security exit, wearing a wide smile tempered only slightly by her speculative expression. Mary Elle supposed she couldn't blame her. Six months earlier she was a single, high-school language teacher barely making ends meet. Now here she was returning from a summer in Paris, an admittedly famous artist, and engaged to a wealthy Frenchman. Of course Crystal couldn't know of the latter. Mary Elle couldn't wait to see her expression when she told her the news.

"It's so good to see you," she exclaimed as the two exchanged a heartfelt hug.

"You too. You look amazing, all sophisticated and polished," Crystal assured her, pulling away to examine Mary Elle from top to bottom. Crystal brushed aside Mary Elle's laughing protest. "No, I'm serious. I swear it must be something in the Parisian air. Of course, your hottie French lover probably has something to do with the glow in your cheeks."

Blushing, Mary Elle looked around to make sure no one else heard her friend's embarrassing comment. "Could we leave the personal part of this afternoon's catching up to a more private venue?"

Grinning at her flushed face, Crystal linked her arm with Mary Elle's and led the way to the baggage carousel for her flight. "Sure, as soon as you explain this."

Confused, Mary Elle looked at the copy of the newspaper article Crystal was holding up in front of her face. It was written in French and there was a picture that looked remarkably similar to the display case in the museum where Luc retrieved her engagement ring from. Her left hand curved instinctively into a fist to make certain the heavy solitaire did not slip off her finger. Maybe she was going to be arrested as a jewel thief after all. The panicked thought crowded out her shock as she grabbed the paper from Crystal's outstretched hand and hurriedly translated the article.

'The Bordeaux Sapphire recently went missing from its usual display case. Is it possible Luc Bordeaux, one of the world's most eligible bachelors, has finally decided to take a wife?'

The rest of the words blurred before her eyes and Mary Elle raised a stunned glance to Crystal's knowing one.

"Well, know anything about a missing sapphire?" Mary Elle felt the telling blush rise in her cheeks.

Crystal latched onto the evidence presented by her flushed face and panicked expression. "Ha! I knew it," she screeched, reaching for Mary Elle's left hand. She wasn't fooled by Mary Elle's desperate act of deception and immediately turned her hand over, gasping when she caught sight of the ring. "Oh, my God!"

Fortunately, her friend's astonishment escaped in a hushed whisper rather than another loud and attention-grabbing screech. Mary Elle quickly pulled her hand free of Crystal's stunned, slackened grip. "Can we talk about this after we pick up my luggage and get in the car? I can't believe this. Luc promised not to make a public announcement. It never occurred to me someone would notice the ring was missing. Did you see what they called it? The Bordeaux Sapphire. What a mess. Do you think Luc's angry?"

Crystal seemed to have trouble following her string of nearly incoherent confessions, but it didn't take her long to realize Mary Elle was genuinely upset. She grabbed her by the hand and led her towards the carousel where the baggage from her flight was just beginning to appear. Fortunately they didn't have long to wait for Mary Elle's suitcase. Retrieving it, Mary Elle set the wheeled luggage down on the linoleum floor and looked almost frantically about for the nearest exit.

"This way," Crystal announced, grasping her arm and leading her towards the parking lot.

Mary Elle paused to check the identity of the caller responsible for the insistent ringing of her phone. When she saw Luc's name flash across the screen she stopped completely, and collapsed on top of her luggage.

"Luc?"

At her anxious greeting, Luc replied in a resigned voice, "I take it you've seen the article."

"Yes, Crystal greeted me with it in baggage claim. I'm sorry. I told you we should have put the ring back. Have you spoken with your grandparents? Are they very angry?"

"Mary Elle," he interrupted her mid-stream. "I informed my grandparents of our engagement the morning after you agreed to marry me. They are not the least bit angry, and are in fact, very anxious to meet my fiancé. I was actually calling to make certain you were all right and the American press did not pick up the story and put two and two together. I assure you, it will not be long before the identity of my fiancé is leaked to the French press."

"Who would do that?" Mary Elle asked, appalled at the thought.

"We never made a secret of our relationship, my love. You lived in my home in Bordeaux for several weeks. We were seen together in Paris. There's any number of people who would be only too happy to make a quick profit from such a disclosure."

"Oh, God," she whispered, dazed at the thought of the American press picking up the story. Maybe she was too hasty in declining Aman's company, not to mention his protection. "I'd better go. Crystal's here. We're heading to the car now."

"Perhaps you should stay with your friend for a few days," Luc suggested somewhat cautiously.

"I can't. You know why I'm here. I'll be careful, I promise and make sure I lock my doors at night."

"Is that supposed to reassure me?"

"All right, all right. Maybe I was too hasty in declining Aman's company, but this is Pittsburgh, Luc. No one cares about the engagement of a wealthy European bachelor here. I can understand why your engagement would be news in Paris, but I'm certain you're wrong about the American press picking up the story. Why would they? I'll be fine. I need to go. Crystal's waiting. I'll call you tonight."

Luc finally broke the long silence on his end. "Sometimes, my love, your innocence terrifies me." At her muttered protest, he added seriously, "I will be expecting your call later this evening and promise you will be careful."

"I promise. I love you," she tacked on in an embarrassed whisper.

"And I you. Come home soon, my love."

Mary Elle disconnected the call with a hand not quite steady and looked up from her perch on her luggage to meet Crystal's curiosity. "Let's go. I'll fill you in on the way."

As much as Mary Elle enjoyed catching up with her best friend, she was distracted and anxious to get home. She needed to climb the stairs to the bell tower and find the answers she sought. More and more she was convinced they were waiting for her there.

An hour later, she was blessing her intuitive friend, who sensed she needed some time alone. Mary Elle didn't bother with unpacking or going through her mail she arranged to have delivered in anticipation of her return. Instead, she waved goodbye to Crystal at the entrance to her home, and promised to call her in the morning. Nothing appeared to have changed in her absence, and yet to Mary Elle everything was different. In an instant, she realized this place was no longer home to her. Home for her was wherever Luc was.

There was no reason for her to unpack her suitcase. She was here for one thing and one thing only...to find what she lost, or hopefully, simply misplaced for a while. She crossed the room and began climbing the narrow stairs to the bell tower. There was no blank canvas waiting for her this time. The unadorned easel stood empty in the center of the room.

Avoiding confronting it, Mary Elle retreated to the corner of the small space where her sketch pads still sat propped up in the corner.

Retrieving one, she dropped to her knees, and then sat on the floor. Crossing her legs, she wedged herself between the two walls and waited, for what she wasn't certain, but she was sure she would recognize it, or her, when it happened. Nothing. Like the canvas, there was nothing but emptiness. She was alone inside her thoughts. *She* was really gone.

Shaking her head to stop the flow of tears filling her eyes, she opened the pad on her lap and retrieved a charcoal from the box next to her, hoping maybe she would feel her again, the way she did the first night, when she stood at her shoulder, watching her recreate the visions from her dreams on paper. But it wasn't the young virgin's eyes coming to life on the paper beneath her hands. It was Luc's. Dark eyes alight with amusement, his lips curved in a semblance of a smile as he looked out at her from the page. Her own lips curving in response, she traced the curve of his lips with her fingertips, wishing he was there with her.

The unwelcome reminder presented itself for her consideration. Now she was here and alone, she felt safe in taking it out and examining it. She couldn't help but wonder if her relationship with Luc was the reason her talent and the one responsible for it deserted her. Did the virgin somehow regard her falling in love with Luc as a betrayal?

The unanswerable questions chased themselves around and around inside her head. Finally she leaned her head back against the corner where the two walls met and closed her eyes, for the first time hoping *she* would return to her in dreams.

She woke at some point in the dead of night, cramped and disoriented, realizing unhappily no dreams of a supernatural origin disturbed her exhausted slumber. Shifting her position and slowly regaining her feet, she wondered what had brought her back to the surface of consciousness. She thrust a hand through her hair. Easing the cramps from her limbs, she realized just how deep she slept.

An unfamiliar, rustling sound coming from the first floor attracted her attention. Mary Elle felt her pulse spike in reaction. Still a bit dazed from sleep she attempted to rationalize away her suddenly pounding heart and racing pulse. She must have imagined the sound she thought she heard. There was nothing there. It was quiet now. She was half asleep.

When her silent reassurances were interrupted by what sounded like someone bumping into a piece of furniture in the dark, her hands clenched instinctively into defensive fists, all pretense of denial abandoned. There was someone in the house with her. Acknowledging the terrifying truth did nothing to relieve her rising panic. Stark terror paralyzed her ability to think and come up with a plan. The darkness below was absolute. The only source of light in the tower where she was trapped with only a single way in or out was the moonlight shining through the stained glass windows, throwing off dark, threatening shadows dancing around her, mocking her fear.

Maybe it was Crystal. Maybe she used her key to come and check on her. Mary Elle was so anxious to get back to the house; perhaps her friend concluded something was wrong. As much as she would like to believe it was Crystal downstairs, Mary Elle instantly rejected her hopeful explanation. Her friend would have turned on the lights. There would be no reason for her to sneak around in the dark, even if she refrained from calling out thinking not to disturb Mary Elle if she was asleep.

Maybe whoever was downstairs wasn't intent on hurting her. Perhaps some homeless person realized the house was empty for the past few months and was using it for shelter while she was away. The minimally comforting possibility warred with Luc's darker warning about the American press picking up the story of their engagement and stalking her.

Following quickly on the reminder of Luc's worry, was Jean Paul's warning about unscrupulous art thieves breaking into her home back in the states. Realizing standing there debating the identity and motives of whoever was downstairs wasn't doing anything to extricate herself from the unpleasant situation, Mary Elle reached for her phone in her pocket, sighing with relief when she realized she still had service.

'Oh, please, Mary Elle, get a grip. Do you honestly believe someone took out an entire cell tower so they could follow you home for an exclusive interview, or force you to paint another *Young Madonna* for them to steal?' A little relieved by the force of her own arguments, she slid the phone back into her pocket. Who was she going to call anyway? She could just imagine Luc's reaction if she called and told him she thought someone broke in and was downstairs waiting to pounce on her.

Smiling at the thought, her amusement momentarily chasing away her fear, she headed towards the stairs, half convincing herself a wild animal breached one of the windows and was rooting around downstairs. The comforting rationalization was shattered a moment later by the thud of something or someone heavy stumbling over an obstacle in its path and falling to the floor. The vivid curses trailing up the stairs confirmed the someone in question was not a wild animal. The fact they were vivid, adult male curses froze her back into the corner between the two walls.

She desperately searched the tiny, shadowed space for any kind of a weapon she could use to defend herself. Her heart shuddered when she realized the best she could do was a paint brush. There wasn't even a door she could use to barricade herself in the tower until the police arrived.

Realizing she'd yet to call them, she reached for her phone and turned to face the wall, hoping to prevent the echo of her voice from reaching downstairs and giving away her presence in the house and dialed 911. She felt the color leach from her face when she concluded the intruder likely tripped over her luggage she left just steps inside the door. It wouldn't take him long to realize the home's occupant returned and he might not be alone in the house. Maybe he would take it as a sign to run away, or on the other hand, he might take her luggage as confirmation he no longer needed to wait for her to return.

Heart racing, Mary Elle prayed she would hear the sounds of the front door opening, then slamming behind whoever was downstairs on his way out the door. The 911 operator waited with her silently on the other end of the line. Mary Elle clutched the phone to her heart as if it could defend her against a violent intruder. When her prayers about the intruder running away went unanswered, she prayed even more frantically for the blare of police sirens to shatter the deafening silence as they speeded to her rescue. Unfortunately, she decided God must be otherwise occupied at the moment, because the silence seemed to descend heavily around her and was filled now with the chilling intent of a predator stalking its weaker prey.

Mary Elle huddled closer into the corner resisting the self-pitying urge to collapse to her knees and cover her face with her hands. Her only hope now was to evade the intruder's reach. She had a better chance of accomplishing that on her feet. The distinct creek on the third step leading up to the second floor reverberated like a shotgun blast in the dark. He wasn't running away. He was coming up the stairs looking for her.

Her fight or flight instincts kicked in, but she resisted the urge to run for the door, recognizing doing so would only hasten the impending confrontation with whoever broke into her home and was now searching for her in the dark. If there was any luck to be salvaged from this night, the intruder would assume she was sleeping in one of the bedrooms on the second floor. If he went down the hall in search of her, she would risk making a run for it. If he followed the stairs straight up to the tower room, she just didn't know. Hopefully she would find the courage to fight when the moment was upon her, because right now she was so terrified she could barely summon the strength to force oxygen into her lungs.

Police sirens pierced the still night, followed moments later by the sound of tires speeding up her graveled drive. Hearing them, Mary Elle stopped fighting her panic. She collapsed to her knees and whispered a heart-felt prayer. "Thank you, God, thank you, God."

At the same time, heavy booted feet descended the stairs at a run, followed swiftly by the sound of her back door slamming. The next sound she heard was almost as welcome as Luc's voice would have been.

"Police! Is anyone here? Are you hurt?"

Mary Elle's answer came out in a husky whisper, "Yes, I'm up here." Then gathering her courage, she yelled out, "Yes, I'm here. Upstairs."

There was the sound of running feet ascending the stairs this time and then the taut, hyper-vigilant face of a uniformed patrol officer, gun drawn, appeared at the entrance to the bell tower.

"I'm here," she called out from the corner. Moments later, a flashlight pierced the darkness and found her huddled on the floor.

"Miss, are you hurt?"

"No," she breathed, fighting tears. "There was someone in the house, wasn't there?"

The policeman crossed the distance between them, holstering his gun after sweeping the room with his flashlight and calling downstairs to his partner. "She's up here. Did you get him?"

"No, he got away."

Mary Elle's wide eyes met those of the young policeman as he reached down to help her to her feet and finally answered her earlier question. "Yes, Miss, there was someone in the house. I'll need to take your statement."

"Yes, yes of course. Would it be all right if I call my friend, first? No, first I have to call my fiancé, then my friend?"

From the sympathetic look in his eyes, she could tell she

appeared as shaky on the outside as she felt on the inside.

"Go ahead, Miss. I'll wait for you downstairs."

"No!" At her panicked protest, the officer stopped and turned back to face her. "Would you mind just waiting here with me for a minute while I make these calls? Then I'll go down with you."

"Of course."

It was only then she realized the 911 operator was trying to get her attention. "Yes, the police arrived. Thank you," she informed the concerned woman on the other end of the line.

After the operator disconnected the call, it took Mary Elle a few tries to get her fingers to depress the button to Luc's number. Seconds later his familiar voice came across the line, instantly closing the great distance between them. Hearing it, Mary Elle lost the control she so desperately tried to hold onto. Before she could respond to his greeting, she burst into hysterical tears.

"Mary Elle? Mary Elle, what's wrong? For God's sake, stop crying and tell me what's wrong!"

She tried, but she couldn't make the gut-wrenching, terrified sobs stop long enough to answer Luc's frantic demand. With a trembling hand she held the phone out to the officer, who accepted it from her outstretched hand.

"Sir, this is Officer Neilson. There's been a break-in at your fiancé's house. She's unhurt. Perhaps you could meet us here. Yes, sir. We'll wait with her until you arrive."

At the officer's promise, Mary Elle's sobs turned to hysterical laughter.Luc probably didn't mention it would take him a while to get there.

"Miss, your fiancé would like to speak with you."

Gathering herself, Mary Elle accepted the phone from his outstretched hand. "Luc? I'm sorry I didn't listen to you. Do you think someone followed me home?"

"Mary Elle, sweetheart, listen to me. I'm on my way. Call Crystal to stay with you. Or better yet, have the police drive you to her home. Do you understand?"

"Yes, yes, I understand," she whispered.

"Hand the phone back to the officer."

Blindly, she held the phone back out to the police officer. "He wants to talk to you again."

"Yes, Sir. We'll make certain Ms. McGann is not alone."

Crystal must have been watching for the police car from her third story apartment. As soon as they pulled into the driveway she flung open her door and ran down the stairs, reaching for Mary Elle as soon as she emerged from the back of the cruiser.

"Oh, thank God, thank God, you're all right," she whispered into Mary Elle's hair as she wrapped her close against her. "Did you call, Luc?"

"Yes, he's coming."

"Good, good. What happened? Never mind, you can tell me later. I should have stayed with you, especially when you told me Luc was afraid something like this would happen. Was it some low-life member of the press looking for an exclusive?"

"I don't know, I don't know. That's crazy. Who would break-in to take my picture? Who cares about such things in Pittsburgh? I thought it was a homeless person who was using the house while I was away. I think he tripped over my luggage at the door, and then when he realized the house wasn't empty I hoped he would run away, but he didn't. He started coming up the stairs. I didn't have anything to defend myself with. If the police didn't get there when they did…"

Crystal broke through her breathless account, "Don't think about it. They did get there and you were smart enough to call them when you did. Thank God. Let's get you inside." She turned towards the police officers as she shuttled her to the stairs. "Are you finished with my friend for the night? Does she need to make a statement or something?"

"Her fiancé requested we wait for him to arrive before taking Miss McGann's statement. I believe, under the circumstances, there's no harm in doing so."

"Thank you. I'll have Mr. Bordeaux get in touch when he

arrives."

The officer nodded and held out his card, which Crystal took and shoved in her back pocket, while ushering Mary Elle towards the stairs. Mary Elle stopped abruptly, pulling away from Crystal and turning to face the men who saved her from God only knew what. She held out her hand to first one then the other. "Thank you," she told them tearfully. "Thank you for being there and chasing him away."

Taking her hand, the officer who found her in the tower room nodded in acknowledgement of her gratitude, and responded with a slight smile, "We would rather have caught him, but I guess chasing him away was the next best thing."

"I don't understand why anyone would break into my house," Mary Elle exclaimed for what seemed to Crystal to be the thousandth time the following morning. She replied just as gently as she did the first nine hundred and ninety nine times she answered her.

"Honey, the world's not all sunlight and fairytales. There's evil out there. It doesn't need a reason to hurt people."

And when she did Mary Elle just turned to her with a look of inexplicable confusion in her eyes Crystal didn't know how to break through. She thought she was as relieved as her friend when an impatient pounding sounded at her front door. Seeing the fear in her friend's eyes, she reassured her gently, "I'm sure it's your knight in shining armor riding in on his white steed to rescue you."

At her teasing, Mary Elle jumped up off of the sofa and ran towards the door, flinging it open without the least bit of caution and throwing herself into the waiting arms of the man on her doorstep. Crystal retreated to the kitchen to give the couple a few moments of privacy and to catch her own breath. She was nearly as relieved as Mary Elle at Luc's arrival. He would take her friend back to his castle in France and keep all the bad guys at bay.

"Are you all right?" Luc asked, tenderly framing Mary Elle's face between his hands.

Mary Elle nodded, and impatiently brushed away the tears threatening to fall. "Yes, I'm fine. I don't know why I'm such a mess. The police arrived in time. I wasn't forced to confront him. I don't even know what he wanted. Maybe he was just lost or something and looking for a handout or a place to spend the night."

"Don't you dare try to minimize this. When I think what might have happened if the police didn't arrive when they did..."

"I know. I'm sorry for insisting I needed to be alone. I thought you were overreacting. Besides, as it turns out I didn't need to come back at all. She wasn't there. Maybe she really is gone."

"I know the thought distresses you, Mary Elle, but at the moment I can't be sorry," he told her.

"You think this has something to do with my work?"

"I don't know," he admitted thrusting a hand through his hair. "Your work, our engagement, random chance? I'm not thinking particularly clearly at the moment. Maybe we should both sit down and have a cup of tea."

She laughed, grateful for his teasing. Yes. Let's."

They called out for a pizza delivery while they waited for the police to arrive to take her statement, since no one was in the proper frame of mind for food preparation. The same officer and his partner from the previous evening arrived along with the pizza.

"Join us, please," Crystal insisted, smiling at the officers. "My friends are too polite to eat in front of you, so if you won't join us, the traumatized victim might starve to death while you question her."

"Anything we can do to help," the senior officer replied with an easy smile and an admiring glance in Crystal's direction.

Mary Elle exchanged a knowing glance with Luc, who

smiled back at her and lifted a piece of pizza from the box and handed it to her on one of the plates Crystal provided.

Accepting it from his outstretched hand, she asked curiously, "Have you ever eaten pizza from a box?"

His eyes flashing with amusement at her question, he conceded, "Way back in the dark ages of my misspent youth I might have indulged in a slice or two."

Laughter greeted his admission. The purpose of the gathering was put aside for a few minutes while the pizza was consumed. Mary Elle couldn't manage more than a few bites, which tasted like cardboard in her mouth, but she knew if she didn't at least pretend to eat, Luc and Crystal would worry.

When the pizza boxes were empty and the plates cleared away, Mary Elle felt her tension rising and instinctively scooted closer to where Luc sat next to her on the sofa. He gripped her hand and gave it a reassuring squeeze.

Mary Elle took the two officers through the events of the previous evening, waking up disoriented and hearing the sounds of someone in the house below her.

"You did the right thing Ms. McGann, by calling us. Do you have any idea who might have been in the house with you last night?"

She shivered slightly at the question. "No. I thought maybe it was a homeless person who noticed the house was empty for a while. I hoped when he realized someone was there he would run away. Instead, he started up the stairs looking for me, I suppose."

Luc's grip on her hand became almost painful until she covered their clasped hands with her free one, encouraging him to ease his grip.

Aware of the subtle exchange the officer turned toward Luc. "Mr. Bordeaux, when we spoke last evening, you didn't seem particularly surprised by the break-in."

"No, I was not. I imagine my fiancé has neglected to inform you she is a famous artist who is engaged to a wealthy and influential man. There was a break-in at the gallery brokering her initial offering on the very night the auction took place. The thief was never apprehended."

Mary Elle was aware of the almost accusatory look cast in her direction by the stunned policeman. "You're right. Your fiancé neglected to share those details with us."

"I didn't think they were relevant," Mary Elle confessed in an apologetic voice.

"Not relevant?" Luc echoed, abruptly standing from his place next to her, almost as if he felt the need to put some distance between them. He turned to regard her with an incredulous expression. "And how are these gentleman supposed to do their jobs when you keep such important details from them?"

"I'm sorry. I know you're angry with me for insisting on coming back alone. In retrospect, Aman's presence would have proven useful, to say the least."

When Luc failed to respond to her half-hearted attempt at humor, one of the officers inserted, "Who is Aman?"

Luc turned and explained, "He is in my employ. Had my fiancé seen fit to take my advice about this trip of hers, your presence here today would not have been necessary."

No one said anything. It was obvious Luc was struggling to hold onto his temper. Mary Elle never saw him angry before. She raised her glance and braved his, aware of the sympathetic and somewhat amused glances being cast her way by the others. She stood from her place on the sofa and approached Luc, framing his face between her hands. "You're right. I'm sorry, but it never occurred to me something like this could happen."

"I distinctly remember pointing out to you just such an occurrence is exactly what could happen if you insisted on returning to your home alone."

The two patrolmen were struggling to control their grins. Mary Elle did her best to ignore them. "I know. Are you trying to make me feel even more foolish than I already do?"

He reached up to clasp her wrists, where her hands still

framed his face. "No. I am merely trying to instill in you an understanding the real world is not the one you seem to believe is out there waiting for you. Not everyone walks with the angels, my love. There are plenty of evil men in this world who prefer the company of demons."

"Amen!" Crystal proclaimed into the silence following Luc's rather depressing assessment.

CHAPTER THIRTY-ONE

They left for Paris the following morning. Mary Elle declined Luc's offer to return to the house and collect her things. There was nothing left for her there. Crystal promised to pack up her art supplies and her few personal possessions she left behind. The furniture belonged to her landlord. It was rather depressing to admit, she'd yet to purchase a single piece of furniture for herself. She certainly didn't expect to purchase any for Luc's homes. She couldn't imagine having the nerve to disturb their perfection. What did it say about her she might go through her entire life and never make a true home for herself?

Aman was not alone when he picked them up in Crystal's driveway earlier. There was another man with him, who rode in the front next to him. She suspected his addition was solely to keep the evil men, Luc seemed to believe were everywhere, at a safe distance. The jet was fueled and ready for take-off as soon as they ascended the steps and took their seats in the luxurious cabin. It was as if Luc couldn't see the last of Pittsburgh soon enough.

Mary Elle stared out the window, wishing she'd taken the time to give her notice and offer her goodbyes to the sisters at St. Mary's in person. She would miss them…and her students. Her lips curved in a reminiscent smile of Patrick's assumption Luc was a drug dealer.

"Did you inform your parents of our engagement?"

Luc's question distracted her from her silent musings. She cringed in anticipation of his reaction to her confession she'd yet to do so. He didn't seem to realize it wasn't the kind of announcement you could just drop on a parent's unprepared head out of the blue. "No. If you remember I was only home for little more than a day," she defended herself.

He nodded. "You might wish to call them when we land. The notice of our engagement will appear in the evening papers. I realize Americans are not particularly interested in the engagement of a wealthy European, but I imagine you would not want your parents to learn of their daughter's engagement from a stranger, or worse, on the Internet."

Mary Elle cringed at his tone. She didn't realize how furious he still was with her over nearly allowing herself to become a victim of a crime. She recognized his anger was driven by his concern for her safety, but the prospect of sitting next to him on a cross-Atlantic flight while he was in his current mood was more than a little intimidating.

Summoning her courage, she reached across the distance separating them and covered his hand with one of hers. Eyeing their joined hands, Luc released an audible sigh and then turned his hand over to clasp her fingers and raise them to his lips.

Holding his glance she apologized again, "I'm sorry. I should have listened to you. I still can't believe someone would follow me home, or some random stranger would have attacked me."

The grip on her fingers tightened. "That is exactly my point. You are so naïve, love, you actually believe good always triumphs over evil, despite the overwhelming evidence to the contrary."

CHAPTER THIRTY-TWO

The news of their engagement exploded across Europe and ricocheted back across from the Middle East, just as Luc predicted it would. All of a sudden Mary Elle couldn't leave the house without being a target for paparazzi tracking her every move. Not that anyone managed to get close enough to actually shove a camera in her face, but there were enough long range camera lenses out there she and Luc avoided taking their breakfast on the terrace outside Luc's suite of rooms, as was their custom in nice weather.

Their precautions didn't keep her image out of the press. Clearly she didn't understand how slow news was in August. Nor did she realize how closely Luc was followed in it. Thank God she called her parents before the news went public. Luc's habit of always turning out to be right was beginning to irritate her a little.

After the first week under siege, she stopped reading her own press. No one seemed particularly delighted with Luc's choice of brides either in France or the Middle East. American. Catholic. An ordinary school teacher until short months ago, when Luc made her famous by purchasing the *Young Madonna* at auction for the incredulous and unprecedented sum of one million euros.

There was speculation the painting was as ordinary as the artist, and M. Bordeaux ironically fell victim to a woman's wiles after avoiding those cast by far more beautiful and fascinating feminine predators over the years. Several of the articles Mary Elle read predicted their marriage wouldn't last a single year, and those were the charitable ones. The others speculated M. Bordeaux would come to his senses and extricate himself from his impulsive engagement before their vows were exchanged. Her self esteem, never particularly strong, was decimated after a few days.

When Luc returned home from work one afternoon, he found her fighting tears. He gently removed her laptop from her reach and deliberately closed it without glancing at the page she was perusing.

"Don't subject yourself to such rubbish, my love. It is nothing. It means less than nothing."

"I know. You're right. I need to work. I need to paint."

Desperation drove her back to her knees beneath an empty canvas. Behind her were sketchpads filled with her remembered impressions of the Nativity, of Joseph, even of St. Ann and her determination to send her daughter to safety with her cousin Elizabeth, but none of them inspired her to dip her brush into paint and put paint to canvas. She was actually downstairs waiting for Luc when he arrived home from work. One look at her face was enough to reveal to him the day had not gone well for her. He opened his arms and she stepped into them.

"Patience, love. Perhaps she is being considerate and giving you time to plan our wedding."

She drew back unsettled at what she chose to interpret as his teasing. Luc was dropping pointed hints more and more often lately about her reluctance to set a date for their wedding. "We haven't really talked about a wedding date."

"No, we haven't, and not due to a lack of trying on my part. I must confess my grandmother is calling me almost daily, hounding me about a date."

CHAPTER THIRTY-THREE

Mary Elle couldn't still the butterflies fluttering around in her stomach. Luc, apparently wearying of her delaying tactics, announced he invited his grandparents for dinner on the evening of the opening of the Madonna exhibit at the museum. Seated at Luc's right at the table in the mansion's formal dining room, Mary Elle only pretended to eat each course as it was laid in front of her by one of his uniformed household staff. Mostly she just pushed the food around her plate.

She was doing her best not to be a disappointment to Luc's family, but try as she might she couldn't relax in their company. The elegant couple, who were regarding her both kindly and expectantly from across the table, filled the role in Luc's life of both parents and grandparents. Mary Elle kept her responses to their gentle curiosity to a minimum. She figured there was less chance of putting her foot in her mouth that way.

"So, have you and Luc decided on a date?" Luc's grandmother asked, her blue eyes intent on Mary Elle's response.

"A date?" Mary Elle, lost in her thoughts, echoed, confused.

At the puzzled look Luc's grandmother shot her grandson and his answering grin, Mary Elle belatedly realized the older woman wanted to know if they set a date for the wedding. Flushing, feeling the telling blush creeping up her cheeks, Mary Elle inserted into the expectant silence, "No, no. We haven't had a chance."

Luc's grandmother smiled kindly in her direction. "I'm not surprised. You've been so busy with the exhibit opening, moving to Paris, and of course, your work."

"Yes," Mary Elle confirmed, relieved by the evidence of her understanding. The way Luc kept prodding her to set a date, using his grandmother as an excuse, she half expected the older woman to demand she set one on the spot.

"Luc tells us you were a teacher in the states," Luc's grandfather made a valiant attempt to join the rather stilted conversation.

"Yes."

Smiling a little at her abbreviated responses, he prompted, "You must miss it."

Mary Elle raised her eyes to meet his probing glance, surprised by his perception. Of course, she was missing her former life. It helped to explain why she felt so out of step lately, "Yes, I do. I didn't realize how much."

"It must be difficult leaving everything behind," his wife added. "So much has happened in the past six months: your phenomenal success with your art, meeting Luc, getting engaged, moving to Paris. It must seem almost like a dream."

Sighing, relieved there was an obvious, rational explanation for the way she was feeling lately, Mary Elle replied with her first natural smile of the evening, "Yes, that's it exactly. Or more like a fantasy. It's almost like finding myself suddenly plopped down in the middle of the life I dreamt of as a little girl. I always wanted to paint, and what little girl doesn't dream of growing up and marrying Prince Charming and living happily ever after in his castle?" They laughed. Mary Elle felt herself beginning to relax and added, "But I never realized... it was stupid of me, wasn't it? I never realized there was loss too, even when you find your dreams. You have to give something up to claim them. Nothing comes without price."

"That's very discerning of you," Luc's grandfather inserted. "Do you wish you could go back?"

"Oh no, no. I never meant to imply that. I don't even remember who I was back then. I've already moved passed that part of my life. I have my art, and finding Luc, falling in love, was this incredible bonus I never even thought to dream of. I just didn't realize in any choice, even a wonderful dream-come- true kind of choice, there's grief too."

"I've had to let go of the life I built for myself after college. I miss my friends and my students. I miss the discipline of my old life, of getting up each morning and having some place to go. There was never a thought of, 'What am I going to do today?' My life was so regimented. I taught, grocery shopped, paid bills, did laundry, graded students' papers. I'm not used to having so much unstructured time on my hands."

She fell silent, and after a moment mused, "I guess it's why it takes nine months to have a baby...to give the mother a chance to get used to the new life coming, and to let go of the life she led before."

Unaware of the heavy silence in the room at her statement, she looked up to see Luc fighting laughter, and wondering what she missed, she turned to see the uncomfortable, speculative expressions on the faces of his grandparents. Confused, she went back over in her mind the contents of their conversation. "Oh, no, no, not me!" She rushed to reassure them. "I'm not pregnant. I was thinking of the nativity... what it must have been like for her."

The tension in the room was broken by relieved laughter.

"Of course we're looking forward to a great-grandchild at some point," Luc's grandmother was quick to assure her.

Mary Elle grinned. "Well, wouldn't an unplanned pregnancy add another juicy nugget for the gossip mill?'

Smiling in empathy, Luc's grandmother added, "Is the nativity the next painting you're working on?"

Mary Elle grimaced. "Not actively. I've made a few attempts, but they weren't right. I'm stuck and I can't figure out why. Actually my difficulties with the painting are a fair representation of my life at the moment...stuck between my old life and my new one. I'm still finding my way. It must have been the same for her too, don't you think? There must have a come a day when she realized she was pregnant. I've never been pregnant before but I have to assume eventually a woman, even an innocent one, knows definitively she's pregnant."

"Yes," Luc's grandmother confirmed with a smile.

"Can you imagine what the moment must have been like for her? The suspicion growing on her over weeks, months. She would have experienced the various stages of disbelief, from denial to eventually an acceptance of what was happening to her. Then her very understandable fear must have grown in concert with the realization until it escalated to stark terror at the thought of what she'd done... at what she agreed to. She likely obsessed over what she was going to do. She kept waiting for him to come back...to tell her what she was supposed to do, but he never did. Eventually she was forced to gather her courage enough to confide in someone. It's hardly surprising she chose her mother."

"Ann was terrified for her. Mary didn't just suddenly decide to run off for a visit with Elizabeth the way her story has been passed down to us. It was Ann who sent her. Ann, who was so desperate to protect her daughter from the law. She never doubted Mary's account of the visit from the holy one and his message to her she would bear God's son. Didn't she always suspect her daughter was special? Surely she must be precious to the Almighty? Now this. She never expected anything like this. How was she going to tell Joachim, Mary's father? Was he even still alive? Or was Ann alone too, carrying the burden of trying to protect her beautiful, innocent daughter without her husband to lean on?"

"There's so much we missed. So much was lost. The way the scriptures tell it, Mary received a visit from the Archangel Gabriel one night and the next day there she was giving birth to God's son in a stable in Bethlehem...like it was easy for her... as though she was on board the whole time...as if she knew everything would be all right in the end. But that's not the way it was for her. She was afraid for nine months. She faced her parents, her betrothed and watched the doubt and disbelief and incredulity enter their expressions and fear they must think less of her. She hated the thought of disappointing them. She felt like God abandoned her. First he sends his holy one to her. Then he gets her with child and disappears."

"Those nine months were her test... wondering if Joseph would subject her to the law, living with the terror in her mother's face, both of them knowing Ann would be unable to protect her, knowing Joseph doubted, he flat out didn't believe her, and meant to cast her off."

"She was alone. She was so alone. People don't realize... they forget she was an ordinary young woman. She wasn't divine, she was chosen – even created for the purpose given her, but she was a human child, a daughter of Eve. She was innocent of men, of evil, and yet she was forced to face it down, confront her fears and do her best to hold onto her faith in the Lord for nine months. Can you imagine what it was like for her? How terrified and desperate and alone she must have felt?"

Empty of words, Mary Elle fell silent and reached up to wipe the unshed tears from her eyes, uncomfortably aware of the silence around the table. She lifted an apologetic glance to Luc, who was regarding her tenderly. "Sorry," she whispered, realizing Luc's grandparents must be wondering what in the world was going on, and who was this woman their grandson was engaged to. She clasped her hands together in her lap and offered miserably into the heavy silence. "Maybe we should leave now."

Luc reached for her hand. "It appears she hasn't abandoned you after all."

She nodded, and then Luc's grandmother asked, puzzled, astonished, "How do you know all of that? It's like you were there. You took us back and gave us a glimpse into those months in the virgin's life. How?"

Mary Elle exchanged a questioning look with Luc. Seeing he was willing to leave to her the contents of the explanations for his grandparents, sighing she confessed, "I guess Luc didn't tell you everything about me."

"Apparently not," his grandmother agreed dryly.

Mary Elle lifted one shoulder in a slight shrug and explained, "I dreamt of her the first time about the scene depicted in the *Young Madonna*. I could feel her anxiety over leaving everything she knew behind. She didn't want to shame her parents, but she didn't really want to go and live in the temple."

"And *The Annunciation*?" Luc's grandfather asked.

"Yes, it was the same, but more. Mary was growing up. She was no longer simply possessed of a child's understanding. She was aware of the repercussions to her if the angel's proclamation turned out to be true. She was honored of course, and like any teenage girl she suffered through riotous swings of emotion... one minute so proud and perhaps even full of herself she was chosen by God to bear his son. In the next, worrying about what everyone would say when they found out she was pregnant and what would happen to her. And she was afraid. Each time she's afraid, even terrified. Yet each time she accepts His will for her. That's the miraculous part, maybe as miraculous as God sending his only son to be born to a daughter of Eve in order to wash clean the face of the earth."

"And the nativity is next?"

"Yes," Mary Elle confirmed. "Though in sequence the next Joyful mystery of the rosary would be The Visitation, but I don't believe that was Mary's idea. It was Ann who sent Mary to her cousin, Elizabeth, to buy her time to think of a plan to save her daughter from the consequences of the law. For Mary, even if her time with Elizabeth was a welcome sanctuary, she was restless and afraid. You know how it is when you're facing something unpleasant, a part of you just wants to get it over with? I think that's what it was like for her. She recognized the time away from Nazareth was just delaying the inevitable. She went because her mother was terrified for her. She was scared too, but she understood, more than Ann by then, her mother couldn't shield her from God's will any more than she could protect her from the judgment of the so-called righteous ones. She agreed to His request. Her life was in the Lord's hands. There was some peace for her in the realization. It was done. She was carrying His son. There was no turning back. She couldn't change her mind. She didn't fail Him."

Desperate now to escape their speculative, shocked glances, Mary Elle added anxiously in Luc's direction, "Shouldn't we leave now?"

"Yes," he replied and stood to take her hand and assist her to her feet.

The museum gleamed luminously in the autumn night. There was a chill to the air, a harbinger of winter's approach. Mary Elle felt the changing seasons in her heart as much as she did the changing weather and bitterly regretted the relentless march of time. Somehow she knew her allotted time in communion with the divine was slipping away from her grasp while she was distracted with more mundane human concerns.

There was a sense of urgency building inside her, just as Mary must have watched her expanding middle with a mixture of awe and terror as the time approached for her to give birth to God's son. Advent was just weeks away, marking the beginning of the church's celebration of the Christmas season. Mary Elle understood if she couldn't translate the nativity to canvas by Christmas morning, the opportunity would pass her by. Her subject would no longer be a virgin terrified of giving birth; she would be a mother whose fears would shift from anxiety over her own fate to fear for her child's. She needed to go back to Bethlehem. She was too quick to give into her fears when the visions came over her the moment she touched the star beneath the altar under the church floor.

She turned to where Luc sat beside her in the back of the limo, watching her. Luc's grandparents took their own car to give them time alone. Mary Elle was glad of the opportunity to gather her composure. "I need to go back. I'm running out of time."

"Go back where?" Luc asked, puzzled at her abrupt announcement after the extended silence between them.

"To the Church of the Nativity. I need to go back."

"Then I'll take you. Perhaps while we're there, we can spend some time in Egypt with my grandfather."

Mary Elle hesitated, and then surrendered to the inevitable with an audible sigh. "Yes, all right. I'm looking forward to meeting him," she tacked on, so Luc wouldn't feel as though she was reluctant to meet the rest of his family. Then at the reminder of how her initial meeting with his French family went, she apologized softly, "I'm sorry. I didn't intend to make things difficult for you at dinner."

"What do you mean?"

"You know, everything I said about the nativity and what it was like for her."

"And you believe my grandparents were offended?" Luc asked.

"Offended, no, but if they don't call you this week and suggest perhaps you should reconsider this engagement of yours, I would be astonished."

He chuckled and countered, "Actually, I predict I will indeed receive a call tomorrow but for the exact opposite reason. My grandparents will congratulate me on my choice, and encourage me to set a date for the wedding without further delay."

"You're delusional," Mary Elle muttered.

"That's actually funny, considering the source."

Her lips twitched at his quick wit, and then she gave into the urge to laugh.

He grinned back at her. "You don't do that enough."

Smiling, she shook her head in bemusement. "I've been

feeling so restless and out of sorts lately. I attributed all my angst to my disappointment over *The Nativity* not flying off the end of my brush like the first two paintings did. I never connected...I never realized I was grieving the loss of my former life. Not that I have any regrets," she added quickly, so he wouldn't think she was having second thoughts about their marriage, "I just miss the routine of my old life...and I miss my students, and the sisters, and Crystal."

"I know, Mary Elle. I recognize I'm asking a lot of you to simply walk away from your former life and insert yourself into mine. I keep expecting you to conclude I'm asking too much, it's not fair for me to keep my life largely intact when yours has been so completely overturned."

Moments later the car pulled to a stop in front of the entrance to the museum. Aman emerged from the car and walked around to hold open the door for them. Mary Elle was unprepared for the flash of bright lights erupting around them as soon as she emerged from the car.

Luc cursed softly under his breath, and gripping her arm, led her quickly to the entrance of the museum. Aman flanked her other side so no one could get close. When they passed through the entrance, Luc turned to look down into her face, his concern and self-reproach evident. "That was remiss of me. Are you all right?"

"Yes, of course. It was nothing. They'll give up after the novelty of your engagement wears off."

"They would give up sooner if we were an old married couple simply going about our boring married lives."

Grinning at his persistence, she met his pointed glance. "Maybe we could just get through tonight first."

"Excuses, excuses," he replied, smiling.

The salons displaying the art for the evening's special event were crowded with formally attired attendees. It seemed to Mary Elle as if everyone in attenance was staring at her. She couldn't resist the urge to dip her glance down toward the neckline of her not particularly daringly cut gown to make certain she wasn't falling out of it. She wasn't used to being the center of attention and the unremitting scrutiny she was receiving made her extremely uncomfortable.

"Breathe, Mary Elle," Luc bent to whisper in her ear as they paused in front of the salon hosting her work so others could emerge from the crowded room.

"I guess it's too early for us to leave?" she asked hopefully.

"Much too early, my dear," another voice inserted itself into their conversation.

Startled, Mary Elle swung around and heaved a relieved sigh when she saw Luc's grandmother's smiling but sympathetic expression. "My grandson is enjoying the opportunity to show off his lovely and extremely talented future wife far too much for you to deprive him of his fun so quickly."

"Thank you, *Grand'Mere*. You are absolutely correct, as always."

"Who is the woman staring at us?" Mary Elle asked, distracted from their bantering exchange by the almost menacing expression on the face of a woman watching their entrance into the gathering from across the room. Their glances met briefly, but the other woman didn't appear to be the least concerned to be caught staring. Rather her eyes slid over Mary Elle's face, her figure, her hair, before returning to lock with Mary Elle's and nodding slightly in mock salute.

Mary Elle suspected the other woman was letting her know in the way only another woman could, she and Luc were lovers prior to Mary Elle entering the picture. The amusement giving life to her dark eyes was very similar to Luc's when he was entertained by her naivety. It was as if she was aware of Mary Elle's faith in her fairy tale ending with Luc, and knew it was destined to implode beneath its own crushing weight.

"You'll have to be a little more specific, my love. I'm not certain we could find a woman in the room who isn't staring at you," Luc's teasing brought her back to the present.

"Thanks," Mary Elle offered with less than subtle sarcasm, then tacked on. "I was referring to the woman in the plum gown, near the entry to the far salon directly opposite us. Dark hair, plunging neckline, wearing a king's ransom in jewelry around her neck."

Luc turned slightly to see who she was referring to. Mary Elle didn't miss the subtle change in his expression, or the tightening around his lips when he replied, "What about her?"

"For a moment she looked as though if she had a sharp blade handy she would have cheerfully slit my throat and then without missing a step, turn with the blood still staining her hands to comfort my grieving fiancé."

Luc's grandmother laughed at Mary Elle's graphic description. Enjoying her grandson's discomfort, she inserted, "I believe you are referring to Madame Renard. There's been speculation for years Luc would marry her. I, for one, am thrilled he waited for you to enter his life."

Touched, Mary Elle turned to the older woman. "Thank you, what a lovely thing to say, especially considering... earlier."

"Don't be silly, my dear. I am in awe of you. Perhaps if the two of you set a date for your wedding, all the former-Madame Bordeaux want-to-bes would give up their designs on your fiancé."

"An excellent idea, *Grand'Mere*. I will even forgive you for distressing Mary Elle with old gossip," Luc interjected.

"Oh, my dear, I never meant to distress you. I imagine you are not blind to the fact Luc was considered quite a catch on the marriage market."

Mary Elle laughed. "No, you're right. I would have to be blind, deaf and dumb to have missed that," she confirmed.

"Why don't we go see what M. Jacques has done with your paintings?" Luc suggested, changing the subject.

Mary Elle nodded and let him lead her into the salon, unable to resist the urge to glance back in Mme Renard's direction. She was not surprised to find the other woman still regarding them with a knowing expression in her eyes and a slightly derisive, mostly amused smile curving her lips.

"Luc's right. Come my dear," his grandmother urged, reaching for Mary Elle's arm to draw her away from Luc's side. "I wish to renew my too-brief acquaintance with your work. I am still quite upset Luc changed his mind and elected to retain the *Young Madonna* for himself. I am even more upset by its loss now I have met its creator." When Luc was out of earshot, she added in a softer voice, "I hope I didn't upset you with my foolish gossip about Luc and Mme Renard. I never for a moment believed my grandson would fall victim to such an obvious cliché."

Mary Elle's lips twitched at the other woman's cutting remark. She couldn't resist the urge to giggle. "Obvious cliché? Ouch!"

The two women exchanged amused glances. "I know. It was catty of me. I meant it when I said I was glad he waited for you. It's obvious he's fallen in love for the first time in his life."

"Oh, oh, what a wonderful thing to say to me," Mary Elle exclaimed, reaching for the other woman's hand. "I hope it's true."

"Surely you cannot doubt it?" Luc's grandmother echoed incredulous.

"It's not I doubt he loves me, precisely. It's just I can't imagine what he sees in me. I mean look at plum gown. She's stunning and sophisticated and apparently wealthy, if the necklace around her neck is real."

"Plum gown?" Luc's grandmother parroted delighted, then dissolved into laughter. They paused at the entrance to the salon to give her a moment to regain her control. "Oh, I do like you. I think we are going to be great friends. I was determined to love whoever Luc eventually brought home to us, but I'm so happy to discover how much I like you."

Smiling, Mary Elle replied, "Me too."

"Since we are destined to be friends I feel I should confide plum gown is fluent in Arabic."

"Well, point for her."

"I think she only studied the language to increase her chances with Luc," the older woman confided in a conspiratorial whisper.

Mary Elle laughed. "You really don't like her, do you?"

Sighing, Luc's grandmother admitted, "It's true I cannot like her. Her single-minded pursuit of Luc always seemed so calculated. If she loved him the way you do, I would have learned to like her. But he never laughed with her, or with any of the women he dated, at least as far as I recall, until he met you. Certainly he never offered to represent the family in my place at a charity event, of all things he most despises, just so he had an excuse to chase after a lovely, young artist whose painting he recently acquired."

"You knew about his detour to Pittsburgh?"

"Of course, my dear. And I was quite thrilled at the prospect."

"You were?" Mary Elle echoed astonished.

"Yes. I hadn't met you by then, of course, but it was so out of character for our Luc. It always seemed to me he was determined to find a wife who would please both sides of his family. I can't tell you how happy I am he chose a wife without regard to either." At Mary Elle's crestfallen expression, she added quickly, "No, no, I didn't mean it to come out the way it sounded. I only meant his grandfather and I are both thrilled Luc fell in love with a woman who loves him as you do and then decided he wished to spend his life with her. I find it very telling no one in his family met you before your engagement was announced."

The crowd in front of her two paintings parted at their approach, and seeing her subject there, all decked out in a truly fitting setting, surrounded by admirers, Mary Elle smiled. She was glad she gave her permission for the two paintings to be displayed together. She realized suddenly it was the first time she was able to see them side by side and she stepped closer to take them in. Luc's grandmother remained behind. Mary Elle was aware of the others holding back, giving her the opportunity to renew her acquaintance with her own work.

From the entrance of the crowded salon, Luc kept a close eye on Mary Elle. He watched the way she stood as if mesmerized before her own work, and couldn't help but wonder if she was silently conversing with her subject.

"Your Mary Elle is an incredibly talented artist," his grandfather remarked from where he stood at Luc's side.

"Yes," Luc agreed, pulling his attention away from Mary Elle to meet his grandfather's considering look.

"I always believed you would marry a woman who shares your faith. I've been preparing your grandmother for such an eventuality since it was obvious your heart and your faith remained behind in Egypt even though you chose to make a life for yourself in France."

Luc's eyes drifted back to Mary Elle before meeting his grandfather's frank curiosity. "Yes, so did I. Then I met a woman whose talent intrigued me, whose faith exceeded my own, and whose beauty and view of life I found irresistible. Suddenly, in an unguarded moment, all of my carefully constructed plans for the future dissolved around me."

"Just as your father's did, I imagine, when he met your mother."

Luc laughed, appreciating the irony. "Yes, well, Allah will enjoy his little jokes on his humble subjects."

Mary Elle turned from her paintings and noticed M. Jacques standing just beyond her shoulder, waiting for a chance to capture her attention. She smiled and approached him with both hands outstretched. He took them and raised one to his lips, bringing a grin to her face.

"Mlle McGann, I think you are as large an attraction this evening as your magnificent work. I trust Mademoiselle our lady is pleased with our efforts on her behalf?"

Mary Elle turned back to her paintings and then met M. Jacques' surprisingly anxious expression with a reassuring smile. "Oh, yes, though she was not accustomed to such grandeur in her earthly life, she says she is still human enough to appreciate all of the attention she's receiving and to be grateful for the care taken to provide her with such a beautiful setting."

After a moment's hesitation, M. Jacques replied in all seriousness, "You relieve my mind, Mademoiselle. Certainly our lady will be well looked after for her visit with us. From the response to her presence this evening, I predict we will need to move her to a larger, more prominent salon in order to accommodate all of the visitors she will no doubt be receiving."

Mary Elle laughed, assuming he was teasing her. "I will leave such details to your expert judgment." Over M. Jacques' shoulder she saw Crystal's Uncle Drew and Jean Paul waiting to have a word with her.

The two men both wore wide, indulgent smiles at her approach. She hugged them both and exchanged the expected double cheek greeting, then waited while Jean Paul introduced Drew to Luc, who caught up with her when she sought out the two men. "Oh, Jean Paul, I'm so happy I agreed to loan *The Annunciation* for the exhibit. It's so amazing for the two paintings to be displayed together, don't you think?"

"Indeed, the viewer is immediately drawn into the virgin's story and its progression. After tonight there will be even greater anticipation for the next in the series."

"You mean the Nativity?"

"Presumably, given your recent journey to Bethlehem. Am I wrong?"

"No," she admitted on a sigh, "but the painting isn't going particularly well. I wasn't happy with my initial effort and haven't gotten around to starting on the next."

At the disappointment in her voice, bordering on self-disgust, he commented dryly, "You were unhappy with your initial effort? Yes, I can see where that would be quite frustrating for you after your first two offerings to the art world are currently on display in one of the most famous museums in the world."

When she looked up to see the three men fighting grins, she released an audible sigh, "All right, point taken. I guess I gave up too easily. I'll try again."

"And again and again and again, I trust. Our lady deserves nothing less."

"Now, there's the Jean Paul we all know and love," she remarked bitingly.

"*Touché*, my young protégé. I am relieved to see you are not without some defensive instincts." Then, quickly changing the subject, he added, "May I congratulate you on your engagement? M. Bordeaux clearly recognizes a great treasure when he sees one."

Luc lifted the hand he still held to his lips. "Indeed."

CHAPTER THIRTY-FOUR

They were scheduled to leave for the Middle East at the end of the week. Mary Elle lost count of the numerous attempts she began and discarded of the nativity painting. They started out promising. There appeared to be no lack of inspiration on her part. Each feminine face coming off the edge of her brush was remarkably similar, but unfortunately none of them resembled the Mary of the Annunciation. She didn't have any idea who she was, but after beginning her latest attempt and seeing the same unfamiliar eyes staring back at her again from the canvas, she decided to finish the painting and see where it led. She couldn't recall her subject from any dream or vision from her visit to Bethlehem, but maybe she simply forgot, or missed her significance in the first place. Whatever the case, since the nativity didn't appear to be about to fly off her brush anytime soon, she decided it wouldn't hurt to practice her technique with her current effort.

Mary Elle didn't share her continued struggles with her work with Luc, so when he eyed the wood case for the nearly finished painting of the strange woman, Mary Elle knew he assumed it was protecting her latest effort at the nativity. She didn't bother disabusing him of his mistaken conclusion. He wasn't completely wrong. The case actually held three works in progress. The almost completed painting of the strange woman, her latest effort on the beginning stages of the nativity, and her Christmas present for Luc.

She wanted to surprise him. Certainly, it was a surprise to her, a gift from her benefactress. Or simply a gesture to let Mary Elle know she didn't desert her after all. Regardless of the reason behind its inspiration, Mary Elle was feeling more hopeful about her work. She couldn't wait to return to the Church of the Nativity and hopefully discover what she missed during her initial visit.

Before they left for the Middle East Mary Elle wanted to stop by the museum to check on her two paintings still on display there and make sure all was well with their subject. She also wanted to let her know she would be away for several weeks since Luc persuaded her to spend Christmas with his grandfather in Egypt. When they drove up to the entrance to the museum she was surprised to see a line snaking around the block.

"Is there a new exhibit opening today?" Mary Elle wondered, turning to where Luc sat beside her in the rear of the limo.

"No," he responded with familiar amusement lighting his eyes. Then at her puzzled look, he added smiling, "They're all waiting for their chance to view your work."

Mary Elle swung back around, observing the resigned faces of the hundreds of people waiting in line to enter the museum. "No, you must be mistaken," she exclaimed, her heart leaping in inexplicable panic at the thought Luc might be right.

"Look at the signs," he suggested.

Since their progress was slowed by the heavy traffic near the entrance to the museum, Mary Elle easily located and read the signs he referred to. Luc was right. The hastily erected signs indicated the line led into the salon hosting the two paintings by American artist, Mary Elle McGann: *The Young Madonna* and *The Annunciation*. Seeing them, awed tears filled her eyes. She couldn't resist the urge to retrieve her phone from her purse and snap a quick photo. She turned to where Luc was regarding her with an amused smile and shared the picture with him. "Mary Elle McGann, American artist. I still can't believe it."

"You sound as if you still believe it's all a dream."

"It still feels like one. Look at all of those people," she commented, turning back around still disbelieving there were so many people lined up to see her work. "They look really cold."

"Obviously they consider their temporary discomfort worth the opportunity to view your art."

Mary Elle nodded uncertainly, her gaze resting on the faces of the people in line. Young and old, they bundled in warm coats against the stiff breeze. There were restless young children whose hands were being held by their impatient but resigned parents. What were they doing there? What did they expect to find at the end of their long wait? She could only hope whatever it was; they found what they were looking for.

"Stop the car," she demanded abruptly. At a word from Luc, Aman pulled as close as he could to the curb and stopped the car in the middle of the slow moving traffic, ignoring the annoyed honking of the cars behind them.

Without pausing to offer an explanation, Mary Elle scrambled out of the car and hurried over to where an elderly nun, in full habit, stood shivering in line.

"Sister? Are you waiting to see the Madonna paintings?"

With a gentle smile the older woman met her concerned glance when she answered her, "Yes, my dear. Me and everyone else in Paris it appears."

Mary Elle reached for her hand, offering, "Come with me and I'll take you in to see them."

Surprised delight, tempered by a tiny hint of suspicion colored the sister's grateful expression. "How can you do that?"

Blushing, Mary Elle confessed, "I'm the artist. We were just going in to check on her and saw you standing in line."

The sister glanced behind her to where Luc emerged from the limo. Aman stood at his side. Her smiled widened, all hint of suspicion relieved, leaving only the surprised delight in her eyes. "Is that your car?"

Mary Elle turned to follow her gaze, met Luc's amused glance, and turned back to the elderly nun. "Well, not mine, but we can ride in it up to the entrance, if you like."

The older woman laughed. "I would indeed, my dear. Wait until the other sisters hear about this. Everyone said it was too cold to come today, but something told me today was the day for my visit. And see, I was rewarded for my faith."

Seeing she was a little unsteady on her feet, Mary Elle took her arm and guided her back to where Luc and Aman waited for them. "Sister, this is my fiancé, M. Luc Bordeaux and his friend, M. Aman. Gentleman, this is Sister..?" She turned an inquiring glance in the sister's direction to complete the introduction.

"Sister Marie Conradine. It's a great pleasure to meet you both."

After the courtesies were exchanged Mary Elle met Luc's smiling glance over the sister's diminutive head. "Sister Marie would like to see the Madonna paintings. Since we were going there anyway, I thought she would prefer a ride in your nice, warm car."

"But of course," Luc agreed readily and with great flourish swept out his arm and held open the door for their guest. "Sister, your carriage awaits."

Laughing, the sister made a very correct curtsey in Luc and Aman's directions, threw Mary Elle a laughing glance over her shoulder than climbed a bit awkwardly into the rear seat. Mary Elle whispered in Luc's ear as she climbed in beside the sister, "Perhaps we can take the long way around to the entrance."

After a ride up Rue de Seine and around the next block, they pulled up in front of the main entrance to the museum. They waited for Aman to exit the driver's seat and come around to open the rear door. Mary Elle could see Sister Marie absorbing every little detail of the luxurious car's interior and

Aman's elegant and respectful bow as he assisted her from the car.

Her eyes shining with pleasure Sister Marie thanked Aman profusely and assured him she would include him and his loved ones in her daily prayers. Her promise was greeted with a gratified smile and a respectful bow by Luc's driver. Sister Marie was even more gratified when they walked right passed the line for tickets and headed directly to the salon housing the Madonna exhibit.

M. Jacques was either given notice of their arrival or he was already in the salon checking on things when they made their way across the crowded room. He motioned to one of the guards to push back a little further the red velvet ropes holding the encroaching crowd a safe and untouchable distance from the paintings. The usually unflappable M. Jacques appeared a little overwhelmed by the popularity of his latest coup. When the guard, seeing them, informed him of their presence, he swung around and strode across the distance separating them, a pleased smile on his face.

With his typical French flourish, he gripped both of Mary Elle's hands in his and exclaimed, "Mlle McGann what a very great and unexpected pleasure. As you can see, I was not mistaken when I foresaw the need for a larger salon to host your work." At the same time he exchanged a nod of greeting with Luc.

Shaking her head, still awed by the crowd, Mary Elle agreed, "I imagine you are rarely wrong," she said, bringing an appreciative smile to the older man's face. "May I introduce our guest, Sister Marie Conradine? She is eager to see the paintings. Sister, this is M. Jacques. He is in charge of the Madonna exhibit."

"A pleasure, Sister. Come, I am quite certain you will not be disappointed." With a peremptory motion of his hand, he directed the guard to hold back the line so the elderly sister could look her fill. Given her small stature and the humble and somewhat guilty smile she cast in the direction of those whose place she took at the front of the line, no one seemed to mind the added delay, especially since they were so close to the front. Even the young mother holding the sleeping infant in her arms smiled indulgently in the elderly nun's direction.

Mary Elle watched Sister Marie's face when she caught her first glimpse of the paintings, anxious to see her reaction. Her audible gasp brought tears to Mary Elle's eyes. Their eyes met for a moment and the sister held out her hand to her. Mary Elle stepped forward to clasp the other's smaller, frailer hand in hers. Together they turned to face the paintings.

"Tell me about her…about them," Sister Marie invited and Mary Elle nodded, but before she could begin, M. Jacques, interrupted, suggesting, "Perhaps Mlle McGann would be willing to speak for the benefit of the crowd waiting to see her work."

Meeting his half-pleading glance, Mary Elle nodded reluctantly and waited while he turned to announce to the crowd, "*Mesdames and Messieurs* we have an unexpected but most fortuitous surprise. The artist, Mlle McGann is with us this morning and is willing to spend a few moments sharing the story behind her work."

Blushing at the polite applause following his announcement, she met Luc's approving glance across the distance separating them, and waited for M. Jacques to hook her up to a microphone so she could be heard throughout the entire salon. After his announcement, patrons from some of the other exhibit areas within ear-shot, who were not inclined to wait in the line to view the two Young Madonna offerings, filled in the open areas behind the snaking line so they could hear her speak.

Drawing a deep, steadying breath, Mary Elle began her recitation, "As I'm sure most of you are aware, the two paintings are representations of pivotal events in the life of the young virgin who would become the mother of Jesus Christ." For a moment, she met the intense and attentive gaze of Sister Marie, and noticed behind her stood a young priest. Mary

Elle didn't notice him earlier, but he looked familiar, as if she attended a Mass at some point where he was the celebrant.

She felt like a fraud, lecturing these two faithful religious, who devoted their very lives to their faith, on the subject of the Virgin Mary. She paused for a moment to gather herself and abandoning her teacher persona chose instead to speak about her personal experiences with the virgin. Turning to face the young girl in the first painting, she began to share her story:

"When I was a little girl I dreamed of growing up and becoming a famous artist. I considered it a great tragedy I lacked the talent to fulfill my dream." There was a surprised rustle through the crowd at her admission. "It's true. I studied for years and years before I was finally forced to accept the unpleasant truth no matter how much you want something, or how hard you work for it, sometimes your most treasured dreams remain out of reach. It was a difficult lesson for me to accept. I suppose for most of us such an acknowledgment represents the defining moment separating childhood from adulthood. We pack away our childhood dreams and get on with the reality and responsibility of adult life. That's what I was doing when the little girl in the first painting came to me in my dreams and asked me to paint her a picture. I found her request depressingly ironic, even a little bit cruel, I was being forced to confront my greatest failure even in my dreams. I told her I couldn't paint, she made a mistake and needed to find someone else."

Mary Elle looked up from the painting and met Sister Marie's understanding glance, where unshed tears shimmered. Turning again to face the crowd, she continued, "She wouldn't go away. I finally gave in, if only to prove her wrong and make her go away. The last thing I wanted to do was dwell on my shortcomings. I was getting on with my life. I was doing all right. I had a job and a roof over my head. I was behaving like a grown-up, living the life of a responsible adult. It wasn't fair for her to come around and break my heart all over again."

When Mary Elle paused to catch her breath, she noticed

a hushed, expectant silence hovered over the room. "I don't know why she came to me. I don't understand what all of this means or who is behind these paintings. I know it was my hand holding the brush and mixing the paint... it was my back and shoulders and legs and fingers cramping from kneeling on the hard floor, hour after hour, gripping the brush and bringing the paintings you see before you to life on canvas. I know what I felt when I painted them... she spoke to me, but I will leave it to each of you to draw your own conclusions. That is the singular promise and beauty of art. The experience of it is unique to each of us."

She stopped speaking and switched off the microphone, reaching out to hand the equipment back to M. Jacques' waiting hands. The heavy silence hovering over the crowded salon was broken by prolonged applause from the gathering. Surprised and gratified by their response, Mary Elle turned to lift a hand in acknowledgement of their tribute, smiling in astonished surprise.

Then she sought Luc in the crowd. He was still there, watching her, and she realized for perhaps the first time, how much she needed him to still be there. He was her rock, the foundation beneath the shifting sands of her life. When she turned away from the crowd she saw Sister Marie conversing with the young priest she noticed earlier. The sister motioned for her to join them and she reluctantly did so, feeling suddenly exhausted, drained from the emotions of sharing with strangers her recent experiences with the virgin. "Mademoiselle McGann, this is a great admirer of your work, Father John. He traveled here all the way from the holy land to see your paintings."

Startled, Mary Elle met the young priest's humble smile and realized why he looked so familiar to her. "Father John. You were the priest at the Church of the Annunciation. You were there the day of my visit."

He greeted her announcement with a slight bow of acknowledgement. "Yes, and when I learned the finished painting would be exhibited to the public for perhaps only a brief time, I had to make the trip to see it…to see them both."

Overwhelmed, Mary responded, "I hope you're not disappointed in the end result."

"No, Mademoiselle, far from it. I count myself blessed to be able to see them in person."

Turning back towards where the paintings stood side by side on their simple easels, she echoed his sentiment. "Yes, so do I. It probably sounds silly, but I need to come by and check on her whenever I can…just to make sure she's all right. Even knowing God has assigned her a far more formidable protector."

Father John laughed and admitted, "I feel the same way. As you can see I spend as much time as I am able to here, nearby."

Mary Elle swung back to face him. "I don't understand."

Father John indicated the single wooden kneeler tucked away in a corner of the salon. "M. Jacques is so kind as to allow me and some of my fellow priests to sit with our lady and pray after hours."

"He has?"

"Yes. You need not be concerned, Mademoiselle. Our lady is never alone."

"You feel her?" He nodded and Mary Elle released an audible sigh. "Then I'm not going crazy."

His grin flashed and he teased, "Well, as to your psychological health I am not qualified to speak, but I would be more inclined to conclude you have been blessed."

"Thank you, and thank you for being with her. Sister Marie, would you like us to drop you somewhere?"

"No dear, you go home with your young man. I believe I will stay for a while and visit with our lady."

Mary Elle nodded and turned to where Luc waited for her. She barely took a step in his direction before a soft feminine voice interrupted her, "Pardon, Mademoiselle. If I could ask a small favor of you."

Mary Elle swung in the direction of the voice and recognized the young mother with the sleeping infant in her arms.

Smiling in response to her hesitant expression, she replied somewhat cautiously to her appeal, "What is it?"

"Will you bless my son?"

Mary Elle so was stunned by the other woman's peculiar request and the look of hope stirring in her pleading eyes, she instinctively retreated a step. "No, no, it's not me. You made a mistake. You should be asking Father John or Sister Marie for their blessing upon your son."

The woman nodded in the direction of the father and sister, who were unabashedly listening in on their conversation. "I would be happy to also have their blessing, but my heart tells me it is yours I am here to seek."

Shaking her head in denial, with tears blurring her vision, Mary Elle protested, "No, I'm sorry, you don't understand. It's not my blessing you seek. I am nothing. She's the one you should be speaking to."

The young mother nodded and there was renewed certainty in her eyes when she explained, "I have prayed and prayed to the virgin. It is she who sent me here today. Now I know why. My son is very ill. He will not be with us much longer." At Mary Elle's aghast expression, the other woman continued quickly, "No, you misunderstand. I do not expect you to heal him. It is only her gentle touch I seek to comfort my son with on the journey he will soon undertake. A mother's soothing hand. She has spoken to you. I can see she has touched your heart. I only ask you share what you have been given with my dying son."

Tears streaming down her face, Mary Elle knew she could not deny such a small request in the face of the awful grief the young mother would soon be facing. She reached out and accepted the infant's slight weight from his mother's outstretched arms. His eyes were closed and he appeared to be sleeping. She placed a gentle kiss on his forehead and whispered a soft prayer for the virgin's blessing upon him. He stirred slightly in her arms.

Then she kissed each of his eyes and silently wished him a safe journey home to heaven. As if he heard her wish for him in his heart his eyes popped open and he smiled into hers. Mary Elle was overwhelmed with the emotion flooding her at the innocent trust she read in his pure blue eyes. He reached out to grip one of her earrings dangling from her ear and grinned when he caught ahold of it. Mary Elle grimaced when he tugged hard and hurriedly shifted his slight weight to one side so she could remove the earring from her ear before he tore it from her lobe. He immediately accepted her gift and reached up to put it in his mouth.

"Oh no, don't put it in you mouth, you'll choke," she admonished, retrieving the earring now covered in baby slobber and casting an apologetic look in his mother's direction. The look in the other woman's eyes made her realize something was wrong. "I'm sorry, I should have been more careful."

Tears spilled down the young mother's face as she leaned closer and brushed her lips across her son's soft hair. He immediately turned and held out his arms to his mother. Their eyes met and the other woman's closed on a prayer of fervent thanksgiving.

Confused, Mary Elle exchanged a puzzled glance with Father John and Sister Marie, and then seeing they shared her confusion, the woman explained, "My Gabriel has been blind since birth. Now look, he sees. For the first time, he sees my face. He will not leave this world without knowing, without seeing my love for him in his mother's eyes."

White-faced Mary Elle backed away. "Did you say your son's name was Gabriel?" She asked in a hushed voice.

"Yes." The young mother confirmed smiling.

Mary Elle turned to stare at the painting and she knew. "It was him. It was her Gabriel who gave your son this gift." She looked up to where she last saw Luc and felt panic rise in her chest when she couldn't see him. Maybe all of this finally became too much for him. She couldn't really blame him. Then just when the fear began to take hold at the thought, she heard his quiet voice.

"Are you finished here?"

She swung around and nodded tearfully in response. He reached for her arm and drew her to his side. "You must excuse us. We are late for an appointment."

Mary Elle didn't hear their responses. It was only his voice she clung to, speaking quiet reassurances into her ear as he led her trembling across the room, passed the hushed crowd staring at her in amazement as word of the recovery of the infant's sight spread through the crowd. "I can't do this anymore. I don't want to do this anymore," she whispered as they finally exited the building and he settled her into the back of his waiting car before joining her there.

She met Luc's concerned glance and wondered, "Why are you still here?"

"What do you mean?"

"Why haven't you left yet? Why haven't you distanced yourself from all of this?"

Not unlike the young mother with her infant son, he brushed his lips across her forehead and drew her into the comfort of his arms. "Don't be foolish, my love. Where am I to go to escape my own heart?"

She burrowed closer in his arms and let the scalding tears fall, for the first time wondering about Father John's conclusion her gift was a blessing.

"How would you feel about moving up our trip to Egypt?"

"Can we leave yesterday?"

CHAPTER
THIRTY-FIVE

The Church of the Nativity. Even after what happened at the museum Mary Elle couldn't not come. A church official was waiting for them. Just like at the museum, there was a line of faithful waiting for their turn to brush up against the divine. Not surprising given Christmas was only weeks away.

The line was halted at a gesture from the official who accompanied them to allow Mary Elle an opportunity to descend alone. The blush rose in her cheeks in response to the resentful stares she received from those in line and her own feelings of guilt at taking their place at the front of it.

"We will wait for you here," Luc assured her, drawing her attention.

Mary Elle nodded and paused briefly at the top of the stairs, remembering what happened the last time she was in this same spot and trying to prepare herself for the impact of the visions she anticipated. She was running out of time. She couldn't afford to be overwhelmed by her own reaction to the point she missed the gift being held out to her from the mortal woman who gave birth to God. Seeing her hesitation, Luc asked, "Do you wish me to accompany you?"

She met his questioning glance and shook her head. "No. I just needed a moment. I'm ready. I won't be long."

"Take whatever time you need, Mary Elle. There is no need for you to hurry."

She nodded, her glance touching on the faces of those

waiting in line, and then she began her descent. It was easier being alone, without worrying about taking too much time and depriving one of the other faithful their opportunity to experience what she did. She knelt for a moment before reaching inside the opening, bowing her head in prayer.

Even before her fingertips reached inside to touch the silver star embedded in the floor, she felt their approach. Like a tidal wave speeding towards her, she could see it coming, knew its impact would kill her, and accepted with surprising equanimity she would be unable to run away fast enough to escape its deadly path.

The screams came first. The agonized screams of a woman in childbirth as she tried to expel the baby from her writhing body. Then fear arrived in equal measure. There was so much blood. No one prepared him for the blood, or the terror or agony on his young wife's face as each contraction took hold of her. Of course, never in a thousand years did he expect to find himself in this position, helping his wife bring a child not his own into the world.

If he didn't completely delude himself with his dreams of an angel's visitation, the child would be a boy, who he was to name, Jesus. The next contraction refocused his thoughts on the moment, and he held steady his young wife's small hand and whispered soothing words of useless comfort to her as sweat beaded and dripped down her face, mingling with her frightened tears. It seemed to him as if she was being torn apart and all he could come up with were futile words and a work-roughened hand for her to cling to in her pain.

"The baby's coming, Joseph. God's son is coming now....."

Joseph froze. Even as Mary struggled to lift her head and strained with all of her waning strength to push the child from her. A child's angry cry broke through his terror and he jumped up from where he knelt at her side and hurried to see to the child....

Mary Elle sank back on her knees and crawled across the floor of the confined space to rest her back against the wall.

Her breathing escaped in short gasps. She leaned her head back as the vivid images began to recede. The echo of the young mother's agonized cries was slower to fade.

She was uncertain how long she sat there, stunned, unable to move, unable to think. She couldn't gather her thoughts, or the energy to regain her feet and ascend the stairs to where Luc waited for her. She didn't think any thoughts remained inside her head. How could anything but the memory of what she just experienced ever intrude on her consciousness again?

From some forgotten recess of her jumbled brain, came the recognition of Luc's voice calling down to her, asking if she was all right. She tried to move her lips, to force sound between them in order to reassure him, but none emerged. Moments later he descended to where she sat leaning back against the far wall. Their eyes met. His were wide with astonishment. She knew hers remained dazed and uncertain. Then he was there, kneeling in front of her, gently brushing the hair from her face.

"Are you all right?" he asked softly, as if he feared the sound of his voice might frighten her.

She met his concerned glance, still unable to form ordinary words in response. So she nodded instead. At least she thought she did.

"Mary Elle?"

"Yes?" Oh good, she heard the sound this time. Soft and husky and unfamiliar, but she recognized it as her own voice.

"Are you ready to leave now?" He continued to address her as if he was addressing a small child who underwent some trauma, slowly, in a gentle, reassuring tone.

"Yes."

Oddly, Luc seemed to hesitate a moment before touching her, then his hands closed around her arms and helped her to her feet. She swayed unsteadily and he held onto her to keep her from falling.

"Do you want me to carry you?" He asked and Mary Elle felt her lips curve in response to his foolish question.

"No. Everyone would stare," she explained.

Luc couldn't find any words to reassure her. He wasn't sure how Mary Elle would react if he informed her everyone was going to stare regardless of whether he carried her out of the ancient church or she walked out. Her face glowed with a light not of this world. Her eyes probing his were clearer than he'd ever seen them. They appeared like fine, clear crystal peering out at him. Her skin was luminous, shining softly in the dim light where they stood steps away from the spot Christians believed their Christ was born. Not willing to examine his own beliefs at the moment, he placed a gentle arm around Mary Elle's slender shoulders, encouraging her to lean against him while he led them back up the stairs.

CHAPTER THIRTY- SIX

Their arrival in Cairo necessitated passing through customs. After reading up on a little bit of his family history on the Internet, Mary Elle thought she understood about Luc's near celebrity-status in France. Apparently, in Cairo, his status ramped up a few more notches. Feeling enormously out of place, Mary Elle stood silently by his side while Luc was greeted and their party whisked through the formalities of customs with barely a cursory glance at passports and other necessary paperwork.

There was frank curiosity in the eyes of those they encountered but no one spoke to her. It wasn't until they were once again settled in the rear of a waiting limousine on their way to Luc's grandfather's home an uncomfortable notion struck her.

"Does your grandfather speak French?"

Smiling at her anxious query, Luc confirmed, "Yes. He also speaks fluent English."

Relieved, considering, Mary Elle replied, "Yes, but I bet he spoke English before you came along."

"Yes, he did."

"He learned French for you."

Brows raised in surprise, Luc confirmed, "We learned together. How did you know?"

"Because he loves you and he wouldn't want to lose that connection with you."

Luc's grandfather was waiting for them on his impressive doorstep at his large estate situated along the Nile River outside the limits of the bustling, crowded, capital city. Mary Elle waited anxiously in anticipation of her upcoming introduction while Luc and the older man embraced. When the two men pulled back, frank gazes assessed the changes since they last saw each other.

Turning to reach for her hand to pull her to his side, Luc presented her to the man she knew in his heart, stood in the place of his father, "Grandfather, may I present my fiancée, Mary Elle McGann? Mary Elle, this is my grandfather."

Mary Elle could detect no hint of the rejection she feared in the older man's eyes and in his still strong hands reaching for both of hers. "Welcome, my dear. I am so pleased my Luc has finally brought you home to me."

"Thank you. I'm so happy to be here and to meet the man who stands as both father and grandfather to Luc."

Delighted, he turned to Luc, who returned his smile, then squeezed her hands and replied, "And I am pleased to meet the woman who has captured his heart and made him whole."

Later the evening of their arrival as they gathered around the dining room, Mary Elle was overwhelmed by the veritable feast laid out in the formal dining room. From her brief experience with Middle Eastern cuisine on her previous trips with tour groups, it was obvious her host went to a great deal of trouble to include Western offerings for her benefit. She hoped he didn't expect her to consume all of them as even the prospect of politely helping herself to a small sampling of each was somewhat intimidating. Still she would do her best. It was obvious Luc's grandfather was doing everything in his power to make her feel welcome. She was determined to relax and enjoy herself.

"Do you have any special Christmas traditions you would like to celebrate while you are with us?" Luc's grandfather asked from where he sat at the head of the table.

Mary Elle shook her head, smiling at his kindness. "Please don't go to any additional trouble on my behalf. I'm sure Luc told you my parents divorced when I was young, so most of my memories of Christmas are of being shuttled back and forth between families."

"Surely, you must have fonder memories of such a special day before your parents divorced," he urged her.

Mary Elle let her thoughts drift back to the Christmases she shared with her parents when her family was still intact. A smile curved her lips as she volunteered, "I do remember when I was little, my mom and I spent the whole day baking cookies on Christmas Eve. There were hundreds of cookies. Since there was only three of us there was no way we could possibly eat so many cookies, but it's what I remember most about Christmas Eve. We would attend midnight Mass and I always felt so grown-up, even though I slept through most of it. Then of course there was waking up Christmas morning and running downstairs before my parents woke up just to make sure Santa didn't forget us. There was always a mountain of presents under the tree, most of them with my name written on the tags." She turned to Luc, and added, "I'd like to give those memories to our children."

"Then, we will certainly do so."

Mary Elle lost no time returning to work on her paintings the following morning. Luc went into the city to attend to business matters and his grandfather didn't seem the least put out by her desire to paint. *The Nativity* was patiently waiting its turn for her attention. It was the painting of the strange woman she was anxious to finish. She finally knew who she was. Mary Elle couldn't wait to see Luc's reaction when he saw her.

Her days took on a peaceful routine. She would retreat to the garden to paint each morning, have lunch alone with Luc's grandfather as more often than not, Luc spent most days in the city working. Then she would spend several more hours painting before dinner. One evening in the week preceding Christmas she returned to the house to find Luc in genial conversation with his grandfather. The two men turned at her entrance.

Luc, catching the wide smile on her face, remarked puzzled, "I'm not certain I recognize that smile. I'm hoping it means you're happy with the way your work is progressing."

She skipped into the room and bent to kiss his lips, before settling down on the arm of his chair. "I am happy. I finished her."

"You finished?' he echoed, stunned.

"Yes, would you like to see her?"

"Very much."

She turned then to Luc's grandfather, who was a silent witness to their exchange, and asked, "Would you like to see her?"

He popped up from his chair with the speed and agility of a much younger man. "Yes, if I would not be intruding."

"On the contrary, I would very much like your opinion."

The three of them trailed out to the cool, fragrant air of the garden. Luc's grandfather exclaimed, "I don't know why, but I'm actually nervous."

Smiling, exchanging a glance with Luc over his grandfather's shoulder, Mary Elle echoed his sentiment, "Yes, me too."

She stopped at the entrance to the garden alcove where her easel was set up and turned around to face the two men, holding her arms out and addressing Luc's grandfather, "You have to close your eyes now."

"I do?"

"Yes, I want to make sure you get the proper perspective. First impressions can't be recaptured."

Smiling, the older man obligingly closed his eyes and allowed her to lead him forward a few steps and position him in front of the painting. She stopped Luc from following by holding out her hand. "It's not your turn, yet."

He nodded graciously and then grinned when his grandfather joked, "Is my grandson trying to intrude on my moment?"

"Yes, but he has agreed to wait his turn. You may open your eyes now."

His reaction was everything she could have hoped for. He gasped, then raised his hands to his face and covered his mouth. His eyes filled with astonished tears as he gazed at the completed painting, then turned his stunned glance to Mary Elle's smiling face. "Miriam. You painted my beloved Miriam?"

"What?" Luc echoed astonished, then stepped forward to see for himself. His eyes wide with amazement, he turned to meet her anxious gaze. "This is what you've been working on?"

"Yes."

"I don't understand. I thought you were working on *The Nativity*."

"*The Nativity*? This is the next painting in your Madonna series?" His grandfather interjected.

She turned away from Luc to answer his grandfather. "Yes."

Luc demanded her attention again, "Mary Elle, how did you do this?"

Bemused, she shook her head, "I don't know. I must have seen a picture of her in one of your homes."

Shaking his head, Luc looked over her shoulder to where his grandfather still stood as if he was mesmerized by the painting.

"May I purchase this from you? Money is of no concern," the older man offered, waving his hand in a dismissive gesture of such a trivial detail.

Smiling, Mary Elle responded, "No, I can't sell her. I hope you will accept her as the gift she was intended."

"For me?" he confirmed. "You did not paint this for Luc?"

"No, the painting is yours. You knew her. You remember her. You miss her."

"Yes," he blinked back his tears and for the first time turned from the painting to look at her.

Mary Elle could see he was still overcome with emotion, so she simply returned his smile and cautioned, "The paint's not completely dry. You shouldn't move her for another twenty four hours."

He nodded his understanding. "Then I think I will sit with my Miriam and keep her company for a while."

"Yes, I think she would enjoy catching up."

With Luc's hand leading her along the stone path back to the house, she waited until she was certain she wouldn't be overheard by his grandfather and commented, "You don't have to pretend it's the same as the others."

"What do you mean?"

She smiled, guessing he knew exactly what she meant. "M. Jacques would not offer to display this painting in the museum."

"Perhaps not," he conceded, "but it's the work of an incredibly gifted artist. Every painting you produce can't be a masterpiece, my love. Not even the great masters aspired to such heights."

"I know. I think maybe this is her gift to me. Maybe when this is all over I won't be producing masterpieces, but the look on your grandfather's face when he saw the painting was more than enough for me to be content."

CHAPTER THIRTY-SEVEN

Even though Christmas is celebrated in the Middle East on January seventh in accordance with the Orthodox churches and the Julian calendar, Mary Elle and Luc's grandfather were happily engaged in baking Christmas cookies throughout the day on December twenty fourth.

She looked at the dozens and dozens of cookies between them on the industrial sized kitchen island and laughed. "What are we going to do with all of these cookies? Are there any orphanages close by we could donate them to?"

He laughed and chose a colorful star studded with sprinkles and white icing from one of the long rows of cookies and raised it to his lips. "I cannot imagine how I have missed out on this delightful tradition all of my life," he announced and finished the cookie in two swift bites.

Their shared laughter was interrupted by Luc's appearance in the doorway. Seeing him, Mary Elle held up the gingerbread man she just finished decorating for his inspection. "Would you like to sample our wares?"

When he didn't respond to her teasing, and his lips failed to curve in the expected smile, Mary Elle searched his face, finally taking in the seriousness of his expression. Panic filled her. "Is something wrong? What happened? Is she all right?"

Sighing at being forced to disturb her joyful endeavors with his grandfather, Luc swiftly crossed the room to where Mary Elle stood with a large white apron wrapped around her middle, covered with flour, sugar and various shades of icing.

He gripped her hands and said into her suddenly colorless face, his intent gaze holding hers, "Your paintings are fine. There was an explosion at a Christian church in the city. There are no reported injuries, but the church and grounds sustained considerable damage."

Mary Elle stepped back, stunned at Luc's news. She could almost feel the color drain out of her cheeks. "What was the name of the church?"

Luc hesitated and then admitted reluctantly, "Our Lady of Faith." Mary Elle jerked away from him. "I have to go."

"Mary Elle…"

She instantly cut him off. "No, no. I know you want to protect me, but you can't protect me from this. I need to go and see her."

Sighing, as if he already calculated his chances of changing her mind and conceding there was none, he agreed, nodding. "All right. I will take you."

Mary Elle shook her head in instinctive denial. "No, there's no reason for you to go. I realize how awkward this is for your family, having me here. You should stay here…have someone drive me…or call a cab."

For perhaps the first time in their relationship Mary Elle rendered Luc speechless. Stunned anger appeared to silence his tongue for a moment before he recovered enough to berate her. "Do you have any comprehension how insulting your suggestion is? That I would remain behind and send my future wife into danger?"

"I'm sorry; I didn't mean to insult you." Her apology was an automatic response to his anger, but she couldn't deny she still wanted Luc to remain safely behind on his grandfather's estate when she went into the city.

"And yet you continue to do so though I can assure you your former presumption I was only interested in you because of your artistic talent pales in comparison to the offense you just offered me."

"I'm sorry. I'm sorry. I couldn't bear it if anything

happened to you."

"And you do not credit I would feel equally bereft if something were to happen to you?"

"You're right. I'm sorry. Can we not talk about this now? I need to change and then you'll take me?" She confirmed tearfully, aware her hands were shaking with reaction, unwilling to take the time to offer any further protest, recognizing any such continued objection to his accompanying her to the scene of the damaged church would prove pointless.

"Yes, I will take you."

Mary Elle nodded and hurried passed him. She ran up the center stairs leading off the main foyer to their suite of rooms. She changed quickly into a modest silk dress and matching jacket. Then she rushed into the adjoining bath where she braided and knotted her hair at the base of her neck, before scrubbing her face clean of flower and sugar, and applying a light make-up. She turned back into the room, grabbed a scarf to cover her head and rushed back towards the stairs.

Luc was waiting for her near the front door with his grandfather at his side. Both men wore concerned, serious expressions. She assumed Luc's grandfather was there to say goodbye but would remain behind. When it became obvious he intended to accompany them to the site of the attack, she protested frantically, "You can't come with us."

When he merely raised an imperious brow in response to her dictate, she turned to Luc for assistance in convincing him. "Luc, you need to make him stay home."

"I would have no more success at persuading him to do so, than I would you."

"But..." With tears in her eyes, she turned back to face Luc's grandfather, unable to put her fear into words. What if something happened to him because of her? She would never be able to face Luc again.

"You are my granddaughter now, Mary Elle. We are family. You also insult me by thinking I would remain behind."

She nodded tearfully, then met Luc's glance. "I'm sorry. I'm really sorry, but I have to go."

Mary Elle took in the chaotic scene with stunned disbelief. She'd seen such sights before of course. In the times they lived in it was impossible to avoid the evidence of almost daily violence perpetrated around the world against the innocent, unarmed, and unsuspecting. She witnessed the aftermath of a terrorist attack, but it was always from a safe distance away and always through the sanitizing filter of a television screen.

To witness the results of such destruction from only a few meters away was another thing altogether, she realized, as her shocked gaze took in the broken windows, and the scarred concrete. The smoke still hung over the air, and brought home to her, in this part of the world, as in no other place on earth, God was used as an excuse to kill.

Even with the windows up she could not avoid breathing in the acrid remnants of the explosives used to bomb the small church. She supposed she should be grateful whoever was behind the attack was either too ignorant, or was going for maximum shock value for the benefit of the western media and chose December twenty fourth, the date Christmas Eve was celebrated in the west, rather than in January when the Egyptian faithful, along with the majority of Orthodox churches, celebrated Christmas. Puzzling over the discrepancy in the dates and the timing of the attack, Mary Elle was horrified and instantly rejected the awful possibility presenting itself for her consideration. She turned an uncertain, pleading glance in Luc's direction.

"This didn't happen because of me, did it? Because I'm here? Because you announced your intention to marry me? Right? Please tell me this has nothing to do with me."

Her frantic pleas trailed off into dismayed silence when Luc's hands bit into her shoulders and he shook her gently, "Do not be ridiculous, Mary Elle. The violent do not need an excuse for such abominations."

Mary Elle remained unconvinced. Panic was closing her throat, making it hard for her to swallow. In frantic desperation she tried to convince both men to remain behind in the car, "You shouldn't be here. I need to be here, but there's no reason for you to put yourselves at risk like this." At Luc's shuttered expression, she added, tears in her eyes, "This is your home. This is your family's home. Your uncle is not going to be happy at your presence here."

"Is that supposed to be less insulting?" Luc replied coldly.

Mary Elle looked passed Luc to his grandfather, "You need to speak to him, explain to him why he shouldn't come with me."

Luc's grandfather simply smiled gently in her direction and reached for one of her icy hands. "In Luc's eyes, you are already his wife, Mary Elle, and my new granddaughter. We are a family now and family supports one another through difficult times."

Sighing, defeated, Mary Elle turned to open the door and found it already being held open for her. Aman stared down at her with sympathy in his glance. She whispered her gratitude and emerged from the car on unsteady legs, aware of the additional men she didn't recognize surrounding them, and of Luc and his grandfather climbing out of the car behind her. Their presence was already attracting a great deal of attention from the crowd gathered both to mourn and gawk; it seemed to Mary Elle, in equal measure.

She began walking towards the entrance to the church where an older priest stood, staring blankly around him, dazed and shell-shocked by the aftermath of violence in the sacred place. In the background, being held back by armed police, protestors' angry voices shouted in Arabic for the entertainment of the television cameras being thrust in their direction. Hearing them, Mary Elle shivered; glad she couldn't understand their screaming protests.

Swallowing her own grief, Mary Elle approached the priest, who thankfully appeared unharmed. His eyes warily watched their approach and she noticed his eyes widen in recognition of Luc and his grandfather. She didn't know what she was going to say to him until the words left her mouth, "Father, will you still be celebrating the vigil Mass this evening?"

He looked down at her from his greater height, seeming stunned by her query, and then his gaze swung passed her to where Luc and his grandfather stood in silent witness to their exchange. Gathering himself, the old priest turned his attention back to her and replied in answer to her query. "Yes, of course. The city officials have declared the church structurally sound, despite all appearances to the contrary."

Mary Elle summoned a smile for his small attempt at humor and let her eyes wander over the tiny church. Most of the stained glass windows were broken. The stone façade had chunks gouged out of it, and the front door hung slightly askew from the force of the explosion. The priest stepped aside to allow her to enter. She was surprised to discover the inside appeared largely intact.

The altar was untouched, the pews still lined up in orderly rows. The tabernacle glowed softly despite the lack of candlelight. Mary Elle stepped into the deserted sanctuary and approached the altar following the center aisle, genuflecting and making the sign of the cross before it. To the right of the altar stood an old organ, pushed up almost against the wall, but she managed to squeeze through the narrow opening to sit on the simple wooden bench placed before it.

Mary Elle thought it would please the virgin if there was music in the little church. Music healed, music restored, music was a form of devotion and prayer crossing all faiths. Drawn by her memories of earlier, happier Christmas celebrations, she raised her hands to the keys and let her heart decide what her fingers would play. As her hands ran across the keyboard and tears spilled from her eyes, the haunting melody of the devotional hymn, *Ava Maria* pierced the night. She raised her voice to fill in the words.

Luc remained near the entrance to the church, blinking back tears at the purity of Mary Elle's voice, remembering her claim she sang only for Allah. He heard the old priest's astonished gasp beside him and turned to assure himself its cause was no more than the sound of the beautiful music filling the little church.

Responding to the curiosity on Luc's face the priest explained, "As you can see the interior of the church survived almost unscathed from the attack."

"Yes, it seems incredible, one might say even miraculous, given the date," Luc agreed.

"Yes, I thought the same when I first inspected the sanctuary after the explosion, but what I find truly miraculous about this night is the fact the organ your fiancé is playing hasn't been used in years. Most of the keys are broken and we haven't had the funds to repair them."

"What are you saying?" Luc demanded harshly.

A slight smile curved the older man's lips and he shook his head in wonder, as if he was still coming to grips with what he was witnessing, "I don't know where the music is coming from, but if it's coming from the old organ your fiance' is playing, then we are indeed witnessing a small Christmas miracle."

Luc searched the other man's expression for some sign of deception then turned to meet his grandfather's incredulous, fascinated gaze before returning to Mary Elle's face. She seemed unaware the organ she was so expertly playing was in disrepair. Suspending his disbelief for a moment, and uncomfortably remembering the young mother's claim of Mary Elle restoring her son's sight, he stepped into the sanctuary, bowing his head and took a place in the back row of pews, and his grandfather settled beside him.

Luc kept his attention on Mary Elle, but he was aware of the slow trickle of faithful parishioners entering the church and beginning to fill the pews. The trickle became a steady stream, as if those gathering inside the sanctuary were drawn by the music filtering outside through the broken windows. By the time the priest was preparing for the start of the liturgy the tiny church was filled to overflowing. The television crews, who arrived to report on a terrorist attack against a Christian church on Christmas Eve in the predominantly Muslim country, were now confronted with a story to captivate the imaginations of viewers around the world. Luc could not shake the uncomfortable realization Mary Elle was at the center of it.

At the conclusion of the Mass, Luc waited for Mary Elle at the entrance to the small church. She approached him with shining eyes, her heart filled with reverence, so grateful he put aside his concern for her safety and brought her to the church. She supposed his grandfather already returned to the car to give them a few moments of privacy.

"Thank you for bringing me and for being here," she said softly, and at his acknowledgment of her gratitude, together they turned and exited the church. Mary Elle noticed the older priest who celebrated the Mass was surrounded by a small gathering of the faithful. She was happy to notice his complexion no longer appeared grey and shaken. Sighing, relieved, she leaned thankfully against Luc's side, suddenly exhausted. He wrapped his arm around her and led her towards where his grandfather waited near the limousine speaking to a few men she assumed were acquaintances of his.

As they approached the car, Mary Elle saw a small statue of the virgin marking the entrance to the church grounds. She was dismayed to discover the statue was badly damaged by the explosion. Disturbed at the sight, she pulled away from Luc's side, explaining softly, "It's all right. I'll meet you at the car. I just need a few minutes to make sure she's all right."

Glancing over her head, Luc sighed and nodded, bending to drop a kiss on the top of her head before reluctantly releasing his hold on her. Mary Elle crossed the small distance to the statue, aware of the tears filling her eyes and a sadness descending on her spirit all but taking her breath away. She made no effort to brush aside the tears streaming down her face as she knelt before the young girl, captured somewhere on the brink of womanhood, but Mary Elle thought it was before the events of the Annunciation.

The sculpted face of the young girl was joyful, her expression playful, her heart light. The artist's vision was in sharp contrast to the stone torn from her outstretched hand by the force of the blast. One of the girl's ears was missing and there were great chunks carved out of her lower half until it appeared as if a strong wind might topple her over. From the looks of it, a casual observer might assume the statue was the epicenter of the explosion.

With a hand trembling from the depths of the despair she couldn't shake off, Mary Elle reached up to gently brush the dust from the virgin's face. For a moment the stone eyes seemed to come alive and vacantly met her gaze, as if she didn't understand what happened, or why anyone would seek to hurt her. Mary Elle didn't know how to reassure her. Instead she bowed her head to evade the agonizing questions she read in the young girl's eyes.

Shoulders shaking with suppressed sobs, Mary Elle removed the diamond necklace Luc gave her, an early Christmas present he called it, and looped it around the outstretched stone stump where the virgin's missing hand was previously attached. The diamonds twinkled in the night and she thought she felt a lessening of the heavy desolation surrounding the girl. When her trembling hands reached up to remove her earrings, Mary Elle felt a strong hand cover her own, stopping her.

"Come love, it's time to leave now," Luc's pitying voice urged her.

Mary Elle raised devastated eyes to his. "I can't. I can't leave her like this. I can't leave her alone."

Ignoring her protest, he reached down to lift her to her feet and turn her to face him, promising, "We'll repair the damage done here."

Mary Elle shook her head, denying his assurance, "They'll just destroy it again."

"Then we'll rebuild it again." When she would have protested, Luc interrupted, "And again, and again and again. They won't win, Mary Elle. Evil won't win this battle for the hearts of men."

"What if it already has?" she countered miserably.

His lips curving in a slight smile, he asked, "How can you of all people ask me such a question?"

When he would have drawn her away, Mary Elle resisted, still reluctant to leave her alone. The old priest approached, encouraging her, "Miss McGann, it's all right. Our lady will not be alone. I will remain with her." Mary Elle surrendered to their joint pressure. "Thank you, Father." Reaching into her purse she emptied her wallet into the stone basket at the girl's feet. When he would have protested her generosity, Mary Elle shook her head. "Please let me know what else I can do…if you need anything…."

When she would have reached up again to remove her earrings, Luc's grip prevented her.

"Mary Elle, I will see to it the church and the statue are restored."

At her hesitant nod, he reached into his jacket and removed his wallet and proceeded to empty it into the basket, a much more generous contribution than Mary Elle's small offering. She was aware of Luc's grandfather joining them, and watched as he too emptied his wallet into the stone basket at the girl's feet.

Nodding her gratitude, Mary Elle allowed herself to be led away towards the waiting car. She was too upset and too empty inside to notice the stream of bystanders, both Muslim and Christian alike, who followed their example and approached the statue to empty their wallets into what became an impromptu offering basket to rebuild the tiny church.

CHAPTER THIRTY-EIGHT

Mary Elle woke Christmas morning alone in bed. She rolled over to check the time on her phone and was amazed at how long she slept. She climbed out of bed and dressed in what she considered her painting uniform, dark Capri leggings and an over-sized smock. A little casual for Christmas day perhaps, but she didn't feel much like celebrating. She needed to work. She brushed her teeth, combed out her hair and let it fall unencumbered to her waist. She didn't bother with make-up.

Drawing a deep breath, trying to keep the desolation from the night before at bay, she turned away from the mirror and left the room in search of Luc. She found him in the dining room with his grandfather and another man, along with a woman and two teenagers, a boy and a girl. She stopped at the entrance, thinking she might be able to retreat back upstairs before anyone noticed she was there. Too late, her hesitant gaze locked with the stranger's across the table. Except he wasn't a stranger. Mary Elle was fairly confident in concluding it was Luc's uncle who was regarding her with a look of speculative curiosity from his dark eyes so like his father and nephew's.

Seeing his uncle's distraction, Luc turned in her direction, then rose to his feet. As if sensing her hesitation, he stepped towards her and reached for her hand. She wasn't fooled by his concerned gesture. She suspected Luc was merely making certain she didn't turn around and run back in the other direction.

"Sleep well?" He asked, drawing her back into the room with him, smiling slightly at her obvious reluctance.

"Yes, thank you," she whispered, tugging on her hand. "I should go change. I'm not dressed for company."

"They're not company. They're family," Luc informed her, refusing to release her hand.

At the amused sparkle in Luc's grandfather's eyes, she realized she was making a fool of herself and releasing an irritated, audible sigh, stopped struggling against Luc's hold.

Aware of her annoyance, he grinned down at her and turning to his uncle, offered, "Uncle Basil, may I present my fiancé, Mary Elle McGann? Mary Elle this is my Uncle Basil, his wife, Farah, and his children, Nabil and Nina."

Mary Elle thought she muttered something appropriate, but she couldn't be sure. She was too busy contemplating her escape. Luc's uncle rose to his feet and nodding in her direction, said, "I am pleased my nephew has finally brought his intended wife home to meet his family."

Mary Elle couldn't decide if he was expecting an answer from her or not, so she remained silent. Luc pushed her down into the chair next to him and took his seat beside her.

"Merry Christmas. Did you sleep well, my dear?" Luc's grandfather asked gently.

"Yes, thank you," then added when Luc began heaping food on her plate, "I'm not hungry."

"Mary Elle," he warned, but she interrupted him.

"I'm sorry. I need to work." She was close to tears. She bent her head to hide them. She so wanted to make a good impression on Luc's uncle and his family, but her head was full of images she needed to transfer to canvas before she lost them.

He reached over to lift her chin so she would meet his eyes. Then seeing her distress he stretched out one arm to the center of the table to retrieve a Christmas cookie and held it up to her lips. She obediently took a bite.

"*The Nativity*?" he asked.

"Yes," she confirmed, and then added, "I have a Christmas gift for you, too. Would it be all right if I give it to you later?"

"Under the tree?"

"There's a tree?" She echoed stunned.

"We waited for you to show us how it is to be decorated," Luc's grandfather inserted.

"Oh, oh, you have a Christmas tree for me?" Her eyes searched his.

"Along with a mountain of presents," he confirmed smiling.

"You remembered, but I don't have presents for anyone... except Luc and you."

"You already gave me a priceless gift," he reminded her. "One my own for you could never match."

"Oh?" Luc's uncle asked, curious.

Luc's grandfather jumped up from his chair. "Ah, let me show you." He rushed out of the room, and returned carrying the painting Mary Elle gave him of his daughter.

"What is this?"

Luc's grandfather grinned triumphantly and turned the painting around to proudly show his son and his family.

"Miriam," Luc's uncle announced stunned, turning an almost accusatory look in her direction.

"I didn't know who she was when I was painting her." Even as the instinctive excuse left her mouth she knew her words were wasted on him.

"Indeed?"

Mary Elle felt Luc stiffen at her side at his uncle's sarcasm. On her other side she saw the tightening around the mouth of Luc's grandfather. She was in the room less than five minutes and she was already causing division between Luc and his family. Hoping to avoid a further deterioration of family unity, she jumped up from her chair, turned a pleading glance in Luc's direction and excused herself, "I need to work."

She didn't escape fast enough. Just as she passed out of

ear shot, she heard Luc's grandfather's rebuke of his only son, "That was ill done of you, Basil. Mary Elle is more than a guest. She is Luc's future wife and my new granddaughter. I will not have her feel as if she is unwelcome in my home."

Mary Elle kept going. She was grateful for Luc's grandfather's defense of her, but she didn't wait around to hear his son's response.

In the stillness of the garden, Mary Elle knelt before the easel holding the partially completed rendition of the Nativity. So far this attempt made it through the initial challenges to its continued existence. Perhaps because she had yet to bring her subjects to life within it yet.

This was the first painting where she began with the background setting rather than the main event. The dimly lit stable was there, filled with straw. There was a hint of livestock just out of sight. It was a lowly setting for the exalted nature of the event about to take place there. Along with the poor light, was the intense stench of manure and feed. Underlying it all was the acrid scent of fear. She could feel it as if it was her own, not only hers, but Joseph's. She could hear his thoughts echoing through her mind, 'What were they doing in this filthy, crowded stable?'

Suddenly she could see what was withheld from her before, what she was incapable of understanding until now. In all of her earlier efforts she tried to impose the typical representation of the nativity, with the young Madonna holding the infant Jesus at her breast, or asleep in the crèche with Joseph standing at her shoulder, both of them regarding the sleeping infant with a mixture of awe and parental love.

Apparently the young virgin was about to set the record straight. With a new sense of urgency, Mary Elle picked up a paintbrush, hurriedly mixed the paint and began filling in the main scene. First came the face of the young virgin in the throes of labor. It wasn't a peaceful gaze she looked out on the world with, nor were her lips framed in an adoring, reverent smile.

No, her features were contorted, grimacing in agony. Her lips parted on a scream of tortuous pain and her terror of the unknown. She longed for the reassurance of her mother's presence, or for any other woman to be there to comfort her. At the same time, even in the midst of her agony, she recognized Joseph was possibly even more terrified than she was, and both of them were doing their best to hide their fears from the other.

Mary Elle lost track of the time as her brush flew across the canvas. After long intent hours, she paused, set down the brush in her hand, stretched out her cramping fingers, and let her gaze wander over what came to life beneath her hand.

The young woman was still the central focus of the painting. Her skin was beaded with sweat, her features contorted in her pain, and her hair lay lank and sweat-dampened around her face, but the expression in her eyes was altered from the one of Mary Elle's earlier vision. The young Madonna was not looking at Joseph, but staring straight ahead out of the current view of the observer to where another stood, watching her struggle to bring her babe into the world. The terror of her earlier gaze gave way to a desperate relief, and overwhelming gratitude to see him there. She hadn't seen him since the evening he appeared to her on the roof outside her window, when he proclaimed to her she would bear the child she was about to bring into the world.

She thought he was angry with her and he deserted her because of her hesitation to accept God's will. She feared she angered God and He called his holy one home to heaven and she would be forced to do this alone. But he was back. Tears filled her eyes knowing everything was going to be all right now. He wouldn't let anything evil happen to her.

For the first time since she fell into whatever this was, Mary Elle was glad of his presence. She felt the same sense of relief she saw reflected in the virgin's eyes at his arrival and the same feeling of peace filled her. Everything was going to be all right now. She was safe. She could let down her vigilance.

At peace now after her desperate need to transfer her impressions, to convey 'her' story on canvas, she leaned back on her knees, and then curled up at the feet of the Mother of God and her yet to be painted, angelic protector, and fell asleep.

Luc found her there, not long after. He checked on her periodically throughout the course of the day until it wasted away into late afternoon, but didn't disturb her when she was immersed in her work. His astonished gaze dwelt on the genius of her creation, the starkness of the depiction, the very humanity of the virgin so often lost in the usual portrayal of the nativity, which all too often showed the peaceful aftermath of the birth, and not it's painful, bloody, frightening reality for those suffering through it.

He turned his gaze to the woman who lay sleeping at his feet. He was not blind to the similarities between the two women. There was an innate innocence they were both allotted by their creator. Though he suspected Mary Elle would deny it, he recognized the two women also shared not merely a faith in God's existence, but a certainty He remained active and present in the affairs of men. A faith, despite her claim she was not devout, continued to evade him, and one he suspected remained elusive to all but Allah's chosen ones.

His lips curved in a smile of almost humorous acknowledgment of the Almighty's choice of the innocent, of the defenseless, to stand against the great evils at work in the world today, likely no less than the evil present in the world at the time of Jesus. Luc couldn't help but wonder where Joseph was in all of this. Was he even going to make an appearance in this painting? Did he have an important part to play in history or was he merely in the scene to provide background, and not a particularly colorful background at that?

Luc doubted the Almighty left the choice of Mary's husband and companion, not to mention Jesus' earthly father, to chance. No, Joseph was chosen just as Mary was, but not to play a direct role in events. Instead, he was tasked with protecting the young family. It was Joseph who stood in front of the innocent, who navigated the troubles confronting the young virgin, the threats facing his young family so his wife and God's infant son would not be defiled by the sins of this world.

Luc recognized his own role was turning out to be not so very different from the biblical Joseph's. For a moment he felt a pang of sympathy for the missing earthly father of Christ in the canvas and hoped he would make it into the painting illustrating such a critical juncture of history. Luc was cheering for Joseph and thought he should be given his rightful due, but even as his thoughts took shape in his head, he was aware of a feeling of resistance emanating from outside of his own consciousness. It was as if he misinterpreted Joseph's role, or at least his assumption he felt slighted by the way he was sidelined into near obscurity by scripture. Wasn't Joseph known as the 'silent prophet' because not a single word of his was recorded in scripture?

Shaking off his fanciful descent into the thoughts and hopes of Biblical figures, he bent to lift his sleeping fiancé into his arms.

"Luc?"

"Yes. You've been holding out on me," he charged, smiling down into Mary Elle's drowsy glance.

She blushed guiltily. "I told you I was stuck," she reminded him, and then she turned to the painting and lifted anxious eyes to his face, "I don't think she's what everyone is expecting."

Luc let his glance return to the painting, taking in the harsh evidence of the pain etched across the laboring woman's face. The image was gritty, and yes, one might even say shocking in the face of the world's typical impression of the immortal virgin. Surely a virgin could never struggle with the terror and the very real pain of childbirth. History and scripture both glossed over the actual birth, as if Jesus's arrival into the world was as miraculous as his conception.

He suspected the world was not comfortable delving too deeply into what it must have been like for the historical Mary. It made her too human, too far removed from the remote pedestal the faithful placed her on. It was as if they feared by confronting her humanity, she would become too much like the rest of mankind. And if she was like the rest of the children of men, then her place in God's plan would be threatened.

Withdrawing his focus from the painting with an effort, he realized Mary Elle was still waiting for his response to her comment. "No, I don't believe she is what anyone is expecting for the next installment of the Madonna series."

CHAPTER THIRTY-NINE

They returned to the house where Luc's family was gathered. In an attempt to relieve the uncomfortable silence at their entrance, Mary Elle asked, "Are there any leftovers? I'm starving."

Luc's grandfather smiled, relief in his gaze and proceeded to ply her with every delicacy his research must have indicated might be served somewhere in the world on Christmas Day.

Mary Elle was so touched he went to such trouble to make her feel at home. He steered the conversation along innocuous lines to avoid a repetition of the day's earlier tension. Even Luc's uncle made an effort to be charming.

After their late lunch, Mary Elle turned in Luc's direction and offered apologetically, "I need to get back to work. He's getting snippy."

"Snippy?" Luc echoed, grinning.

She shrugged and muttered beneath her breath, "You know what I mean."

When she rose to return to the garden, Luc reached out a hand to stop her. "Before you retreat to biblical times, will you answer a question for me?"

"Of course."

"Where's Joseph?"

Smiling, Mary Elle squeezed his hand and suggested, "Come along and I'll tell you about that night."

Luc's grandfather interrupted, "Would we be intruding if

we accompanied you?"

Mary Elle turned to reassure him, "No of course not. Please, join us."

The entire family rose to follow her into the garden and gathered around the half-finished painting. Gasps of surprise echoed from her audience. Ignoring their audible reactions, Mary Elle faced the painting, sinking to the ground before it, already retreating from her surroundings to the pivotal night captured in the painting. Her account began tentatively, and then picked up speed as she became lost in the past and in the events of that night.

"She knows Joseph is furious at what he considers the ridiculous intrusion into their lives by the Roman emperor's command every Jew return to his place of birth to be counted in the Roman census. Joseph is a patient man, a good man, but he is also a devout Jew and he resents the Roman occupation of his country."

"In spite of the presence of the Romans he has gone about his life to the best of his ability, but this latest demand was challenging his inclination to accept with his usual equanimity the reality of Roman rule. Mary's afraid of what he'll do, of what his reaction will be if she confesses to him she's in labor. They were on the road for long, dusty weeks and she spent most of the time trying to hide the baby's impending birth."

"In addition to her fears of Joseph's reaction, she's fighting her own terror about the birth itself. Never in a million years did she imagine she would find herself in this situation, on the road, alone with her husband, with no woman to attend her. She wants her mother. She does her best to hide her fear, because she can see it echoed in Joseph's eyes every time he looks at her. She knew he was as anxious to reach Bethlehem as she was so he wouldn't be faced with the prospect of being alone with her in the wilderness. At least in the town, he assumes there will be other women around to assist with her laboring."

"She doesn't blame him. What does a man know about such things? An older man at that. Mary wanted to reach town for the same reason. If she couldn't have the comfort of her mother to attend her at least there would be some comfort to be found with another woman to help her with the birth. She didn't expect any help from the holy one who announced God's plan for her and then disappeared. She hadn't seen him since the night on her parents' roof."

Curious Luc bent to whisper in her ear from where he stood over her, her back leaning against his legs.

She lifted her face to meet his glance and responded, "Yes. She thinks he's angry with her, that she disappointed God when she hesitated before giving him her answer. She assumes he left her, disgusted with her human weakness and he wasn't coming back, and she would be totally alone for the birth. Even in her fear, she's afraid to confide in Joseph because she's even more terrified of what he'll do."

"When they finally arrive in Bethlehem she's filled with an enormous feeling of relief, she'll be able to lie down in a bed and ask Joseph to find a midwife to assist her. She'll finally be able to confide in Joseph the babe would be born that night. She wanted to tell him. She needed to share her secret with someone. Then there's no room at the inn. Joseph, at the end of his rope, loses his temper. She exchanges a pleading glance for understanding with the offended, harried innkeeper."

"When he offers them room in the stable, Joseph is not appeased, but when he meets Mary's hesitant glance, she realizes he wasn't fooled by her pretense. He knows she's about to give birth. She reaches for his hand and whispers to her husband, "It is God's holy will. It is not for us to complain about our circumstances or to question Him.""

Joseph realizes his anger and fear and resentment at the Romans is nothing compared to what his young bride must have been through traveling on the back of a donkey while she was heavy with child. Yet she voiced no word of complaint. His rage, his sense of self-importance, and his feelings of having sacrificed so much of his former life, of his plans for his future to comply with the angel's demand, the one who appeared to him in a dream and advised him to take Mary into his home, coalesced into a frustrated, impotent rage."

"Hadn't he done enough? Hadn't he sacrificed enough? When was this craziness ever going to end? Didn't he bow before God's will? Didn't he already do more than any righteous Jew would have done in his shoes? Didn't humble himself and swallow his pride at the angel's urging and take his young bride into his home, knowing she carried a child, he, her husband, wasn't the father of? How much more was God planning on demanding from him? When was he going to be able to return to his former life?"

"He was a simple man, a carpenter. He had no place in the course of great events. Those were for others... for prophets and priests, not for men like him. What in the world was he doing in the middle of this insanity? Fantasy, more like. The son of God. The promised savior of the Jews. The absurdity of it all was beyond what he could take in. He was tired of being pulled in so many different directions."

"Then just when his doubts and his anger would get the better of him, he would meet his young wife's anxious eyes and would once again doubt his doubt. He would recall the angel's visit to his dreams and he would once again accept regardless of the truth of the origins of the child his wife carried, she was a young and gentle woman, little more than a child herself, who was incapable of fending for herself and her child in the world of men. He accepted her into his home. She was his wife. He was an honorable man. He would do what needed to be done."

"In that moment he accepted what needed to be done was to make his wife as comfortable as possible and to let her know he would be by her side through every step, whatever God demanded of them. She would not be alone. He would not leave his gentle wife to the careless mercy of strangers, or subject her to the merciless laws of his own Jewish faith, or that of the enemy Romans."

"He doubted?" Luc asked surprised.

Mary Elle's glance remained on the painting. "Yes of course. What reasonable man, no matter how devout his faith would not have doubted?"

"So they were alone?" Luc confirmed.

"Not exactly," Mary Elle admitted.

"Ah, I sense her angelic companion is about to make an appearance."

"Yes, but not immediately. First he tests Joseph. He wants to see if he's truly going to stay with her, to determine whether or not he's worthy of the Almighty's choice. He's aware of his doubts and fears and resentments. He knows of his self-pitying complaints…his questions of why me? So he waits."

Sighing, Luc offers, "He wants Joseph to suffer for his sins."

Mary Elle shrugged against his legs. "I wouldn't be surprised if that was part of his intent, but I think the greater part was he was giving Joseph a chance to redeem himself in Mary's eyes, and in God's. I think he was actually trying to be nice."

"Leaving a desperate man, terrified for his wife's sake alone with his fears is his way of being nice?"

"Yes. Joseph was more than he knew. More than has been captured by scripture. Gabriel was giving him the chance to become the man he already was."

"I'm not sure I follow you," Luc interrupted.

"There's no destiny at work in life, but there is potential. There are new heights to be reached and an evolutionary advancement possible in a soul's life, but it is up to each individual whether or not they choose to develop and manifest their potential. It's up to the individual to decide whether they will strive to reach beyond their current limitations and become more than they were; even more than they are in the very moment they are confronted with the choice to say yes to God's will in their lives or to turn away, to make excuses, to tell themselves what He asks is ridiculous, they're too busy, they must be imagining things. Mary wasn't the only one asked to make a choice. Gabriel was giving Joseph a chance to reaffirm his, or walk away. No one in his world would blame him if the truth came out he was not the father of his wife's child."

"People assume Mary was confronted with a single choice. Joseph made one choice, but that's not the way it works. They were confronted with their choices over and over. God gives us an out. We can walk away. This was Joseph's chance to go back to who he was...to step away from the insanity he was complaining about...to turn his back on the crazy turn his life took when he thought he was so lucky to have been the man chosen by the temple elders to be Mary's husband. If Joseph considered himself cheated, that God tricked him, here was God's messenger giving him an out. If Joseph believed he was pushed into making a commitment without all the facts in his possession, without knowing or fully comprehending what would be expected of him, now was his chance to walk away."

"Yes, but at what price?" Luc wondered.

"None."

Luc shook his head in disbelief. "He could just walk away? Without punishment? And the angel wouldn't strike him down for deserting God's chosen one?"

"No," Mary Elle answered with a certainty she rarely felt. "Joseph was given a rare gift, but he was under no obligation to accept it. There is no punishment for declining a gift."

"But he accepted the gift and the consequences accompanying it when he agreed to take Mary into his home," Luc protested.

"Lord Gabriel was giving him a chance to unmake his choice, to in essence choose again."

"Can he do that?"

"Yes of course. He is the holy one of God."

"What would have happened if Joseph changed his mind?"

Mary Elle shrugged and admitted, "I don't know. I don't get to see what would have happened."

"But Joseph didn't change his mind."

"No, and when the child's birth was approaching, Gabriel took pity on them both and made his presence known. Mary was so relieved to see him standing there at her feet, so happy he came back. The tears you see glittering in her eyes are happy tears. You can see the relief in her expression, because she knows everything will be all right now."

Mary Elle finished her recitation then returned her focus to the painting. There was still work to be done. Joseph could wait. Her earthly husband could not protect either his wife or the child she was about to give birth to with the same effectiveness of God's holy one. The truth was Mary needed the Archangel Gabriel more than she needed her husband in the moment.

Nodding, as if in response to a silent urging only she could hear, Luc watched Mary Elle reach down to pick up a paintbrush and begin mixing fresh paint. As much as he longed to watch the scene continue to unfold before him, he recognized their continued presence would be a level of intrusion Mary Elle would be uncomfortable with. So he reluctantly turned to usher his family away from the garden and leave his wife alone with her heavenly companions.

CHAPTER FORTY

It was late in the evening before Mary Elle returned to the house. She found Luc's family gathered in one of the large salons, and gasped delighted when she saw the large, artificial tree set up in the corner. Luc and his grandfather were unwinding a string of Christmas lights and wrapping them awkwardly if enthusiastically around the base of the tree. As promised, a veritable mountain of gifts was piled up in the corner, no doubt waiting to take their proper place beneath the tree once the decorations were complete. Smiling, Mary Elle thought this might turn out to be one of her best Christmases ever.

Hearing her surprise, both men turned to see her standing, smiling in the doorway. "We thought to wait for you, but Luc said there was no telling when you would finish your painting for the night."

She crossed the room and planted an affectionate kiss on Luc's grandfather's cheek. "Thank you for going to so much trouble for me. It's the most beautiful tree I've ever seen." She took the string of lights from his hand and made quick work of wrapping them around the tree and reaching for the strand in Luc's hand, connected the two and continued placing the lights around the tree. When she was finished she stepped back to admire her handy work.

Luc's grandfather looked ridiculously pleased with the effect. Mary Elle turned to smile at Luc and noticed even his uncle watched the process with what could only be described as an indulgent expression on his face.

"Can we help decorate the tree now?" Nina, Luc's niece

asked, her voice brimming with enthusiasm.

"There's more?" Mary Elle asked surprised, turning to Luc, who pointed in his grandfather's direction, where the older man was rooting around the wide base of the tree opening boxes containing extravagantly and clearly, expensively, decorated Christmas ornaments.

"Oh, my goodness. They're fabulous. I've never seen such beautiful ornaments." She exclaimed, and then hurried over to kneel next to Luc's grandfather to help him unpack the boxes.

The entire family got into the spirit of decorating the tree. When it was finished, Mary Elle stepped back to admire their teamwork. "Isn't this the most beautiful Christmas tree you've ever seen?"

"Certainly it is the most beautiful one I've ever had a hand in decorating," Luc replied.

The others laughed, agreeing with his ironic sentiment.

"Now, it is time for gifts?" Luc's grandfather inserted hopefully.

It took them over an hour to open all the gaily wrapped presents. Mary Elle was overwhelmed by the generosity of Luc's family. There were even gifts for her from Luc's uncle and his family. She was grateful Luc took care of reciprocating for both of them, so she wasn't alone in opening gifts.

"I wanted you to open this one last," Luc grandfather told her, handing her a small box, wrapped in silver and gold.

She met his anxious glance, and accepted the surprisingly heavy box from his hand. Her hands trembled slightly as she tore back the wrapping and lifted the lid off the box. Inside was a heavy gold necklace, in a purely Egyptian style. She suspected the large stones adorning it were genuine and felt the same awe of it as she did when Luc placed her sapphire and diamond engagement ring on her finger. "Oh, it's spectacular, but surely, you cannot mean to give me this. It's too much. I couldn't possibly accept this," she protested, lifting her gaze to his.

He waved off her protest. "You will accept my gift. This

necklace belonged to my wife. It would have passed to Luc's mother, my Miriam. It is yours now. I think my Miriam would approve, just as she would approve her son's choice for his wife."

"Oh, oh," Mary Elle brushed tears from her eyes and stood to hug the older man. His arms closed around her and she whispered in his ear, "I'm so happy Luc wanted to spend Christmas here. I was so nervous about meeting you, but you make me feel as if you're not disappointed he didn't choose a Muslim woman to marry."

He drew back to meet her tearful glance. Reaching up, he framed her face and assured her, "I too am glad my grandson persuaded you to share Christmas with us." Then he bent and whispered in her ear, "Disappointed? You bring him such joy, a joy I have never seen on his face before. I couldn't be more pleased with the new granddaughter he has given me."

He kissed the top of her head, and then released her. "If we are finished with the gifts, how about some Christmas cookies?"

Everyone laughed, but Luc protested. "I am not opposed to Christmas cookies, or the quintessential hot chocolate to accompany them, even though it is quite warm out this evening, but before we proceed, I believe my intended has forgotten something."

"I have?" Mary Elle asked confused.

"Something about a gift for me," he reminded her of her earlier promise.

"Oh, yes, of course. I can't believe I forgot. I'll be right back," she promised and dashed out of the room and up the stairs. She returned a few minutes later carrying a large, rectangular box, wrapped with heavy paper depicting the nativity, and a large red bow.

Luc accepted the box from her outstretched hands, eying her speculatively. She grinned back and urged him to open it. He sat in a chair and placed the heavy gift on his lap, then neatly removed the bow and tore off the wrap. Beneath the paper was a locked wooden box used for transporting paintings. Seeing it he raised his glance to hers and commented, "I must confess if this is a trick to disguise the true nature of your gift, and there is not a painting by American artist, Mary Elle McGann, inside, I am going to be severely disappointed."

Only grinning in reply, Mary Elle waited with butterflies in her stomach, while Luc unlocked the box and drew open the lid. His expression gave nothing away as his eyes took in the contents of the box. Finally, he raised his gaze to hers and Mary Elle expelled a sigh of relief at the look of pleasure she read in his.

"How did you know?"

She shrugged, not pretending she didn't comprehend what he was asking. "She knew you were wondering about him."

"The two of you discussed me?"

"Not exactly," she denied.

Grinning at her half denial, Luc returned his attention to the painting. "He is not going on loan to the museum to be included in the display of the Madonna exhibit."

"All right," she agreed smiling, when Luc referred to the painting as 'he' rather than it.

"May we see it?" Luc's grandfather asked, interrupting their cryptic exchange, unable to contain his curiosity any longer.

"Yes, of course, as long as we all understand this painting will be returning to Paris when we do."

Laughing at Luc's pointed possessiveness, his grandfather stood and came to stand behind Luc's chair to get a look at the painting on his lap. "Joseph," he announced in awed wonder.

"Yes," Mary Elle confirmed, her eyes glancing down at the painting where Joseph stood in his element, at work in his shop. Mary stood in the window of his house calling to him. Their eyes each held the other's glance, and what passed between them, was not to be dissected by others.

"Will you tell us about this painting the way you explained the nativity to us?" Luc's grandfather asked.

"No," Mary Elle replied softly, her glance meeting Luc's surprised one. "They are man and wife. What is between them should remain so."

Luc reached up to squeeze her hand and no one pressed her to provide context for the painting. "It's magnificent, every bit as good as the first two in the series. Jean Paul will be disappointed not to get his hands on it, but I intend for this to go immediately into my private collection and to never see the light of a museum. Unless you object to my plans for him?"

She shook her head. "No, I painted him for you." She was pleased he understood.

It was after midnight when they returned to their rooms. Luc caught her around the waist as the door closed behind them and pulled her back against him.

"I have to take a shower," Mary Elle demurred. "I'm a mess."

Luc swept her hair to the side and bent to kiss the nape of her neck, "Good idea," he said, against her flesh, his lips trailing up to nip her ear lobe. "I'll join you.

After their shared shower, Luc helped her dry her hair with a large bath towel and Mary Elle leaned into him and hugged him close and walked with him to the bed. Yawning audibly, she snuggled naked against Luc's warmth and admitted, "I'm so tired. I think I could sleep for a week."

Luc smiled at the ceiling, his arm wrapped close around her softness. He was aware of the request he was about to make forming in his mind. Mary Elle seemed in no hurry to exchange their wedding vows. He realized he had not been completely opposed to her delaying tactics. Maybe he was suffering from a case of temporary obsession. Maybe he would recover his prior discipline before it was too late, before he tied himself for life to this maddening, alluring woman. "Mary Elle?"

"Yes," she responded sleepily. She was feeling very relaxed after their shared shower. Her work on *The Nativity* was going well. Luc's grandfather didn't seem disappointed Luc had gotten himself engaged to her, and even Luc's uncle seemed to be coming around. All in all, it was a very good day. "I'm very pleased with your gift for me."

"I knew you would be," she said on a happy sigh as she drifted off to sleep.

"I have one more gift I would ask of you," he confided.

Mary Elle's brows scrunched together in confusion. She forced her heavy lids open and half rebuked him. "You do realize, don't you, the tradition at Christmas is to give gifts, not ask for them."

He chuckled. "I shall keep your advice in mind for next year, but for now, there is one more thing I'd like you to do for me."

"What is it?" The caution was back in her voice. Hearing it, Luc smiled. She evaded looking at him. He really must be losing his mind, as she so often accused him of.

"I want you to marry me."

There was a long pause after his request and then she replied, puzzled, "I don't understand. I thought when you asked me to marry you and I said yes, we moved past the asking part."

Luc smiled at her confusion then switched their places so he leaned over her where she lay in his bed, bracing his weight with his elbows. "True, but no matter how hard I nudge, you are still reluctant to set a date for our wedding." At her silence, he added, "I assure you, my love, I am not going to change my mind and decide my desire to marry you is a mistake. So there is no reason for us not to be wed without further delay. Here, in Egypt."

"You want to get married here?"

"For my grandfather. It would mean a great deal to him, especially since he was unable to witness his only daughter's wedding."

"That's not fair," Mary Elle protested.

"I know, love, but unfair or not, it doesn't diminish the truth of my assertion. We can have a second ceremony in France for the benefit of my grandparents and your parents, in the Catholic Church."

"You want us to have an Islamic wedding ceremony?" She echoed, and then at his confirming nod, added, awed, "Is that allowed?"

When he only grinned in response, she added, "I meant, are you allowed to marry outside your faith?"

"Are you?" he countered.

"Yes, as long as you agree to raise our children Catholic," she confessed miserably.

"Islam has the same requirement," he informed her.

"So what are we going to do?"

"Get married in both religions, and then raise our children, as I was, in the tenets of both Catholicism and Islam. When our children are old enough, they will decide for themselves which faith, or another, they wish to practice."

"You're serious?"

Luc shrugged. "It's how I was raised. I count myself fortunate."

"Isn't that cheating?" Mary Elle asked, awed by his audacity.

"I don't see how. We will keep our word and raise our children to respect the beliefs of both religions."

"I never considered raising our children in both religions an option," she admitted.

"And was this one of the reasons you were reluctant to set a wedding date?"

"Yes," she admitted, sighing.

"Now, you have run out of excuses. Marry me, Mary Elle. Let us begin our life together."

Still she hesitated, cautioning him. "It's not over yet."

"What's not over?"

"Whatever this is. Whatever I started with the Madonna

paintings. It's not finished. If we get married, I need you to promise me you won't try to stop me from finishing what I've started."

"Why would I?" He countered, perplexed.

"I don't know where all of this is leading. Remember Jonah?"

Luc smiled, "I doubt your work will lead you to share the prophet's fate, my love."

"Let's hope not, but I promised her I would see this through. If we're going to get married here, before I know where this is going, I need you to promise me you won't try to stop me from keeping my commitment to her."

His eyes probed hers, suspecting she was holding back some knowledge of what was coming to trigger his protective instincts. "I will give you my promise, if in return you will promise not to keep secret from me anything that could lead you into danger."

"All right, I promise. It's an easy promise for me to give you, Luc. I can't imagine how continuing the Madonna series could lead me into danger."

"And yet your home was broken into on the very night you returned to Pittsburgh."

She waved off the unpleasant reminder. "I really think the incident was just some random coincidence."

When she saw he didn't share her conclusion, she changed the subject. There was one more condition she wanted him to agree to before they were married. "Before we return to France, would it be all right if we stopped in Rome first?"

"I suspect your desire to visit Rome is not solely motivated by your wish to spend an entire day staring up at the Sistine Chapel," he commented, reminding her of a previous exchange between them.

"No, not entirely."

"You just promised me you would not keep secrets about your work," he reminded her, then added before she could interrupt, "Why Rome?"

Sighing, Mary Elle confessed, "Maybe because I won't go to Jerusalem and I know she won't let him force me to go."

He was silent for a moment after her disclosure, and then asked, "Why are you reluctant to visit Jerusalem? You've been to both Nazareth and Bethlehem."

"It's not the same. Don't you see? I can't bear to witness what she was forced to, to be forced to feel what she felt when her son was..."

"When her son was crucified."

"Yes."

"So why Rome? The virgin was never in Rome, was she?"

"I don't know. How can I know such a thing? I thought maybe she wants me to go to Rome because there's a substitute there."

"What do you mean?"

"Michelangelo's *Pieta* is on display at St. Peter's Basilica."

"The artist's sculpture of Mary holding her son's body after he was taken down from the cross."

"Yes," she confirmed, then asked anxiously, "Do you think she's disappointed in me because I won't go to Jerusalem? Because I won't let her show me? Do you think I should go?"

"No. I don't believe she's disappointed in you. How can you entertain such a worry?"

"You didn't answer my question. Do you think I should go to His holy city?"

He hesitated, then evaded answering her directly, "When you are ready to go, I will accompany you."

She shook her head and whispered, "I don't think I'll ever be ready to go. I can't have that in my head. It doesn't go away...what she shows me...it never goes away."

"Then after we are married, and have thoroughly enjoyed our honeymoon, I'll take you to Rome. Yes?"

Who was she trying to convince she could hold out against him? Luc or herself? "Yes."

CHAPTER FORTY-ONE

Mary Elle's hope they could visit St. Peter's as merely anonymous tourists was dashed before they even finished passing through security. Luc seemed amused by her disappointment at being recognized. A middle aged priest wearing a welcoming smile waited for them at the entrance to the basilica.

"Signorina McGann and Signore Bordeaux, it is both a pleasure and an honor to welcome you to Vatican City. I am Monsignor Antonio Citino. I cannot express to you Signorina how much I admire your work and how eagerly I and my fellow priests await your next offering. We are all speculating on whether or not the next installment will be the Visitation or a completely different moment in our lady's life."

"The Nativity," Mary Elle responded to his curiosity, and the priest clapped his hands together.

"I will be among the first in line when it is available for public display."

"Thank you."

"How may I serve you today? Have you visited with us before? Would you like me to arrange a tour?"

At Mary Elle's imploring look, Luc stepped in to fill the silence. "Thank you, for your kind welcome, Monsignor. I believe my wife would prefer to simply take in the magnificence of the basilica at her own pace."

The Monsignor nodded his understanding, "Yes, of

course and forgive me, Signore Bordeaux, for my earlier misapprehension. I had not heard Signorina McGann was now officially Signora Bordeaux. My congratulations."

"Thank you."

"I will leave you to enjoy your visit. Please alert one of the guards if you are in need of anything. They will find me. We are honored to have you."

Michelangelo's *Pieta* was their first stop. Luc stood silently behind her as Mary Elle took in the magnificence of the artist's genius. Upon its completion in 1499 the artist was criticized for the youth of the virgin depicted in the work. Michelangelo answered his critics by explaining the virgin's youth represented the incorruptible nature of the chaste. Mary Elle agreed with the artist's vision. The work was so much more powerful a contrast with the young, beautiful woman holding the broken body of her dead son across her lap. It resonated with her particularly because all of her interaction with the virgin was as a young woman. Mary Elle felt tears prick her eyes as she beheld the sculpture but no visions assailed her of the actual event, and the virgin's eyes, while undeniably beautiful, remained vacant and fixed on her fallen son.

Mary Elle looked up to meet Luc's glance, and shaking her head in answer to his silent inquiry, let him lead her away. They wandered around the huge structure in no particular order, pausing before Bernini's baldachin directly under the dome of the basilica, marking the spot of St. Peter's tomb underneath. She was overwhelmed by the artistry, awed by its genius and history, by the way reverence and art were merged into a single complementary whole, but she felt no particular attraction to any single piece.

Discouraged, Mary Elle sought refuge in a small chapel along the north aisle. There was a sign at the entrance admonishing those who sought entrance to remain silent within, as the chapel was reserved for prayer and reflection. There was a guard at the door, who nodded in their direction as they passed the threshold. The chapel was circular, with rows of chairs across the back wall, and a small shrine to the virgin on one side, with candles burning before it. Fresco paintings lined the walls, but there was no singular spectacular work by a famous artist to attract visitors. In fact there were less than a dozen other people in the room, none of them giving Mary Elle more than a passing glance. She crossed the small space to light a candle before the shrine to the virgin. Luc took a seat in the gallery and waited for her.

Still smiling, she fished her offering through the slot and lit a candle, kneeling in front of the painted statue of the virgin and bowing her head. "I'm not sure where we go from here. Maybe I misunderstood and I didn't need to be here, after all. I have this impression we're not finished yet, but maybe it's because I just can't bear the thought of letting you go."

She waited, hoping for a sign, but there was nothing. Sighing softly, she added a prayer of thanksgiving for all she was given and slowly rose to her feet. She turned back to where Luc sat waiting for her and her heart stuttered when their glances met. How was it possible a year earlier she was a simple, high school teacher back in the states? She looked around her, overwhelmed. Here she was in Rome, at a chapel in St. Peter's Basilica and the man she never dared dream could be hers was now her husband and was sitting there, waiting patiently for her to finish a crazy errand, the purpose of which was unknown to both of them.

Offering another, more heartfelt prayer of thanksgiving, Mary Elle felt a subtle change come over the atmosphere of the small chapel. It was as if the chapel itself recognized the presence of the one to whom its simple shrine was devoted to.

Drawn as she was at the Church of the Annunciation in Nazareth, Mary Elle stepped towards the center of the circular space, glancing around, looking for any sign of the reason she was brought here. Sensing movement near her, she looked down to see the little girl from the first night smiling up at her through her dark eyes holding no hint of the fear evident at their first introduction.

Mary Elle squatted down so they were eye to eye, but her heart was too full to force any words to pass through her lips. She watched as the young virgin spread her arms wide and then spun in circles like a little girl unable to contain her happiness.

Smiling, catching a hint of her carefree mood, Mary Elle watched overjoyed at the girl's light-hearted display but was puzzled by the circumstance of her being a little girl again. When she stopped spinning and dropped her arms to her waist, she stood staring up at Mary Elle with an expectant, pleading look in her eyes.

"What is it? What do you want me to do for you?" Mary Elle asked softly, aware from the lack of reaction of the few remaining visitors in the small chapel, no one else saw what she did.

"I want you to paint me a picture," the girl confided.

"All right," Mary Elle readily agreed, smiling. "What do you want me to paint this time?"

The young virgin stood there smiling for a moment, then holding Mary Elle's glance, she swung her arm out wide, and repeated, "I want you to paint me a picture."

Confused, Mary Elle followed the motion of her arm, and then gasped incredulous at what her eyes beheld. The small chapel was transformed before her vision, scene after scene from the virgin's life was captured and played out in the depictions of the mysteries of the rosaries. There were dozens of paintings, maybe hundreds of them.

It was too much for Mary Elle to take in and she dropped to her knees. When she raised her glance to the center wall above where the rows of seats were lined up like pews, there was a large unadorned panel. It was out of place in her vision, where every other square inch of wall was filled with painted images. Puzzled, she turned to see the virgin followed her glance and stood staring up at the wall, then she turned to meet Mary Elle's questioning glance.

The look she gave her was filled with sadness and compassion. Mary Elle understood without words what the missing scene depicted. It would be given her when she returned to Jerusalem to follow the winding path of the *Via Dolorosa* to its bloody consummation. All of her evasions were for naught.

She drew her eyes from the empty wall and took a final look around the chapel before the visions slowly faded, restoring the humble chapel back to its current state where it reflected what was, rather than the possibilities of what could be. If she was intimidated by each blank canvas she confronted on her simple, single easel, there were no words to describe what she felt now.

The anxious, hopeful expression was back in the young virgin's eyes when their glances met. Mary Elle knew she was waiting for her answer. 'I want you to paint me a picture. You are the chosen one. If you will not help me there is no one else.'

So, this was her test, her moment of truth. She made no attempt to deceive herself she could honor her commitment to the virgin and return to France with Luc and begin their married life together. Their divorce could be easily arranged. She wouldn't blame him. Already mourning her incomprehensible, inconsolable loss she nodded in answer to the little girl's unspoken question. A brilliant smile bloomed on her young face and then she left her.

Mary Elle sat back on her knees and covered her face with her hands, unable to process the depths of her grief. When she struggled clumsily back to feet, Luc was there, concern in his glance as his eyes took in her white face and shaky stance. Her dazed glance met his, but no words formed on her lips. What was there to say? How could she explain their life was over before it even began? "Mary Elle?"

"I can't tell you, not here, not now. Can we go?" she asked, a hint of the desperation she was feeling evident in her voice and in her glance.

He hesitated, and then replied, "Yes, of course."

There was no one else in the chapel. Mary Elle didn't realize it was Monsignor Citino's doing until she saw him standing guard at the door. She tensed when they approached the exit and Luc squeezed her hand reassuringly.

"Signora Bordeaux, I will not ask you to share with me the contents of the revelations you received from our lady, but before you leave us, I would like to relate the history of this chapel to you."

"Another time, perhaps," Luc interjected.

"We will be ready, Signora Bordeaux, when you are."

Mary Elle nodded, and leaning into Luc's comforting strength she passed through the guarded entrance to the chapel without a backward glance.

Luc didn't press her on the way to the airport where his plane waited for them. Nor did he prod at her during the flight back to Paris. Later as they prepared for bed, Luc gathered her in his arms and pulled her close against his chest, reminding her of her promise to him, "No secrets, *Mon amour*. Tell me what the virgin asked of you." Mary Elle hid her face against his chest.

"Mary Elle?"

Without warning she burst into hysterical, heart-wrenching sobs. Luc made no effort to calm her. Instead he lifted her in his arms and carried her to bed, cradling her against his chest, his fingers threading through her hair in long soothing strokes and simply waited for the tears to exhaust themselves.

"We shouldn't have gotten married," she whispered through her slowing sobs.

Luc lifted her chin so she was forced to meet his glance. "You do not wish to be my wife?"

"I didn't say that."

"No, forgive me, your claim we should not have gotten married sounded like regret to me."

"You don't understand."

"Agreed."

Mary Elle pulled away from his restraining arms and crossed her legs, facing him. "She said she wants me to paint her a picture."

"I do not think such a simple request would lead you to conclude you should not have married me."

Mary Elle threaded her fingers through her hair. "It's not *a* picture. It's dozens, hundreds even. She wants me to cover the chapel with scenes from the mysteries, and other scene not yet acknowledged mysteries, but will be, I think. We've lost so much. She plans to fill in the missing gaps."

"And what does the virgin's request have to do with our marriage?"

"I can't paint the chapel from Bordeaux. It's fresco. What am I talking about? The church is not going to just let me paint over the paintings already on the walls of the chapel. They're probably the work of some famous renaissance painter."

"I would not attempt to deceive yourself with your argument, my love. I believe Monsignor Citino made the church's position on the matter very clear."

"But he didn't know. How could he know what she would ask me?"

"Didn't wish to relate to you the history of the chapel? Perhaps they've been expecting you."

"Maybe," she conceded, and then added, "What are we doing to do?"

"Mary Elle, do you remember the promise you asked of me, before you would agree to marry me?"

Too upset to think clearly, Mary Elle shook her head.

"You made me promise I would not interfere with your commitment to the virgin."

"Neither of us was expecting this."

"It doesn't matter. Do you have so little faith in me? Did you truly believe I would let you go?"

"You won't try to stop me?"

"No."

"But my work is in Rome."

"Yes. We are not the first couple to work in different cities."

"How about different countries?"

"We will work this out."

"You don't want a divorce?"

He laughed. "Is that what you thought?"

"Yes."

"Do you remember your commitment to me? Always, forever. I will never let you go. You were willing to give up your former life for me. I will offer no less to you."

CHAPTER FORTY-TWO

The Vatican issued a press release today announcing American artist Mary Elle McGann Bordeaux, wife of French industrialist, Luc Bordeaux, was selected to oversee the renovation of a chapel in St. Peter's Basilica, devoted to the Virgin Mary. The renovation will consist of original fresco works by the artist inspired by the mysteries of the rosary. Once complete the chapel will be re-consecrated to the virgin.

CHAPTER FORTY-THREE

Ironically, as soon as she learned Luc would not stand in her way of keeping her commitment to the virgin, Mary Elle was in no hurry to return to Rome. She couldn't bear the thought of being separated from Luc for long stretches at a time. Since Luc was in no hurry for her to leave France their time together stretched from long weeks into months. The truth was she was afraid to begin. Memories of the small chapel were imprinted on her brain. The thought of delving into each small square and pulling from it the fleeting vision the virgin revealed to her and translating it fresco style onto the chapel walls was overwhelming.

She never even attempted a fresco project. She did some research into the process since returning to France, but she honestly wasn't sure she was capable of fulfilling the virgin's request. It was as if she stood at the edge of very steep cliff face. It would take a leap of faith to step off of it. She wasn't sure she possessed such faith.

Her delaying tactics were not without price. Her resistance to the will pulling her back to Rome was proving exhausting. She could barely get through the day without retreating to their rooms for an afternoon nap. She battled both headaches when she fought against the visions and nausea when she surrendered to them. It took her several weeks before she realized the cause of her symptoms wasn't brought about solely by her reluctance to return to Italy. She was pregnant with Luc's child.

The realization gave rise to all sorts of conflicting emotions within her. One minute she was ecstatic at the prospect of having Luc's baby, the next she was nervous about his reaction. They hadn't really discussed children yet. The one reaction she wasn't expecting was a compelling sense of urgency to return to Rome and begin her work on the chapel. It was as if the virgin understood, better than she did at this point, a baby would prove a true threat to Mary Elle's work on the chapel.

She vacillated back and forth about whether or not to share the news of her pregnancy with Luc. He was the baby's father. Of course he deserved to know as quickly as possible. He would be thrilled, wouldn't he? What if he wasn't? What if he tried to stop her from returning to Rome?

In the end she compromised. She began making concrete plans to fulfill her commitment to the virgin. She contacted Monsignor Citino and informed him she would arrive by the end of the month to commence work on the chapel. He seemed generally thrilled with her pledge, and expressed his assurance the church would provide everything necessary for her work, including an apartment in Vatican City for as long as she needed one.

She was as prepared for her upcoming separation from Luc as she ever would be, which was not at all, she acknowledged readily enough, but she was now committed to return to Rome. The only thing left for her to do was to tell Luc she was leaving…next week. She was waiting for him on the terrace, where they dined their first night together. Even though the early spring made it a little chilly to have dinner outside, it seemed a fitting place to inform Luc he was going to be a father.

He caught up with her there in the early evening when he returned home from work. She was wrapped up in a quilt on one of the chaises. She fell asleep waiting for him. His lips brushed her skin, bringing her awake. Their eyes met, his tender, hers wary.

"You're home," she whispered, bringing a smile to his face.

"Yes. You sound surprised," he replied. "Are we dining on the terrace this evening?"

Mary Elle struggled to sit up and clear her head from its lingering fuzziness from her nap. The temperature had dropped another ten degrees, making Luc's question not a purely rhetorical one.

"It was warmer earlier," she defended her plan.

Smiling, Luc sat down beside her on the chaise, lifted her onto his lap and pulled her back against his chest. Sighing, Mary Elle snuggled close against him. "Was there a particular reason you wished to dine on the terrace this evening?"

She lifted her head from his chest so she could meet his half curious, half amused glance. "We have to talk."

"You wish to return to Rome," Luc stated, his eyes probing hers.

"Yes. I have to go back. Staying here pretending it's not going to be awful to leave you isn't going to make the eventual goodbye any easier. If anything, it's only prolonging the inevitable."

"Yes, but now you are ready?"

"I don't think I'll ever be ready, but I know I can't walk away from this, so it doesn't make sense to continue putting things off," she hesitated, and then admitted anxiously, "I informed Father Citino I would arrive in Rome by the end of the month. He said they would have an apartment waiting for me for as long as I needed one."

"Thoughtful of him," Luc replied with only mild sarcasm in his voice, "but you will not be availing yourself of the good Father's generosity."

"I won't?" Mary Elle countered confused.

Luc shifted her on his lap so he could reach into his pocket. From it, he retrieved a heavy iron key and offered it to her. Mary Elle eyed it, confused, accepted it and then raised an inquiring glance to Luc's. "What is this?"

"It is a key to the villa I purchased for us in Rome. It is within walking distance to the basilica and is staffed and waiting for us."

Mary Elle was so overwhelmed by his generous gesture she burst into tears. To think he made all the arrangements, knowing she would one day gather the courage to return to Rome. He even purchased a home for them and staffed it, showing her in no uncertain terms he meant to honor his commitment to her. Yet she was dishonest with him; afraid to confide in him the truth about the baby.

Luc didn't seem the least bit surprised by her emotional display. He merely smiled and held her while she cried against his chest. When her tears subsided, he asked, gently teasing her, "You would prefer to live in the Vatican apartment?"

Miserably, she shook her head. "There's something else I have to tell you," she confessed, warily meeting his glance.

"You've decided you wish me to grant you a divorce, after all?"

"This isn't funny. I should have told you before. I didn't know how. I was afraid you wouldn't let me go back."

Luc didn't seem particularly concerned about her rambling confession. "What is it you wish to confess to me?"

"I'm pregnant." The admission left her lips in a soft whisper. Her eyes were downcast so she couldn't see his reaction.

"I know."

"What?!" Her head shot up to meet his glance. "How do you know? I didn't even know."

"I've been waiting for you to consider the possibility. You've been displaying all the symptoms." He ticked them off on his fingers, "You've been sleeping more, you're nauseous most mornings, your breasts are more sensitive and slightly larger in my hands and you've been more emotional than usual. I was hoping all of these clues pointed to you being pregnant, but then you never said anything. What is it, love?

Are you not ready to become a mother? I know we haven't discussed children except in the vaguest of terms…"

Mary Elle shook her head. He knew. He recognized the signs before she did. She supposed she shouldn't be surprised, but she was, and confused. "Are you happy about the baby?"

His eyes filled with pleasure. "Very happy, but I'm waiting for you to tell me why you're not."

"It's not that I'm not happy about the baby, but I have to go back to Rome. I was afraid you would try to stop me."

"Admittedly, there's a part of me that would prefer to keep you locked up and all to myself with me in France, but I recognize such an attitude is, regrettably, no longer acceptable in these modern times. So I will ask you to be very careful and not overdo, and for your promise you will eat and sleep regularly, and not protest too much when I insist Aman remain with you in Italy the weeks I must return to Paris to work."

"But…"

He held up an imperious finger, silencing her instinctive protest. "No buts, my love. I would not be able to focus on my work if I left you completely alone in Italy. I would prefer Aman remain with you."

She sighed, and offered only a minor objection to his insistence, "I would hardly be alone at the Vatican. There are thousands of visitors every day."

"Yes, I know. I would prefer none of them bothered my wife."

Mary Elle nodded, surrendering. All in all she couldn't believe how reasonable Luc was being about all this. "You're really happy about the baby?"

He laughed. "How can you doubt it?"

"Your grandfather will be thrilled," Mary Elle remarked, thinking about Luc's grandfather's reaction to a new great-grandson or daughter.

"He already is," Luc confided grinning.

"What?" Mary Elle countered, "You told him before you

told me?" Her protest sounded ridiculous even to her own ears and she really couldn't blame Luc for laughing in her face.

CHAPTER FORTY-FOUR

They left for Rome at the end of the week. Mary Elle was delighted with the villa on the river Luc purchased for them, though she considered villa a somewhat understated term for his gift. Estate came closer to the mark. The property was gated, no doubt a reflection of Luc's obsession with security, but it was also magnificent, magical, a Renaissance era mansion with lots of open air terraces and patios. The gardens were just beginning to come to life in the warming temperatures provided by the longer days of early spring. Mary Elle couldn't wait to see them in full bloom.

Best of all, the property was only a short walk to St. Peter's, though Luc had no intention of allowing her to walk among the crowds milling daily around St. Peter's Square near the entrance to the basilica. She was so happy he was being reasonable about her returning to work on the chapel given her pregnancy, she submitted with only minimal protest to his dictate Aman would drive her each morning to work in the basilica and return for her when she was ready to leave for the day. He made his feelings on the matter of her mode of transportation very clear. She was not to walk home alone in the evenings.

Mary Elle's independent streak wanted to assert itself against what she considered his somewhat draconian dictates but she accepted he was worried about both her and the baby. After what happened when she returned home to Pittsburgh alone, she knew any protest on her part would fall on deaf ears, anyway. So she surrendered to his conditions with good grace, and reminded herself she should be grateful for his care and concern for her and the baby.

Luc stayed with her the first few weeks while she settled into her new routine. Mary Elle knew his other reason for remaining in Italy with her was to assure himself she was eating and sleeping sensibly and not putting in too many hours working. More than once he appeared at the entrance to the chapel in the early evening hours searching for her. When he spotted her perched thirty feet above the ground, with paintbrush in hand and her arm stretched over the railing towards the image she was working on, he climbed the scaffolding set up for her use and all but dragged her back down to earth, berating her all the way down.

"If this is your idea of eating regularly and not overdoing, we need to reopen this discussion."

Mary Elle would dutifully apologize, only then realizing how exhausted and hungry she was. She would lean gratefully into his side and let him tuck her into the rear of the limo and take her home.

Today was one of those days she became so wrapped up in her work Luc was forced to retrieve her once again from her perch on the scaffolding. She sat opposite him at the table on the terrace with the failing evening light reflecting off the river, struggling to keep her eyes open.

"You must eat something before you fall asleep, Mary Elle."

She nodded and forced herself to sit up straighter in her chair and reached for her fork. "I know. I'm sorry, it's just so overwhelming. I'll settle in. I did eat the lunch Signora Merrelli sent. The doctor says we're doing fine," she reminded him at his doubtful look.

"He also said you need to take care not to overdo," Luc reminded her.

"I know. I'm really trying," she promised him.

He nodded, sighing in resignation, and then broached the

subject he'd been avoiding, "I will be away for the next ten days. I need to return to Paris to work and then I have business in both London and Vienna."

Mary Elle tried to hide the stunned tears she could feel stinging her eyes. She knew this day was coming. Before they left Paris, they agreed Luc would work from Rome for two weeks of each month. He was already there four. He needed to return to his own routine and his own work. She respected that, but the thought of him leaving her and not being able to be with him at night and wake up the next morning wrapped close in his arms, was devastating.

"Mary Elle?" he prodded, at her continued silence.

She forced a stilted smile to her lips and bravely met his glance after first blinking away her betraying tears. "Yes, yes of course you have to go. I really appreciate you staying with me for so long and helping me get settled."

He rose from his chair and pulled her from hers, hugging her close and bending to drop a kiss on the top her head, where it was nestled close beneath his chin. "I will return a week from Thursday. Aman will remain with you." When she would have protested, he cut her off, "We've already agreed on this."

Sighing audibly, she nodded and wrapped her arms close around his waist, clinging to him even as she acknowledged silently this would be only the first of many such painful partings.

A month later, she climbed out of the rear of the limousine after her regular appointment with her and the baby's doctor. She was happy to be able to report to Luc Doctor Martella confirmed everything was going well with her pregnancy. Even though she was not yet in maternity clothes, the baby was growing and moving regularly now. They elected not to learn the sex of their baby in advance. Both of them wanted to be surprised.

Smiling, she hung up with Luc and began weaving her way across the crowded square towards the entrance to St. Peter's.

She preferred to arrive in the early morning hours before the basilica opened to the public, but her morning appointment with the doctor delayed her. She kept her head down so as not to attract any attention and made her way across the wide square only just beginning to fill with tourists.

She heard the sound of running steps behind her, but she didn't turn around, preferring to remain as anonymous as possible. There were a few times since her arrival in Rome when she was recognized, but each time Luc was with her and his presence was seemingly intimidating enough to put off even the most enthusiastic fan.

"Madame Bordeaux!" The sound of her own name shouted in Aman's familiar voice, reached her above the noise of the crowd. The unfamiliar sense of urgency it contained startled her enough to halt abruptly and turn around to try to locate him in the crowd. The small, sudden movement on her part probably saved her life.

It wasn't Aman she heard running towards her. No the figure looming over her, his features contorted into a mask of hatred was screaming at her with the voice of a madman. "Filthy Muslim whore! Blasphemer! Devil's spawn!"

Shocked, horrified, Mary Elle put her hands out in front of her in an instinctive, defensive gesture even as she tripped over own feet in her awkward hurry to back away from the evil affronting her. Too late she became terrifyingly aware of the wicked-looking knife he brandished wildly in one hand even as the filthy rampage he directed at her continued to pour forth from lips that almost frothed with fury.

Her eyes locked onto the knife as it descended towards her. Her breath stopped. Time froze even as her feet and limbs were suddenly rooted in place. She couldn't make her hands move fast enough to block the rapid approach of the blade glinting dazzlingly in the bright sunlight of a cloudless spring morning. Her legs felt like lead beneath her. Panic rose within her chest and choked off whatever self-preservation instincts she possessed that were even now urging her to take a stand or take flight. Either. Anything but to just simply stand there and allow herself to be slaughtered like some sacrificial lamb at the center of an ancient, barbaric ritual.

Her inner voice was screaming at her desperately to move…to do something, anything before it was too late. It felt like an eternity she watched the point of the steel stalking her, knowing when it struck, the pain would be horrific, unlike anything she ever endured. She supposed it was only a matter of seconds, even fractions of a second, before the blade met soft, yielding flesh, inches below her left shoulder. Part of her recognized her attacker was aiming for her heart. His intent to kill. Somehow her slight, sudden movement managed to deflect his aim somewhat. The realization was her last rational thought. She was instantly and completely overwhelmed by the ghastly sight of her own blood erupting in deep, thick red from the wound he inflicted on her to splatter in a wide arc over both of their faces and cover the hand still holding the blade buried to the hilt against her chest.

The pain was instantaneous. Hideous. Horrendous as the blade struck and sank deeper, seeking her heart through flesh and bone, all the while the echo of her assailant's filth spewed from his mouth, competing for her attention against her agonized pain and her terror for her life and for that of her unborn child. She tried to reach up her arms to push the blade away, but her left arm was dead.

Even as she saw over her attacker's shoulder Aman's anguished, pleading face rushing towards her, further resistance was beyond her capabilities. Her legs simply refused to keep her upright any longer. She thought she must have screamed her outrage at the appalling pain assaulting her and at her assailant's angry, vicious rage. No one had ever struck her before. She couldn't even recall a single instance when her parents spanked her as a child.

Her last thought before the blessed darkness stole over her was a simple plea to God, "Please don't let this be the end. I need to see him again. I need Luc. I need our baby. Don't let me die."

CHAPTER FORTY-FIVE

Luc was there when she woke up. God must have heard her prayer after all, or maybe she was already in heaven. That must be it. How else could Luc get there so quickly? It couldn't be heaven. Luc wasn't dead. Where was this place? Then the memories returned with a suddenness and a viciousness leaving her reeling. She gasped in fear, struggling to sit up, wincing against the pain of trying to move her left side.

"You're awake, thank Allah. How are you feeling? Are you in pain? What can I get for you?"

The questions poured out of Luc one after the other unchecked, not pausing to give her time to answer one before the next flooded forth. Mary Elle had never seen Luc in such a state. She was so happy to see him, to realize he was really there with her; she leaned back against the pillows and just lay there smiling up into his beautiful, anxious face. Her lips curved in a radiant smile as she remembered thinking when the lunatic attacked her she might never get to see him again. "Aman saved me. I'm so glad you're here."

Luc briefly closed his eyes at her words and his lips moved in what looked like a silent prayer before he reached out a trembling hand to smooth the tendrils of her hair back from her forehead. "Where else would I be, love? I should never have left you," he told her in a voice filled with regret.

"Don't be silly. You have your work, your life…" She broke off when she saw his fierce expression.

"You are my life, Mary Elle. Do you have any conception what I went through when I heard you were attacked and I couldn't reach you?"

"For a moment I was afraid if he killed me, I would never get to see you again," she confessed and then it was as if everything hit her at once... what might have happened if Aman wasn't there to save her. She burst into tears and seeing her distress, Luc climbed into the hospital bed with her and carefully gathered her into his arms while she sobbed against his neck.

"Sh, sh, it's all right now, you're safe, our baby is safe. I'm here now and I will never let you go again."

Awash in gratitude at the realization of how close she came to losing this, to losing Luc, Mary Elle's sobs quieted and she closed her eyes, drifting in a lovely half sleep with the soothing sound of Luc's promises filling her mind and chasing away her fear. She understood what he vowed was impossible. Of course they would be forced apart again by the demands of life, even the demands of just an ordinary life, but still they comforted her.

She was only half-listening to what he was telling her. It was enough for now just to be alive. Then something Luc was saying caught her attention and she shook her head dazedly to clear her confusion, trying to catch up with what he was telling her.

"....the doctor says you won't need additional surgery and there is no reason we cannot return to France in a few days. They would like to keep you for another night or two for observation, but they assure me it is purely a precautionary measure."

"Return to France?" Mary Elle echoed, confused.

"Yes of course. Unless you prefer we return to Cairo. My grandfather is frantic and has been calling me every few hours for an update."

"But, Luc, I can't return to France. My work is here."

Her protest fell on deaf ears. "Your work will be here waiting for you after you are fully recovered." There was a hardness in his voice she couldn't recall hearing before.

"So I'll return to Rome in a few weeks." She threw out just

in case she was misinterpreting his intent.

His jaw tightened at her persistence. "We'll discuss your return at a later date."

Beginning to panic at his implacable tone, Mary Elle countered, "I think we better discuss it now, before I agree to return to France with you."

"Agree to return with me?" He echoed incredulously. "You are my wife. There is no question of you remaining in Italy. You are not safe here."

"Don't be silly. There are fanatics everywhere. I imagine there is even one or two lurking in the bucolic Bordeaux countryside."

"You dare to joke about this? Do you have any conception of what I've been through? Do you honestly expect me to allow you to put yourself at risk again for another lunatic to take a slice out of you? What if Aman wasn't with you? What if I had not insisted he remain with you at all times… and I seem to recall you fought me every step of the way on that precaution."

"You were right. I'm really glad he was there to save me, but I'm not sure I understand exactly what you mean about not allowing me to put myself at risk again. This is my work. I can no more walk away from it than you could from what you do."

"No one is trying to kill me for running a business."

"But they could."

"When they do, we can re-open this discussion. We're leaving Thursday."

"No."

"No?" Rather than raising his voice, Luc's dropped an octave when he was angry. She had to admit it was very effective as an intimidation tool. Since it was the first time she could recall him employing it with her, the tactic was all the more effective.

With an effort, she stood her ground. "I can't leave Italy until you promise me you won't stand in the way of my returning to finish my work on the chapel once my arm is healed."

Luc stood in one swift movement, his frustration evident at her stubbornness. He even retreated a step from her bedside, as if he couldn't trust himself to remain in close proximity with her, and at the same time resist the temptation to shake some sense into her. "Mary Elle, you are my wife. You carry my child. I will not permit you to put yourself and our child at risk by continuing to be a target for every extremist Christian fanatic or Islamic jihadist who has decided your continued existence is somehow a threat to his cause."

"Our baby is fine," she protested.

"By the merest stroke of providence."

"So because I'm pregnant, I can't paint," she threw back, equally frustrated.

"You can paint in Bordeaux."

"Oh really? How am I supposed to paint the chapel in Bordeaux?" She abandoned all attempts at placating Luc's temper. She was having a hard enough time controlling her own.

"You can paint the canvases at the estate and they can be transported to Rome once they're complete."

Realizing incredulously he was completely serious, Mary Elle struggled into a seated position, wincing at the weight she carelessly placed on her injured side. "The chapel is fresco. Unless you can figure out a way to transport the entire chapel from Rome to Bordeaux and back again, it is impossible for me to continue my work on the chapel in Bordeaux."

She was so upset she didn't realize she was nearly shouting by the time she finished her mocking protest to his assumption she would simply fall into his plans for her life and abandon what she knew would be the most important work of her life.

"You can simply inform the church fresco is no longer an option. They'll adjust."

She was stupefied by his calm assurance he could simply order the Catholic Church around as easily he presumed he could her. "They'll adjust? Just like that? It's not that simple and I would think you of all people would understand. What makes you think this is your decision anyway? How dare you presume you can order my life around as though I were a child!"

"If you would stop behaving like a child, I wouldn't need to order you're life as though you were one."

Then it hit her. He was worried about the baby...his child. He meant to keep her in France until after the baby was born. Then he would come up with another excuse and another. 'The baby was too young to be without its mother. Surely she could see that...' And what would happen if there was another child after this one? If Luc had his way she would never return to Italy to finish her work on the virgin's chapel. "I think you should leave now before one of us says something we can't take back."

"Mary Elle..."

"No. I can't talk to you about this anymore right now. I know you love me and you're afraid for me and our baby. I'm afraid to, but right now I'm more afraid of you than of what awaits me out there."

The color drained from Luc's face at her quiet accusation. Pulling himself together with obvious effort, he retreated behind a wall of calm stoicism. "I see. Then I will leave you safely alone."

Mary Elle bit down on the urge to call him back the second he turned away from her and passed stiffly through the door. Bare minutes later, a nurse came in to make sure she was comfortable. The expression in her eyes told Mary Elle she heard her argument with Luc. Recalling how they were practically shouting at each other, Mary Elle guessed the entire floor heard their argument.

Wouldn't the revelation add a little more fuel to the media storm no doubt brewing outside her sanitized hospital room? Signora Bordeaux was pregnant. The artist behind the Madonna series was soon to be a mother herself. Maybe the lunatics should just form a line for their turn to carve a slice out of her, as Luc so graphically put it.

She waved the hovering nurse away and then turned over on her uninjured side. Facing the wall she wept until she fell into a fitful sleep. She tossed and turned in her sleep, attempting to find a comfortable position. The pain medication must have worn off, because her shoulder felt like it was on fire.

She woke in the middle of the night. Her room was dark, but a dim light burned over the door, casting a soft glow over the shadows in the room. She searched them almost frantically, but Luc hadn't returned. A desolate sob escaped her and she suddenly felt terribly alone. She muffled the sound of her tears with the blanket so as not to alert one of the attentive nurses and eventually cried herself back into a fitful sleep.

The drugs made her dreams vivid, chaotic, and mixed with the violent memories of the attack. There was blood everywhere. She looked around desperately for Aman to save her, but she was alone. Maybe Luc didn't care if anyone saved her this time. Her attacker's accusations echoed in a bizarre cacophony through her confused dreams, '...devil's spawn... Islamic whore....evil masquerading as the virgin's servant...'

Terrified, Mary Elle tried desperately to escape the point of the knife coming towards her. It was shiny and pure, as if the madman wielding it prepared it especially to use on her flesh. Shaking, horrified, she finally pulled herself free of the bloody dream. Sweating from the exertion she painfully sat up in bed then turned her attention to her trembling hands when she realized they felt sticky. Confused, she raised them to her face. They were covered in blood.

Frozen with fresh fear, she tried to scream but the sound of her terror got stuck in her throat. Terrified her attacker managed to escape police custody and sought her out to finish his bloody intent, only this time making sure her baby didn't survive, Mary Elle forced the next scream past the blockage in her throat, and then another and another.

They heard her this time. They all rushed into her room at once. The white-coated doctors shoved an astonished Aman out of their way as they hurried to her side. From the horrified, pitying looks on their faces, she knew her baby was dead. He won after all. She felt the pain then, as if his blade pierced her stomach and carved her child from her womb. It didn't matter how much medication they pumped into her. There was no solace to ease the pain of her loss.

When she regained consciousness, Mary Elle thought she heard the sound of Luc's voice. She looked around eagerly, needing him, then confused when she couldn't find him by her side, she heard him again, standing just outside her door.

"How is my wife?"

She thought she heard a regretful sigh in response to his worried question and wondered if doctors were taught the technique in medical school along with anatomy and physiology. A vaguely familiar voice replied cautiously to Luc's inquiry, "She is fragile, Signor Bordeaux."

"May I sit with her?"

"Yes, of course."

Mary Elle quickly closed her eyes, feigning sleep as the door widened and Luc entered. 'Fragile.' She hated the word. She especially hated it being applied to her. 'Fragile. What did that mean anyway?'

She was aware of Luc lowering himself into the chair by her side and reaching for her hand. He clasped her chilled one between both of his, and then bent his head to rest its weight on her captive hand. She felt his tears seep between his fingers and onto her skin, then felt the sting of her own in her eyes, and immediately abandoned all thoughts of feigning sleep.

"Oh, Luc! I lost our baby. I'm so sorry. I'm so sorry."

His pain-filled eyes met her desolate ones. "Beloved, it wasn't your fault. I shouldn't have upset you. I'm sorry. I should never have left you alone, again. Will I ever be there for you when you need me?"

She burst into tears, shaking her head. "Don't say that. How can you say that? You're always there when I need you. It was my fault. Of course you would be worried about the baby. Now, I can't undo it, I can't take it back. The baby's gone. Our baby's gone."

He joined her in the bed and gathered her gently into his arms, comforting her as she sobbed against him, her heart broken. He tried to console her with whispered words of love and comfort, but she refused to be comforted. "I'm sorry I'm fragile. I'm sorry I'm so much trouble to you. I've been nothing but trouble to you since the day we met. Don't you ever get tired of rescuing me?"

"Ssh, love. Don't say such foolish things. You've brought nothing but joy and light to my life since the morning we met. I will never tire of rescuing you. I only regret I failed to do so this time. I swear to you, I will not fail you again."

She pulled away from his arms so she could look into his stricken eyes. "It is you who shouldn't say such foolish things. You didn't fail to protect me. You left Aman behind and he saved me. Sometimes bad things happen and there's nothing we can do about them. Let's not fight anymore. I can't bear it." She leaned back against him. "I hate waking up alone."

He kissed the top of her head and stroked her hair in a gentle caress along the length of her back. "You will not be alone again, love."

It was the second time in the past few hours he made the same promise. It was no less foolish a promise than the first time he made it. He was a busy man, after all. Of course there would be times when she slept alone, but still his promise comforted her. Neither of them brought up the subject of her work. It was as if neither of them could bear to look beyond the tragic loss they suffered.

CHAPTER FORTY-SIX

"How is she?"

Mary Elle assumed she must still be dreaming, or the pain meds were making her more dazed than she realized, because she would swear she heard her mother's voice just outside the door. Confused, she turned to where Luc should be. Didn't he promise she wouldn't wake up alone anymore?

It was Luc's voice responding to the woman with her mother's voice. "She's out of danger. She lost a lot of blood. They want to keep her a few more days for observation, and then I would like to take her home for a while so she can escape all of this. At least until the press coverage dies down. Unfortunately, she will have to return to testify at the trial."

"Can I see her?"

"Yes of course. She's resting."

"Then I'll just go sit with her if that's all right."

Mary Elle closed her eyes when the door opened and the woman came in. She sat in the chair next to the bed and gently stroked her cheek before taking one of Mary Elle's hands between both of hers, the way Luc did. Then her mother raised her hand to her face and rubbed it against her soft cheek. For the second time in the past twenty four hours, Mary Elle felt the dampness of tears shed for her on her skin.

"Mom?"

"Oh, Mary Elle, I'm sorry, did I wake you? Baby girl, how are you feeling? You're so pale."

"I'm fine, Mom. You didn't have to come all this way."

"Don't you dare tell me you're fine. I suppose you're in this hospital all bandaged up because you're fine and some crazy maniac didn't try to kill you."

"It's all right, Mom."

"No, don't do that. You were always the one trying to comfort me, even when you were a little girl. I can still hear you telling me not to cry, everything was going to be all right. Sometimes I wish I didn't have you so young. I swear I'd be a better mother to you now than I was capable of being then."

"Mom, don't be silly. You were a wonderful mother...the best."

"Well, we both know that's a lie, but I tried my best. The truth is I never understood you. I never understood how special you were. Even though you gave us plenty of hints," she continued on, waving off Mary Elle's instinctive protest. "And look at you now, a famous artist, with people lining up for hours to see your work. You're painting a chapel in St. Peter's. In St. Peter's, Mary Elle!" She repeated as if she still needed convincing. "My daughter and Michelangelo. I should have known. The first time you called him Daddy, I should have known you were destined for something like this."

"What are you talking about?" Mary Elle asked, confused.

"Don't you remember, Mary Elle? When you were a little girl you used to call God, Daddy. One day you came home from preschool at St. Paul's and they talked about how God was everyone's heavenly father. From then on, it was Daddy said this, and Daddy said that. I should have known. I should have realized when you said you told Daddy you wanted to paint pretty pictures. Stupid me, I never put the two together. I assumed you were going behind my back and you and your father were conspiring to soften me up so I wouldn't object to you giving up your music. I felt like such a fool when I read about the *Young Madonna* being auctioned off for a small fortune. I don't I blame you for not telling me. After all, I was the one who told you not to waste your time majoring in studio art in college. Now they're calling you the next great American artist."

"You weren't the only one, Mom."

"Not that I make a habit of defending your father, but in this case I'll confess. It was me who was so opposed to you giving up your music. Your father only wanted you to be happy. He was ready to rush right out and buy you those art supplies you asked for."

"He was?" Mary Elle echoed stunned.

"Don't you remember, honey? You were always his little girl. If you set your heart on flying to the moon, I'm sure your father would have been on the phone to NASA the next morning trying to figure out how to make it happen."

"Oh, Mom, I'm so glad you told me."

"I know, it was selfish of me to make your father pretend he agreed with me. I thought I was doing the right thing at the time."

"Mom, I never blamed you. When I said you weren't the only one who wanted me to choose a more practical major, I wasn't referring to Dad. My art professors in college advised me I didn't have the talent to pursue a career in art."

"They did?"

"Yes."

"You never told us."

"I was too embarrassed …and devastated," Mary Elle admitted softly, still unable to completely put aside the pain from that day.

"Well, I guess they were bigger fools than I was. Thank God you never did listen to anyone."

"Truer words, Mary Jane, truer words."

"Dad!"

"Jake!"

Astonished, mother and daughter turned identical eyes to the man standing in the door.

"Dad, what are you doing here?"

"What am I doing here? What the hell kind of question is that? My daughter gets attacked on the steps of St. Peter's, for God's sake. Where else would I be?"

"Oh, Dad." Tears filling her eyes, Mary Elle returned her

father's gentle embrace.

"How you doing, Baby doll? And don't you dare try to convince me you're fine because I gotta tell you, you don't look so good. These sheets have more color than your pretty face."

"All right, I won't say I'm fine, but I'm getting better."

"Fair enough."

An awkward silence fell between them. Luc, as if waiting out of sight to give them some privacy for their family reunion, appeared in the doorway. Their eyes met across the room. His scanned her face, as if reassuring himself she was still there, and wasn't in any great pain and didn't need him to slay a dragon for her, or something else equally impossible, at the moment. Mary Elle realized she almost lost him. The belated recognition brought home to her how much she loved him, more than she would have ever believed she was capable of loving or needing anyone.

She felt like such a fool for arguing with him over returning to France. She should have known he was only trying to shield her from the press and the repercussions to her of a trial. Without another thought, she dismissed their previous argument. She wanted to apologize, to tell him how much she loved him and how stupid she'd been. Unfortunately, the opportunity was lost to her with her parents' presence.

"Is someone going to make the introductions?" Her father's slightly mocking voice asked into the heavy silence that fell over the room upon Luc's entrance into it.

Blushing, seeing the amusement light in Luc's eyes at her discomfort, Mary Elle offered into the expectant silence, "Mom and Dad, this is Luc Bordeaux. He's sort of my husband."

She caught sight of Luc's grin, right before she turned in response to her mother's protest, "Sort of your husband? I realize they do things differently than they did back in your father's and my day, Mary Elle, but things aren't that different. There's no such thing as being sort of married, just as there's no such thing as being sort of pregnant. So which is it?"

In a rare show of unity among her parents, Mary Elle could see her father's nod of agreement as he swung his glance back and forth between her and Luc. She smothered the sharp stab of pain at the reminder of her recent loss. "Yes, to the former and no to the latter, at least not after yesterday."

"What?"

Sensing her pain, and sharing it, Luc stepped forward to stand beside her and stroke her hair. "Mary Elle is my wife. We were married in an Islamic ceremony in Egypt. I have tried to persuade her to have our union blessed by one of the priests who reside in great abundance in Rome, but she has yet to consent. Mary Elle lost our child she was carrying after the attack."

"Oh, Mary Elle. I'm so sorry," her mother cried, sharing her pain.

"I know, Mom, thank you. It's awful and it hurts so much more than my shoulder, but what can I do? What can we do except grieve and try to move forward? It's not as though I'm the first woman to ever lose a baby."

"It doesn't mean it doesn't hurt as if you were."

Tears shining in her eyes, Mary Elle nodded her agreement with her mother's empathy.

Seeing she was no longer in the mood for company, Luc ushered her parents out of her hospital room and then returned to her a few minutes later. He sat down on the edge of the bed and their glances met. He pulled her into his arms when she leaned towards him. Sighing, she rested her head on his chest.

"Did they tell you?" she asked softly.

"Tell me what?"

"Our baby. Was he or she a boy or a girl?"

Hesitant to add to her pain, Luc admitted, "A baby girl."

Tears filled her eyes and streamed down her cheeks. She buried her face against his chest and sobbed silently, so as not to alarm the hovering medical staff in the hallway. Luc's arms tightened around her and he bent to rest the side of his face on top of her head.

"I'm sorry. I'm so sorry. Your grandfather would have been so excited to hold his Miriam's granddaughter."

"Yes, and he will be equally excited to hold the next child we bring to him."

"Can we?" She finally dared asked the question she was afraid to ask the doctors.

"What do you mean? Of course."

"No, I meant can we have more children? I was afraid to ask the doctors."

He leaned back and lifted her chin so she would meet his tender gaze. "Yes, love. The doctor assured me there is no reason we cannot have more children. We do need to wait to try again until after you've fully recovered from your injuries."

Relieved, she nodded, releasing a shaky sigh. "All right. I'm ready to go home with you now."

Luc's glance searched hers, almost in disbelief at the abruptness of her surrender. Mary Elle could see the questions swirling in his dark eyes, but he didn't give voice to them. It was almost as if he couldn't credit his good fortune and he was unwilling to probe her unexpected concession too closely in case she changed her mind.

CHAPTER FORTY-SEVEN

The doctor in charge of her care confirmed yesterday evening Signora Mary Elle McGann Bordeaux, the young American artist commissioned to restore one of the chapels dedicated to the Virgin Mary at St. Peter's Basilica was released from the hospital yesterday. The young artist, who last week was the victim of a brutal knife attack carried out by a Christian fanatic on the steps of St. Peter's, left the hospital in the company of her husband, Signore Luc Bordeaux. Presumably she will recover at one of her husband's estates in France. The couple, whose recent engagement shocked the continent, were married in a private ceremony during their recent visit to Signore Bordeaux's family in the Middle East.

CHAPTER FORTY-EIGHT

As they began their descent into Charles de Gaulle International airport in Paris, Mary Elle stirred from her nap in Luc's arms. She cringed at the stiffness in her shoulder and raised her gaze to meet Luc's concerned glance.

"I'm fine, just a little stiff," she assured him and then turned to the window on her other side to watch the city come into view beneath them. Turning back to Luc, she asked him hesitantly, "Do you think you could arrange for another after-hours visit with your friend, the Director, at the museum? I need to stop by and check on her, and let her know I'm fine. I'd rather not visit during normal operating hours."

"Of course."

Their eyes met, but neither knew how to break the silence between them. It was still there, the invisible barrier that rose between them after the attack about her work. Mary Elle was uncomfortable bringing up the topic and she suspected Luc was studiously avoiding it as well. The maniac who assaulted her was still causing her harm, even though she was already recovering from the physical effects of their violent confrontation. She feared the invisible scars were going to take a lot longer to heal, the most grievous of them being the damage it did to her relationship with Luc.

Once on the ground, Mary Elle eyed distastefully the waiting wheelchair at the bottom of the steps they descended to the tarmac. She barely managed to swallow her instinctive protest before giving voice to it. Luc, sensing her discomfort at the evidence of her still fragile state, ignored the wheelchair and swept her up in his arms and carried her to the waiting limousine.

"Thank you," she whispered against his neck.

He bent down and brushed the top of her head with his lips, and whispered in reply, "You're welcome."

A small gesture, a tiny connection, but maybe they were beginning to find their way again.

They spent their first night back in France in Luc's Paris home. He arranged for her visit to the museum the following evening. They passed through the hushed halls and into the salon where the two paintings that started all of this waited for her. Her initial works remained unframed, standing side by side, perched on two workmanlike easels similar to the ones they were brought to life on in her little chapel home in Pittsburgh. The security guard made himself scarce so she had the space to herself. Even Luc remained at the entrance to the salon to give her privacy for her visit.

She stood for a moment before the canvases, examining them with a critical eye, aiming for the objectivity of someone without an intimate connection to them. Of course her aim fell far short of its objective. She couldn't remain dispassionate when faced with the purity of the little girl's faith in her angelic protector and her fear at leaving behind the comfort of her life with her parents.

At the painting by her side the little girl was a young woman whose faith was nourished over her years spent in the temple. Her faith was about to be tested beyond the ability of most of mankind to comprehend. The innocence was still present in her wary eyes but a little more than a decade of life in this physical world honed her purity with a healthy dose of caution.

Her eyes still held awe and reverence when she beheld the angel kneeling before her. But this time her awe was tainted with fear he might not be there for her when she needed him most. Not because he was unable to save her from evil men who would condemn her when they discovered she was with child, but perhaps because he would be unwilling to bestir himself.

Mary Elle understood her fear, in a way she didn't appreciate until she came face to face with a man intent on her death plunging a knife into her chest, all the while raining obscenities over her stunned head and damning her to hell. If faith was a gift, it did not come without cost. The greater the gift, the heavier the price exacted for it.

A little awkwardly because of the sling cradling her injured shoulder, and because the rest of her was still bruised and sore, Mary Elle sank down to her knees before the two paintings.

Even as she knelt before her, the silence remained unbroken between them. Mary Elle guessed it would be up to her to break it, to try to explain what she was doing back in Paris when she was supposed to be in Rome, repaying her benefactress for the gift she was given.

"I'm sorry I failed you. I seem to be failing everyone these days. I'm not giving up. I just need a little time to get myself together and maybe a little more to gather my courage before I go back. I guess that's the part I missed, right? The part I minimized in all of this. It was easy for me when you were the only one in danger. I already knew how your story turned out. It never occurred to me I would ever be in physical danger. I guess my self assurance was both arrogant and naïve of me, don't you think? I never considered my work, this gift you gave me, would be a source of conflict between Luc and me. I always figured without it I didn't have a chance with him. Now the shoe's on the other foot, so to speak. It's my need to finish this, to honor the gift you gave me, causing a breach between us."

"I didn't understand, not really, the sacrifice part. I guess I figured since everything turned out okay for you in eternity, the sacrifices didn't really count. Sorry to be such an idiot. I needed to come here tonight to apologize, and to promise you

I'll go back and finish your chapel. I can't give you an exact date, but a sick maniac armed with a knife isn't going to stop me. Nor is the man I love, who is armed with love and a deep sense of concern and responsibility towards me. The last time we spoke I promised I was all in and I would see this through. Nothing that's happened since has changed my commitment. I just needed you to know."

Mary Elle waited in silence, hoping for a sign all was still well between them, but none was forthcoming. Sighing in regret and resignation, she struggled back to her feet, grateful for Luc's hand as he hurried forward to assist her. For the first time, he didn't ask for and she didn't offer any details about the exchange he was a silent witness of. Instead, she leaned silently against his chest and he seemed content to simply hold her and rest his head on top of hers.

"Can we go back to Bordeaux tomorrow?" she asked, raising her glance to his.

"Yes."

"I guess the press is having a field day with all of this," she offered, not really holding out any hope he would rebut her assumption.

"Yes, they are. You needn't concern yourself with the media, Mary Elle. I will not allow anyone to get close enough to be a threat to you."

Hearing the regret and self-condemnation in his voice, Mary Elle shook her head, allowing a slight smile to come to her lips. "It wasn't your fault, Luc. Even the secret service sometimes loses a president."

His lips twitched at her analogy and then split into a wide smile, familiar amusement dancing in his eyes. "I will try to remember that."

"Let's go home."

CHAPTER FORTY-NINE

Summer faded into autumn. Mary Elle whiled away the days taking long walks over the grounds of Luc's country home, reading, sleeping and trying to be the kind of wife she thought Luc deserved. Things slowly returned to normal between them, or as normal as they could be with the huge elephant in the room neither of them seemed willing to discuss. She supposed Luc was enjoying their time together as much as she was. She thought it must be a relief for him to know he would not be called upon to rescue her from some unanticipated mishap. For her part, Mary Elle avoided the television, the Internet and print media. It was as though she existed in a vacuum of peace and luxury where nothing evil or sordid could reach her.

Of course the dark side to living in a bubble was she was growing increasingly restless to return to work. Luc resumed his normal schedule a month after their return to France, though in consideration of her still *fragile* state, he split his time between the estate and the Paris mansion, commuting back and forth from the private airstrip on the estate when he needed to. There were times when his social obligations demanded he remain in the city for the weekend. It was those times Mary Elle realized if their marriage was to survive they needed to return their relationship to a more equal footing as soon as possible.

Though they resumed their intimate relationship as soon

as the doctors released her from their oversight, they still existed in an odd state of Luc playing the role of her protector with her the child in need of his protection. At first, Mary Elle was so stunned by the attack she gratefully retreated into the safety of the sanctuary Luc was anxious to provide for her. Now, months later, she couldn't help but wonder if he was attending those social obligations alone in Paris. The unpleasant acknowledgement there were any number of women willing to provide him with their companionship for the evening was enough for her to overcome her fear about returning to the city to face the media gauntlet her return would ignite. Coming to a sudden decision, Mary Elle cut short her morning walk and hurried back in the direction of the house. She decided to surprise Luc in Paris, and prayed he would be the only one surprised by her showing up on their threshold unannounced.

"Mme Bordeaux, welcome. I trust your drive was uneventful?"

"Yes, thank you."

"Madame, please come in," Mary Elle found it ironic that Luc's housekeeper felt the need to invite her into what was now her own home. "Would you like to rest in your rooms?" 'As if she was still some fragile invalid.' "M. Bordeaux is at his office. Would you like me to call his assistant and ask him to inform your husband of your arrival?"

"No, I wanted to surprise Luc, thank you."

"M. Bordeaux may be quite late," she warned and Mary Elle nodded, wondering what would keep Luc quite late at his office.

Mary Elle waited all day, and as predicted by a woman more in tune with her husband's schedule than his wife, late into the evening, before finally retreating to their rooms after her solitary dinner. She was tired enough the bed beckoned invitingly, but she resisted climbing between the welcoming sheets, wondering if another woman took her place in her husband's bed since she took up permanent residence at the

Bordeaux estate.

Instead she curled up in one of the chaises on the terrace with a quilt off the bed wrapped close around her. The autumn night was warm and the distant noise of the city lulled her to sleep. Her dreams were troubled.

She thought she heard someone calling her name. She was so happy at the thought *she* returned it took Mary Elle a few moments to realize something was wrong. She hadn't returned to her dreams. It wasn't *her* voice calling to her. The voice was familiar, but it was deeper, masculine.

"Mary Elle, love, wake up."

'Oh, it was Luc. He finally came home.'

"Mary Elle?" She felt his hand gently brushing the hair from her face. The breeze picked up and she shivered in the cold. Feeling her shiver, Luc lifted her in his arms and carried her back into his room...their room. She was his wife. Legally, anyway.

At her continued silence, he sat with her on the bed. "Are you going to continue to pretend to be asleep or are you going to tell me why you're here?"

Reluctantly, she opened her eyes and met his probing glance. "Are you sorry I'm here?"

"No, of course not. Why would you think I would be sorry to see you?"

She might be a married woman now but she was no better at playing the kind of games men and women indulged in than she was the night they met. "Are you having an affair?"

"What?! Why would you think such a thing? Has someone told you I'm having an affair?" Luc seemed genuinely astonished by her question.

"No. I'm not even sure I would blame you even if it was true," she admitted miserably. "I haven't been a very good wife to you. I wanted to change that. It's why I drove to Paris. I wanted to surprise you, but then you didn't come home..."

"My presence was required at a business dinner. One I would have happily foregone if I knew you were here waiting for me," he explained gently.

"I'm sorry. I don't really know what I'm supposed to do now, who I'm supposed to be," she confessed, dejected.

Sensing she needed his comfort, Luc bent to kiss her, patiently, tenderly, until she began to respond. He turned with her in his arms and laid her down on the bed, then followed her, his weight pressing her into the sheets. Mary Elle was reminded of their first night together. Everything seemed so much simpler then.

Now there were shadows filled with ghosts between them, driving them apart. She wouldn't let them win. With new resolve she surprised Luc by rolling him off of her and following until she was straddling him, her robe falling open, revealing soft, perfumed flesh beneath. His hands reached up to part the silk and indulge them both.

"You are my wife, Mary Elle. That is who you are supposed to be now," he told her huskily, his mind clearly not on having a serious conversation about the dismal state of their marriage. How could she tell him that wasn't enough for either of them?

Aroused by her boldness, Luc gripped the back of her head just to make certain she wouldn't retreat from the growing passion between them. If his wife was finally willing to throw open the door to unveil the secrets she kept hidden behind the extended silences growing between them in recent months, he wasn't about to waste this opportunity.

When he returned home alone to find his wife asleep on the terrace outside their suite, Luc drew a shaky breath at the fickleness of fate. He shouldn't be surprised by her insight into his moods. From the very first Mary Elle was attuned to him. The fact was, he considered not returning to his empty bed alone. His realization of what such a lapse would have cost him made him cling to his wife's surprising passionate welcome all the more fiercely. Mary Elle was not the kind of woman who would overlook a small matter of infidelity on her husband's part. To an innocent like his wife, such a betrayal would lead her to conclude he no longer loved her, that he no longer wished her to be his wife.

Even though that was the furthest thing from his mind, in Mary Elle's reckoning, if she caught him with another woman, the bond between them would be irrevocably severed, never to be rejoined. He almost lost her. The realization it was his own roving inclination rather than the blade of a madman that almost deprived him of his wife's love, brought him to a place of self-rebuke and near self-disgust.

Passion spent, Mary Elle, sleepily, was aware of Luc rolling off her and gathering her close against his side, with one arm flung over her back. "Welcome home, wife."

Mary Elle remained in Paris. She began painting again, slowly, and like the portrait of Luc's mother, found comfort in the beauty coming off her brush. Her efforts weren't masterpieces, but like Luc pointed out, not even the great masters aspired to produce a masterpiece with every effort. The topic of her return to Italy to renew her work on the virgin's chapel remained an unvoiced one. It was there, between them, but neither seemed willing to risk the fragile truce they began to piece together between them after her surprise return to Paris.

Tonight she was taking another step towards integrating herself more fully into Luc's life. She was attending a social function with him not centered around her art. When he initially mentioned the event to her, she was reluctant to agree to accompany him. The unappealing prospect of having to face the questions and curiosity of Luc's friends and business associates, particularly given the dramatic events that drove her from Italy was responsible for her hesitation. Luc didn't push her. He just indicated the evening was not an occasion he could excuse himself from and informed her he would be late returning home.

Mary Elle belatedly realized Luc made excuses for her a lot. He made things easy for her, rather than demand she attend the function with him as his wife. It was the realization that brought home to her how self-involved she'd become. Their entire marriage, their entire relationship was all about her, what she wanted, what she needed. She returned to Paris to begin the process of putting their marriage on a more equal footing, including a more equal division of the giving and taking on both sides.

"You take my breath away," Luc's admiring voice reached her from the doorway separating their bedroom and her bath.

Their eyes met in the mirror, where she stood adding the final touches to her hair and makeup. She was thankful it was cool and the cocktail dress she wore covered the still visible scars on her back and shoulder. It was the first time she wore anything approaching formal wear since the attack.

She turned to face Luc, breaking their reflected eye contact, and approached him where he stood framed in the doorway in his dark evening suit. She reached up to brush a non-existent piece of lint from his shoulders, because she felt the need to touch him, and she was still too uncertain of how far they'd come to initiate such contact without an excuse.

"It seems only fair," she responded to his admiring comment. "I haven't been able to catch my breath around you since the morning we met."

He captured her hand and linked their fingers, before bringing their joined hands to his lips. He brushed his lips across the sensitive skin of her inner wrist, sending a tingling reaction through her entire body. "We won't stay late," he promised her.

"Is it so obvious?" she asked with a sigh.

"You are nervous about tonight?" At her cautious nod, he smiled, and added, "Yes, but knowing you are nervous only makes me more grateful for your willingness to accompany me."

"I'm trying to be a better wife to you," she confessed.

His eyes lit with pleased wonder and one arm slid around her back, drawing her close. He bent his head to breathe in her perfume and to let his lips tease the suddenly swiftly beating pulse at the base of her neck. "Mary Elle, my love, no man dares even pray to Allah for such a wife as you are to me," he assured her.

Mary Elle wasn't letting herself off the hook so easily this time. She pulled away from his warmth with an effort and caught his face between her hands. "You keep saying things like that, you make me believe them, but it's not true." When he would have protested, she placed her fingertips across his lips. "No, you have to be honest with me about what you need from me. You haven't been. I realized today this is the first social event we've attended together not revolving around me or my art. That is so wrong on so many levels and you never called me out on it, so I'm calling myself on it. I'm going to be a better wife to you."

The tenderness in his glance took her breath away. When she recovered enough to string two thoughts together, she inwardly hugged herself. They were finding their way back. Everything was going to be all right.

CHAPTER FIFTY

The following week Luc sat behind his desk in his Paris office attempting to concentrate on a proposal to convert the family factories to solar power. He gave a muttered curse when he realized he was having difficulty focusing on the pages in front of him. He didn't recall ever having such difficulties before, even in the wilder days of his youth. It was hardly surprising Mary Elle was responsible for his distraction. No other woman had the ability to so completely consume his thoughts or his life as his young wife.

Her sudden return to Paris was as welcome as it was surprising. His lips curved at the reminder of her professed intent to be a better wife to him. If she was any better of a wife to him he might not see forty, but he would die a contented man. He recognized the current state of marital bliss between them could not last forever. Mary Elle hadn't pushed him, but he knew she was anxious to return to Rome to renew her work on the virgin's chapel. He also recognized he had no right to attempt to prevent her from doing so.

He was almost insane with worry in the initial hours after he learned of the attack on his wife. His worry was laced with guilt he'd been unable to protect her from the sharp blade of an intended assassin. He was still nearly mad with worry at the thought of her returning to the very scene of the assault in order for her to continue her work. The recognition there wasn't any shortage of crazed, religious fanatics in the world who might find an excuse to target his innocent wife, if for no other reason than the media coverage such an assault would generate, kept him up at night. The thought of letting her go again while he remained behind in France, too far to reach her if she needed him, was not one he'd been able to find a solution for.

So for now they existed in the gloriously passionate and blissful state of honeymooners everywhere. The fact that their current happiness was based on denial and an avoidance of the issues they would eventually be forced to confront did not trouble him overly much. They were entitled to a few months of evading the harsh glare of reality after what they'd been through.

The intercom on his desk buzzed, interrupting his distracted musings. "M. Bordeaux, there's an American Detective Nielson, on the line wishing to speak with you."

"Put him through," Luc instructed harshly at the unpleasant reminder of yet another attempted assault on his wife.

"Mr. Bordeaux, forgive me for interrupting your day," the detective's disembodied voice came over the line. Luc brought the other man's face to mind and idly wondered if anything ever came of the interest he read in the detective's eyes in regards to Mary Elle's friend, Crystal.

"You have news about the break-in at my wife's home, Detective?"

"Perhaps," he hedged. "It's a long shot, but I thought one worthy of a call. We have a suspect in custody on an un-related drug distribution charge. He's a third time offender, facing a lengthy sentence, so he wants to cut a deal. He indicated he had information about the break-in at the famous artist's house near the edge of town. It was an interesting claim since the break-in wasn't exactly front page news at the time."

"And was the information he provided you useful to your investigation?"

"Not to us, but I thought I'd run it by you first before concluding he was just blowing smoke."

"What did he have to offer?"

"Does the name J. Renard mean anything to you?"

At his former lover's name, Luc was so enraged he literally saw red flash across the canvas of his mind. He looked down and discovered his hand was clutching the phone so tightly he was surprised it didn't snap in half.

"Mr. Bordeaux?"

With an effort Luc drew a calming breath, clamping down on his barely suppressed fury. "Yes, Detective, I am acquainted with someone by the name of J. Renard. You may strike your deal with your suspect. As the person responsible for the break-in at my fiancé's home is beyond the reach of your American justice, please rest assured J. Renard will pay dearly for terrorizing my wife."

Luc disconnected the call. Unable to remain seated behind his desk, he regained his feet so swiftly and in such a state of rage, his office chair ended up on its back on the floor, the wheels spinning chaotically like a turtle flipped onto its back and unable to right itself. Luc strode to the window and gazed out over the city. As much as the prospect of exacting revenge against his former lover appealed to him, he recognized the pleasant fantasies drifting through his furious thoughts would be denied him. He was a civilized man, after all, and he had no desire to spend the rest of his life in a French prison.

Besides, Mary Elle would likely blame herself for his spectacular fall from society's good graces. He would not further distress his wife by forcing her to confront the fact a former lover of his was so unbalanced she somehow managed to employ a foreign criminal to break into her home from across the Atlantic.

No, he wouldn't harm her, but he would exact his revenge. Just as he intended to exact his vengeance against the sick bastard who plunged a knife into his wife's soft, unmarred flesh. First though, before he pursued either, ultimately satisfying objectives, he needed to regain control over his driving fury. If there was any truth behind old clichés, it was purported revenge was a dish better served cold.

Setting aside his reckless wrath was one thing. Overcoming his feelings of self-disgust at the realization he almost married a woman capable of terrorizing a rival for his affections was another challenge entirely. The fact that he both pleasured and taken pleasure from such a woman as a lover made him so sick he was struggling not to lose his lunch.

The proposal on his desk forgotten, he swung around and headed for the door. He needed air. More, he needed to rid himself of the filth of the stain of his relationship with Janelle before he returned home to his wife. The wife, who was so desperately trying to become a better wife to him...to in essence be the kind of wife Janelle would have been in her place.

The disturbing, sick irony of the situation was not lost on him. Shaking his head, Luc slammed out of his office with no clear direction in mind.

CHAPTER FIFTY-ONE

He took her to Bordeaux. He needed to remove Mary Elle from his former lover's reach, at least until he could think straight and decide how he was going to proceed. An inquiry to the detective in charge of the investigation into the attack on Mary Elle in Rome forced him to conclude the two events were unrelated. He wasn't certain if he should feel relieved Janelle wasn't behind the assassination attempt in Rome, or worried there was more than one crazed lunatic intent on harming his young wife.

He stayed with her, keeping such a close eye on her he was certain Mary Elle would grow suspicious, but she never asked. She just regarded him hesitantly from out of the depths of her clear grey eyes and assured him she was no longer fragile. He would smile and nod his head in agreement, but inside he couldn't get over the sight of her lying in a hospital bed, bandaged and hysterical over the loss of their unborn child, or the sound of her terrified voice on the other end of the line when the police found her huddled in a dark corner in the bell tower of her home in Pittsburgh.

CHAPTER FIFTY-TWO

Mary Elle was growing increasingly restless to return to Rome. The dreams, after a long absence, returned with increasingly regularity. She hid them from Luc. He was already convinced she was fragile; she was reluctant to add unbalanced to the equation.

There was another reason she was anxious to return to Rome. The suspicion was growing on her she was pregnant again. She hadn't seen a doctor or even taken a home pregnancy test. Back in the states she would have just dropped by the local drugstore and picked up a kit. The dread of the repercussions of her walking into a local pharmacy in Bordeaux, after of course Aman drove her there in the Bordeaux limousine and where everyone within a ten mile radius of the estate would recognize her instantly, was enough to prevent her from putting any such half-considered plan into action. She finally solved her dilemma by confiding in Crystal and asking her to purchase and send the kits to her. Crystal laughed at her quandary, teased her about her fame, congratulated her on the new baby, and promised to send the pregnancy test kits out the following morning.

"What has you smiling?" Luc asked from across the table on the terrace where they were enjoying the warmth of a spring day.

"I was just thinking about my conversation with Crystal earlier," Mary Elle demurred. "She said she was sending me a package from the shop. Remember, Cinderella?"

At his smiling nod, she added, "The same company expanded their line and she just unpacked a fairy godmother and a prince with a glass slipper in his hand. She thought we might like to add to our collection."

He laughed. "I'll look forward to it."

Mary Elle sighed relieved. Crisis averted. Besides, Crystal mentioned the fairy godmother and the prince in the course of their conversation. Mary Elle would text her after dinner to make certain her friend didn't forget to include them in the package.

Later Mary Elle cried out in her sleep.

Luc shook her awake. "It's all right, love, you're safe. You were having a nightmare."

Dazed, Mary Elle nodded and burrowed against his chest, seeking his warmth. She was so cold. It was dark in her dreams. "I'm sorry, did I wake you?"

He bent and kissed the top of her head. "You haven't been sleeping well."

She pulled back far enough to see his face. "I need to go back." There. She said it.

He framed her face. "I know. I'm going with you."

"What? You'll let me go? You won't try to stop me?" Mary Elle was shocked. She expected him to fight her every step of the way and here he was telling her he would take her.

"Will you give me a little more time to make the necessary arrangements?"

Mary Elle shook her head, convinced she must still be dreaming. "Of course. You're serious. You'll come back with me?"

"You must return and I can't let you go."

Mary Elle launched herself at him, and Luc laughingly accepted her stunned gratitude.

The following morning they enjoyed their morning ritual on the terrace outside their bedroom suite. Luc looked up from his paper as she joined him at the table, blushing when his eyes swept appreciatively over her clad only in his shirt.

"I have to return to Paris for a business obligation and for a dinner on Friday evening," he informed her. "I was hoping my beautiful wife would accompany me."

Mary Elle's expression fell at his playful request and tears welled in her eyes. "Oh, Luc, I'm sorry. I want so much to be there for you, especially since you ask so little of me, but I can't. It's holy week. You go. I'm sorry. I can't leave her alone on Good Friday, of all days. I'm sorry."

Friday morning, Mary Elle left the house before dawn split the darkness hovering over the horizon and made her way across the expansive grounds to the chapel. A blank canvas awaited her there in the center of the circular space, resting against her old college easel. She put it there after Luc left for the city earlier in the week. He didn't object to her staying behind, only assured her he understood, and for her not to worry. He would attend the event he requested her presence at alone. Mary Elle felt almost worse he was so understanding about everything.

She didn't tell him about the baby. Crystal's package arrived as promised. Luc laughed at the contents and promised to add the new additions to the Cinderella collection to the originals where they were displayed on a shelf in his office. Mary Elle kept to herself the remaining contents of the package and performed the test confirming her pregnancy when she dressed for dinner.

She felt guilty about not telling Luc he was going to be a father, especially knowing how much the news would mean to him, and his grandparents, but she was afraid to share the joyful news with him. At least not yet. She was so stunned by his promise to take her back to Rome she feared the news of her pregnancy would change his mind.

Carrying a flashlight to illuminate her way across the dark grounds, she entered the dark chapel and paused to light the candles before the shrine to the virgin, before making her way up the narrow stairs. The canvas was there waiting for her, with paint tubes lined up neatly in rows beneath it. She reached up to retrieve and light the oil lanterns, then hung them on the hooks around the small space before retreating to the corner where she slid down between the two walls and leaned her head back against the hard stone, and closed her eyes.

The silence hung heavily in the sacred space and Mary Elle drifted off to sleep. There were a few, fleeting moments of blessed peace, then the visions assaulted her as suddenly and violently as the madman sprang his attack on her in St. Peter's Square. She was helpless to fight them off. Trapped in dreams, she was unable to free herself from their vise-like grip on her consciousness. She finally surfaced at the sound of her own smothered sobbing. Shaking her head in an attempt to clear the lingering visions, she held her head between her hands, but they refused to release her. Scene after scene of the events rocking the world two millennia earlier erupted like explosives detonating inside her head.

Unable to resist, unable to break free, she sought to cling to her faltering grip on her own sanity the only way she knew how. She crawled on her hands and knees to the waiting canvas, and with her hand shaking noticeably, she mixed the paints, uncertain what would come off her brush when it met the blank canvas.

There were no preliminary sketches to work from. No plan. No clear vision. Tears all but blinding her, desperation all but paralyzing her, Mary Elle filled the brush in her hand with paint and reached out to the canvas to purge herself of the bloody visions in the only way she could think of.

Stark desolation poured out of her. A mother's tears mixed with the blood of her son's broken body as they took him down from a wooden cross and placed him in her waiting arms. She kissed his brow and smoothed the matted, blood-soaked hair from his face, using her tears and the cloth of her robe to cleanse the stains left by blood and sweat, and the violence inflicted against him by lesser men, from his beloved features. With gentle hands she removed the cruel thorns still clinging to his torn flesh from the primitive crown mockingly placed on his head by his Roman executioners.

Though her tears and gasping breaths were ripped from the depths of Mary Elle's soul, none escaped the virgin's eyes. Her loss, her desolation was too great to give voice to, too devastating for tears. In their place was a hollow, vacant grief reflected in her dark eyes ripping at Mary Elle's heart. She was barely conscious of filling in the details of the painting as her brush flew across the canvas. She painted the torn, bloodied and bruised flesh where the nails pierced his wrists and ankles, and the sword was thrust into his side to assure the witnesses of his sentence he was truly dead.

Overhead the sky was dark and threatening. There was fear on the faces of those surrounding where a mother sat beneath a wooden cross, cradling the body of her dead son. A fear brought about by the odd rumors surrounding the dead prophet and by the way the sky appeared as though it was about to unleash the wrath of heaven upon them for their sins.

When the last of it poured out of her, Mary Elle threw the paintbrush from her hand and collapsed on the floor beneath the easel, deep and painful sobs shaking her slender form.

Luc found her sobbing when he hurried up the stairs from his watchful vigil in the chapel below. Alarmed, he raced over to where his wife lay with her head resting on the stone floor, her whole body heaving with the force of her heart-wrenching sobs. He bent down to lift her into his arms, and then he saw it, and was struck numb, mesmerized by the painting with its wet paint glimmering in the early evening light of a setting sun reflecting through the stained glass windows looking down upon them from above.

For perhaps the first time, Luc thought he understood a hint of his wife's reluctance to travel to Jerusalem and the price exacted from her for the gift she was given. He managed to draw his focus away from the fresh evidence of his wife's genius only with a willful effort on his part and then he drew her closer against his chest.

Confused, Mary Elle raised her glance to meet his

concerned one. "Luc? What are you doing here? What about your dinner? You had plans."

He smoothed her hair away from her damp cheeks. "Did you think I would leave you? I've been downstairs, Mary Elle, sharing your vigil of this day in the only way I could."

Fresh tears filling her eyes, she reached up to trace the outline of his face with the tips of her fingers, smearing his features with the wet paint still staining her hands. "I don't deserve you. I'm really trying to be a good wife to you, but I can't make it stop. I don't know how to make it stop."

CHAPTER FIFTY-THREE

Easter morning dawned bright and clear. Luc arranged for Easter Mass to be offered in the little chapel on the estate. Afterwards they went upstairs to the bell chapel to retrieve her Good Friday painting.

"I plan to make a gift of this painting to the church," Mary Elle announced as they stood before it.

"I hope the church is suitably grateful," Luc replied, not without a trace of mockery.

"It's the best work I've ever done. She would want her son's church to be its steward."

Luc bent to kiss the top of her head. "Yes, I believe she would."

They returned to the house for breakfast. Mary Elle was surprised to find a small gift-wrapped box next to her plate. Curious, she lifted it in her hands where they sat on the terrace overlooking the gardens just beginning to come to life with spring's official arrival.

"What is this?"

"An Easter gift for my lovely wife."

Smiling, Mary Elle held up one finger and said, "I have a gift for you, too. Wait here."

Grinning, he caught her by the waist when she would have dashed past him. "You do realize Muslims do not celebrate Easter, don't you?"

"I hope you'll celebrate this one," she told him and slipped from his hold.

She returned moments later wearing a wide smile and carrying a small box, decorated with a large bow.

"This is for you. I promise it's not a chocolate Easter bunny."

Luc grinned and accepted the box from her outstretched hand, eyeing it a little warily.

He placed it on the table in front of him, and said, "Since this is a Christian holiday, it seems appropriate you open my offering to you first."

"All right," Mary Elle agreed, retrieving her own gift from where it sat near her plate. She unwrapped it, expecting from the size and lightness of the box, Luc added to her already generous and growing jewelry collection. When she opened the lid, she raised her glance to Luc's gentle one, her own a mixture of hope and confusion."It's the key to the villa in Rome." She couldn't stop the flow of tears filling her eyes.

"We can go back?"

He reached over to wipe her tears away with his thumb. "Yes, whenever you wish. Tomorrow if you like."

"Oh, Luc, you better open your gift now before I start making plans. You might change your mind when you see what it is."

Brows raised, he unwrapped the small box he held, but before he lifted the lid, he met her worried glance and assured her, "No matter what this box contains, I will not change my mind about taking you back to Rome to finish the chapel."

Her lips curving in a slight smile at the sincerity of his commitment, Mary Elle replied, "I'm not going to hold you to your promise until after you see your present."

"You make me very curious to discover what's hiding under this lid." He eyed her and the box with no little trepidation, making Mary Elle laugh.

"Open it and see."

He lifted the lid and removed its contents, obviously uncertain what he held in his hand. Grinning at his confusion,

Mary Elle reached over to turn the little stick so he could read its significance. His reaction was everything she could have hoped for. Eyes wide with shock, he lifted his gaze away from her gift to meet hers.

"Mary Elle, what is this? Are you telling me you're pregnant?"

She smiled into a glance both incredulous and filled with hope. "Yes. We're going to have a baby."

He jumped up from his chair and swung her into his arms, spinning them round and round until she laughingly protested the dizzy sensations swamping her.

"Happy Easter!" She proclaimed, when he sat back down at the table, still holding her in his lap.

"Indeed!" Luc agreed, and then added, "When?"

"I waited to tell you…just in case, you know. I didn't want you to have to go through that again. I'm about eight weeks along. I think our baby is due at the end of October."

"Would you mind very much if we delay our departure for Rome a few weeks until I grow accustomed to the idea?"

"I can still go? You won't be angry with me if I still want to go back?"

"We will go, Mary Elle. I can work from Rome."

"But…"

"Never again, Beloved. I promised you we would never be apart for such long stretches again. As you pointed out before we returned to France, it is impossible for me to transport the basilica here for you to continue your work, so you must return to Rome, and I will accompany you."

CHAPTER FIFTY-FOUR

It actually took Luc more than a month to grow accustomed to the idea he was going to be a father. Mary Elle didn't mind his pampering. He flew his grandfather in to surprise her for her birthday and Crystal as well. Even her parents flew over to congratulate her. Luc's grandparents hosted a large party for her at their Paris mansion, and the house was filled with wellwishers. Her pregnancy was just beginning to show by the time they returned to Rome.

The papers were full of stories about the return of the artist of the virgin's chapel, and how she was soon to become a mother herself. For the most part Mary Elle was able to ignore the curious glances when she was recognized and pointed out as she made her way to the entrance to the basilica. Though Luc saw to it she was never alone when she stepped foot outside their villa. Aman shadowed her every step, and a second man drove the limousine transporting her back and forth. She wouldn't be tremendously surprised to learn Luc arranged for the car to be bullet-proofed in her absence. She didn't raise any objection to the added security he insisted on, and only grinned into his stubborn face when she realized Luc was expecting her too.

Her eyes filled with wonder, she smiled at the guard manning his post at the entrance to the closed chapel. Climbing the scaffolding, she knelt down to mix fresh paint and on a prayer, lifted her face to heaven. "What should we paint today?"

...EPILOGUE

The old woman waited patiently in the long line for her turn to enter the *Capella del Rosario* in St. Peter's Basilica. It was more than five decades since she saw the interior of the chapel. She wasn't certain what to expect. Would *she* be there to greet her? Mary Elle doubted it.

She left her when Mary Elle's third son was born and the chapel was all but complete. Mary Elle returned to France with Luc and their sons. She gave the chapel and the virgin what remained of her twenties and then surprised the world, and her husband most of all, when she proclaimed she was finished. No one dared ask her about the single, remaining blank panel centered over the gallery where the faithful could sit and enjoy the chapel in quiet contemplation and prayer. Luc least of all. He knew what the vacant panel was destined to contain. Mary Elle guessed he was relieved when she didn't ask him to keep his promise and return with her to Jerusalem.

Now it was too late for him to keep his promise. Luc, the other half of herself, the other half of her heart, passed from this life peacefully a year earlier, after a long illness. She loved him passionately until the moment they bid a final farewell at the family estate in Bordeaux. She hoped her own passing would swiftly follow his, but the gift was denied her. There was one final task left for her to complete, a task she evaded for more than half a century.

Her work hung in every major museum in the world and was still largely sought after by collectors. No doubt they were eagerly awaiting word of her eventual death to boost the value of their collections. Her lips lifted in a smile. She wasn't done yet. Her family's private collection would be worth an enormous amount of money, yet she considered what she did here, in this sacred place, her life's work. She gave the world this; always conscious of M. Jacques' chastisement art touching the hearts of so many shouldn't be reserved for those who could afford to pay enormous sums for it.

She took a few weeks at their villa in Rome, insisting to her children she needed time alone with her grief, but she already came to terms with her husband's death. At least to the extent one could ever come to terms with losing the other half of one's soul. No, she was in Rome for quite another reason. The time had come for her to make recompense for the gift she was given. She thought she was finally ready, but first she would pay her respects to the one who bestowed so much upon her unworthy shoulders.

When she finally reached the front of the line she entered the chapel and gazed in awe at the portrayal of the mysteries of the rosary spread out in the circular chapel: the original Joyful, Sorrowful, Glorious and Luminous mysteries were all represented. Other events captured the yet to be named mysteries, but that was not her concern, nor did she ever wade into the debate over the years about their significance.

Every inch of available space in the diminutive chapel was filled with her work, except the blank wall opposite the small shrine to the virgin. Mary Elle followed the other faithful pilgrims around the path of one of the basilica's most popular exhibits. Her eyes filled with tears at the acknowledgement she had a part in creating this. She gazed up at the walls and breathed it all in, wandering through the various phases of the virgin's life and those of her son's: a new depiction of the annunciation, the visitation, his birth and presentation at the temple, his baptism in the Jordan, the first miracle at the marriage feast at Cana, his transfiguration, the last supper. Finally, her gaze rested on the depiction of the Sorrowful Mysteries: the agony in the garden, the scourging at the pillar, the crowning with thorns, the carrying of the cross, before falling on the blank wall waiting to be filled in with what would be the chapel's final image.

Vatican officials contacted her no less than annually over the years, asking her to return and finish the chapel. Luc handled all of those requests for her, merely informing the Vatican she was not yet ready to complete the chapel. The contacts grew more frequent recently, as she grew older and the church recognized, no doubt wondering if perhaps she didn't, her time in this physical world was growing short, and if she was going to complete the chapel, surely she needed to begin soon. After all, it took years for her to bring it to its current state and she was no longer a young woman.

She paused in front of the blank wall and dared to raise her head, afraid of the condemnation and recrimination she expected to rain down upon her, but there was nothing, only the same silence she experienced since *she* left her. The silence and emptiness she confronted now was only an echo of the emptiness she experienced whenever she thought back on the time she was blessed to spend with the virgin. Ignoring the crowd, she sank down to her knees before the blank wall, drawing curious glances from the faithful surrounding her.

It was intimidating in its starkness, as each empty canvas had been she confronted in her little tower room back in the states when she first began this journey. She bowed her head and offered a prayer.

She thought she heard a whisper of a memory in reply, "Are you ready then to walk with me now?"

Her shoulders began shaking and tears slid from between her closed eyes. She instinctively wrapped her arms around her middle to still their shaking and to comfort herself since Luc was no longer with her to offer his much-needed comfort.

"Yes, I'm ready," she whispered out loud, and struggled to regain her feet.

Stronger arms than hers reached out to assist her and she turned to offer her gratitude, assuming it was one of the visitors to the chapel who took pity on an old woman and politely came to her assistance. When their eyes met, she was taken back to a spring afternoon six decades earlier, in Nazareth.

"Thank you, Father," she repeated her words to him then.

He nodded and replied, his eyes glancing around the room. "During the active years of my ministry, I came here as often as I could to be with our lady. After I retired, I moved to Rome to be near her. All of these long years I waited to see its completion. I thought perhaps the gift would be denied me; that I would be like the faithful Jews of the first testament who waited for the birth of the savior and were not among the chosen ones to live to see such times. I am not well, you see, and I've often wondered at our Lord's delay in calling me home to Him. Then I come here today and you are here, and I think our beloved heavenly Father has generously revealed to me the reason for his delay in summoning me. I think my part will be not unlike the role of the faithful Simeon, who was promised he would not taste death until he beheld the savior of the Jews. I think, Madame Bordeaux, you will finish the work you were called to in this life."

Gripping his hand, she stared back up at the blank wall, recognizing while she was not unwell; her strength was beginning to fail. She only hoped she retained enough for the duty ahead of her. Turning back to the old priest she said, "I don't know if I will complete her work she has shared with me, Father, but I do know I am finally ready to begin."

Their eyes met and he asked smiling, "May I have the privilege of informing my superiors of your intent?"

Returning his smile, Mary Elle happily assented, "Yes, please do. I have a trip to make first, but when it is complete I will return directly here and begin. I think a few weeks should be enough time. Is a few weeks sufficient notice to close the chapel to visitors for a while?"

He squeezed her hand in response. "A moment's notice would be enough time, Madame. I do not doubt you are well aware of how anxious the church is to see the chapel completed."

"Especially given my advanced years?" Mary Elle quipped.

Smiling, he shared in her amusement and together they turned towards the exit.

Later, she was forced to deal with her sons' anxiety over her plans. They heard of the church's intent to close the virgin's chapel. She supposed she should have called and informed them of her intent, but she hoped to already be on her way to Israel before a public announcement was made, mostly to avoid this very conversation with her eldest son, Luc.

"Mother, I realize you feel a responsibility to finish the chapel, but are you certain of this decision? You are no longer the young woman who created the works gracing the chapel walls. Haven't you given enough?"

She didn't bother trying to convince him there was no such thing. Luc was the one of her children most like his father and followed him into the business arena. His young shoulders bore the heavy burden of an international conglomerate along with the livelihoods of the thousands of men and women the family businesses employed. He felt the weight of his responsibilities, and like his father, took them seriously. But Mary Elle feared her oldest son lacked his father's faith and his willingness to accept what he had not personally experienced.

Their middle son inherited her love of art and was the one who handled the details of her legacy. He dealt with the museums wishing to arrange special exhibits of her work and private collectors interested in acquiring any new paintings that still occasionally came off the end of her brush.

Her youngest son stunned them all when, after graduating from university and working for three promising years tending the family lands, he announced his intention to enter the seminary and become a Catholic priest. The older two followed their father's religious affiliation into Islam and were appalled by their younger brother's announcement.

She still remembered the pivotal morning as if it was yesterday, instead of decades ago. She was overjoyed by his announcement, but she would never forget his father's reaction, the one she knew her youngest most feared. Luc rose from the table where the family was gathered and walked around to stand before his youngest son. He placed his hands on his son's shoulders and asked if he was certain of his decision. When Joseph assured his father he was absolutely certain he was called to serve in the priesthood, Luc embraced him, kissing him on both cheeks and assuring him seriously, "Then we will support you in every way we can. We are family and family supports one another."

Mary Elle thought the gift Luc gave her that morning was more precious to her than any other he bestowed on her. It was her youngest who would take these last steps of her journey with her. He arranged to meet her in Jerusalem and for her to stay at the Franciscan retreat house there.

The day finally arrived. She would walk the *Via Dolorosa* along the route her Lord took two thousand years earlier on the way to his crucifixion. Joseph walked silently beside her as they approached the Lion Gate in the Muslim quarter of the old city closest to the First station of the cross. Looking ahead she saw her two other sons waiting for them there. Curious, resigned, she raised her glance to her youngest son, but he merely shrugged at the questions he read in her eyes.

It was Luc who broke the silence between them. "You never spoke about your experiences with the virgin, but Dad explained to us how it was for you. Before he died, he made us promise if you ever decided you were ready to return to Jerusalem we would accompany you and fulfill his pledge to you if he could not."

"He promised he would take me when I was ready," Mary Elle told them.

Her middle son, Aman, told her, "He is here in us."

"Why did you wait so long to come? Dad was always

expecting you to ask him to bring you here," Luc told her.

"I know. Part of me regrets waiting so long. It would have been easier if he were here to be with me on this last stage of my journey. He was there every step of the way. I hope he doesn't feel cheated he's not here for this part, but the truth is, I never expected him to leave before I did. He was always there. The one constant in my life besides my work. After we realized how serious his illness was, I wouldn't come even though he urged me to. I couldn't ask him. He took care of me our entire lives together. It was my turn to care for him."

"You did, Mom. You were there for him in a way we couldn't be. I don't think I ever told you how grateful I was, we were, for your care of Dad."

She raised a tearful glance to her oldest son's. "I loved him, more than this life. If I could have left with him, just lay down beside him and crossed the final threshold hand in hand I would have done so, but my wish was denied me. There was still work for me to do. And now I'm ready to finish it."

"You still haven't explained why you waited so long," he reminded her.

She hesitated, then admitted, "Because it stays inside of me, what she shows me. I couldn't bear the thought of living with those visions for decades. I was afraid they would consume me and steal away my life with your father and the three of you. So I waited. Now the time for waiting is passed. Maybe I delayed too long, but I'm determined to finish her chapel before I leave this world. I'm weary of this life. I miss your father. So you must promise me you won't interfere today. No matter what happens, you cannot interfere."

"You're going to have to be a little more specific, Mom. What is likely to happen so we can prepare ourselves?"

She laughed. "One doesn't make demands of God, Aman. The premise is true in both Islam and Christianity. He's been very patient with me, but now it's time for me to fulfill my end of our bargain."

At her sons' reluctant, resigned agreement, they turned

and began walking with her in the direction of the First Station of the Cross, where Jesus was condemned by Pontius Pilate. Mary Elle retrieved the rosary from her bag Luc had made for her for their tenth wedding anniversary. It was fashioned of similar medieval workmanship to the rest of the Bordeaux Sapphire collection, but the sapphire, diamond and heavy silver rosary would not be joining the display at the Paris museum. She intended to leave it in the care of her youngest son for the length of his life, and then it would be put on display in the Chapel of the Rosaries.

Mary Elle was aware of her sons' presence behind her as she walked, and was even grateful for it. Her beloved, Luc's sons were well known in the Muslim world, and at the sight of them at her side, the crowds in the busy streets parted, allowing them to pass through without harassment. The way of the cross was not for the faint of heart, nor did it lend itself to quiet prayer and contemplation as it wove through the narrow streets of the old city where tourist shops and snack bars lined the way...and crowds, always crowds, filled them.

Even so, the competing, often shouted voices in Arabic, Hebrew, English, French and just about every other language known to man could not hold her attention for long. The faces of those in the busy streets turning to stare at her as she passed, her fingers working the rosary beads in her hand, her lips moving in silent prayer, soon faded into the anonymity of the street scene along with the stalls of shops filled with exotic wares, and strange smells.

She was falling back to a day millennia ago. With each step Mary Elle felt the tide of visions and emotions beginning to rise within her, but she fought against the swells, fearing she would be swamped by them before she reached her final destination.

At the Fourth Station at the Armenian Church, Mary Elle's lips stilled as she sank to her knees. Tears welled in her eyes as she stretched out her arms in an imploring gesture as her beloved son passed by. He turned and for a moment their glances met. His was resolute but filled with pain from the stripes on his back and the burden he carried. Their glances locked and he managed to summon a reassuring smile for her benefit. His love for her shone in his eyes. Somehow, from the depths of her despair, she forced her own lips to curve in response. Then he turned away from the reminder of his earthly life and began walking again, bent beneath the burden that would be the vehicle of his death, eager now to bring about its consummation. With his attention set firmly on the way ahead, Mary Elle let her smile of love and longing slide from her lips. She bent over in her grief and agony, until her head rested against the warm cobbled street.

She remained there for so long, her shoulders shaking with silent sobs, her eldest son finally bent to assist her to her feet. She nodded at his concerned expression, leaning into his side for a moment. Then pulling away, she summoned a reassuring smile for her younger sons' benefits, and then followed the way he had taken. When he stumbled, so did she, unable to remain upright when her beloved son and lord was on his knees. But each time he forced his feet back beneath his legs, so did she. Together. They walked this way together.

Maybe she wasn't the one whose flesh was pierced by nails securing her to a wooden cross, but her anguish was perhaps worse to be a mother asked to stand silently by as a witness to her beloved son's condemnation and torture. At the entrance to the Church of the Holy Sepulchre, Mary Elle hesitated, staring unseeing at its ancient stone façade. Though her mind instructed them to continue moving forward, her feet seemed either unwilling or unable to proceed.

"Mom?" She heard a dim echo of her son's concerned voice, but it was as if a stranger spoke to her. She wasn't there with him. She was still trapped in the distant past. This was it. This was the moment she avoided for six decades and still she hesitated, but she would not turn away, not again. Unwilling to turn back and unable to move forward she stood there unaware of the concerned, questioning glances her sons exchanged over her head.

"Madame Bordeaux?" It was another voice from her past cutting through her dazed impasse. She turned in its direction and for a moment her lips curved in wonder.

"Aman?" Her eyes filled with tears and she held out her hands to him. He took them in his still strong grasp.

"My very good friend asked me to walk these last steps with you," he explained, tears glistening in his own eyes as he squeezed her hands.

Mary Elle shook her head. How did he know? How did he figure out this would be the sticking point for her? Even from beyond this life he was still watching out for her.

"Are you ready?" he asked and she nodded. He held her arm and steered her up the stairs to the right of the entrance to the church where the Tenth Station was located. He held onto her as she leaned against the stone wall and wept as she watched her son being stripped of his clothes, then led her inside where he was nailed to the cross. Mary Elle couldn't completely smother the sob erupting from her lips at the echo in her mind of the reverberation of the executioner's hammer striking the head of the nails, its progress slowed only negligibly by the resistance of flesh and bone.

She collapsed to her knees and wiped away the blood splatters she could feel staining her face and hands, unseeing as the brutal visions assaulted her mind's eyes. Aman, with Luc's help all but carried her to the next station where she watched from a safe distance as her son gave up his life for mankind's sake.

It was done. She didn't need to see where they took him down from the cross. She already gave the world that legacy, on a Good Friday sixty years earlier when Luc kept vigil with her at the chapel at the Bordeaux estate. Nor did she need to see where they laid his physical body to rest. His spirit did not rest there and its depiction would not grace the chapel walls.

...EPILOGUE

She faced its emptiness a final time before she would fill it with the visions granted her, but she was no longer intimidated by its emptiness. No, she looked around the virgin's chapel and was relieved her work in this life was all but done. Resolute, she climbed the scaffolding and began mixing the paint.

It took her longer than she expected, particularly as the painting of its aftermath poured out of her in a single, brilliant afternoon. But she was older now, and there was no denying, physically at least, she no longer possessed the strength and endurance for her legendary all-nighters of her youth. Day after day, week after week, with always one of her sons, or Luc's beloved Aman, in the gallery, she worked, bringing to life for the world, what was given her in the silence of her mind.

It was all but complete now. There was only a single offering left for her to make. It would be her last to the chapel...to the gift she was given. She reached to retrieve a fresh painting knife from the scaffolding floor at her feet. Gripping it tightly she brought the sharp serrated edge to her wrist. When she would have drawn blood, a familiar, slightly mocking, but affectionate voice stopped her,

"Come, Daughter, let us not add any more drama to the situation than necessary."

"Daddy?"

"Yes, beloved."

"I'm ready to come home now."

"I know. Finish your work for me."

Smiling, Mary Elle shifted the knife in her hands and

pricked her finger tip, then allowed her blood to drip onto the palette beneath her and merge with the red paint already mixed there. Picking up her brush she dipped it in the paint and filled in the final bloody evidence of man's sins against God.

When she was finished, she bowed her head and whispered softly, "I lied to the priest."

"I know."

"I didn't know what to tell him. I wanted to get to wear my pretty white dress and have my First Holy Communion. I was afraid he would be mad at me if I told him the truth. I knew he wouldn't believe me."

"I know, Mary Elle. It's all right."

"Do I still get to come home?"

"Yes."

...EPILOGUE

A Bordeaux family spokesman reported today Mary Elle McGann Bordeaux passed away peacefully this morning in her sleep. Her three sons and eight grandchildren were reportedly at her side. The family was gathered in Rome for the scheduled re-consecration of the Chapel of the Rosaries at St. Peter's Basilica, which the artist only recently completed. The restoration was largely completed half a century ago when the artist was a young mother in her twenties. The final panels, which are believed to depict the Crucifixion of Christ, have been eagerly awaited by Vatican officials and faithful Christians all over the world.

The announcement earlier this year by Vatican officials the artist had resumed work on the chapel was greeted by almost unanimous sighs of relief around the art world, particularly given Madame Bordeaux's advanced years. The final panels were only completed in the past several weeks. It's reopening to the public is being eagerly anticipated by art experts and faithful Christians alike. Tourism to Rome spiked immediately in anticipation of the chapel's re-opening to the public next month.

Unfortunately the artist did not live long enough to see the public's reaction to what the privileged few of the art world who have been given the opportunity to preview the completed chapel are already hailing as the modern equivalent to Michelangelo's Sistine Chapel.

...EPILOGUE

Mary Elle McGann Bordeaux was laid to rest today in St. Peter's Basilica beneath the newly re-consecrated Chapel of the Rosaries she made her life's work. The Holy Father himself presided at her funeral mass. St. Peter's square was filled with thousands of faithful devotees who were in Rome for the public opening of the chapel and observed the Mass of Christian burial on large screens set-up to serve the massive crowds, some of its members carrying signs calling for Signora Bordeaux's immediate canonization as a saint of the Roman Catholic Church.

...The End

I hope you enjoyed The Young Madonna. If so, I hope you'll take a moment to leave a rating or review on Amazon. Just click on the link below to take you to the review page on Amazon.

Review Your Purchases (amazon.com)

Interested in other books by Lynn?
Keep Reading for a Preview of *...The Catalyst*

PROLOGUE...
THE CATALYST

The new gendarme whiled away the hours of his first official assignment flirting with the pretty young cashier who occasionally paused to assist a tourist with his or her purchases. Though the assignment of keeping watch for suspicious activity among the visitors to the historic site was not exactly what he anticipated when in a burst of patriotic enthusiasm following a terrorist attack on his beloved Paris he joined the ranks of the gendarme, he accepted the drawn out boredom of his first placement as part of his initiation into the service. With the increased threat of terrorism around the world, France's military police was called upon to play a more visible and active role in protecting their country's national treasures.

Certainly the ancient abbey Mont St Michel qualified as a national treasure. It's history dated back to the early eighth century, and the abbey survived numerous attacks to its continued existence, including the Hundred Years War, fires, the French Revolution and two World Wars. Jean was not particularly concerned about the prospect of an imminent terrorist attack, particularly since Mont St. Michel was located on a remote island a four hour drive from heavily populated Paris.

While the lovely Marie's attention was currently focused on assisting a tourist with her selections, Jean looked about him, concluding after a brief examination of his surroundings there was no discernible threat for him to worry about. His glance fell on a young girl standing before the statue of St. Michael in the alcove near the exit. The statue was the plaster model for the depiction of the archangel crowning the structure's fleche and stood almost fifteen feet high, towering over the child. The girl's long golden curls fell almost to her waist and when she turned her head to assure herself her mother was still close by, he could see even across the distance separating them, her eyes were an astonishing, piercing blue.

Her mother collected her purchases and strode towards the exit to where her daughter now stood staring intently up into the face of the statue. When her mother took her hand to lead her away, the child shook her head in denial, turning to look up at her mother to presumably explain her reluctance to leave just yet. Whatever she said to her mother apparently surprised the woman, because her eyes widened and she cast an apologetic look to those in ear-shot of her conversation with her young daughter, who were all wearing indulgent smiles at the child's declaration. Curious, Jean stepped closer to the pair so he could eavesdrop on their exchange.

"It's true, Mommy, Lord Michael is angry," the child insisted.

Jean felt his own lips curving in an amused smile at the girl's claim as he watched her mother kneel down so she was face-to-face with her young daughter. "Who is the Archangel angry with, Noelle?" She inquired patiently in the voice of an adult indulging a child's imagination.

"France." The child replied without hesitation, bringing amused chuckles to the lips of the bystanders who, like Jean, had drawn nearer to listen in on the conversation between mother and child.

Jean noticed the mother cast another apologetic look in the direction of their amused audience before returning to her earnest, very young daughter. "Why is the angel angry at France?"

"Because they took it away. They have to give it back," the

young girl insisted.

"They took what away?"

"His home. It's supposed to be a house devoted to God. He said so. What does devoted mean, Mommy?"

Sighing, perplexed, the woman explained, "It means loving service."

"Oh. France has to give his house back. Michael said so."

Jean noticed no one was laughing now and the crowd around the young mother and child was growing larger with each fantastic proclamation out of the young Noelle's innocent lips.

"I don't understand, Noelle." Her mother gave voice to the confusion they were all feeling.

The little girl turned her focus back to the statue of the archangel, then swung her arm wide in a gesture encompassing everything in sight. "This, Mommy. This place is one of his homes on earth. France took it away and now Michael wants it back."

The young mother looked at a loss as to how to answer her daughter. She stood, reaching for her daughter's hand, only just becoming aware of the amount of attention they were attracting. "I'm certain if the Archangel Michael wants his home back he won't have any difficulty in retrieving it."

The woman's frustrated comment brought fresh amusement to the expressions of those witnessing their exchange. The young Noelle, however, seemed not to hear her mother's response. She suddenly lifted her gaze to the ceiling and spun around in a slow circle, then stopped and reached for her mother's hand, attempting to pull her towards the exit.

"We need to leave now, Mommy. He's coming. Lord Michael is coming. He's going to show them what they did."

"Noelle, what are you talking about?"

The young girl tugged harder on her mother's resisting hand. Jean felt the tension in the crowd surrounding them ramp up in response to the desperation in her childish voice.

"Mommy, please. He's coming. He's coming now. We have to leave."

At the same instant as the girl's desperate plea to her mother, a loud crack split the undercurrent of voices among the observers surrounding them, silencing them as everyone looked around in fear, seeking the source of the loud noise still reverberating around the room. The young girl covered her ears and hid her face against her mother's legs. The woman bent down to lift her shaking, slender form into her arms even as the prior amused witnesses to their odd exchange froze in place. In the next instant the head of the statue of Michael separated itself from the rest of his body and fell with a loud crash to the floor. Still intact, the head rolled a few feet from where it landed and came to rest at the feet of the mother holding her terrified child in her arms.

"See what they did, Mommy?" The child cried out, staring for a moment down into the vacant eyes of the decapitated head.

"Noelle, sweetheart, no one did anything." The woman clutched her daughter close and spoke in soothing tones in an attempt to relieve her fear, but the girl was beyond comfort. She clenched her eyes tightly closed and once more raised her small hands to cover her ears.

"I don't want to see anymore. I don't want him to tell me anymore. Make it stop, Mommy. Make him stop...."

Jean was too stunned to do anything but watch as the young mother still clutching her daughter close against her chest, hurried through the exit. He turned his astonished gaze to the head of the angel resting on the floor, the little girl's words replaying through his thoughts. Looking down at the archangel's decapitated head he couldn't help but recall the defacement of the religious statues that occurred during the French Revolution. Mont St. Michel was converted into a prison for the use of the revolutionaries, but only after the monks in residence were evicted and the oppression of the church and clergy had begun.

I hope you enjoyed this preview of The Catalyst, here's the link to purchase the e-book and paperback.

The Catalyst - Kindle edition by Wood, Lynn. Romance Kindle eBooks @ Amazon.com.

The Catalyst: Wood, Lynn: 9781545535288: Amazon.com: Books

Happy Reading!

Thanks so much for spending your precious time in my stories.

Best Regards,

Lynn

Coming May, 2024 is the exciting first book in the new Honor and Protect Series:

Secrets Lies and Betrayals

Secrets, Lies and Betrayals - Kindle edition by Wood, Lynn. Romance Kindle eBooks @ Amazon.com.

Printed in Dunstable, United Kingdom